THE
STARS
OF
HEAVEN

A NOVEL

JESSICA DALL

The Stars of Heaven
Red Adept Publishing, LLC
104 Bugenfield Court
Garner, NC 27529
http://RedAdeptPublishing.com/
Copyright © 2020 by Jessica Dall. All rights reserved.
Cover Art by Streetlight Graphics[1]

---

1.   http://StreetlightGraphics.com

*To Niles, without whom this book would never have been
written*

Part One: 1755

Chapter One

Tia Ema had barely made it through the door before her quick, sharp voice filled the front hall. "Dores? Dores, where are you?"

Cecília didn't hear her mother answer before Tia Ema continued: "*Querido São José!* The crowds out there... and Aloisio! I'm not sure what I will do with that brother of mine. *Meu Deus.* I—"

"Is that you, Ema?" Mamãe's voice finally came from deeper inside the house.

Cecília slowed on the steps, moving just enough to be able to argue that she wasn't eavesdropping. Again.

Tia Ema barely took the time to say "yes" before she was back into her ranting. "Oh, Dores, I'm not sure my heart can take much more! Aloisio sent his boy this morning, and you wouldn't believe, he said—"

"Is Aloisio still not well?" Mamãe had long learned not to wait for Tia Ema to take a breath before responding. She'd likely learned *that* before the priest had finished the nuptial blessing the day she'd married Papai.

Tia Ema finally hesitated. "What?"

"He sent word that he wasn't well enough to attend vigil with us last night."

"*Querido São José*," Tia Ema repeated her favorite exclamation. "That man tells me nothing! That useless boy of his wouldn't answer me a thing this morning. Just looked at me with those wide eyes the entire time I was speaking and said Aloisio wasn't coming over and over. I had half a mind to..." Tia Ema continued, word after word spilling out when Mamãe didn't stop the onslaught.

Cecília reached the landing before the bottom flight of stairs and paused to brush herself off, even if there was no possible way her new gown had gotten dirty on the short walk between her room and the stairs.

Just making sure it's lying correctly, she tried to convince herself. Made from a French pattern specifically for All Saints' Day, with ruffled ends on her elbow-length sleeves and a full pannier holding out the hips, the gown was quite a change from the simple day dresses or Turkish robes she wore around the house. If making sure that it fit perfectly before heading downstairs meant pausing a little longer out of sight, where she could hear her aunt and mother talking, it was hardly her fault.

"Has anyone been sent to check on him?" Mamãe finally asked as Tia Ema started on her fourth or fifth tirade against Tio Aloisio's errand boy. "He hasn't been feeling well since he returned, has he?"

"He certainly has been relying on that *boy* to take care of things." Tia Ema huffed. "I should have gone down to that house of his the second Aloisio docked. He's always a touch peaked when he returns from abroad. He really needs to—"

"How bad are the crowds?" Mamãe asked. "If Aloisio isn't coming, should we still go to São Vincente? The Palmeiro's service—"

"No!" The word escaped Cecília's mouth before she managed to catch herself, and the voices in the entryway went ominously quiet.

"Cecília?" Mamãe's far-from-pleased voice echoed up the stairs.

Cecília grimaced, but the damage was already done. She moved into sight, trying to look as innocent as possible. "Good morning, Mamãe. Good morning, Tia Ema."

Mamãe's pale face pinched. "What have I told you about lingering, Cecília Madalena?"

"I wasn't—"

"You obviously have an opinion about what we're discussing?"

Cecília refrained from bunching the fabric of her gown in her hands at the dark look flashing through her mother's blue eyes. Mamãe had once been a beautiful woman.

She still would be, Cecília imagined, even though her fair hair was fading from gold to white and the lines on her face were growing deeper, *if only she didn't look so severe all the time*. Cecília straightened her shoulders. She had already been caught. Denial wouldn't help anything. "We told Francisco we'd go to São Vincente. He'll be looking for us."

Mamãe shook her head. "I'm sure he'll have plenty of other things to be worried about today."

"But—"

"Are you arguing, Cecília Madalena?"

"No, Mamãe." Cecília bit her cheek to keep herself from adding anything else.

"Go to the *oratório* and think about what you've done. We'll let you know when we're leaving."

"Yes, Mamãe," Cecília murmured and turned toward the room holding their little wooden shrine. It made sense that Mamãe no longer wanted to go across town to attend High Mass. Cecília had been shocked Mamãe had agreed to go to São Vincente in the first place. Her pride at having a son take the cloth had obviously overtaken her need to never go more than twenty steps from their front door. Since one thing had gone wrong, of course she would want to go to the Palmeiro's private chapel down the street instead. No doubt, if Mamãe had ever had the finances to build their own chapel, Cecília would have forgotten what the outside world looked like entirely.

Careful to keep her skirts from wrinkling, Cecília knelt in front of the *oratório*, crossed herself, and said a quick prayer for forgiveness. As far back as her first confession, she had struggled with the commandment to *honor thy mother*. Before Papai's death three years before, Mamãe had loved saying that Cecília had too much of her father in her. Cecília had to admit that was likely still true. Unlike her younger sister, Bibiana, who seemed entirely happy at the prospect of spending the rest of her life indoors like a proper Portuguese lady, Cecília had inherited far more of her father's wanderlust than any daughter should have been cursed with. But after three years of being lucky to get outside long enough even to go visiting, Cecília imagined the Palmeiro's confessor had to be growing tired of hearing Cecília atone for all the ways she had disobeyed her mother week after week after week.

After lighting a votive candle to place in front of Mamãe's most prized possession, the golden reliquary that held a lock of blessed Santa Inês's hair, Cecília stood and blew out a tense breath. She hadn't heard the bells since they had chimed nine, but it had to be inching toward the half hour. If they didn't leave soon, they would have no choice but to go to the Palmeiro's service at eleven.

If she could get Tio Aloisio to join them, though, she might have enough time to change Mamãe's mind and get all of them across town to São Vincente.

Cecília moved for the back door, listening carefully to make sure she didn't come across any of the servants as they worked to get things ready for dinner. Beyond dodging where Bibiana was playing with one of her dolls, however, the way was clear. Cecília sent off a quick prayer of thanks and grabbed a black outer robe to wear over her gown. With the pannier under her gown, the robe wouldn't let her blend in quite as well as she normally did when she slipped out, but with the crowds that always arrived on All Saints' Day, she would likely be able to make it to the river unnoticed.

Crisp autumn air blew in as Cecília cracked the door, and a rush of excitement pulsed through her. She couldn't stop herself from smiling. Lord knew how many acts of contrition she would be doing that night for sneaking out, but for the moment, she couldn't bring herself to feel remorse. How *anyone* could stand staying inside on such a beautiful day—proper lady or not—Cecília would never know.

From the state of the streets, it seemed the rest of Lisbon agreed. Cecília stepped away from the alley behind her house and was swept into the mass of bodies on the main road without a second look. The one time Cecília had managed to lure Bibiana outside on a feast day, Bibiana had hated every minute of it. The crowds had scared her, the tight, winding streets had confused her, and the only good memory she seemed to have from the experience was looking at all the colorful sheets and banners hanging from windows to decorate the cobblestone streets.

That's what makes Bibiana a better daughter, Cecília supposed. As it was, Cecília could have spent all day moving along with the chaos, looking at the little tent cities that had popped up overnight wherever there was space, and listening to cart women trying to sell sardines to anyone who would stop long enough to listen.

Two more turns and a few stinking brown puddles later, and the Tagus came into view. Cecília's breath caught. Brilliant blue, the river called to her as it always had, looking all the more beautiful in the midmorning light. All of the white stone buildings facing it looked as though they had been painted gold by the sun, as though God had seen fit to decorate the city far more majestically than the *lisboetas* had managed with measly banners. For all of Mamãe's complaints about dirt, thieves, and beggars out on the street, all Cecília could see was the beauty.

Tio Aloisio's house sat on the bank of the Tagus, close to the strait where the river narrowed before reaching the Atlantic. Not as grand as many of the buildings that had been built close to the king's riverside palace, the house was still an impressive structure, nearly as tall as Cecília's home in the Baixa, with similar white walls and a red roof.

"More than enough space for a single man in town," Tio Aloisio had claimed when he'd bought it a year before so he would have a place to stay closer to the docks. He'd needed one, as often as he'd taken to going on trade missions after inheriting Papai's ship. He couldn't very well travel back and forth from his country vineyard.

Pulling her skirts up an inch, Cecília crossed the last street at a jog and came to a stop in front of the wide door. She knocked and waited for someone to answer.

No one did.

Frowning, she tried again. Even if Tio Aloisio had fallen so ill that he couldn't make it out of bed, the house certainly shouldn't have been empty. A servant, his cook, the boy Tia Ema cared for so much... someone would be up and about. Cecília lifted her hand to knock a third time. The door opened as if timed to her forward swing.

Cecília jerked her hand back, barely avoiding hitting the man filling the doorway. She froze in surprise. A second later, she realized she no doubt looked idiotic with her fist hovering in the air and dropped it to her side. "Pardon me."

"My fault, I'm sure," the man answered with a crooked smile, his words accented in a way that made them sound discordant.

Cecília tried to get her mouth to say something else as her mind whirled, attempting to figure out who was standing in front of her. His clothes looked too well-made to be a servant, but in a simple brown waistcoat, jacket, and breeches, he didn't look like one of Tio Aloisio's merchant friends, either. Then again, it didn't seem he had entirely finished his morning toilette, with his auburn hair clubbed behind his neck with no sign of a wig—or even powder, for that matter.

An assistant, perhaps? He looked at most half a decade older than her—twenty-two or twenty-three, if that.

"May I help you?" he asked when she continued to stand there, mute.

Cecília started and caught her hands in front of her stiffly. "I'm looking for my uncle, Senhor Aloisio Silva Durante?"

"Oh." The crooked smile came back. "You must be"—he seemed to reach for a name—"Bibiana?"

Cecília puffed up slightly. As little as what the man thought of her mattered, she would have hoped, with seven years separating them, she didn't look like her ten-year-old sister. "Cecília. Cecília de Santa Rita e Durante."

His hazel eyes crinkled at the sides. "Everyone here does have very impressive names."

Cecília released a breath through her nose, trying to hide her discomfort at the entirely odd situation by straightening her spine fully, even if he remained at least half a foot taller than her that way. "Is my uncle here?"

The man nodded as he took a step back. "He's finishing dressing, I believe. Would you like to wait for him?"

Waiting didn't make Cecília feel wonderful, not with time ticking down. She still tried to focus on the positive. "He's feeling better, then?"

The man's eyebrows furrowed. "Better?"

"He was ill yesterday?"

The confused look didn't move off the man's face, but Tio Aloisio's voice broke in before he could speak again. "Cecília? I thought I heard your voice."

Cecília released a relieved breath as her uncle's familiar—and healthy—face came into view. "Tio, I'm glad to see you looking so well."

He cocked an eyebrow as if he had no idea what she meant, either, before understanding flashed over his expression. "Oh, yes. I'm glad to say my illness was nothing dire. You never know what it will do to your health, being somewhere as damp as London in the fall."

"I'm glad," Cecília repeated then rushed on. "Where are you going to Mass, then? Tia Ema said you weren't coming to São Vincente anymore?"

"I'm afraid I don't have the time today, Cilinha." He moved around to gather his things. "I have a business meeting I can't miss."

Cecília blinked. "But it's All Saints' Day."

"We were delayed getting back." He picked up his walking stick. "I find I'm still working to catch up. Especially with getting Bates here settled."

Cecília glanced at the younger man, who was still lingering in the entryway.

He offered a quick smile and a short bow. "John Bates. Pleasure to meet you, Senhorita Durante."

So the man was English. That explained his accent. Cecília didn't have time to think too much about it. She turned back to her uncle. "But you're going to Mass? It's a Holy Day of Obligat—"

"Of course," Tio Aloisio said then finally stopped moving long enough to look at her straight on. "Does your mother know you're here?"

"I..." Cecília's mind didn't switch over quickly enough to come up with anything that wouldn't be a blatant lie. "She said since you weren't coming, we couldn't—"

"You know better than that, Cilinha." He shook his head, the curls of his own long white wig bouncing back and forth. "Wandering on your own?"

Cecília wrung her hands in front of her, nothing about the situation turning out how she had hoped. She tried to salvage something out of it. "You can walk back with me. Maybe you can convince Mamãe—"

"What time is your meeting, Bates?" Tio Aloisio cut her off.

Mr. Bates's eyebrows rose, but he answered, "Ten, sir."

"You wouldn't mind walking my niece back home this morning, then? She could likely point out Rua Nova dos Mercadores for you on the way."

Cecília frowned. "Tio Aloisio—"

"It would actually be my pleasure," Mr. Bates said over her. "I admit the streets here quite confound me."

"They do some lisboetas who have lived here their entire lives." Tio Aloisio clapped Mr. Bates's shoulder as if they were old friends then turned back to Cecília. "Your mother will be looking for you."

"Tio..." Cecília started, not certain how she was going to finish her sentence.

Tio Aloisio didn't give her the chance to, anyway. He checked the time on his gold pocket watch then motioned Mr. Bates outside before stepping through himself, forcing Cecília back onto the street. "I'm running late, as always. See you tonight, Bates."

"Have a good day, Senhor Durante." Mr. Bates lowered his head respectfully then swept on a cocked hat and turned to Cecília. "As you please, Senhorita Durante."

With Tio Aloisio already heading the opposite way down the road at a good clip, Cecília was left with little choice but to go with the Englishman or slip off into the crowd by herself to head back home. She couldn't quite determine which would get her into less trouble, should anyone Mamãe knew spot her. Unable to decide, Cecília spun on her heel and started back the way she had come. If the Englishman could keep up, she supposed she would point him toward the row of shops that lined Rua Nova dos Mercadores.

New to the city or not, Mr. Bates didn't seem to have an issue with the crowds. He stayed close at hand, matching each of Cecília's movements a second after she made them to maneuver around slower clumps of travelers on the street. She watched him out of the corner of her eye, debating whether she should offer any kind of conversation.

He beat her to it. "Is there a reason so many of you wear those black cloaks?"

Cecília frowned. "Pardon?"

"When I first arrived, I thought there were only priests on the street. There are still more priests here than I've ever seen in my life, I'm relatively sure, but it seems everyone wears those." He motioned briefly at her cloak. "I've been meaning to ask your uncle about it."

She shrugged. "Even the less virtuous think twice before attempting to rob someone who has taken holy orders. This is safer than flaunting fine clothing."

"I take it that's why your uncle insisted I keep a dagger with me, then?"

"Most men carry a sword if they can afford one." She didn't bother to look at him as she swung out wide to avoid those who were kneeling in front of a niche carved into the side of a building dedicated to São António. The builder had included a relic from the blessed saint himself when the niche had been created, or so Cecília had heard whispered. She crossed herself quickly.

Mr. Bates didn't.

She continued to study him out of the corner of her eye. "You came with my uncle from London, Mr. Bates?"

"Indeed, I did."

"Are you *from* London, then?"

"London by way of everywhere else," he said and smiled when she sent him a questioning look. "I was born in Southampton but jumped a ship as soon as anyone would let me. Have been to the far reaches at this point. London was just my most recent stop."

She fought down the rush of excitement the idea of travel sent through her, keeping her voice level, properly disinterested. "You're a merchant? Like my uncle?"

"More a sailor who had the good fortune to make friends in high places. I owe your uncle a great debt for all the help he's offered in getting me settled in Lisbon."

Cecília pursed her lips slightly. Many of her uncle's business partners were English, part of the British Factory as they were called, but she couldn't understand why Tio Aloisio would take it upon himself to bring another Englishman—an English Protestant, she was willing to assume—back to Lisbon.

"It's a beautiful city." He kept the conversation moving when she didn't answer. "It is as they say: he who has never seen Lisbon has never seen a good thing."

At least he and Cecília could agree on that. Glancing at the parishioners spilling out the door of Nossa Senhora dos Mártires into the square in front of the basilica, Cecília was left with the sinking feeling that it was getting far closer to ten than she'd originally estimated. Even if she had convinced Tio Aloisio to come to the Baixa with her, they would have had no chance to make it to São Vincente in time for High Mass. All she could hope was that no one had noticed she'd gone, and the entire morning would be one more thing she would have to privately confess at the Palmeiro's. She slowed them to a stop just outside the square by another niche—one holding a thick wooden crucifix—and pointed east. "Rua Nova dos Mercadores is that way, if you'd like to part ways here."

"I'm more than happy to walk you the rest of the way home, Senhorita Durante."

Because after everything, she needed someone from her *bairro* seeing her wandering about alone with an Englishman. "With the crowds, I imagine that would make you late for your meeting."

A conflicted expression moved over Mr. Bates's face as he scanned the crowd for himself, no doubt seeing she was right.

She saved him the trouble of having to weigh whatever duty he felt to her and however important he considered his meeting. "I've lived in Lisbon my entire life, Mr. Bates. I'm certain I'll be able to make it home without your assistance."

Mr. Bates began to give one more halfhearted objection before a low rumble moving through the ground made him trail off. Cecília frowned, looking for an approaching coach, though from the way the sound was growing, it would have had to have been a line of coaches barreling toward them.

"What's that?" Mr. Bates followed Cecília's gaze.

Cecília shook her head, not having any better idea than Mr. Bates. The rumbling grew stronger, making loose pebbles rattle around her feet as the sound neared a roar.

Earthquake. The thought registered a second too late as the street under her rolled. Cecília tipped forward as shouts went up, mixing with discordant clanging church bells. She put her hand out to brace herself, but the ground lurched again. Her shoulder slammed into the curve of the niche then bucked the other way. She hit cobblestone hard.

The wall of the building across from her split, chunks of white plaster raining down across the street. Rough brick showed through as the ground continued its assault. Then the brick started to tilt. Eyes widening, Cecília curled into herself, everything happening too quickly to make sense. The wall fell. Hard chunks pelted her as it kicked up a cloud of dust so thick that she had no choice but to close her eyes.

Slowly, the shaking slowed, and the roar was replaced by a cacophony of the most horrible sounds Cecília had ever heard—screaming, crying, panicked whinnies of horses. Cecília's body seized. She tried to unfurl, but her muscles wouldn't release.

Shock kept her curled, eyes squeezed shut as though everything would stop if she didn't look, as though she would wake up in her bed, the morning a dream. A new roar rose over the screams a second before the rumbling returned. Crying, she dropped her forehead to the ground, mumbling some prayer for mercy as Hell rose up around her. "*Misericorda. Misericorda de Deus.*"

There was more screaming, more crashing, a loud *snap,* and pain shooting across her back. Somewhere, her mind registered that something hard had landed on top of her. She choked on dust as she gasped, trying to suck in what air she could under the crushing weight. Time began to blur. Nothing existed beyond the roar and rocking and pain.

The ground slowly stilled once again—after how long, Cecília couldn't begin to imagine—but she still couldn't breathe. She struggled to reach whatever had pinned her. One hand touched smooth wood—the crucifix from the niche. She pushed, but it wouldn't shift. Something had to have been on top of it, pressing into the cross as it pressed into her. Her sight began to blur, her chest not able to expand enough to take in air. As hard as she fought to remain conscious, her mind turned fuzzy.

The third roar barely registered until the crucifix shook loose. Cecília gasped. She ended up coughing, thick dust coating her throat. No longer completely pinned, she still had to fight to free herself. Rough bricks scraped her palms, but they shifted as the shaking stopped, letting Cecília inch her way forward. She could find her way out, if she just kept moving...

Reaching out once more, her hand hit nothing. She froze, the sensation not making sense until she realized she had reached open air. The day had simply turned pitch black.

And the Lord said unto Moses, Stretch out thine hand toward Heaven, that there may be darkness over the land of Egypt, even darkness which may be felt. The words floated through Cecília's mind, and she crossed herself before she realized how much pain the movement caused. She couldn't bring herself to rise from her knees. God had thrown her and the whole city down into the earth. There was no other explanation.

Slowly, some light began to filter through the haze in the air, and Cecília's eyes struggled to adjust. The sight was worse than the darkness. Bodies poked through piles of stone—men with their heads dashed open, mangled limbs reaching out as if trying to free themselves even without the bodies to which they had once been attached. Others were still alive, and some cried for help, some already fleeing over the rubble. They weren't in Hell. But Lisbon seemed worse.

As the reality filtered through her shock, a new thought registered in Cecília's mind. *Bibiana. Mamãe.*

Cecília scrambled to her feet, pain muddling with the panic to the point where she couldn't feel her body at all. Unthinking, she started stumbling over the piles of brick and wood and bodies.

"The Day of Judgment has arrived!" A priest's voice carried over the awful screams still echoing from the rubble. "Remember the Apocalypse of John: *And there was a great earthquake, such as was not since men were upon the earth.* The sixth seal has been broken! Repent for your sinful souls."

Cecília's legs shook. The pain in her side grew as the words worked their way inside her.

"Senhorita Durante?"

Her name registered blankly in her mind. She tried to turn, but her knees gave out. The dirty, bleeding man in front of her reached out as if he was trying to catch her then stopped short, shouting as he cradled his own arm instead. Cecília hit the ground, the jar somehow more painful than anything she had ever experienced and dulled to where she barely felt it.

The man recovered, and he looked around before bending, off-kilter, toward Cecília. "We need to get back to your uncle's."

Recognition registered in the mess of Cecília's mind. "Mr. Ba..."

Another rumble went through the ground, not as strong as the others but enough to send up a new round of shouting. Cecília whimpered. She couldn't let herself think about the Apocalypse, the man in front of her, or the pain shooting through her body.

Mamãe, Bibiana... She needed to make it back home. God was punishing her. She deserved it. *Sneaking out, lying...* But He wouldn't punish them. Not Mamãe. Certainly not Bibiana. Good, innocent little Bibiana.

She forced herself back up to standing, even as every inch of her fought against it, and turned for her best guess of where home might be in the shell that was Lisbon.

Mr. Bates called after her, his voice mixing into the awful clamor filling the dusty air. Cecília moved faster through the horrifying jumble of ruins. Dead eyes stared up at the brown sky, and prostrated living pulled at their hair or kissed painted saints and rosaries. Her foot caught on something. She stumbled but couldn't bring herself to look. Whatever it had been, she didn't want to see.

She cleared a pile of rubble only for a wave of smoke to sweep over her. She coughed and moved the lace from her mantilla to cover her mouth in some vague attempt to breathe, but even then, the smoke seared her lungs. Something was burning. No, many things were burning. She had to turn back around, but she didn't know where else to go.

"Senhorita Durante."

She started at hearing her name so close to her side. Mr. Bates had followed her.

"We need to make it back to the river. The city's alight. If we can get on your uncle's ship, we might have a chance."

"I can't... My family..." Cecília shook her head, unsure if she was about to laugh or cry. Nothing made sense. *How he can plan...* Her mind couldn't carry her through a thought.

"You won't find anyone dead." He grabbed her wrist with his good arm. "Please. Perhaps your parents will go to the river too?"

Papai would have. The thought appeared somewhere deep in Cecília's mind. As little as she could believe Mamãe would, as well, it was enough to let her follow the way Mr. Bates was leading. Her body ached more and more with each step.

Chapter Two

No matter which way Cecília tried to go, she couldn't find any landmark, anything familiar, anything that looked like home. Cracked shells of buildings poked out in chunks of plaster and stone. Twisted metal railings rose like deadly snakes from piles of bricks, empty spindles when Cecília was lucky and impaled mangled bodies when she wasn't. After Lord knew how long of walking through the horror, Cecília couldn't absorb any more. She fell into the rest of the beaten, bloody mass of humanity, trying to find a way out of town. Even Mr. Bates had fallen silent as the enormity of it all appeared to hit him as well.

Somewhere outside the walls of Lisbon, Cecília's body suddenly jolted back to reality, the dull ache she had been feeling turning into breathtaking pain. She stumbled slightly.

Mr. Bates snapped out of his own daze. "Senhorita Durante? What's the matter?"

The question nearly made her laugh. She didn't waste the breath it would take to state the obvious. "I... I need to sit."

Mr. Bates took her elbow with his good arm, as though worried she would tip over where they stood, and looked around before leading her to a large stone sitting off the main road. No one else so much as bothered to look. Cecília supposed she couldn't blame them. She had long stopped listening to the cries for help. There were too many who needed aid while everyone needed to protect their own.

Mr. Bates took a seat on the ground next to her, looking as exhausted as she felt beyond the gray ash that had plastered itself to his face and hair.

No powder or too much. The weak thought bubbled up as she looked at his hair, the humor quickly dying off as she realized the absurdity of it in current circumstances. Instead, she tried to take stock of herself. Her ankle was stiff and swollen. Her left side throbbed where the crucifix had fallen on top of her. Her eyes started to water. If God wanted to make his displeasure known, He had, beyond the shadow of a doubt. The throbbing spiked as a sob escaped. But perhaps it was supposed to. Perhaps it was God multiplying her sorrow as He had Eve's for her sin.

A muffled grunt startled her enough to look up again, and she turned just in time to see Mr. Bates pushing himself back up to sitting, rubbing a shoulder that didn't look quite as disformed anymore.

He met her eyes silently for a moment, some sort of determination burning behind the exhaustion, pain, and worry, then asked, "Do you know where we are?"

She tried to blink away her tears. "What?"

"We can't get to the river. We can't stay here. We need some sort of plan."

"Plan?" Cecília's voice tipped up, incredulous. "The world is ending. The Lord—"

"Has left us both alive," Mr. Bates completed for her. "It would be a poor show of faith to let ourselves die, don't you think?"

Cecília looked back the way they had come. The mass of dirty, bleeding people seemed unending as smoke continued to rise from what had once been Lisbon, turning the beautiful golden sunlight a sickly brownish orange.

"Your uncle has a vineyard, doesn't he?" Mr. Bates continued. "Somewhere in the country?"

The calm practicality in his tone helped make its way past the haze of despair in Cecília's mind. "Near Queluz."

"Where's Queluz?"

"Half a day northwest," she recited then properly looked around at the land and realized they were on the road west toward Belém. "North from here."

"That's where he would go, don't you think?" he said then added, "Where your family would go?"

Mamãe, Bibiana, Tia Ema... The thought shot a new wave of panic into her stomach. She tried to keep her breathing under control as each sharp breath drove an even sharper pain through her side. *They can't be dead. God wouldn't punish them...* "There or to my grandparents' in Loures."

A conflicted look passed over Mr. Bates's face. "Which is closer?"

"From here, the vineyard."

Visible relief washed over him. "We should go there, then. Hope that everyone else does as well. Do you think you can lead the way?" His eyes dropped over her. "Do you think you can walk?"

Mamãe and Bibiana are alive. They have to be. Being farther up in the Baixa than Cecília and Mr. Bates had been, though, would mean they likely would leave the city going north, putting them somewhere between Queluz and Loures, nowhere near Belém. Who knew how much longer Cecília's body would last, but she had to try to get somewhere she would be found.

Forcing herself up with a wince, Cecília nodded. "I think I can."

CECÍLIA HADN'T BEEN to her uncle's vineyard in years, not since Papai had died and Tio Aloisio had taken over Papai's business. Not for a year or two before that, even. Still, she recognized the landmarks as she and Mr. Bates made their way north, even though it seemed to take untold ages to move from one to the next. The half-day carriage ride she remembered stretched on hour by hour, as her already sore body tried to collapse. As stiffly as she moved, it was a miracle that any light was left in the sky by the time they reached the little valley holding Tio Aloisio's vineyard. With the pinkish glow still clinging to the hills on the horizon, Cecília could make out the boxy shape of her uncle's home surrounded by the scattering of storage houses and lodgings for the men who worked on the vineyard. Everything still seemed to be standing, but the buildings, the trellised grapevines lining the hills around the house, the placidity of it all felt cruelly mocking.

"That's it?"

Cecília nodded, not sure she was breathing well enough to speak.

Releasing his own relieved breath, Mr. Bates helped her down the last hill, and they walked up the path leading to the home's front door. Though a lit lantern had been hung from a hook out front, the rest of the home remained dark. The emptiness made Cecília's stomach turn. The vineyard hadn't been leveled, but it seemed as though all the people who kept the vineyard running while Tio Aloisio was away had disappeared.

Mr. Bates moved up to the wooden door and knocked. After a moment, he knocked again before looking back at Cecília. "No one seems to be home."

"Do you think something happened to them?" she asked breathlessly.

He studied her, his gaze concerned before he took the lantern off its hook and held it closer to the building.

A long crack snaked up from the door, and Cecília stepped back at the thought of the house crumbling. "Maybe we should stay out here."

Mr. Bates frowned. "What?"

"If it"—she couldn't bring herself to say most of the words passing through her mind—"cracks more?"

He turned back to it and prodded at the spot.

"Mr. Bates..." She took another step back.

Some of the plaster flaked off, but the building remained standing. Cecília realized her fists were clenched tightly enough that her nails were biting into her palms. She forced them to relax.

Mr. Bates studied the home for another moment before he lifted the latch on the door and pushed. It swung open without protest. He called inside, "Anyone there?"

No one answered.

He looked back at Cecília. "It's likely safer staying inside than out here in the dark. We can stay by the door, if you like."

Cecília tried to convince herself she was being silly, but she found herself still frozen in place.

"Senhorita Durante. We need to sit. Find something to eat."

Cecília suddenly realized she hadn't had a thing to eat all day. They had been fasting, of course, before Mass, and everyone in the kitchens had been so busy preparing a feast... Her stomach soured as her thought trailed off before she could decide if she was actually hungry.

The light wavered slightly as Mr. Bates stepped over the threshold with the lantern. He moved around, the light catching the window to the left of the door—what Cecília vaguely recalled was a salon—then to the right before he stepped back up to the threshold. "A few things look as if they were knocked over, but it doesn't seem bad. I think it's safe for you to come in."

Cecília swallowed but forced herself forward, limping worse than before, her protesting muscles beginning to seize from standing still.

"Could I help?"

"You're hurt yourself." She somehow managed to keep walking.

"I'll get by." He nodded to the left room. "There's a settee in there. You should sit."

Cecília turned without argument. "Your shoulder?"

"Stiff. It will be for a while. But I got it back in place. Nothing I haven't dealt with before."

She twisted as much as she could to give him a questioning look.

"It's been…" He hesitated. "*Dislocado*? Is that the right word?"

"Des*locado*?" she corrected.

"I'm getting tired. My Portuguese and Spanish are running together." He offered a weak smile. "My shoulder's been out of joint before, more than once. I'll get it in a sling when I can."

"You're not in pain?"

"I didn't say that." He stepped into the room after her and set the lantern on a small round table.

Cecília paused. The salon, she remembered, had been decorated much like hers was—like hers had been—in the Moorish fashion, with thick pillows and rugs. That salon had been entirely redone. Tall-backed chairs and dark-wood tables filled the space, all surrounded by shelf after shelf of leather-bound books. "What is all of this?"

Mr. Bates looked back at her. "What's all of what?"

It's a wonder Tio Aloisio had any room for trade, bringing all of this with him. She shook her head, doubting she would be able to explain the oddity of seeing the room so changed in her current state. She limped to a long bench with a padded back and lowered herself as carefully as she could. She still grimaced as pain shot up her side. Eyes watering, she bit down a whimper.

"What happened to your side?" Mr. Bates moved closer to her.

"Something fell on me." She placed her hand gingerly on the spot and gritted her teeth, not wanting to think what it had meant, having a crucifix nearly kill her.

"Would you like me to look?"

She lifted her eyes back to his.

"Something may be broken," he said quickly. "I know how to wrap it, if so."

"Are you also a physician, Mr. Bates?" She shifted slightly. She would have to do something about her clothes. Since she was seated again, the boning in her stays that had kept her upright was pressing too hard on her side, and she felt the splintered framing of her pannier jabbing into her hips. She couldn't let herself consider what state her new dress had to have been in.

"Ships are dangerous places. Saw a man get blown straight out of the rigging once. Cracked his rib. Did something wrong a few days later. Suddenly couldn't breathe and dropped dead."

Cecília's eyes widened.

"Not that I think you're going to die," he said in a rush. "Just a reason to check on it. Especially after that walk. You should have been resting far earlier than this."

Cecília managed a nod even if words wouldn't come, and Mr. Bates moved to the spot behind her on the bench. His hand gently touched hers. She gasped as he pressed a hard piece of boning tighter to her.

His hand jerked back. "I'm sorry."

"Sailors don't tend to wear stays, I take it." Cecília did her best to keep her voice light, though her discomfort made the words too terse.

Mr. Bates gave a short, equally awkward laugh. "No, I can't say they do."

The room went quiet again, silence stretching out as the obvious settled in. Cecília cleared her throat lightly. "You can't do anything with my gown on?"

"I... Well, I'm sure I could..."

She had already accepted that she couldn't stay dressed as she was and moved to trying to convince herself there was no reason to worry about impropriety. Twelve hours before, her mother would have become apoplectic at the idea of Cecília doing anything as shocking as being alone in a room with a man not related to her. But there was nothing to be done for it, just like she could do nothing about her clothing without his help. Resigning herself to the situation, she undid the clasp of her black robe. "It's fine. The stays hurt, and I'll need help..."

Mr. Bates didn't answer for a moment. Then he stood. "What do you need?"

"I can do most of it." She slipped the black robe off stiffly and focused on looking herself over, so she wouldn't have to watch Mr. Bates watch her—or politely try *not* to watch her. Though her hands were scratched raw, and her arms were already mottled with deep-purple bruises, it seemed her robe had taken the worst of what had happened. The lace at the elbows of her gown was perhaps even salvageable. She tried to keep her mind on that thought as she unpinned her stomacher and set it aside with her dirty, ripped robe. Carefully, she pulled her arms free of the gown and turned her attention to the layers of petticoats that were draped limply over her broken pannier. Grimacing, she forced herself back up to standing to undo the ribbons holding each layer around her waist. The throbbing in her side grew as she worked to unwrap each tie, but she somehow managed, leaving a puddle of the beautiful fabric she had been so pleased with that morning around her.

Favor is deceitful, and beauty is vain: but a woman that feareth the Lord, she shall be praised. The verse the Palmeiro's confessor loved to recite whenever she confessed a sin of vanity flittered through her mind.

Sending up yet another quick prayer for forgiveness, Cecília finally lifted her eyes to Mr. Bates. The man had thoughtfully turned to study the books lining the far wall as she worked, though Cecília imagined it had to be too dark to make out what the books were. Cecília swallowed, trying to fight down how exposed she already felt with her stays still wrapped tightly around her, standing there in her thin *camisa*. She imagined she wouldn't feel much better when she was down to *just* the camisa.

She cleared her throat to bring Mr. Bates's attention back to her. "Could you help...? My stays are laced in the back. You should be able to, with one arm...?"

Mr. Bates's eyes dropped over her for a split second before he seemed to catch himself, and he nodded. Silently, he moved to her side, and she turned to let him get to the lacing, her heart pounding uncomfortably in her ears. As much as she tried to tell herself it was necessity, every sermon she had heard about immorality and lust of the flesh flew through her head at once. Necessity or not, letting an Englishman undress her had to be its own terrible level of damnation, and Heavens knew her soul didn't need any more of that.

With a final few awkward tugs, the stays gave way. Cecília took a grateful breath as the boning stopped pressing into her injured side then immediately regretted it, as the expanding air sent a new wave of pain through her. A small grunt sounded from somewhere in the back of her throat.

"Did I hurt you?"

Mr. Bates's voice brought her back to the present. Cecília shook her head, still holding the front of her stays protectively to her chest, as though that would change the fact that she was practically naked. "Breathed too deeply."

Mr. Bates nodded, taking a step back from her as he rubbed his own shoulder self-consciously. Or perhaps he was simply in pain as well. "Sit again?"

She didn't need to be told twice. Though it was blissful, no longer having the boning pushing into her, she suddenly realized how much she had been relying on it to remain upright. Without the structure of her clothes, her body was trying to crumple in on itself. She sat back on the little bench, leaning her less-hurt shoulder against the padded back to leave her hurt side open.

Mr. Bates took a breath as if he was going to speak again, but instead, he silently moved back to his place behind her on the bench. The touch of his fingers on her side made Cecília tense, but he moved quickly, professionally, feeling along her ribs.

She cried out as he reached where the crucifix had landed.

"Sorry." He pulled back. "But I think there is a break."

She took as deep a breath as she dared. "You'll want to wrap it, then?"

His words stumbled slightly as he rushed. "I'm sure I can do that over your... your..."

"Camisa?" She looked at him.

He nodded. "I'll look for something I can use for that and a sling and see if there's anything to eat."

Cecília shook her head. "I'm not hungry."

"You should still try to eat." He headed toward the door of the room.

"Please, don't go." The words escaped before she could stop them. She added at a near whisper, "I don't want to be alone."

He pressed his lips into a thin line then said, "We have to eat."

Cecília frowned but didn't answer, fingering her gold cross—the one Papai had given her from one of his trips to Brazil—where it sat near the neckline of her camisa. Mr. Bates's eyes dropped just long enough to make Cecília's hand still before he caught himself and moved back into the front hallway. Cecília went back to rubbing the metal, finding dents that had formed when she'd fallen. Too tired to think anymore about what that meant, about what any of it meant, she let her eyes drift closed and vaguely hoped she would wake up and find that everything had been an awful dream.

Chapter Three

Cecília ached so deeply she half wished she'd never woken. It dug down to her bones, straining every muscle and ligament to the point where she thought she might snap apart. Slowly, she forced her eyes open, and the reality of everything crashed back down on her. Somehow, it made the pain worse.

Though her eyes searched the room, she couldn't bring herself to move from how she had ended up curled on her side on the little bench. Her eyes settled on an open bottle of wine sitting next to a bowl that held part of a loaf of bread.

Releasing a shallow breath, Cecília steeled herself to move. Her body fought against every shift, the sharp pains from the day before joining with muscles that had gone so tense that they refused to stretch. Somehow, she managed to get herself more or less up to sitting, even if her teeth felt as if they might crack from how tightly she had clenched her jaw.

Across the room, Mr. Bates was sleeping in a high-backed upholstered chair, his head leaning at an awkward angle against one of the wings protruding from the side. Though Cecília had the lingering suspicion that Tio Aloisio had brought a fair deal of the new furniture back with him from England, she had to imagine the Englishman would have fared better with the old Moorish pillows on the floor.

As if he could feel her eyes on him, Mr. Bates stirred awake. He winced, and Cecília noticed the bruise that had formed along his jaw and neck. She imagined she couldn't look much better in the daylight, at least not if the ugly splotches on her forearms were any indication.

"You didn't get your sling." Cecília said the first words that came to mind.

"Couldn't manage it by myself. I figured I'd survive a night." He seemed to attempt a smile, though it didn't entirely form. "There's bread there. It's stale but not bad if you soak it in the wine. Your uncle has an impressive vintage, though I imagine you already know that."

"Mamãe never let us drink wine." Somewhere, her mind realized she had spoken in the past tense, and her stomach twisted. She tried to ignore it by focusing on the confused look Mr. Bates once again fixed on her.

"Your uncle owns a vineyard, and you don't drink wine?"

"Mamãe says it isn't fashionable for young ladies to drink."

"What is fashionable, then?"

"Water, mostly."

Mr. Bates released an incredulous breath. "That's a new one."

"Not in Portugal." Cecília looked back down at the bottle, bread, and bowl. With the grain shortage they'd had, the fact that someone had left the better part of a loaf of bread sitting around to grow stale was nearly as unsettling as the emptiness of the house itself. *Where is everyone?*

"You take communion, though?"

Cecília came out of her thoughts with a frown. "Of course."

"That's wine."

"That's the blood of Christ."

"Ah. Yes." Mr. Bates shifted forward in the chair and looked himself over. "I mean no disrespect, Senhorita Durante, but I believe you'll find that the blood of Christ tastes much more like that bottle of wine than blood, whether or not one believes in transubstantiation."

Cecília's muscles attempted to spasm with the new wave of tension moving through her. She let the disdain in her voice say she had no interest in hearing a Protestant's opinions on her religion. "You can say 'transubstantiation' but not 'dislocated'?"

Mr. Bates's eyes lifted to her again. "Frankly, I'm impressed I got to Spanish, as late as it was last night. When I lose a word, my mind tends to find French."

Cecília continued to frown, but her curiosity won out. "French?"

"First language I picked up," he said. "After English, obviously."

Cecília realized she hadn't thought too much about how Mr. Bates spoke. Outside his harsh accent and the single slip the night before, his Portuguese had been flawless. Far better than many of the foreigners who had lived in Lisbon for years. "How many languages do you speak?"

"With some fluency, five. I can get by in a few more, if need be."

Cecília stared at the man. "You speak *five* languages?"

"I've always had a gift for it." He prodded his shoulder gingerly. "Part of why your uncle offered to bring me here. He was impressed by how quickly I picked up Portuguese. Of course, I already knew Spanish, and as you can see, they're rather close. I wager you'd understand me for the most part if I spoke Spanish slowly enough."

"And how long have you known my uncle?"

"A couple of years now. I happened to receive an invitation to a dinner he was attending in London. An odd confluence of events, really, took me off one ship and then eventually brought me here."

"Not exactly serendipitous, coming here just for this."

"So goes the *Rota Fortunae*, I suppose." He offered another small smile, though it didn't entirely hide the tension sliding into his tone.

Somehow, the small crack in Mr. Bates's calm practicality made Cecília feel better. She looked back at the bread and wine, trying to decide if her battered body would even let her eat. It had been more than a day since her last meal, and she still wasn't hungry. "So what do we do now?"

"Now?"

"I need to find my family."

"They could still be making their way here. In all the chaos yesterday, it's very possible we're just the first to arrive."

"And if they aren't?"

Mr. Bates looked at her for a moment before he said, "I know you're worried, Senhorita Durante. You have every right to be, but we have more than enough to worry about right here and right now. We should get ourselves settled. You still need to eat. We should wrap your side. Then, if no one else shows up today—maybe tomorrow—we can make further plans."

"You want us to sit around an empty house for two days?"

"Can you honestly say you're in any shape to go elsewhere?" He held her eyes as if waiting to see if she would argue before he continued, "I told your uncle I would see you home. It seems that's just going to take longer than originally thought."

Not certain what else she could say, Cecília picked up the bottle of wine and sniffed it. The smell brought back memories of chapels and Mass and things she certainly didn't want to remember as long as she wasn't kneeling next to her mother and sister. In her mind, all of them were alive and well.

"I can look for a well, if you want water." Mr. Bates had obviously misinterpreted her expression. "But we have that right now, and it's going to make you feel better than water will, believe me. If you feel anything like I do this morning, you could likely use something even stronger. It's been a long time since I've ached like this."

She took a drink, trying to keep her thoughts off her face as she felt him watching her. Her stomach only churned worse as the warmth of the wine slid past her chest. She tightened her grip on the neck of the bottle. "You're Protestant."

Mr. Bates's eyebrows furrowed. "Does that matter right now?"

"It feels as though it should."

"I have no desire to convert you, if that's your worry. Or anyone else for that matter. I wouldn't have come to *Portugal* of all places if I did. Again, no offense meant, but you are considered a rather backward part of Europe."

"Backward?" Cecília's hackles rose.

"It's a lovely country. Don't mistake my meaning," he said, "but the rest of the world out there? It's a new age. We're learning, studying, growing. You, well, you still have a bloody Inquisition going." He caught himself. "Beg pardon my language."

"Why'd you even come, then," she snapped, "if the rest of the world is so wonderful?"

"Money." He said the word as though it should have been obvious. "Your uncle offered the me the chance to set up business here. I would have had to be mad to turn that down."

"Greed is a mortal sin."

"The love of money may be the root of all evil," Mr. Bates said, "but the need of money is simply practicality. The only ones who can pretend *that* isn't a fact are ones who have never struggled for it."

Cecília forced down another gulp of the wine, having to admit the warmth was helping her muscles to relax, though she still found herself grinding her teeth. *No use wasting your breath arguing scripture with an Englishman.* She attempted to force her mind to something more productive to talk about before she ended up in an argument she didn't have the stamina to maintain. If Mr. Bates was content with the state of his soul, that was entirely his business. He had nothing to do with her or—the thought registered—"Tio Aloisio..."

"What?" Mr. Bates asked.

"My uncle." Cecília's eyes snapped back to his face. "Was he going to Mass when he left yesterday?"

Mr. Bates hesitated long enough to leave Cecília with the sickly feeling that she had her answer. He finally shook his head stiffly. "Your uncle's faith is his affair, Senhorita Durante, not mine."

"But you know where he was going."

"Senhorita Durante—"

"Mr. Bates"—she kept her voice hard—"is my uncle still Catholic?"

Mr. Bates released a breath. "I couldn't say what he considers himself, Senhorita Durante. But no, he wasn't going to Mass."

Cecília felt the air leave her lungs, nearly as strongly as when the cross had landed across her back. It was no wonder that Lisbon had been cast so low, filled with the likes of her and greedy Englishmen and whatever was happening with Tio Aloisio...

"Do you know what a Deist is?" Mr. Bates continued, clearly attempting to sound kind.

Cecília shook her head slightly, her mind still racing far too much to talk.

"It's... the religion of the new age, I would argue. Theology that doesn't discount man's inherent ability to reason."

"I don't want to hear this," she whispered.

"There are natural laws that govern the universe, laws that man can study. Newton's calculus, thermodynamics... arguably, if man could only find the right equations, we would be able to understand the very fabric of the universe."

"You're talking heresy!" she snapped.

Mr. Bates hesitated for only a second. "You may think so, if you wish to call it that, but the very fact that man is able to find reason in what was once thought inexplicable proves that the world follows a scientific set of laws over being controlled by constant divine interference. The hand of God is not what stops a ball rolling into a thick patch of grass. It is the static force of the grass itself."

"You're saying there's no God?"

"Not at all. Someone had to set the laws and put the universe into motion. I'm just saying there is reason behind natural philosophy. It isn't the Almighty reaching down to move every chess piece in all of our lives."

"And what *reason* could there be behind what happened yesterday?" Cecília's hands started to shake. Clenching them around the wine bottle, she attempted to stop them before she damaged some other part of her that she didn't know could be hurt. "All those people dead? The city burning? What *natural law* would cause that?"

"I..." Mr. Bates paused, though she wasn't certain if he was searching for reasons, questioning himself, or simply reacting to her anger. "I'm not certain. I would have to research—"

"Research." Cecília released an incredulous breath.

A door slammed toward the back of the house, followed by a deep male voice. "Senhora Santiago?"

Realization that she was sitting in her camisa with a bottle of wine, arguing with a heretical Englishman, hit Cecília like a bucket of cold water. She set the bottle down and crossed her arms as well as she could, attempting modesty, but her robe was ruined and the rest of her clothing too complicated to straighten out without help. A second later, the man stepped far enough inside the front hallway to be seen. He slowed as he saw them, and Cecília got a good look at his face. Though he certainly looked older than the last time she had seen him at the vineyard, he was still familiar enough for her to pull up a name. "Jorge?"

The man's brown-black eyes swung from where they had settled on Mr. Bates to Cecília. The slight furrow of his thick eyebrows said he didn't recognize her, though she supposed she looked far more different, no longer twelve or thirteen, than he did still in his twenties.

"Cecília," she said. "Senhor Durante's niece?"

Recognition moved over his face. "Senhorita Cecília." His eyes bounced between her and Mr. Bates. "What in Heaven's name has happened?"

"You must have felt the quake?" Mr. Bates saved Cecília from having to answer. "Lisbon's in ruins. We came here in hopes that Senhor Durante would as well."

"This is Mr. Bates," Cecília added, her voice much more civil than she would have thought she could have managed just a minute before. "One of my uncle's business partners. Mr. Bates, Jorge…" Cecília realized she had never learned the man's last name, so she continued, "He's worked at the vineyard for years."

Jorge lowered his head, though it seemed less than respectful, before he looked back at Cecília. "English?"

She nodded.

"All seem to be, these days," Jorge murmured.

Cecília didn't bother to delve into that. "Where is everyone?"

"The church bells came down in town and damaged part of the chapel roof. Most of us stayed to help there, but Senhora Santiago was supposed to be back…" Jorge trailed off as he went back to looking at Cecília and Mr. Bates. "You said Lisbon…?"

"The quake destroyed it," Mr. Bates said, matter-of-factly enough that it felt like a punch to the stomach.

The worst of the carnage flashed through her mind, as fresh as if she were reliving it. A stab of pain shot through her side as she took a gulp of air, and she bent sharply.

"Senhorita Durante!"

"Senhorita Cecília!"

Both of the men shifted toward her, but another door opened.

"Susana?" a woman's voice echoed through the hall. "Where are you?"

Jorge paused and asked, "Senhora Santiago?" His eyes followed Mr. Bates as the Englishman moved beside Cecília on the bench.

"Jorge?" Tio Aloisio's housekeeper's voice came closer.

Cecília tried to control her breathing before her rib pierced her through.

Mr. Bates placed a hand in the middle of Cecília's back, careful to stay away from her injured side. "Slow, steady breaths. Just remain calm. You'll be fine."

Calm... Cecília refused to look at him. "I need to go home. Lisbon... my mother..."

"I'll get you home, I promise." He kept his voice low, soothing.

"*Minha nossa senhora!*" Senhora Santiago's exclamation cut through the room. "What in Heaven happened?"

Cecília lifted her eyes to look at the tall, broad woman standing in the doorway. Though gray was taking over her dark hair, Senhora Santiago remained exactly as imposing as Cecília remembered from her childhood, down to the stark black dress she wore.

"They came from Lisbon," Jorge supplied. "Senhorita Cecília and"—his eyes slid to Mr. Bates—"Senhor Durante's associate."

Mr. Bates stood from his place on the bench, leaving the spot on Cecília's back suddenly cold. "John Bates, ma'am. We were hoping Senhor Durante would find his way here as well, along with Senhorita Durante's other family. Lisbon is..." He hesitated for a split second, as if planning something more tactful than last time. "The quake hit it much harder than here. Senhorita Durante's side is injured. It should be wrapped. If there is a physician—"

"You poor dears." Senhora Santiago looked between them. "You were here all night in such a state?" She turned to Jorge. "Help Mr. Bates to one of the guest rooms then see if you can find Senhorita Serafina's old things for Senhorita Cecília." She faced Cecília, pursing her lips slightly. "Let's get you patched up and into something decent. We can't have you sitting about in such a state."

Cecília's head felt too thick from the pain, the argument, and the sudden flurry of action, so she let Senhora Santiago cluck over her as they made their way deeper into the house, toward what had once been Tia Serafina's room.

CECÍLIA RAN HER FINGERS along the dented cross on her chest and stared at the dark ceiling. Whatever Senhora Santiago had had Cecília drink to help her sleep had worn off, leaving her alone in her late aunt's ground-floor bedroom with nothing but far too many awful thoughts. She reached out to the little table at her bedside and found the rosary that had been mixed in with the rest of Tia Serafina's things. As much as it still hurt, Cecília slid so she could kneel by the bed and crossed herself.

I believe in God, the Father Almighty, Creator of Heaven and earth; and in Jesus Christ, His only Son, our Lord; Who was conceived by the Holy Spirit, born of the Virgin Mary, suffered under—

A loud creak from the ceiling made Cecília's eyes fly open. Little rumbles had been moving through the ground all day, as though God wanted to remind them of His anger, but nothing had caused damage out in the countryside. Still, Cecília couldn't relax until she heard footsteps that said the house wasn't going to come down around her. Someone else just happened to be awake.

Cecília tried to find her place in the Apostle's Creed. *Born of the Virgin Mary, suffered under Pontius Pilate, was crucified, died, and was buried...*

The footsteps had moved out to the landing on the second story and started down the stairs. Carefully pushing herself up to standing with a soft whimper, Cecília got her feet under her and limped toward the doorway, blindly feeling for the wooden frame in the dark. Her hand found the latch, and she swung the door open a crack in time to see a familiar tall shape retreating down the hall, toward the back door.

"Mr. Bates?" she whispered as loudly as she dared.

The shape turned, the candle he held giving Cecília enough light to see his face. He frowned and took a few steps toward her so he could whisper as well. "Senhorita Durante. Did I wake you?"

"I couldn't sleep." She shifted the rosary beads in her hand slightly, not feeling the need to bring his attention to them after their discussion that morning. "Where are you going?"

"Couldn't sleep either," he said. "I was going to get some fresh air."

Cecília glanced down the rest of the hallway, the door leading out the side just far enough beyond the candle's circle of light to be hidden in the dark. Being outside, away from the creaking building, seemed far preferable to remaining in the pitch-black room. "May I come?"

Mr. Bates hesitated. "You shouldn't strain yourself."

"You're hurt as well."

"I also have a fair deal of experience at it. The ocean's a dangerous place."

Not as dangerous as the land at the moment. She pressed her lips together. "I've been sleeping all day. I can't stay in there."

Understanding flashed over Mr. Bates's expression, as though he had picked up the explanation she couldn't fully give.

He would, she supposed. Something was driving him back outside as well.

He motioned slightly toward the door with the hand holding the candle. "If you would give me the honor of your company?"

She offered as much of a smile as she could manage and followed him down the hall, doing her best to hide her limp.

After jockeying slightly so Cecília could work the latch as Mr. Bates held the candle with his good arm, the door swung open. A cool gust of air swept inside, and the tightness in Cecília's chest lessened just enough for her to feel like she could breathe again.

"We likely shouldn't go wandering in the dark." Mr. Bates set the candle on the steps, using the outside wall to protect the flame from the wind, and pulled the door up behind them.

Getting away from the house seemed preferable, but between her injuries and not knowing how Tio Aloisio's garden might have changed in the past few years, Mr. Bates's suggestion was certainly the most prudent plan. Cecília nodded and started to lower herself, accepting Mr. Bates's help to remain balanced at the top of the stairs.

The silence of the night settled down on them. With only the pinpricks of stars and the smallest sliver of a crescent moon, the rest of the vineyard might as well have not existed beyond the circle of light the candle cast around the steps and patchy grass below.

Cecília looked out over it, searching for the line where the hills met the sky in the dark. "Is this what it's like at sea?"

"What?"

"The darkness like this. Back home, before…" She forced herself off the thought before it could take hold. "I'd look out my bedroom window at night to see all the other windows that were lit, and I'd wonder what it had to be like for my father out in the middle of the ocean. It takes over fifty days to Brazil, he once told me. Fifty days of nothing but water."

"I've never been to Brazil," Mr. Bates said, "but the open sea is an experience. Even darker, though not so quiet. Waves hit the hull. The ship creaks. And that's just above deck. Add a dozen men sleeping in a room a third the size of your uncle's library, and you don't get much quiet."

"I always wished my father would take me with him when he'd go," Cecília said.

Mr. Bates laughed lightly. "I'm not certain you would have liked it much. You start with these grand notions of how it'll be, sailing off to the Orient, seeing the world, and then you find out what it's really like. Being at sea for weeks at a time. Tight quarters. Bad food…"

"You still do it."

"True, but it takes a special level of madness to be drawn to it. I imagine most women would be far too sane for any of that."

"Who says I'm most women?"

He smiled at her. "Had plans to steal a pair of trousers and sail with Anne Bonny, did you?"

"With whom?"

"Anne Bonny. Famous pirate. Dressed like a man to go sailing off with her husband."

"I wouldn't be a pirate." Cecília shook her head derisively. "I *would* have gone with my father, had he let me. It never seemed fair that João got to go, and I had to stay home."

"João's your brother?"

Cecília nodded. "We lost him in the same storm that took my father."

"I'm very sorry to hear that."

She gave a weak shrug, that grief seeming oddly far away.

"Though, perhaps for the best you *weren't* with them, then?"

She met his eyes, the conversation suddenly feeling too personal. She'd only met the man a day ago, and there she was, alone with him once again, discussing her family and desires she'd kept bottled up since her father had explained she'd never be able to go with him when she was a child. She looked down at her hands, covering the rosary with one palm over the other as she changed the topic. "I... I should likely apologize."

"For what?" he asked.

"For earlier," she said. "I shouldn't have been so rude. While we were talking." *Bibiana wouldn't have been...* Then again, Bibiana never got angry in the first place. She was far too good-natured for that.

"I can't say I considered anything rude," Mr. Bates said.

Cecília looked at him. "I was rather curt."

"Passionate, perhaps"—he offered a crooked smile—"but that's to be expected when discussing politics or religion. And you're, by far, not the first person to consider Deist views heretical."

"And you aren't worried about that?"

"I'm not Catholic. Your Inquisition has no power over me. And if you lot are right, I'm already damned, simply being Protestant. I can't say I'm worried over the state of my soul."

Must be nice. Cecília ran her fingers over the little coral beads of the rosary. She took a shaky breath. "If something happened to Tio Aloisio... I don't want him to be in Hell."

"I think it's early to give up hope, Senhorita Durante. Your uncle could be on his way here as we speak. And even if the worst happened, your uncle is a good man. A great man, some would say. It would be a very cruel God who would damn him for eternity just for being willing to *listen* to modern ideas."

You don't think He can be cruel? "Have you worked out what *you* believe yesterday was, then? If not His divine displeasure?"

"I actually found an interesting work by Aristotle in your uncle's library today while you were resting. He postulated that there are vapors underground that need to be vented at times. Like a tea kettle whistling when the steam builds up."

"And so all of *that* was... vapors venting?"

"It makes logical sense, I would argue. Volcanos show there is fire under the earth, and even the Church would agree with that, assuming that is where Hell is. It seems quite plausible that fire could lead to steam that would thus become trapped and cause tremors."

Cecília shook her head. "I'm sorry, Mr. Bates, but I don't believe we're going to find agreement on that."

"I can't say I expected us to, Senhorita Durante."

Cecília studied his face, most of his profile in shadow from where he'd placed the candle. "Do you ever wish you'd become a scholar rather than a sailor, Mr. Bates?"

"Never would have had the money," he said. "Anyway, I'm sure I've learned much more traveling than I would have at Oxford. And it doesn't pay especially well, being a deckhand, but you at least *make* money, learning on a ship."

Cecília nodded, not having any good response to that. As silence settled over them, she ran her fingers over the silver cross at the bottom of the rosary. The small figure of Jesus hung there, face entirely placid for all of His suffering. Her fingers stilled.

"Were you scared?" she finally asked in a small voice. "Yesterday?"

"Terrified," he said. "You?"

"I still am," she admitted.

Mr. Bates nodded slightly, his face showing understanding even if he didn't answer. In the quiet, he placed his hand over hers and squeezed gently. Even if she should have, she didn't pull away, accepting the comfort in the little island of light they'd created on the back steps.

Chapter Four

Cecília prodded her ankle experimentally and grimaced. The worst of the swelling seemed to be retreating, but the pain was still there. She huffed. After four days of sitting around a vineyard that was slowly returning to business as normal with no sign of new visitors, she was starting to move from simple bouts of panic to pure irritation. If Mamãe had left town, she had to have gone to Loures. Or perhaps Cecília's memory had it wrong, had made everything that much worse than it really was, and Mamãe and Bibiana were back home, fixing whatever damage the quake had done there. Perhaps she and Mr. Bates had just ended up in the worst of things, and Mamãe was now sitting around, worried sick, hoping Cecília showed up again.

"Senhorita Cecília."

Cecília snapped out of her thoughts and focused on the man in front of her. "Jorge."

He set a bucket down near the back stairs. Cecília imagined he'd been drawing water from the well halfway between the house and the kitchen, and she had been too wrapped up in her own thoughts to notice. Pushing some of his curly black hair away from his forehead, he straightened again and looked Cecília over. "Should you be out here without a wrap? There's a cold wind starting."

"I'm fine." Cecília smoothed out the bottom of the simple day dress she had taken from Tia Serafina's things so it would cover her ankle. There was a crispness to the day, suiting for early November, but it was certainly not as cold as she'd grown used to, sitting with

Mr. Bates out on the back step while the rest of the house was asleep every night. She glanced up at the hills. The bright sunlight showed the lines of grapevines stretching out around them in a way Cecília hadn't properly seen on their moonless nights. She nodded toward the men walking along the rows. "What are they doing?"

Jorge twisted to follow her eyes to the hill. "We're still checking the trellises to make sure none of them were damaged."

"Have any been?"

"Nothing that can't be fixed. Save the church bells, it seems the worst that's happened is a few smashed bottles and the well running a little low." Jorge smiled. "If anything, it might help drive up the price of a few years' vintages."

"I'm not certain attempting to profit off a disaster would be taken well by many people." Mr. Bates's voice came from the doorway, and Cecília saw Jorge's eyes narrow with thinly veiled loathing.

"There's some damage," Jorge said, "but I wouldn't call it a disaster."

"Did *you* have a building fall on you?"

Cecília's stomach twisted as the memory threatened to come back. "Mr. Bates."

He obviously caught the tone of her voice, brushing the back of his hand against her shoulder in a quick apology.

The way Jorge's expression darkened said he hadn't missed the brief touch, and the look didn't make Cecília's stomach feel any better. "You know, I am a little cold," she said. "I think I'll go inside."

"Do you need assistance?" Jorge asked.

"I have it." Mr. Bates turned slightly.

"I'm fine." Cecília held her hands up as both men seemed about ready to swarm her in some attempt at proving Cecília didn't even know what. Stepping around the Englishman, she moved back inside. Without looking, she could hear Mr. Bates following her a moment later.

That will help... At least it didn't sound as though Jorge had decided to follow as well. She waited for the door to fully shut before she turned to face him.

Mr. Bates slowed as he searched her face, looking genuinely confused at her dark expression. "What's the matter?"

"You shouldn't touch me in front of people." *You shouldn't touch me at all,* she had to admit to herself, but as each night had passed, sleepless and tense, it had seemed more and more pointless to deny what little comfort they could get from the small brushes and moments resting into one another. Things were just different in the dark.

"When did I touch you?"

"My shoulder?"

"That was barely a graze." Mr. Bates shook his head.

"Jorge obviously noticed." Cecília crossed her arms, keeping one a little higher to protect her injured side nearly without thinking. "People will talk."

"I think people have other things to worry about for the moment than shoulder grazes."

She narrowed her eyes.

"As you wish, Senhorita Durante," he said, the words—polite as they were—sounding as though he was just refraining from rolling his eyes at her. *That* familiarity also felt vastly more irritating in the middle of the day than during one of their sometimes-meaningless, sometimes-profound nighttime discussions. The front door slammed open before Cecília could snipe at him.

"Santiago? Senhora Santiago?" Tio Aloisio's voice echoed through the house.

Cecília froze, half-certain she was hearing things. Mr. Bates's body went stiff before he recovered and turned for the front hall. Cecília followed him.

"Senhora Santiago?" Tio Aloisio had moved to the staircase, calling for the housekeeper.

Cecília opened her mouth but couldn't get words out as she watched her uncle's back. Clothes ripped and dirty, Tio Aloisio didn't look as though he had changed in days. And without one of his wigs, his shock of short white hair made him look so... old.

"Senhor Durante," Mr. Bates said, sounding just as shocked as Cecília felt.

Though he can speak.

Tio Aloisio turned, his thick eyebrows furrowing for a moment before he seemed to register who was standing in front of him. "Bates. Cecília."

Cecília's stupor broke, and she threw her arms around her uncle's neck, her relief at seeing him overshadowing anything else she should have been feeling.

"Cilinha." Tio Aloisio's hands went to her waist. The pressure on her side made her jerk back.

"She has a broken rib, sir," Mr. Bates explained for her. "We were unfortunate enough to have the better part of a building fall on us Saturday."

Once again, the matter-of-fact way Mr. Bates talked about it made Cecília's stomach churn. She tried to ignore it. "We were praying you'd come here. Have you seen Mamãe? And Bibiana and Tia E—"

"Aloisio." A new man strode inside, continuing on in what it took Cecília a minute to realize was English.

Mr. Bates's face reacted, and he stepped forward as two more men moved through the door. Though one looked in as rough a shape as Tio Aloisio, the other two were entirely put together. Finely dressed with either round stomachs or stomach padding, they looked far more successful than Mr. Bates. Perhaps more successful than Tio Aloisio. If they continued speaking in English, though, she supposed she would never know.

She turned back to her uncle. "Tio Al—"

"Senhor Durante!" Senhora Santiago appeared from somewhere deeper inside the house.

Tio Aloisio gripped Cecília's shoulder, his eyes already moving between the housekeeper and the other Englishmen who had come with him. "We'll speak in a minute, Cilinha."

"Tio—" She tried to twist after him, but her side stopped her short. She grimaced slightly, placing her hand over her ribs, but Tio Aloisio was already with Senhora Santiago, gesturing sharply as he gave some directions.

Mr. Bates used his left hand to shake the second well-dressed man's, looking entirely engaged in whatever was being said. Cecília pressed her lips together and stepped back against the wall. Whatever Tio Aloisio needed to do, it was obviously important. She would let him finish that and then find out what he knew about Lisbon.

CECÍLIA GROUND HER teeth, standing in the hallway. She had barely understood a word that had been said since Tio Aloisio had arrived, the entire house suddenly seeming to only speak English. She was beginning to understand what Jorge was mumbling about Englishmen.

Cecília straightened as voices began to move toward her. Wearing a fresh set of clothes, though still looking frazzled, Tio Aloisio strode down the hallway with two of the Englishmen no one had bothered to introduce, apparently headed for the back door.

Cecília fell into step beside him as best she could. "Tio Aloisio—"

"Not now, Cecília."

"But—"

"I said not now." He brushed past with the other men, disappearing out the back door a second later.

Cecília blew out an annoyed breath, but she had waited long enough while the men all discussed Heaven knew what. Tio Aloisio obviously knew something of what had happened, and she was going to find out what. She stomped up to the back door as well as she could and threw it open. She froze, looking around in confusion. Tio Aloisio had been walking quickly but not so quickly he should have disappeared in the few seconds it had taken for her to get outside. She walked down the back steps and looked around, trying to work out where the men could have gone. The next group appeared at the back door before Cecília could work it out.

She moved on to the next best thing. "Mr. Bates."

Standing toward the back of the group, Mr. Bates hesitated as all four men looked at her.

Cecília remained focused on Mr. Bates, uncertain how well the others spoke Portuguese. "What's happening?"

Mr. Bates glanced at the other men before looking back at her. "Could we speak later, Senhorita Durante?"

"If someone doesn't tell me what's happening right now, I'm likely to scream." Irritation won out over decorum, Mr. Bates's slightly politer attempt of being rid of her not feeling any better than Tio Aloisio's brusque response.

Mr. Bates hesitated for a moment before he said something in English to the other men with him. Nodding, they moved off, though not without sending Cecília a range of questioning to simply judgmental looks. Mr. Bates watched them leave until they were out of earshot.

Cecília saw no reason to show patience anymore. "What's happening? What's everyone been talking about?"

Something registered on Mr. Bates's face. "Right. You can't understand us."

"No. I foolishly didn't think to learn English before traveling to *Queluz*. I obviously should have known better," she snapped.

Mr. Bates looked toward where the men had gone again. "Your uncle has come back for supplies. One of the king's ministers, a Senhor Carvalho, is attempting to bring the city back under control. Keeping those living in the fields around Lisbon fed will likely go a long way to stopping any more looting or rioting. Senhor Durante has gone to see what we can quickly transport."

"We?"

"I've offered what help I can provide."

Cecília's mind attempted to sort through what Mr. Bates had said. Looting and people living outside the city meant there was a city to go back to, which was better than the worst of her memory. Mamãe and Bibiana could still be waiting for her. "We're going back to Lisbon, then?"

Mr. Bates hesitated. "*We*, your uncle and myself, are. By all accounts, though, it's not somewhere you should be."

"What does that mean?"

"Your uncle can tell you what he likes of his ordeal, but... the city's a ruin. The Paço da Ribeira, Casa da Ópera, Casa da India... all of them are destroyed. Most of the palace was swept out to sea in a giant wave that hit sometime after we left, from what Mr. Broome said. Half the city has been left to live in little dirty tents, and there's nothing like a disaster to bring out the worst in some men. Likely not helped with the prison coming down as well. There are truly the worst sorts of men wandering the streets right now. It isn't anywhere you should be."

It felt as though the air had been sucked from Cecília's lungs. The thought of the beautiful buildings all along the river, gone, the very heart of the city... Her throat threatened to close. She fought to swallow the lump. She wouldn't accept it. She couldn't. She pushed the idea out of her mind. "But my family—"

"They likely have gone to your grandparents' at this point. You said they live close enough by?"

"But if they haven't—"

"Senhorita Durante." Mr. Bates shook his head. "You're aware how many people live in Lisbon? If even just half of them are out in those fields, that's more than a hundred-thousand people. You aren't going to find anyone by wandering the streets."

"I can't just sit here!" Her voice rose dangerously, even as she fought to keep it level. "It's my city. My family. If they're hurt, trapped out there, I can't do nothing!"

"Putting yourself in danger isn't going to help anyone. You're still healing."

"So are you, and you're going." She didn't temper the bite in her tone.

"That's different."

"How?"

He gave her a look that said he wasn't going to waste their time stating the obvious: *I'm not a woman.*

She refused to let it go. "You aren't even Portuguese."

"Senhorita Durante, your uncle has more than enough to worry about at the moment. Could I convince you to attempt writing your grandparents first, at the very least? Your family could very well be there and worried about you."

Cecília ground her teeth, forcing herself to actually think things through, though every emotion pulsing around her body left her wanting to do nothing more than yell. She wasn't certain how far her grandparents were from Tio Aloisio's, as she had never traveled from one to the other herself, but she imagined it couldn't be more than half a day. With how quickly Tio Aloisio was bustling around, though, it didn't seem likely she would have long before he left again—and going with him was her only good chance to return to the city.

Slowly, she began to work out a plan. "I think I need to lie down. I doubt anyone is going to miss me, anyway."

Mr. Bates looked at her as though uncertain that he trusted her sudden switch. With a glance after where the other men had disappeared, though, he apparently gave in to his need to catch up rather than press further. "Try to get some rest, Senhorita Durante. Obviously, neither of us has been sleeping well."

Cecília nodded and silently watched Mr. Bates go. Once he had disappeared from view, she turned in the opposite direction, hoping she would be able to find someone who could make an impromptu ride to Loures.

Thank you, Santo Expedito. She sent a quick glance heavenward as she neared the stable. The saint had to be looking out for her, for there Jorge stood, repairing a cart wheel.

"Jorge." Cecília chanced speeding up, her ankle and side faring surprisingly well, all things considered.

He looked up and offered a quick smile. "Senhorita Cecília."

"I'm glad to catch you." She stopped at the end of the cart. "Are you busy?"

"Senhor Durante asked me to get all the carts ready, but that's done once I get this wheel on straight again. Why?"

"I need to get a message to my grandparents in Loures," Cecília said quickly. "Is that too far for you to ride?"

"Loures?" he repeated and pursed his lips as he considered it. "It's about three hours each way, I think. Perhaps you could make it under that if you pushed."

Cecília did the math in her head. With it already late in the afternoon, six hours would put any rider back well after dark, but if she waited until morning, even if a message left at first light, it wouldn't be back until midday. And assuming Tio Aloisio was planning to leave tomorrow, he certainly wouldn't wait that long with how much time it would take to get to Lisbon, trailing a string of carts. "It is truly a lot to ask, I know, but would you be able to go now? I'm sure my grandparents would give you a room for the night, so you could ride back in the morning. It's an urgent matter."

Jorge studied her for a moment before he lowered his head. "Of course, senhorita. I'll be done with the carts within the half hour, if that isn't too much delay?"

Cecília smiled in relief. "Thank you so much, Jorge. You're wonderful."

He smiled widely at the compliment. "My pleasure. What message do you need delivered?"

Oh, right. In her rush she had forgotten she would need an actual message. She debated finding paper and ink, though as slow a writer as she was, a proper letter would likely take longer than fixing the cart wheel. *Just keep it simple,* she decided. "I need to know if my family is there. My mother and sister. Perhaps my brother." Though Francisco would have been even farther east at São Vincente, so Heavens knew if *he* would have gone to Loures. "If they aren't, ask if my grandparents have heard from them. And you can, of course, tell them I'm here and well."

Jorge nodded. "Anything else?"

Cecília tried to think whether she had forgotten anything but ended up shaking her head. "I just need to find the rest of my family."

Chapter Five

A light drizzle had moved in overnight and slowed the morning packing that was happening at the vineyard. Cecília could only hope that it wasn't slowing Jorge's return. As the hour ticked closer to midday, however, the energy in front of the house changed. The spurts of English she had been hearing got louder and more consistent as people ducked around the carts sitting near the front door. Cecília's stomach knotted as she watched the men work from the corner of the house. She was running out of time to make a decision, and she still didn't have an answer from Loures.

Most holy Mary, Mother of God, through all my weaknesses, please guide me. Give me the help of your grace, for I've never been this lost. I know I shouldn't have left home, but how do I atone? Should I stay here? Do I need to go back? Is this a test of my patience?

She was far too close to failing, if that were the case.

Please, let me know what I should do.

"Senhorita Cecília."

Her name pulled her out of her prayer, and she looked right. Jorge was coming along the side of the house. She looked heavenward—*thank you*—then moved toward him. "Jorge, thank Heaven you're back."

He smiled, though it didn't look happy enough for her liking. He pulled a folded piece of paper out of his jacket. "I'm afraid your mother isn't in Loures, but I thought you might want to know that Senhor Durante spoke to me yesterday, after you did, and asked me to go to Loures as well with a letter for your grandfather. This is the response."

Cecília wasn't certain what she had done to earn Jorge's loyalty over her uncle, but she supposed she shouldn't question it. The Holy Mother had obviously interceded to give an answer. Cecília unfurled the letter. Gritting her teeth, she squinted at her grandfather's loopy handwriting. She read as well as she could, quickly picking up the most important sentences: *We have unfortunately not heard from Maria das Dores, but please do send us Cecília. We are happy to have her until the rest of her family can be located.*

She folded the paper once again and looked back at Jorge. "Do you mind if *I* give my uncle this?"

Jorge hesitated for a moment before he nodded. "Say I saw he was... busy."

Cecília watched Jorge's eyes narrow as he looked at all the Englishmen moving around in front of the house. She started to speak before realizing that Jorge's eyes had settled, and his look had become dark. Cecília turned as well as she could without twisting at the waist.

Mr. Bates glanced over from where he was talking to the portliest of the other Englishmen—Mr. Quigley?—then away sharply as he realized he had been noticed. It seemed it wasn't the first time he had looked toward them.

"Has he been bothering you?" Jorge asked.

"Mr. Bates?"

"He's been following you around."

The fact that the sentence hadn't been a question made Cecília tense. She shook her head. "It's fine. I've barely spoken to him since the rest of the British Factory showed up."

Jorge nodded once.

"Truly, though"—she tried to change the subject—"you have no idea the debt of gratitude I owe you for today, Jorge."

His eyes finally came back to her, and the dark look lessened somewhat. "Of course, Senhorita Cecília. I'm happy to help in any way I can."

"I'll bring this to my uncle." She limply motioned with the letter to excuse herself.

Jorge lowered his head and turned for the back of the house.

Pressing her lips together, Cecília tried to plan her next move. She had to go to Lisbon. She had prayed for guidance, and she had been answered. Her family wasn't in Loures. If she wanted to find them, she would have to go, return to their house, if it still stood, and atone for having left in the first place. Of course, if Mr. Bates had been so fervent about her not going to Lisbon, she couldn't imagine her uncle would be any more enthusiastic about the idea.

Mr. Bates finished whatever he was saying to Mr. Quigley and moved toward her before she'd had a chance to fully decide what to do.

"Something wrong?" he asked as soon as he was close enough to not shout.

She lifted her eyebrows, questioning.

"You look concerned."

"Just thinking," she said then motioned toward the cart. "You're about to leave?"

"Your uncle wrote your grandparents." Mr. Bates seemed to be attempting to placate her, saying the answer was yes. "We can hope you'll have good news from them soon and will be able to go to Loures yourself."

If he could ignore her question, she could ignore his statement. "I need to speak to my uncle."

"He's rather busy at the moment." Mr. Bates twisted to look where Tio Aloisio was talking to another vineyard worker. "But—"

Cecília strode forward, seeing no reason to give Mr. Bates the opportunity to try to talk her out of anything. "Tio?"

Tio Aloisio barely glanced at her. "Cecília, not—"

"I want to go with you."

Tio Aloisio, for perhaps the first time since the Englishmen had walked in the front door after them, fully turned to look at her. Cecília just wished he weren't looking at her as though he hadn't understood a word that had come out of her mouth. Just as she was beginning to wonder if she should ask Mr. Bates to translate into English for Tio Aloisio to understand her, her uncle finally said, "Pardon?"

"I want to go to Lisbon." She squared her shoulders, trying to sound like Mamãe when she intended to brook no argument.

Tio Aloisio shook his head, bringing his hand up to massage his temple. "You can't come with us, Cilinha."

"I can help."

"There is more than enough for us to do without having to worry about you as well."

"But—"

"The answer is *no*." Tio Aloisio sent her a more chilling look than she had ever experienced from the man. "I thank the Lord Almighty that you have made it this far to safety. I am not bringing you back into what Lisbon's become. Now stay out of the way. I've written your grandparents. You should get a letter back tomorrow. I pray your mother and sister are safe there, and you'll be able to join them."

Cecília started to form another argument, but something about how adamantly he had said "tomorrow" made her hesitate. It was almost as though he had specifically planned it so he would be gone before they knew one way or the other.

Before she managed to gather her thoughts, Tio Aloisio dismissed her. "You're welcome to stay here as long as you need, or I have everything ready for you to go to Loures while we're gone. I'll write as soon as I am able to tell you more about the situation in Lisbon. Just trust me, it is no place for a young girl."

"I'm nearly eighteen."

"A young woman, then," he said. "You'll be able to go back to Lisbon at some point. Senhor Carvalho has already taken steps to bring the city under control, but I would not want *anyone's* daughter to be brought into what is happening there, least of all my own brother's." He glanced up at the gray sky. "You should get out of the rain."

It's barely a drizzle. Cecília's frown deepened, but she didn't bother arguing. Between Tio Aloisio and Mr. Bates, it didn't seem likely the men would willingly welcome her along. No, if she was going to follow the Holy Mother's guidance, she would have to sneak along herself. And to do that, she would need a few supplies of her own.

THE CART BOUNCED AS it rolled along the dirt road, jarring Cecília's side enough that she was half-ready to make herself known just so she wouldn't have to remain perched amongst the bags of rice any longer.

Just a little longer, she told herself. Without a watch and under the tarp they had stretched over the wagon to keep off the persistent drizzle, she couldn't tell how long they'd been traveling. They had to be getting close to Lisbon, though, or at least closer to Lisbon than they were to Queluz. She just had to wait long enough that it would be simpler to bring her the rest of the way into the city than to send her back.

The right wheel hit a hole, tipping Cecília onto her injured side. She bit down a yelp, clenching her jaw so tightly her teeth ached. As the pain passed, what was left of her patience evaporated. Carefully, she shifted so she could push the tarp up an inch to see over the side. Her stomach bottomed out. They were closer to Lisbon than she had realized, but the familiar countryside was dotted with sorry-looking shelters. Even-sorrier-looking people sat outside tents made from dirty sheets or awkwardly leaning wood planks, most with their heads down as the light rain continued to fall. As Cecília studied them, the sick feeling grew worse. Some of the pitiful people looked as though they had never lived in a much better state than what Cecília was seeing, but beyond the caked-in dirt and hastily wrapped bandages, many sitting around were as finely dressed as Cecília had been on All Saint's Day. She wasn't looking at the homeless she had always seen on her trips through Lisbon's streets. Poor or rich, they were all brought low, looking sickeningly abandoned.

Is Mamãe out here? Bibiana? Would I...? Cecília couldn't bring herself to finish the last thought as she slipped back down into the cart. Hope tried to flicker somewhere inside her—*Things could be better in the Baixa. We're outside the city. Maybe these people lived where I was*—but with the image of the people sitting out in the rain, the fevered dream that she would find her mother sitting at home, waiting, was slowly dying.

Mr. Bates had mentioned that people were living in the fields around the city. She had accepted that she would possibly have to look for Mamãe and Bibiana in one of the camps, if they had been displaced. Cecília's mind had simply refused to accept the sheer scale of things. Flashes of the quake tried to fight their way out of the dark part of her mind she had been forcing herself to forget. The images came back in all their glory: the tremors, being trapped, the ruins of Lisbon she had almost managed to convince herself were just a dream, a nightmare. Her hands trembled as her breathing became short.

A mix of rising voices and wailing helped snap Cecília from the swell of panic. Swallowing to hold on to her last shred of composure, she rose back up enough to peek past the edge of the cart. A few of the poor souls had found their way closer to the caravan. An equal number argued and pleaded with Tio Aloisio as he seemed to turn them away. The name "Carvalho" reached Cecília, said multiple times with varying effects. A few of the angrier camp dwellers stepped closer to the carts, their insults shifting to the English with them.

"*Estrangeiro!*" Foreigner.

"*Protestante!*" Protestant.

The words mixed with others Cecília wouldn't have dared repeat.

A few of the Englishmen turned back toward the carts, and they started forward again at whatever was said. Cecília lay back against the rice, closing her eyes as the cart painstakingly maneuvered around the growing crowd. She sent up a prayer for safety, half expecting the tarp to be ripped back by an angry, hungry mob at any moment. But they continued to roll forward, past the worst of the shouting. Cecília had to imagine that more than one of the men in their caravan was armed. She couldn't imagine much less would have deterred the vitriol spewing from the people outside.

You prayed for guidance, she reminded herself. *The Blessed Virgin answered herself.* Cecília would have to put herself in God's hands and trust that, whatever happened, it was His will and her atonement. Keeping her eyes squeezed shut and accepting the pain throbbing through her side with the rocking, she prayed for herself, for those outside, and for all of Lisbon.

THE CART STARTED AND stopped repeatedly, to the point that Cecília wondered if they were ever going to reach wherever Tio Aloisio wanted to be. She didn't dare push the tarp up again, not with all the tension still hanging in the air.

Once again, the cart stopped, and Cecília listened, trying to pick out the voices around her. If any of the men were speaking Portuguese, though, she couldn't hear them clearly enough to make out the words.

Finally, the end of the tarp that was tied to the corner of the cart rustled. Cecília tensed. With no shouting, she could be relatively sure that it wasn't an angry mob storming the carts, but that meant—

Mr. Bates pulled back the fabric and froze. He stared at her for a moment, glanced farther off, then looked back at Cecília. "What in the blazes are you doing here?"

Cecília slid forward, keeping her expression haughty as she attempted as graceful an exit from the cart as she could manage—more easily said than done as she pushed her stiff body over the rough, shifting sacks of rice. "My family's here. I'm going to look for them."

"Your uncle just sent a letter to your grandparents—"

"And no one is there." Cecília pulled the letter out of her pocket, the folded paper quite a bit worse for the wear. At Mr. Bates's raised eyebrows, she continued, "I asked Jorge to go to Loures last night. He brought me this back."

A mix of emotions moved over Mr. Bates's face too quickly for Cecília to pick any single one out, and he took the letter from her. The conflicted emotions turned to genuine concern as he read.

Tio Aloisio appeared before Mr. Bates could speak. For one second, he just stared at her as though too exhausted to be angry, then her presence seemed to register. His face went pale before deep-red splotches climbed up his cheeks.

"Mamãe isn't in Loures." Cecília pointed at the letter, as though it would protect her from her uncle's wrath.

His mouth opened and closed for a moment, as if he was trying to yell but couldn't quite manage, before he snatched the letter from Mr. Bates.

As Tio Aloisio read it, Cecília finally looked around. With the sheet tents and sorry wooden *barracas*—shacks—the new camp didn't look much different than the one outside the city. Too many people sat around, dirty, half-dressed, and broken, filling up the landscape. But slowly, as Cecília forced herself to truly *look* at the people around them, the differences became clearer. Rather than the mix she had seen outside the city, most of the people sitting around looked as though they had been well off. Looking farther out through the tents, Cecília even saw a carriage or two that were now obviously being used for housing. Her eyes fell on the river, and some sickly recognition of where they were settled into her stomach. They were back on the road to Belém.

Tio Aloisio flapped the letter at her, pulling Cecília out of her thoughts. "You're going to Loures. First thing tomorrow."

"No one is in Loures," Cecília said. "Mamãe and Bibiana and Tia Ema and Francisco—"

"Trust me, Cecília Madalena, I want to find them as much as you, but you here won't help *anything*."

Cecília Madalena. She wasn't certain she'd ever heard her uncle use her full confirmation name. Her skin pricked icy cold at the sound of it. "I—"

"You nothing. This isn't a game."

"I never—"

"It's too late to do anything now." Tio Aloisio looked at the horizon, as if he would be able to stop the sun sinking in the sky by sheer force of will, before he pointed at Mr. Bates. "Keep her here. I'll have to make arrangements for this now."

"Tio Al—"

Mr. Bates caught Cecília's arm before she could follow Tio Aloisio back toward the tents.

"Let me go." She tried to shake him off.

His grip tightened. "He already has enough to deal with."

"He doesn't need to *deal with* me." She fixed him with as evil a look as she could muster. "He can do whatever *he* needs to. *I* need to look for my family."

"How, exactly?" Mr. Bates looked nearly as angry as Tio Aloisio had, his eyes flashing right back at her. "Wander around in all of this? Hope you run into someone?"

She refused to show her own uncertainty. Things were far worse than she had let herself believe, but she had made it that far. She couldn't simply slink off and not try, already in so deeply. "I know plenty of lisboetas. If I go to the Baixa—"

"The Baixa's gone," he said. "It burned. The only people you'll meet in town right now are people you certainly don't want to. There are Lord knows how many bands of soldiers roaming the streets, trying to get rid of all those people."

The panic from earlier started to build in the pit of Cecília's stomach at the idea of the fires. "Stop it."

"Your uncle didn't want to worry you, but do you really want to hear how bad it is? How people trapped in the rubble burned alive before anyone could help them? How those prisoners who broke out are now robbing and murdering their way through the people who are left? Do you need to hear it all to understand why you can't be here?"

Blood rushing through her ears, Cecília wrenched free and started away.

"Cecília!" He followed.

"Leave me alone."

He grabbed her arm again. "I'm not letting you wander off."

"Let go!"

"No."

Her chest clenched tightly enough that the world spun. She couldn't stay there. Too much was fighting for space in her mind. She had a plan. She had to follow her plan. She had to find her family. Jerking, she tried to get free, but he had her, surprisingly strong with his left hand. The words bubbled up. "*Ajude-me!*" she called for help, glancing aside just long enough to see if anyone had noticed before giving Mr. Bates a desperate, challenging look. "*Estrangeiro! Protestante!*"

Those words certainly got attention. Mr. Bates pulled back as if burnt, and some of the men nearby shifted toward them, obviously ready to intervene. Cecília didn't wait to see what she had left Mr. Bates to, turning away to outrun the horror in her head.

Chapter Six

Cecília stood in the middle of Hell. That was what it had to be. Somehow, she had made her way through the skeleton streets to what had been her home. The last lingering sliver of hope that she would find someone there—that things would somehow go back to the way they had been—shattered, and the emptiness knocked the wind from her lungs. Nothing but the stone foundation and ash remained of her home. The smell of charcoal and burnt flesh coated her nose.

"People trapped in the rubble burned alive before anyone could help them." Mr. Bates's words echoed around Cecília's hollow skull. Her throat constricted, gagging her. Without that hope—without any hope—she couldn't fight off the possibilities. *Was Mamãe trapped? Was Bibiana?* Cecília remembered the votive she had lit before leaving. Such a little thing. Something she had done a hundred times before. *Did that votive topple in the quake? Did I start the fire that burned my family alive? Could God possibly be that cruel?*

Her stomach revolted, and her legs gave out. As she hit the ground, a cloud of ash puffed up. Her Hell coated every inch of her. She fought to breathe. When she finally could, she broke down and cried.

By the time she ran out of tears, the sun had sunk to the horizon. She looked back across the shell of her home in the long shadows. There was no way she would be able to get back to Tio Aloisio before dark. She couldn't bring herself to care. As often as she had sneaked out against Mamãe's wishes, Cecília had never dared leave home after dark. Being left in her nightmare in the shell of her old life overnight seemed only fitting.

A hazy streak of light cut through the ash, and a glint of metal caught the corner of Cecília's eye. Forcing her heavy body to move, she dragged herself forward enough to paw through the ash to the glint. Blackened and slightly misshapen, the silver statue of São Cristóvão she had locked under her bed three years ago as punishment for letting Papai and João die broke the surface. Cecília held the small figure in her ash-covered palm. Another sob swept through her chest, no tears left to join it. She squeezed her eyes shut.

What are You telling me?

If the Blessed Virgin showed God's will for me to go back to Lisbon, what does São Cristóvão, the patron of travelers, mean? She had already traveled too much. After everything else, she wasn't sure she could go much farther.

"What have you found there, *bonitinha*?"

Cecília's hand wrapped around the little statue as she snapped her head to the side.

Three men stood on the street below the cracked stone stairs that led up to the remnants of her scorched home. Wearing ripped clothing coated in ash, they didn't look much different than any of the other lisboetas she had seen haunting the ruins on her way to the Baixa. Something about the malice on their dirty, scarred faces, however, made Cecília's heart jump to her throat.

She slipped the statue into her pocket as inconspicuously as possible and stood. Her legs tried to give out again.

"Found some little piece of gold, hmm?" The man at the front moved up the stairs, blocking Cecília's way back to the street. "Something pretty the rest of us missed?"

Criminals, Cecília had to assume, or at least men who had taken to pilfering in Lisbon's tragedy. Indignation mixed with her need to flee, strengthening her limbs. She glanced to the side. A blackened chunk of wall closed off the far side of the house. She wouldn't easily be able to make a run for the alley—if the alley was there anymore. She could jump from the foundation to the road to her left and avoid the stairs. But even if her aching body could take the jolt from the three-foot fall, she wouldn't likely outrun the men, especially not with one still standing on the street as the second followed the leader into the shell of a home. If it came down to trying or standing there, waiting to see what harm the men would do her, though…

Cecília shot toward the ledge closest to her, praying her body would hold out. The men were too quick. Arms locked under hers before she had a chance to jump and pulled her back.

"Now, now, *bonitinha*, we're trying to be friendly." The leader jerked her around to face him. The sour smell of his breath mixed with the acrid smell of smoke. "You don't want to go so soon?"

She thrashed, new stabs of pain shooting up her side from her rib with each movement.

He swung her again so her back was pressed to his chest and pinned her arms to her sides. "Check her skirts."

"Pleasure." The second man approached.

"Let go!" She kicked, trying to hit the man in front of her, the one behind her. It didn't matter. She needed to break free. She needed—

Her heel connected with the shin of the man holding her. He jerked in surprise, releasing his grip enough for Cecília to wrench loose. Panic pounding in her ears, she ran. Pain, nearly strong enough to dull her vision, shot through her body as she jumped to the ground. Ash flew up around her as she scrambled through the rubble. Her side burned in agony, her breaths coming shorter and shorter as her body tried to give out. Still, she could hear the men behind her, their footsteps getting closer and closer.

She rounded a corner and skidded to a stop at a group of soldiers standing at the other end of the street. She tried to call out for help but found she couldn't draw the breath to speak. Their eyes lifted all the same, some hitting her as others looked over her shoulder. The footsteps behind her slid to a stop.

"*Soldados!*" one of the thieves shouted, and the feet turned away.

"After them!" a soldier at the front ordered some of his men.

Cecília tried to catch herself on a jagged wall as her body slumped. She couldn't manage to lift her arm. Her knees hit the ground again, and she clutched her side, trying to breathe.

A shot rang out somewhere behind her. Then another. The soldier at the front moved up to her. "Senhorita, are you hurt?"

She still couldn't draw enough air to speak.

The man set his musket aside to help her to her feet. "Senhorita?"

She took another gasped breath and finally managed, "Those men... I was at my house"—*what used to be my house*—"and they came. Tried to take—"

The sound of pounding hooves cut her off.

Cecília kept one hand on his arm for balance as she watched a man approach on a horse. Likely around Tio Aloisio's age, he was as ash-coated as everyone else in the Baixa, but the air he gave off said he was someone important.

"What the Devil were those shots?" He looked over the soldiers on the street.

"Three looters, Minister," the soldier standing next to Cecília answered. "They attacked this woman. I sent Almeida and Mendes after them."

"See them on the scaffolding by the river. Obviously, we don't have enough hanging there to get our point across," the horseman said before he looked at Cecília, his piercing eyes studying her from a long, wizened face that was still quite handsome despite his age. "This is a dangerous place to be, senhorita. Especially after dark."

Cecília could only manage to nod.

"I believe she's injured," the soldier supplied.

How the man on the horse had been addressed suddenly registered in Cecília's mind. "Minister."

The man cut off whatever he had been about to say.

"Are you Senhor Carvalho? The king's minister?"

He lifted his eyebrows. "I am."

"You sent for my uncle," she said in a rush.

Senhor Carvalho tilted his head slightly. "And who is your uncle?"

"Ti... Durante. Senhor Aloisio Silva Durante. He brought wine and rice from his vineyard today."

"I'm glad to hear it. Your uncle is a good man," Senhor Carvalho said gallantly then glanced around. "I trust he didn't leave you here alone?"

Cecília swallowed.

"Cecília!"

She jumped, the motion only making her knees buckle again. She clutched the soldier's arm to remain upright and blinked to convince herself that she really was seeing Mr. Bates down the road. She recovered, starting the introduction before he made it to the group of men. "Senhor Carvalho, this is one of my uncle's business partners, Mr. Bates. Mr. Bates, Senhor Carvalho, the king's minister."

Mr. Bates's stride broke for a split second before he continued toward the group. He lowered his head enough to be respectful as he faced Senhor Carvalho. "An honor to meet you, Minister. I was... helping Senhorita Durante look for her mother. Before we got separated."

Cecília didn't contradict Mr. Bates's telling of events, even as she could feel how harshly the soldiers standing around were suddenly judging him.

Senhor Carvalho looked between them. "Is Senhor Durante nearby?"

"He's back toward Belém." Mr. Bates pointed.

Senhor Carvalho nodded once. He shifted his gaze to one of the other soldiers. "Vargas, take Senhorita Durante and Senhor Bates to my house. Carry her, if need be." He looked back to Cecília. "My house survived the destruction, praise be. You can stay there until daybreak. I've done my best to rid the street of looters, but I wouldn't suggest walking through town after dark. I believe you've seen why."

"You're too generous," Cecília managed.

"Your uncle has been a great help to me," he said. "It is the least I can do."

Cecília opened her mouth to answer, but the minister had already turned, issuing the rest of his orders before riding away. Holding her side, Cecília forced herself forward, determined not to be reduced to being carried through the streets. Her muscles fought against her, feeling nearly as sore as they had on the day everything had happened.

The soldier next to the one she'd been using as a crutch stepped with her. "Senhorita Durante?"

She looked at him.

"Are you related to Father Durante? From São Vincente?"

Something fluttered in her stomach, dangerously close to nausea. "My brother."

"I can't say what's happened to him now, but he was ministering to the ill in one of the *campos* on the east side of town. If you're looking for your family."

A lump formed in Cecília's throat that she had to fight to dislodge. Perhaps she was too late to save Mamãe and Bibiana, but it was possible she wasn't entirely alone. "Thank you."

The soldier lowered his head in a quick bow, shouldered his musket, and moved off with the rest of his fellows, ready to face whatever else was stirring on Lisbon's streets.

CECÍLIA STARED AT THE ceiling of the little bedroom, trying not to think. The nine-year-old—whom Senhor Carvalho's wife, Senhora Daun, had quickly introduced as her daughter Teresa Vi-olante—lying on the bed next to Cecília turned over in her sleep. The slight bounce was enough to shoot a new pain up Cecília's side. A flash of the men grabbing her, followed by the burnt shell of a house, the fires, and the quake crashed through her mind. She suddenly couldn't breathe. Whether her rib had finally been driven through her lung and she was dying, or if the weight of what was happening was suffocating her as readily as that crucifix, she didn't know. She sat up, trying to stop her mind from racing.

It was no use, not in the dark. Doing her best not to wake Teresa or the Carvalhos' four-year-old daughter, whose name Cecília couldn't remember, she climbed out of the large shared bed and moved for the hallway. As a guest in the fine house, especially a guest foisted upon an unwitting hostess late at night, Cecília knew she shouldn't go wandering. But she couldn't stay in that room with those beautiful little girls with the awful thoughts of what had likely happened to Bibiana so fresh. Less than a mile from her home in the Baixa, Senhor Carvalho's house in the Barrio Alto looked practically untouched. It didn't feel fair. It *certainly* wasn't fair. Too much tried to press down on her at once—memories, pain, horror. She made it as far down the stairs as the first landing before she collapsed. A sob broke free before she bit it down. The last thing she needed was to wake the entire house.

She gripped her injured side with one hand, holding her knees to her chest with the other. She felt too much hurt to deal with it. She had no choice but to find Francisco. He was the family she had left. He was a priest. Maybe, just maybe, he would know what everything meant. Because it had to mean something. It had to. To think of everything as some twist of fate set in motion by an uncaring God... some natural process...

"Senhorita Durante?"

She squeezed her eyes tightly. Of course he would show up. For the past week, when had there been a moment of weakness where Mr. Bates hadn't appeared? Whether he was helping or hurting, she didn't know. She got control of her breathing enough to talk. "Leave me alone."

"Are you hurt?"

"I said leave me alone." She looked up at him, raising her voice as much as she dared. "What are you even doing here?"

The mix of hurt and anger she had seen since she had left him in the camp—which he had been veiling while dealing with Senhor Carvalho and his family—flickered back to life on his face. "I was worried you were going to try sneaking out again. You seem to have real trouble remaining in place."

"And that's your business?"

"Your uncle told me to watch you. Though I think I've gone rather above and beyond after you tried to get me killed this afternoon."

"You wouldn't have been killed," Cecília mumbled into her knees.

"You know why so many members of the British Factory weren't hurt in the quake?" Mr. Bates's voice tipped up with a hard edge. "Because they left the city to avoid trouble with your lot on All Saints' Day. Don't think we aren't aware of what could happen to us being here."

"Then maybe you shouldn't be here," Cecília snapped, hardening herself to stand once again. "Leave me alone." She made it half to straightening before her side spasmed.

"You are hurt." The anger in Mr. Bates's tone leached out in an instant as he moved up the final step to her side.

She remained half hunched. "I'll be fine. I just aggravated it."

He moved around her so his good arm was closest to her. "You should be lying down."

"I'm fine," she lied, even though she knew her pain had to be evident on her face as every muscle tried to clench at once. "I don't need your help."

"You can barely stand."

She flinched as he tried to touch her. "I can't go back in there."

"In where?"

"With those girls." She dropped her voice as the anger she had been clinging to faltered under the new wave of grief.

"The Carvalho girls?" The frown came through his voice even if Cecília couldn't bring herself to look at him. "Have they done something?"

"It's my fault," Cecília barely whispered. "It's all my fault."

Mr. Bates started to speak then straightened as he looked around. "Please. You need to sit at least."

Cecília didn't fight him anymore. Accepting his hold around her hip below her injured side, she let him lead her down the rest of the flight and to a low bench in the Carvalhos' salon.

Once she was settled, Mr. Bates lowered himself to kneel in front of her. "Now, what's happened?"

"They're dead." She kept her eyes on her hands, doing her best not to start crying again. Her side wouldn't take it, and for as much as Mr. Bates had thrust himself into her life over the past week, she couldn't be that open with her grief with it so fresh.

"The girls...?" he started in alarm before he apparently realized what she meant. "You found something? At your house?"

"They would have been there." It had been too early for the Palmeiro's service, and Mamãe certainly wouldn't have left the house for any other reason. "And I left a candle burning..." Her throat tried to close up. She forced the lump down. "That fire... If they'd been trapped... If they were alive..." The image of that horror washed through her, and all semblance of control broke. She doubled, accepting the pain as her rightful punishment. If she did die, if her rib did pierce her through, perhaps that would be her final act of atonement and, she could hope, her promise of salvation—marked like Jesus, pierced by the Holy Lance.

"Did you see anything that said they were there?" Mr. Bates's voice broke back through. "Cecília." He forced her chin up slightly so she would have to look at him.

"Everything's turned to ash," she said softly.

"So nothing. No bones? No jewelry they were wearing?"

She shook her head as much as she could.

"Then you don't know they were there."

She opened her mouth, but he didn't let her get a word out.

"And even if they were, God forbid, fires broke out in hundreds of places all over the city. You can't blame any single candle for that. It would be like blaming a single locust for blighting a year's crops."

Cecília held Mr. Bates's eyes, studying them in the mostly dark room. "Why are you trying to make me feel better?"

His eyebrows furrowed slightly.

"You were angry with me a minute ago."

He hesitated. "Just because I'm upset doesn't mean I want you to blame yourself for deaths that aren't your fault and possibly never even happened."

"You said people burned—"

"I was upset. Worried. I didn't mean to scare you."

"Worried?" She suddenly realized how close he was, his face only a hand's width from her with how she had leaned forward.

"It's dangerous here," he said. "You're lucky nothing unspeakable happened to you before those soldiers came."

She swallowed. "How did you even find me?"

He gave a one-shouldered shrug. "I asked how to get to the Baixa—since that seemed where you were most likely to go—then followed any commotion I heard. I imagined I'd find you at the heart of one of them."

"Seems like a lot of trouble to go to."

"Your uncle told me to watch you."

"And you traipsed all over Lisbon to do that?"

He paused then finally said, "It seems so."

Cecília studied him for another moment before she straightened. A pained hiss escaped, and her hand went to her side.

"You've done too much today." Mr. Bates moved next to her on the bench, his hand hovering above hers without touching it.

"Do you still believe God didn't do this, Mr. Bates? After seeing all this?"

"Do you still believe He's so cruel?"

She pressed her lips together. "I prayed for guidance this morning. Jorge showed up just then with that letter. You don't believe that is divine intervention?"

"Fortuitous timing, perhaps." He gently shifted her hand out of the way so he could check her side. "Though I'd imagine mortal infatuation played more into that then divine interference, if you asked him to go for you."

Cecília winced as his fingers found the worst of her bruise. "Infatuation?"

"By my estimation, I imagine that field hand was more interested in your favor than in doing God's work." He ran his fingers to the side slightly before he shook his head. "You can't run around like this, Cecília."

She caught his hand so he would stop prodding, and something in the air turned tense. Another second, and he pulled back, clearing his throat. Cecília swallowed, the new pressure still pushing down on her. "You keep calling me Cecília."

He looked up at her. "What?"

"You've been calling me Cecília."

He blinked, fumbling his words for a moment before he managed to properly speak. "I'm sorry. I don't know why—"

"You may, if you'd like." She brought her hand back to her side.

His eyes dropped again. "Did you have someone rewrap that?"

She hadn't. Senhora Daun had already seemed less than pleased to have two strangers show up on her stoop unannounced, even if she had the good breeding to hide it behind a kind smile, and Cecília had been on the edge of collapse after making it up the final hill to the Barrio Alto. The memory of the night they had arrived at Tio Aloisio's, though, suddenly sent a flash of heat through her, embarrassment and something else. A week before, she wouldn't have known the Englishman from Adam. A week before, everything made sense. But a week before might as well have been lifetimes. Her voice came out low, too soft to be authoritative. "I'm not going back to Belém tomorrow. Or to Loures."

Mr. Bates frowned.

"One of the soldiers said my older brother was ministering on the east side of town. He's a priest. People will know him. I should be able to find him."

Mr. Bates looked her over. "You're in no shape to go wandering through any of the camps around here."

"I have to find him." She had been sent back to Lisbon for a reason. Whether or not Mr. Bates would believe that, she had to.

His eyes settled on her face, searching for something there. "You know you can be an infuriatingly stubborn woman?"

"I've been told. Several times."

His eyes settled on her mouth for a half a second before he met her gaze. Tension like a thread pulled tight reverberated inside her, then once again, the air in the room shifted. Suddenly, the gap between them had vanished. Cecília hadn't leaned forward, she hadn't felt him do so either, and yet their lips brushed. What air she had been able to inhale left her lungs. Her entire body tingled from the sensation, from the suddenness, from the deep, internal knowledge that everything that was happening was wrong. And yet she couldn't stop it. For the first time in what seemed like lifetimes, she didn't feel so dreadfully alone.

From the building desperation between them, he felt it too. The brush turned to steady pressure, Mr. Bates's hand going around the back of her neck, guiding her mouth against his. Cecília gave herself over to it, little pleasant jolts shooting down through her, fighting off all the awful feelings lingering there.

His hand moved from her neck, sliding around her as his body began to press her backward. Pain shot up her side. She gasped, a new spasm trying to work through her, and Mr. Bates shot back so quickly he nearly knocked himself off the bench.

He said something in English then switched back. "I'm sorry. I don't know what..." He stood. "You really should rest—"

"Please don't go," she whispered.

He hesitated. "What?"

"You didn't come after me just because of my uncle, did you?"

The question sat in the air between them, hovering on top of the earlier thickness. He finally released a breath. "No." He didn't elaborate.

She didn't want him to. "Then sit with me? I'll even listen to more about your philosophy, if you like. I just... I can't think anymore. Not about today. I will if I'm alone."

Mr. Bates looked at her for another moment before he moved back to the bench. Ignoring how wrong everything had already gone, Cecília leaned into him. After the slightest hesitation, he slid his arm behind her—not quite holding her but letting his fingers brush against her shoulder. Shutting her eyes, she tried to focus on the touch. As always, everything was different in the dark. And dear Lord, she needed whatever he could offer as long as she was left floating in the night.

She imagined he did as well.

"YOU SAW PAPAI?" FOUR-year-old Maria Francisca hovered by Cecília's legs as one of the Carvalho servants helped rewrap the bandage around Cecília's ribs. "Is he coming home now?"

"You know Mama said he's busy." Teresa, still perched on the bed, rolled her eyes. "He needs to help the king help the hurt people."

Cecília offered both little girls a smile, though she wasn't sure if their inquisitive chattering was better or worse than being alone with her thoughts.

"Your cross is broken." Maria Francisca moved out of the way as the servant shifted to tie off the wrapping.

"It's not *broken*. It's bent," Teresa corrected.

Cecília lifted her hand to the poor dented necklace still tied securely in place near the neckline of her camisa.

"Do you want a new one?" Maria Francisca hopped onto the bed next to her sister.

Somehow, Cecília's smile stayed in place. "*My* papai gave me this one. I can get it fixed later."

"Is he helping the king too? Your papai?"

As little as the four-year-old's exuberance fit Cecília's mood, Cecília couldn't bring herself to dampen it while looking at the girl's bright, curious eyes. "He's in Brazil. Have you ever seen one of those big ships they have down at the docks?" Her stomach twisted. *Big ships they* had *down at the docks...*

"When we were coming back from court with Mama." Teresa nodded.

"My papai owns one of those. He sails it all around the world."

"Papai's sailed places too." Maria Francisca's voice rose, not letting her sister talk over her again. "He lived in Low... Lun..."

"London," Teresa supplied.

"London. Then he met Mama in *Österreich*."

"Austria," Teresa translated.

Maria Francisca nodded fervently enough that her dark curls bounced. "She's from Austria. Just like the old queen."

"Dona Maria Ana," Teresa said with an affected somberness that seemed almost comical on her angular little face, "God rest her exalted soul."

Another harried-looking woman appeared in the doorway. "Senhorita Teresa, Senhorita Francisca, why are you still sitting there? Your breakfasts are getting cold. Up, up!"

Maria Francisca popped off the bed. Teresa huffed but stood to follow her sister and the woman Cecília had to assume was their nurse.

The servant helping Cecília moved to the rest of the clothing Cecília had taken from her late aunt's things and began to tie on the petticoats. "That's not too tight, senhorita?"

"It's fine." Cecília tried not to think about the sharp ache that hadn't left her side since yesterday. She was still relying on the wrap rather than stays to avoid the boning pressing into the deep bruise, but if she was going to keep going, she needed to find a way to ignore it.

Of course, she hadn't yet figured out how she would get Mr. Bates to stop from trying to get her back into bed. Heat rushed into her cheeks as her thoughts swung out from what she had originally meant in her own mind. Even though they hadn't kissed again, Cecília still couldn't fight the flush from the mix of that memory and how she had woken before dawn, resting against him.

"The staff will be up soon, Cecília." He had stroked her hair lightly to wake her. "You don't want to be caught down here." *With me,* his tone implied.

She thanked Heaven that the servant girl was too busy tying Cecília's pockets over the petticoats to see how red Cecília had turned. She would have to ask if the Carvalhos had a confessor. She had gone too long without the familiar structure of Mass, prayer, and confession that had marked her days her entire life. That was likely driving her as mad as the rest of what she had lost in the past week. Everything that had ever anchored her was gone. At least she could possibly get confession back.

And before I see Francisco, she hoped. Priest or not, he was still her brother. She couldn't confess to him. Especially not after what had happened last night.

The girl finished with Cecília's gown and took a step back. "Is there anything else you need, senhorita?"

"No, thank you."

"Senhora Daun is taking her breakfast downstairs, if you would like to join her."

Cecília nodded and watched the girl go before she took as deep a breath as she could, testing the new wrap. For all that had happened the day before, she had to admit she wasn't in as bad a shape as she would have anticipated. She apparently had held together so far. She could only keep doing what she had to and see how long that remained true. She slipped her hand through the slit in her skirt and into her pocket to feel the slightly deformed São Cristóvão statue. Trying not to think too long, she moved for the stairs.

She could hear Mr. Bates's voice before she reached the bottom. In a light and congenial tone, he was speaking German, which said he was with Senhora Daun. As tired as Cecília was of not understanding anything that was happening around her, his being able to speak to Senhora Daun in her native language had been the only thing that had truly made the woman smile when they had showed up on the Carvalho doorstep, so Cecília supposed she couldn't complain too much. She moved into the doorway and waited for the pair to notice her.

Mr. Bates looked up first, and he trailed off mid-word before he recovered and finished whatever he'd been saying to Senhora Daun.

Cecília didn't bother trying to pick out any of the words, simply waiting where she was until Senhora Daun looked at her as well.

"Good morning, Senhorita Durante."

"Good morning, Senhora Daun." Cecília performed as much of a curtsey as she could.

"Please join us." The woman motioned across the low table.

Cecília lowered her head and moved to where Senhora Daun had gestured. The intensity with which Mr. Bates was watching her made heat start to tingle into her cheeks again, though he likely was trying to size up how much pain she was still in more than anything else. To distract herself, she focused on hiding her stiffness.

"Did you sleep well?" Senhora Daun focused on her plate, the earlier laughter in her voice replaced by something formal and stiff.

"Yes, thank you," Cecília lied. She shifted her head slightly so a few loose dark curls of her hair would hang forward enough to block Mr. Bates from view. "I was wondering, though, do you happen to have a confessor?"

Senhora Daun's dark eyes lifted to meet Cecília's, giving Cecília a good idea where little Teresa had gotten her sharply pointed features. "We do, but he is helping my husband at the moment."

"Of course," Cecília said as a servant set a plate in front of her. She tried to think if she should say something else. Another servant appeared in the doorway, saving her from needing to come up with anything.

"A messenger for you, senhora."

Senhora Daun nodded and pushed herself up to standing. "Excuse me."

Mr. Bates rose slightly as well. He waited until Senhora Daun had exited before sitting again.

Cecília watched him out of the corner of her eye through the shield of tight curls.

"You want a confessor?" he asked after a beat.

She looked at him.

"Because of…?"

"Because I'm still Catholic."

He looked down at his own plate, apparently willing to leave there the discussion of the night before. "How are you feeling this morning?"

"Better." She pushed her hair behind her ear, not certain if her discomfort was brought simply being in a room with him again or because of the knowledge that they were in a stranger's home, sharing breakfast with the daughter of an Austrian count, with servants circling behind them. The normalcy of a formal meal certainly seemed wrong after what Cecília had seen. "I was hoping to see a confessor then look for my brother today."

The careful treading shattered, and Mr. Bates sent her an incredulous look. "Today? You can't be serious."

"He's likely the only family I have left at this point."

"You have your uncle."

Cecília released a breath through her nose and made herself meet his eyes. "My mother had eight children, you know. My sister Ana Margarida died last year, trying to bring her own son into the world. João died at sea with my father. Gabriel and José passed as infants before I was ever born, and Isabela didn't see her fifth birthday. If Bibiana is gone, it's only Francisco and me. You expect me to go off and wait for Heaven knows how long to actually see he's alive?"

"You're *injured.* You need to rest."

"I'm fine."

"Saying you are isn't going to heal your rib any more quickly."

"Do you honestly think you can stop me if I've already made up my mind, Mr. Bates?"

Mr. Bates fixed her with an annoyed, if resigned, look but finally sighed. "If I agree, will you at least allow me to come with you this time rather than running off?"

"*You* don't need to go back to Belém?"

Mr. Bates shook his head, looking down at his plate. "In for a penny, in for a pound." He met her eyes again. "At least wait until we can send word that you're well back to your uncle?"

Cecília studied him, trying to determine if he was attempting to pull some other trick to stop her going before she nodded. "Fine."

Mr. Bates still looked less than pleased, but he set down his slice of bread and picked up the teacup by his plate instead, as if he needed to signal he had concluded his argument. He paused before he fully lifted the cup to his lips. "You are welcome to call me John, if you like. After everything?"

The heat rushed back into Cecília's face before she could fight it, and she turned to her own plate, letting her hair fall back down to hide her.

Chapter Seven

The ache had once again turned to stabbing pain by the time Cecília made it up the slope leading into the campos on the east side of the city. She did her best to hide it. Mr. Bates—*John?* she tried the name out in her mind—had been watching her ever since they had left Senhor Carvalho's house. If she started wheezing, she had no doubt he would stop hovering and swoop in to make her rest. He had already been carefully mapping their route, obviously trying to steer her away from the most objectionable areas of town. Though Cecília had to wonder how he knew where those places were, she couldn't complain, not when they had already passed two sets of newly erected gallows, both with decaying corpses swinging at the ends of nooses.

"Looters," John had offered as explanation before shepherding her toward another street.

Somehow, though, even as they walked through the shell of the city, the deep sorrow that had all but crippled her the day before had turned numb. Hope had finally died, and in that despair, she had found a way to keep moving. Because moving was her only option. As long as she kept walking, focusing on finding Francisco, she could ignore the destruction around her and ignore everything she had lost.

The same sorry-looking tents and barracas started to appear as they left the last of the hollow shell of Lisbon, yet another tent city built up in what were normally empty fields outside the city. Cecília scanned the expanse, a knot pulling uncomfortably at the numbness she had so recently managed to claim. There had always been home-less in Lisbon. Now Lisbon itself was homeless. *She* was homeless. She had simply been fortunate enough not to have to consider that fact.

"Your brother's name is Francisco?" John looked over the crowd in front of them.

"Yes, Francisco." Cecília forced her mind back to more pressing matters. "Father Durante. He was at São Vincente, if you find anyone from that parish."

John glanced up to check where the sun sat, already high in the sky, made a face, then nodded. "We'd better start asking around."

Even if he had been surly with her all morning, Cecília offered as much of a smile as she could manage. He was unenthusiastic help, perhaps, but having someone else along did make the entire under-taking less daunting. As they worked their way through the mix of people sitting around, she also found it made for an easier time with John being able to talk to the scattering of foreigners mixed in with the lisboetas.

The sun was nearing its zenith by the time Cecília found some-one who recognized Francisco's name. The girl, likely a few years younger than Cecília, looked up from wrangling her siblings in front of their sheet-tent. "Father Durante? He took confession for us two nights ago."

Cecília lost her breath for a moment. She swallowed to recover, hearing John talking in English somewhere behind her past the ring-ing in her ears. "Was he here?"

"That way." The girl pointed before reaching out to stop the lit-tlest of the children running about from wandering off.

"Thank you," Cecília said. "Thank you so much."

The girl nodded and turned to yell at two boys wrestling near what Cecília hoped was a mud puddle.

Cecília angled to talk to John just in time to see the woman to whom he was speaking snap something that didn't seem kind and turn away. Cecília lifted an eyebrow when he met her gaze. "Friend of yours?"

"Irish," he said as though that explained everything, rubbing his temple. Something about his expression made him look younger than she remembered. "Any luck?"

"Yes, actually." Cecília's voice lifted, the joy sounding slightly obscene in current circumstances. "That girl said Francisco took confession for her a couple of nights ago."

"So he is ali..." He trailed off. "He's here, then."

Cecília nodded and pointed. "That way, supposedly."

He motioned for her to lead.

Cecília walked the way the girl had directed, knocking her ankles into each other as she felt a flea bite. She wrinkled her nose but kept herself from complaining, even in her head. Her brother was alive. She could deal with a few bites if it meant finding him.

She maneuvered around a man who was sitting and rocking on the ground, seemingly no longer in control of his faculties, then stopped short. Francisco stood in profile, hunched over a pale man on a blanket. He touched the man's hand and gave a kind, if tense, smile.

"Is that him?" John asked.

She nodded, it taking another moment for reality to set in before she could convince her legs to move. She rushed forward. "Cisco!"

Francisco started, spinning toward her with a frown. She slowed at the confused look on his face. His eyes slid over her as if he wasn't certain what he was seeing.

"Father?" The man on the blanket looked between them.

Closer, Cecília noticed both of the man's legs were missing below the knee. Her smile lessened, but even that wasn't enough to be rid of the elated rush moving through her.

"Ce—" Francis started then motioned her away. "Wait there."

Cecília took a few steps back to give the injured man privacy, but she kept her eyes on her brother. An angry raised gash ran along the side of his head past his temple, and a few places on his face were spotted yellow-green with healing bruises, but otherwise, he was still her handsome brother, all in one piece. Even if the gash left a scar, Cecília imagined there would still be plenty of women cursing him for taking the cloth, as there had been back in the Baixa. With Papai's wavy dark hair and Mamãe's blue eyes, he had always been the most striking of the Durante siblings.

Favor is deceitful, and beauty is vain... she tried to remind herself. It was hardly the time for envy.

As Francisco finished with the legless man, Cecília felt John come up behind her and stand, not close enough to touch, though her skin prickled, overly aware of him. She released a slow breath to fight it off then pressed her hand to her side as the pain there caught up to her. The sudden bursts of emotion that let her forget her injuries were going to be the death of her.

Of course, John immediately noticed. "How's your side?"

"I'll survive." Cecília didn't take her eyes off her brother.

Francisco finished his prayer with the injured man then turned back to Cecília. He stared for a moment, sent a suspicious look at John, then swept up to her. "Cecília, thank the Lord. We thought you had been lost."

A small spark of hope tried to catch in Cecília's stomach, not quite finding purchase. "We?"

"Bibiana and I."

Another rush of elation. "Bibiana? She's alive? Here?"

Something passed over Francisco's face that Cecília didn't know how to interpret. "She was found in the rubble, clutching the reliquary holding blessed Santa Inês's hair. Not a scratch on her."

The world spun. Cecília didn't realize John had caught her arm to steady her until she could focus on Francisco's face again. With his eyebrows fully furrowed at the Englishman, her brother obviously wasn't pleased. She caught hold of herself and nudged John back. "Francisco, this is Mr. Bates, Tio Aloisio's business partner. Mr. Bates, my brother, Father Durante." She rushed on with, "Tio Aloisio was needed on the other side of town, so Mr. Bates offered to escort me."

"A pleasure to meet you, Father Durante." John lowered his head and lifted his hat in enough of a bow to be respectful.

Francisco nodded quickly, though his dark look didn't drop. He addressed Cecília once again. "You've been with Tio Aloisio?"

"He's on the other side of the city," she repeated. "Senhor Carvalho, the minister, enlisted his help."

Francisco's jaw clenched. "Yes, I know the minister."

Cecília frowned, uncertain how she should answer her brother's derision. She let it go. "Where's Bibiana? Mamãe...?"

Francisco's jaw didn't relax, but his eyes softened slightly. "I wasn't there, but Senhora Santana was the one who brought Bibiana here. They found Tia Ema's body before the fire reached the street. And Bibiana, of course, miracle of miracles. Mãe, they couldn't reach..."

The way he trailed off said too much. Cecília squeezed her eyes shut, fighting out the image of people burning, trapped under rubble.

"When they couldn't find you at all... I have been praying for you along with all the other poor souls this past week. Praise God that He has returned you to us."

Cecília forced her way back toward her earlier numbness and opened her eyes—focusing on Francisco's blue ones. *Mamãe's blue ones...* "Where's Bia? Can I see her?"

Francisco opened his mouth to answer then shut it abruptly as he checked over his shoulder. "Let me find someone to see to the rest here." He motioned to the injured scattered about. "Then I'll take you to her."

Cecília nodded, remaining silent as he turned away, the frayed hem of his black robe brushing over the trampled grass and mud.

"Cecília?" John asked, his voice still soft even as Francisco moved away.

A new rush of tears tried to bubble up.

"It wasn't your candle," he continued softly. "If anyone could be rescued before the fires reached the house, you didn't cause—"

"Don't," she said then met the pair of concerned hazel eyes. "I need to see Bibiana."

Bibiana had been saved by the intervention of God and Santa Inês. God had given both of her siblings their lives. He had saved Cecília, even if she was less deserving. She needed to thank Him for His miracle, not question the lives He had taken.

Whether or not John was able to reconcile Bibiana's miracle with his distant God, he still seemed to understand. Nodding slightly, he took a step back a second before Francisco returned.

"This way." Francisco motioned, slowly winding his way through the camp farther north. Cries of "Father, Father" went up wherever they passed, everyone seemingly calling out at once for Francisco's attention. He offered a word here, blessed a child there, but never stopped for more than a second. For all his sorrow and apparent exhaustion, Francisco still made as fine a priest as ever.

Finally, he turned sharply and moved to a grouping of shabby barracas. Not much to look at, made of poorly attached planks of wood stacked high enough for people to walk inside, the huts' frames at least protected the people inside more than fabric. Cecília hoped it meant Bibiana had been placed somewhere better than one of the little blanket tents.

I can take her with me to Loures. Now that I know, Cecília told herself. She would be there for Bibiana if Mamãe had been called to

Heaven. Poor, innocent little Bibiana. She deserved somewhere nice to stay. Cecília would even find it in herself to stay inside all day every day for the rest of her life if her grandparents insisted. She could be a proper Portuguese lady if she needed to be.

"Senhora Garcia?" Francisco called.

A little round woman standing not much higher than Cecília's bust appeared at the open side of one of the huts, brushing her hands on her dirty skirt. "Father Durante, I didn't expect you this early."

Francisco gave the small woman a quick smile then stepped to the side to motion to Cecília. "Senhora Garcia, this is my other sister, Cecília. God has seen that she's found her way here."

"The Lord is good." Senhora Garcia looked genuinely elated at Cecília's appearance.

"The Lord is good," Francisco repeated. "She wanted to see Bibiana."

"Of course, of course." Senhora Garcia stepped out of the way of the open entrance to the hut.

Cecília stepped through when Francisco motioned, only a few inches separating her head and the wooden plank serving as a roof. She glanced back just long enough to see both John and her brother stooping awkwardly to stand inside the little hut. Her eyes took a moment to adjust to the dark shadows cast around the corners of the shelter, nothing quite sticking out in the lumps of cloth and pillows that had been used to cover the muddy ground. In the darkness, she heard her sister's voice before she could pinpoint where Bibiana was.

"*Ave Maria, gratia plena, Dominus tecum.*"

Cecília's eyes finally focused on the mumbling little lump in the far corner. "Bia!"

"*Benedicta tu in mulieribus, et benedictus fructus ventris tui, Jesus,*" Bibiana continued to murmur in Latin, her blue eyes focused on the edge of a blanket in front of her as if she hadn't registered that anyone had entered the barraca.

"Bia?" Cecília slowed her progress across the small space.

"She hasn't stopped since she was pulled from the rubble." Francisco didn't move from his spot by the doorway.

"She's been praying Hail Marys all week?" Cecília frowned, keeping her eyes on Bibiana as the Latin continued to fall from her sister's lips.

"Praying the Rosary," Senhora Garcia said. "Over and over. All in perfect Latin. She is truly *a criança milagre.*"

"The miracle child?" John repeated from his place just behind Francisco.

"She was saved by Santa Inês, the protector of young girls and chastity." Senhora Garcia nodded. "The little one is a beacon to us all."

Bibiana finished her first prayer and barely took a breath before starting into the next. "*Glória Patri et Fílio et Spirítui Sancto...*"

"Does she not sleep?" Cecília turned to look between the senhora and her brother.

"In spurts," Senhora Garcia said, "though she speaks it then as well. The Lord has sent her back to us to pray for all our sins."

Cecília couldn't muster the same enthusiasm as Senhora Garcia over Bibiana's state, but she crossed herself all the same.

"Has she always known Latin?" John asked.

"What?" Francisco looked at him.

"Has she always known how to speak Latin, or is that new?"

Briefly considering lying to prevent his discounting the miraculous, Cecília admitted, "We learned our prayers."

John nodded, wisely keeping whatever thoughts he had on the subject to himself.

Francisco took a step so he had the room to turn to face John, though the awkward stoop still undercut the authority in his tone. "Mr. Bates, I thank you for bringing my sister here. I wouldn't wish to waste any more of your time."

John's eyebrows rose slightly at the less-than-subtle dismissal, and he looked to Cecília.

"Tio Aloisio has a cart." Cecília tried to break the tension in the little hut. "He was going to send me to Loures. If Mr. Bates could get him to bring it here, I could take Bibi—"

"You can't take her from the city." Senhora Garcia's eyes widened. "*A criança milagre* was given back to pray for the sinful souls still being punished in Lisbon!"

John failed at remaining silent. "You think that's a fair responsibility to impress upon a young girl?"

"Santa Inês was a martyr by twelve."

He snorted. "And that's something to which we should all—"

"Mr. Bates." Cecília fixed him with a hard stare. "Thank you for your opinion, but could I speak with my brother a moment?"

John held her eyes for a second then lowered his head. "I'll be outside."

"You're free to take your leave," Francisco said.

John looked at Francisco then back to Cecília, repeating resolutely, "I'll be outside."

Cecília stifled a low groan at the tension she could see in Francisco's jaw even after John stepped out of the barraca. She looked at the stout little woman, who was still puffed up from John's questioning. "Senhora Garcia, if you wouldn't mind?"

She looked at Cecília.

"I need to speak with my brother."

"If you try to take that child—"

"Senhora Garcia." Francisco lifted a hand. "I will handle things."

Senhora Garcia's lips remained pursed, but she bobbed a short curtsy. "Of course, Father."

Cecília waited for the little woman to leave before she pressed a hand into her side and slowly lowered herself to the ground beside Bibiana. The smell of dirt, ash, and old sweat hovered so low to the ground inside the little hovel. Cecília did her best to ignore it. At least she didn't feel more fleas biting.

As quiet as her voice was, Bibiana hadn't stopped her mumbling. From what Cecília could hear, Bibiana was done with her Glory Be and on to announcing the Agony in the Garden. So she was praying the Sorrowful Mysteries. Cecília supposed it was fitting.

"Bates," Francisco finally said.

Cecília looked back up.

"He's English?"

Cecília nodded, trying to work out the quickest way to take the conversation away from that topic. "Tio Aloisio has a lot of associates in the British Factory, since he trades with them."

"He should have better sense than to send you wandering alone with a man like that."

"Mr. Bates has been nothing but helpful." Cecília left it at that. She touched Bibiana's face. The cheek felt unnaturally clammy, more as if Bibiana were a statue coated in dew than a living, breathing person. "Bia? Can you hear me? It's Cecília."

"*Pater noster, qui es in cælis...*" Bibiana didn't even seem to register that she had been touched, moving straight to her Our Father.

Francisco released a breath and seemed to ignore his anger at least for the moment as his voice softened again. "She doesn't speak, Ceci. Not more than her prayers."

It had been years since Francisco had called her by a nickname. Five years older than her, he had either considered himself too mature or had been too serious for shortening names for most of their lives. She had always been Cecília, Bibiana never Bia, and instead of Mamãe, he used the more mature Mãe. The unexpected familiarity didn't make her feel any better. She touched Bibiana's folded hands. As cold as the rest of her, they didn't move other than her fingers slightly twitching as if she were touching invisible rosary beads while she prayed.

"Bia…" Cecília murmured softly before she turned back to Francisco. "I need to take her to Loures with me. She isn't well."

"No one in this city is well," Francisco said. "Spiritually, Bibiana is likely the healthiest of us all. Father Malagrida himself has stopped here to pray with her."

The name registered somewhere in Cecília's memory. Father Malagrida was the Jesuit priest whom Mamãe had regarded as a living saint. They had all heard tell of the miracles he had performed abroad. Supposedly, he had even known the exact minute Dona Maria Ana had passed, nowhere near the palace. Still, whether or not Bibiana had been blessed by the man, Cecília couldn't reconcile the thought of leaving her little sister to the misery of the camp.

"She's freezing cold, and it's only going to get colder with winter. It can't possibly be good for her health, sitting here with the damp and fleas—"

"God does not show his favor through comfort, Cecília. Those most blessed often suffer the worst in their mortal coil. You should know that."

"You certainly can't wish for her to *truly* be martyred?"

"I would not wish it, from my own love for *both* of my sisters, but it is not my, your, or anyone else's right to decide what God has planned for our lives."

Cecília tried to imagine her sister as a living saint. Bibiana had always seemed blessed. But if that meant Bibiana would have to suffer like Santa Inês, dragged naked through the street and beheaded, Cecília wasn't certain she would be able to accept her sister's fate with any kind of grace. She reached out and touched Bibiana's cold arm again, stomach squirming.

"Do you need to give confession?"

"To you?" She turned her head.

"Do you have something worth confessing you don't wish me to know about?"

"No," Cecília lied, adding it to the list of things she *would* have to confess. "You're just... my brother."

Francisco shook his head, but he didn't press her. He moved far enough into the space to lay a hand on Bibiana's head and mumbled a quick prayer himself before his eyes hit Cecília again. "It's almost time for Sext. Come pray with us, and I'll see if Father Juanes has the time to sit with you instead."

Cecília nodded and sent a final look to Bibiana as the girl continued to mumble her own prayers. *I'll make sure you're taken care of, Bia. While you pray for us, I'll take care of you.*

OUTSIDE OF OBLIGING herself through Lent the previous year, Cecília had rarely followed the Liturgy of the Hours when left to her own devices. Too often, time got away from her, and it would already be time for Vespers before she would realize she'd missed None three hours earlier. She couldn't deny, however, that kneeling with the rest of the crowd that had gathered in the camp and listening to the familiar psalms left her feeling calmer and more normal than she had in days.

Still, she could feel John's eyes on her, burning into the back of her skull. He had kept a respectful distance, standing back by the wooden barracas, not commenting or interfering as they had begun. That hadn't changed the fact that Cecília felt him as distinctly as if he had touched her.

The unwelcome flush moved through her again, and she bowed her head lower, pressing her clasped hands to her chest more tightly as she fought to focus on the prayers.

Create in me a clean heart, O God; and renew a right spirit within me.

Cast me not away from thy presence; and take not thy holy spirit from me.

She would need John's help, though, to get Bibiana out of camp, at least if Francisco remained insistent about keeping her in Lisbon. Cecília supposed she didn't have the right to question Francisco about the will of God. He was a priest. He had been studying the Bible and works from great theologians, books that gave her headaches merely from looking at the covers, for as long as she could remember. It would be a sin of pride to believe she knew better than he did. Yet every time she tried to accept the thought of Bibiana staying in that dark little hovel, cold and rocking, a new push of drive radiated from Cecília's chest and all the way to her fingertips.

Is that Your answer? she asked God. *Do You not want her to stay? Or am I trying to see what I want because I'm struggling with Your will?*

Without any apparent answers to her questions, she let her mind drift. If she did intend to take Bibiana to Loures, she would first need Tio Aloisio's cart. Even if by some miracle of her own she found it in her to walk the three leagues to Loures—and Lord was that an *if* with how badly her body ached—Bibiana didn't seem like she could do much more than sit.

Maybe Francisco would listen to Tio Aloisio. She pursed her lips slightly. Tio Aloisio was likely still furious with her, but he would be a stronger advocate for letting Bibiana leave than Cecília could be by herself.

Movement in the corner of her eye jolted Cecília back to reality, and she realized she had missed the rest of the prayers.

Not helping my cause, am I? She crossed herself quickly and stood with only a slight wince. A quick look to the front showed that Francisco and Father Juanes were both surrounded by others in the camp, so Cecília turned to face John.

He straightened at her attention and moved forward before she could think to motion. His eyes glanced to her side.

"I'm fine," she answered before he could ask the question that was quickly growing old. "Francisco won't agree to me taking Bibiana to Loures."

John's eyebrows furrowed. "He can't want her to stay here."

"He agrees that she was sent back to us to pray for the city."

"Ah." John looked as though he had barely refrained from rolling his eyes.

"Your opinions on that aren't helpful right now." Cecília looked over her shoulder. Francisco wasn't looking at them, at least. She pressed her lips together and turned back to John. "I do need your help, though."

John glanced at Francisco. "I don't think your brother's going to listen to anything *I* say."

"But he might listen to our uncle. And Tio Aloisio... How upset do you think he is with me?"

"I imagine he's more worried than upset," he said. "At least with you."

The realization hit her much too late. "Is he going to be upset with you? Because of me?"

"It'll be fine," he said, but the words were tinged false. "What do you need me to do?"

Cecília worried her lip, adding guilt over John getting in trouble to the list of things she had to atone for. "Do you think you could bring him back here with you? My uncle?"

John frowned. "You're staying?"

"I need to be with Bibiana." And she likely couldn't make the walk back without properly fainting. She rubbed her side lightly. "I'm sorry to ask when you've already done so much—"

"I'm happy to do it," he said, scanning the camp. "But... you think you'll be fine here? By yourself?"

"I'm not by myself." She looked back at Francisco, who had finished his conversation and was intensely focused on her. She turned back to John quickly. "Please? It's not going to help, you being here with my brother. I'm so sorry that I've caused all these problems for you. I—"

"Cecília," he said, "I want to help. You don't need to apologize." His arm moved as if he was going to touch her, but then his eyes flicked toward Francisco, and he bowed instead. "I'll be back as soon as I can. You should be with your grandparents, not out here."

Cecília offered a small smile as he turned. The knot in her stomach pulled tighter as he walked away and tighter still when she realized how awful it felt, him leaving at all.

Chapter Eight

Cecília sat in a hazy room, the entire space feeling insubstantial and yet so real. Deep inside, she knew she was dreaming, yet she couldn't bring herself to hope to wake up. The richly colored pillows under her joined with the rosy golden light that wrapped around her. She was in their dining room, which was decorated with a mix of the Moorish style Mamãe found so fashionable and the accent pieces Papai had brought back from his trips. Each one had its own story, fantastic enough that Mamãe would shake her head and tell Papai to stop spinning tales when he told them, even while she smiled.

A new warmth moved into her as an arm slid around her waist. She looked next to her, somehow not at all shocked by John's appearance out of thin air.

She stared in silence for a moment then finally asked, "Why can't you just have faith sometimes?"

"I have faith," the dream figure of John answered. "Not your faith."

"Why?" she whispered.

He simply smiled and ran his thumb over her bottom lip. Warmth rushed through her, and suddenly, all she could focus on was the desire to feel him kiss her again.

"Senhorita Cecília." A hand clamped on her shoulder, tearing her out of the dream.

She half sat in surprise before she remembered her rib. Hissing, she felt the warmth of the dream dissipate in an instant in the dark barraca. Blinking, she tried to accept the difference.

"Senhorita Cecília," Senhora Garcia's voice cut through the darkness. "It's time for Lauds."

Cecília released a breath, trying to rid herself of the tension still humming in her body. At least the dark hid her face, which was no doubt red. "Is it dawn already?"

"Nearly," Senhora Garcia said. "Get up. Prayer will help you with that bad dream."

Cecília froze. "What?"

"I could hear you tossing. You're going to hurt yourself if you don't exorcize those demons soon."

"Just a dream about my old home was all," Cecília mumbled as she sat up the rest of the way, checking the wrap around her side.

Senhora Garcia didn't comment, which was more than fine with Cecília. She had only a few moments to clear her head before she had to leave her little pallet of blankets and start the day. If to sin in thought truly was to sin in deed, she was solidly damned to be buffeted about in Hell with others who sinned in the flesh.

She had yet to confess the actual kiss in the three days she had been sitting in the camp, waiting for John and Tio Aloisio. Perhaps that had been her mistake. The longer she sat with that on her conscience, the more it would fester. Yet for as wrong as they were, Cecília didn't fully want to give up her dreams. In the bleak camp, their warmth was her only relief, outside of prayer.

"*Sálve Regína, máter misericórdiæ: víta, dulcédo, et spes nóstra, sálve.*"

Cecília squinted, trying to see Bibiana through the dark. Her sister had finished yet another pass through her rosary, though the slurred mumble said Bibiana was asleep. Cecília crossed herself, trying to keep her mind from turning bitter at the constant presence of the words in the hut. Cecília had been there for three full days, and Bibiana had not stopped, not even to sleep or eat. They struggled to get anything into her stomach past the mumbling.

Please let nothing have happened to John Bates. Cecília shifted up onto her knees as she brushed herself off. *Please let Tio Aloisio come today. I will suffer here as much as You ask, but this eternal torment...*

She wasn't certain how to end her prayer, and so she let it trail off. As she had wandered through the *campo,* looking for Francisco three days before, she hadn't been fully able to take in just how bad life was for those left in the camp with nowhere to go. She and Bibiana were considered lucky, living with Senhora Garcia with something that could pass for a roof over their heads, although that roof hadn't stopped water from seeping through. Though it hadn't rained again, Cecília's clothing was perpetually damp. She could no longer tell what itching was from the waterlogged linen and what was from the fleas that seemed to multiply by the hour, brought from place to place by the feral dogs that stalked the camp after dark.

"Senhora Garcia." Francisco's voice came through the open doorway. "Are you ready?"

"Coming, Father Durante," Senhora Garcia called.

Finding the shadow that was Bibiana, Cecília kissed her sister's forehead before heading out for the day. She frowned once again at the clamminess, but even if Bibiana seemed no better, she also seemed no worse. Cecília supposed that was all she could ask for the time being.

Outside the little wooden structure, the shadows of Senhora Garcia and Francisco took more form in the predawn light. Cecília fell into line, following silently as they headed for the emptier space where they held all their prayers.

"Word is, Father Malagrida is going to be in camp today," Francisco said into the quiet morning air.

"What?" Cecília's question pushed over Senhora Garcia's exclamation of delight.

"He's been traveling around the campos to help the ill, both physically and spiritually. I heard word that he'll be doing a sermon nearby this afternoon. You should come."

Senhora Garcia agreed enthusiastically, though Cecília had a feeling the sentence had been directed at her.

"Of course," she said, already wondering how far she was willing to wander from the little barraca that had become her home in case that was the exact moment Tio Aloisio arrived. She could only hope, if it were the day Tio Aloisio made it to the campo, he would be willing to wait for Cecília's return.

CECÍLIA HADN'T BOTHERED to give more than single-word answers outside of the prayers that punctuated her day every three hours or so. If Senhora Garcia had noticed, she hadn't seemed to care. The old woman passed Cecília yet another bowl of the bland rice porridge that was the only real sustenance in the camp and turned to Bibiana. Slowly, she forced the girl to eat in between mumbled Hail Marys and Mysteries. Cecília listened as she poked at her own porridge, her appetite entirely gone after days of eating the mush without so much as a spoonful of sugar to improve the taste.

After a few more bites, Cecília couldn't take it anymore. "I'll be outside, Senhora Garcia."

The woman looked up from her work. "Don't go wandering. Father Malagrida should be here soon."

"Soon" had been the line through Lauds and Prime and Terce. They were past Sext, marking midday, and "soon" had yet to come. Cecília offered as much of a smile as she could manage. "I just need some fresh air. I'll be outside the door."

As she stepped through the empty doorway, Cecília saw that the cloud cover of the morning had dissipated, but it hadn't done anything to remove the gloom hovering over the camp. She pulled her robe tighter around her then slipped her hand through the opening to feel the dented necklace still pressed to her chest.

"Your cross is broken." The little voice played in Cecília's head.

"It's not *broken*. It's bent."

A battered gold cross, Tia Serafina's rosary, and the little deformed silver statue of São Cristóvão, beyond the clothes she currently wore, were the three things that made the entirety of Cecília's earthly possessions. Compared to many, she was lucky. She looked at the men standing near the next row of huts. Though they were sharing a pipe, none looked at one another. Their eyes focused on ground that had been churned into mud.

If we can't go soon, I will go mad...

A commotion in the other direction grabbed Cecília's attention. She glanced back at the shabby little barraca then started forward to see what was happening. Even if she didn't dare take so much as her robe off at night, for fear of robbers or worse, she hadn't been harassed in the camp. Word had spread quickly enough that she was the sister of both Father Durante and the Miracle Child. Even if she didn't have either's divine blessing, the association was obviously enough.

She slowed as the cart came into view, blinking just in case she *had* gone mad. Tio Aloisio stood off to one side, talking to Francisco as a curious crowd began to circle. She took a step forward then froze as her skin tingled. Looking to the end of the cart, she met John's eyes. He offered a small smile before bending to straighten whatever he had been unloading.

Cecília caught her own smile, which was far too happy for the grim camp, and schooled it away before she started forward, moving as quickly as she could without breaking into a jog. "Tio Aloisio!"

The dark look her uncle fixed her with said he wasn't any happier with her. He looked back at Francisco. "I think we need to talk, Cisco."

Francisco bristled, his face pinched in the way it used to when he was younger. "It's Father Durante."

Cecília wasn't the only one getting Tio Aloisio's dark looks. He fixed his eyes on Francisco, hard and steady. "Now."

"You have no authority to—"

"With your father not here, your sisters can use all the help they can get. Where's Bibiana?"

Francisco's jaw remained tense, but he spun quickly enough that his black robe flared around his ankles, and he started for Senhora Garcia's barraca with Tio Aloisio close at heel.

Suddenly alone, Cecília hesitated, knowing that she should go with her brother and uncle. Then again, she needed Tio Aloisio focused on changing Francisco's mind, not splitting his time glaring between the two of them. Her body lit up as footsteps approached her.

Get ahold of yourself. She tried to force the flush away, fighting her traitorous body. She was too aware of him, and those dreams... none of it was right or even natural. She worked to keep her voice steady. "Thank you for bringing him."

"You knew it was me?" John took a place beside her.

Cecília released a breath then turned to face him. "I'm glad you're back. I was worried something had happened to you."

His cheek twitched in a way that could have been another small smile or a grimace. "A lot has been happening. It took a while to get free again."

She started to answer then noticed the cloth sling was missing. "Your arm. Is it better?"

"Oh." John brought his left hand to his right shoulder. "It will be a few more weeks until it's entirely back to normal, but it's on its way. I can push through it." His eyes dropped to her side. "You?"

"I'm fine." Cecília swallowed. Something snapped, and she threw her arms around his neck. Beyond the ash and sweat, some familiar, comforting smell clung to him.

He froze for a beat before he placed his hands on her hips and pushed her back awkwardly. "Cecília..."

She came to her senses and stepped away, a flush moving up her neck. "I'm sorry." She glanced behind her to see if anyone had noticed then placed the smell. She turned back to John. "Were you sailing?"

He cut off whatever he had been about to say as his eyebrows rose. "What?"

"You smell like salt. What were you doing?"

He glanced around again as if someone was going to catch them speaking then looked back at her. "Minister Carvalho asked for those with ships to help bury bodies at sea. Your uncle needed help, and I certainly know my way around rigging."

"You were helping... toss people into the ocean?"

"We had a priest with us. Approved by the Cardinal Patriarch, even, I was told. You don't have to worry for their souls."

"What about people's families? If they're still looking, they won't know—"

"The last thing this city needs right now is a plague." John shook his head. "The minister's wise to clear the streets."

She pressed her lips together.

He obviously took her expression as hesitation. "I know I'd prefer a burial at sea to being left rotting in the street, attracting mongrels. I've known good men who have had the same, and I have no doubt they are now in Heaven."

She fought off the urge to embrace him again. "You're well, though?"

"Never better." He didn't attempt something more convincing. "You? You've been well here?"

She didn't call him on the obvious lie. "Tired. It's hard to sleep here, but I've been more worried than anything."

"Worried about me?"

"And everything else."

His eyes flicked down to her mouth, not lingering but not quickly enough to be hidden. The sound of happy, awed voices rose from deeper into the camp. Cecília frowned, the lightness in the air the first break in the misery she had felt since she had arrived.

She held out a hand to stop a woman who was rushing forward. "What's happening?"

She barely broke her stride, calling back, "Father Malagrida is here!"

"Father Malagrida?" John repeated.

"Francisco said he was coming today. He's famous. Some say a living saint."

"I've heard of him." John nodded. "Last I heard, Minister Carvalho had prohibited his sermonizing."

Cecília blinked a little too quickly. "Prohibited?"

"Malagrida and any other priest whose sermons increase anxiety amongst the populace. People need to focus on rebuilding the capital, not fret about the impending end of the world."

"He has no right to censor holy men."

"Whether or not he has the right, you have to admit he has a point."

She met his eyes. "Please don't do this right now, John."

His eyes couldn't seem to find a place to settle on her face. "Do what?"

"We need our faith as much as we need our homes. Don't try to take that."

His gaze settled on her mouth once again, and he wasn't as quick to remove it this time. Her breath caught.

"Cecília." Francisco's voice shattered the moment.

Cecília didn't know whether to be thankful or disappointed. She angled to see him.

"Come." He motioned, turning after the crowd.

John frowned. "Does he always call you like a hound?"

Cecília hesitated, looking at Francisco's back then John. "Can you find out what's happening with Tio Aloisio?"

His cheek twitched in another smile-grimace, and he nodded. "I'll try."

Cecília squeezed his hand quickly, not entirely able to resist touching him a final time even given how tense their conversation had grown. Silently, she turned after Francisco, still feeling John's eyes on her as she walked away.

CECÍLIA STOOD TO ONE side in the mass of humanity that had gathered around Father Malagrida, heart pounding as the rest of the crowd remained so silent that she had no doubt even those a hundred bodies back could hear the priest's stern voice.

"Learn, oh Lisbon, that the destroyers of our houses, palaces, churches, and convents, the cause of the death of so many people and of the flame that devoured such vast treasures, are your abominable sins." The priest's piercing blue eyes scanned the crowd, moving as though he were looking into the soul of every person there, one by one. "Tragic Lisbon is now a mound of ruins. Unrestorable, abandoned. As for the dead, what a great harvest of sinful souls such a disaster has sent to Hell! Holy people prophesied the earthquake's coming, yet the city continued in its sinful ways without a care for the future. Now, indeed, Lisbon is desperate."

Red blotches began to stain the man's face, visible over his stark-white beard even at a distance. Cecília couldn't help but think of the portraits of Old Testament prophets she'd seen emblazoned in stained glass. She pressed her fist into her stomach, trying to keep her breathing steady.

"It is *scandalous* to pretend the earthquake was solely a natural event, though some may wish it to be so, for if that be true, there is no need to repent and avoid the wrath of God. Believe me, Lisbon, not even the Devil himself could invent a false idea more likely to lead us to irreparable ruin.

"Now, it is necessary to devote all our strength and purpose to the task of repentance. Do you think being billeted in the country, outside the city, put us outside the jurisdiction of God?" He pointed skyward. "God undoubtedly desires to exercise His love and mercy, but be sure, wherever we are, He is watching us, scourge in hand. See to your sins before He next sends your souls to Hell."

Cecília's hands trembled. A low panic she hadn't felt in days coursed through her. She squeezed her eyes shut, opened them, then shut them again, but she couldn't fully gain control of herself.

Father Malagrida finished his sermon, his voice rising through the end, growing loud enough that it rattled inside Cecília's head, and she felt hellfire licking her feet. The silence after he finished stretched for what seemed like an eternity. Then it shattered, the crowd shifting as one as Father Malagrida turned to prepare the Eucharist.

Francisco looked at Cecília from his place next to her, his face just as hard as Tio Aloisio's had been earlier. "You understand why Bibiana must remain here now? If you wish to go off with Aloisio and his English friends you seem to like so much, good riddance. I will pray for your soul, but don't try to drag us to Hell with you. Certainly not by calling Aloisio to roar his heresies at me."

"Cis—" she started, but Francisco had already stormed away, making his way to the front of the crowd as it parted before him like the Red Sea.

Cecília looked at their priest-prophet then at the line already starting, waiting to receive communion from a man who had performed miracles.

She hadn't taken communion since she had arrived in camp. Then again, she could hardly say she was in a state of grace—she hadn't confessed the kiss. She hadn't confessed her dreams. She hadn't confessed all the doubts that had been circling in her head in the past ten days or the guilt that wouldn't leave her be. She turned away from the priest. She couldn't say where she was going, but she couldn't stay there.

"CECÍLIA?" JOHN'S VOICE called from somewhere far away.

Cecília didn't unfurl from her spot wedged against the cart wheel, mostly hidden from view as the shadows lengthened.

"And once again," she mumbled. Of course he was the one looking for her—no one else had for weeks. She and John Bates, thrown together as though he were her own Purgatory, leaving her to play out her punishment as she fought to purify her soul. Or maybe it was Hell. At least Purgatory offered a chance of escape.

His footsteps approached then stopped as he apparently spotted her. "Cecília! We've been looking for you for over an hour. It's getting dark."

"I don't know what to do anymore," she said weakly, not sure if she had spoken loudly enough to be heard by anyone but herself.

John hesitated then took a seat next to her. "What do you mean?"

"Do you think my mother was a sinner? Sent to Hell?"

"Are you quoting Malagrida's sermon?"

"Not quoting." She pulled her knees tighter to her chest, her rib not hurting quite as much as before. "I just... I used to know what to think. I sinned. Lord knows I did. But I knew what those sins were. I knew how I needed to repent. At least I thought I did. But all of this... Mamãe suffered so much in this life and bore it all... She was the most devout woman I know. And Bibiana... I know Cisco's a priest. I know I shouldn't question whether what he has said is right. He must know God's will better than I ever could, but as much as I try to accept it or pray to understand, I can't bear the thought of leaving Bibiana here. Not with her suffering so."

John nodded slowly as he seemed to consider his words carefully. "Someone being a priest doesn't necessarily mean he's always right."

She looked at him, wanting to believe him, not certain if it was because he was right or because she couldn't face her own failings anymore.

"You're struggling." He brought his hand to her cheek, brushing it gently. "That's fine. Questioning is an essential part of being human."

"So says your philosophy?"

"So says everything I believe."

She dropped her eyes to the ground.

"Cecília." He tilted her face so she'd look at him again. "You are an amazing woman. Stubborn, infuriating sometimes, but amazing all the same. You fall, you struggle, but you keep going. And after all that, I would trust whatever your conscience tells you over empty words, no matter who is speaking them."

Cecília let her eyes drift closed, focusing on how his hand on her felt. With so much she still had to repent for, another instance of comfort barely seemed worth fighting. "Kiss me?" He didn't answer, so she opened her eyes again. "Please?"

John's eyes focused on her mouth, but he shook his head. "No."

"Oh..." Cecília pulled back from him as a stab of rejection tore into her.

"No, Cecília"—he caught her arm to keep her from entirely twisting away from him—"I want to. Dear Lord, believe I want to. But I can't. Not like this."

"Like this?"

"I'm going back to England."

The words sputtered in her mind, not fully making sense. She fought to find her voice again, feeling as though she'd been slapped. "What?"

"While I was gone, we went to your uncle's house by the river. Where his house was. Everything's gone. Sucked out to sea or already looted. Save the purse I had on me, I'm penniless."

"So am I," Cecília said, emotions tumbling over one another so quickly she couldn't get a hold on any one.

"You have your uncle to take care of you. And your grandparents. I have nothing. Your uncle has offered to pay for my passage back home. I have to go put my life back together."

"You're leaving us here? Me here?"

"What else am I supposed to do?"

"Not leave me?" Cecília knew she was whining. She couldn't bring herself to care after everything else she had felt that day.

John brought his hand back to her cheek then ran his thumb along her bottom lip. "I'm not Catholic, Cecília. I'm never going to be. And even if I were, I have ten shillings to my name. Any other place, any other time, we never would have so much as spoken. The world is upside down for the moment, but it will right itself. There's no place for us there."

"You can't go." Her voice broke. She couldn't take losing one more person—losing him.

"I have to. And if I kiss you, I won't."

The lump in Cecília's throat threatened to keep her from speaking as tears began to sting her eyes. Tucked against the cart, with the long shadows merging into solid darkness as the sun set, they were turning into outlines—features disappearing, cloaked in twilight. She swallowed, fighting to keep some part of herself together. "Will you at least hold me? Just for a little while."

John hesitated then nodded, shifting to move his arm around her. As he held her, she rested her head against his chest and let everything she had been trying not to feel wash over her in a single wave of pain and ecstasy.

CECÍLIA STOOD AT THE end of the cart, folded into herself as though she would disappear if she only grew small enough. Her final moments with John had been cut too short, interrupted by more men calling her name as they joined the search.

He'd told her to go first. Cecília had assumed that John was attempting to stave off more trouble by not having both of them return together, but even well into morning, he hadn't reappeared. She stood with the cart, head down, while Tio Aloisio and Francisco snapped at one another over Bibiana.

The shouting rose as Tio Aloisio appeared outside the little barraca, carrying Bibiana in his arms. Francisco followed with a distressed Senhora Garcia, everyone talking at once.

"He knows if he doesn't get your sister, you're going to sneak away again."

Cecília started and looked to her side. She blinked, wondering how John had appeared so quickly out of nowhere.

"You won't leave here without her."

Cecília pulled her arms tighter around her, pressing her side as if the spark of pain would help anchor her to the world. "I thought you'd gone."

She could hear his frown even if she didn't look at him. "Did you want me to?"

"I just hadn't seen you..."

"I was getting something." He opened his coat and pulled a small book out of his pocket.

Cecília frowned as he held it out to her. "What's that?"

"Since you aren't going to have me talking at you about philosophy every night now, I thought I could at least give you this."

Cecília took it cautiously as though the little book were going to bite her. Printed in black ink, the words stared up at her: *Leviathan, sive De materia, forma, et potestate civitatis ecclesiasticae et civilis.*

"I prefer Locke to Hobbes, and I certainly don't expect you to agree with all of it, but it's in Latin, so I figured you'd have a better chance of reading it than anything in English."

"Where did you get this?" Cecília looked at him.

"I saw that a few of the merchants saved some books when we were looking for your brother. The difficult part was convincing them to part with one." He didn't meet her eyes, instead opening the cover to show something written in pencil inside: *St. Matthias, Parish of Poplar, London.* "And here. One of my sisters lives in London. Attends St. Matthias. It's where I go when I'm in town. If you ever wish to write a letter, it's the safest place to send it. It'll get to me one way or another."

"I..." She struggled with words. "I don't know how to write very well."

"All the same. If you would like the practice, perhaps."

Something deep in Cecília's stomach twisted, and she found she couldn't manage more than, "John..."

Tio Aloisio strode forward, still carrying Bibiana in his arms. "Get in the cart, Cecília."

John took a step away from her and gave a respectful bow. "It's been my honor to know you, Senhorita Durante. I hope I'll hear from you."

"Cecília," Tio Aloisio snapped, lifting Bibiana over the side of the low cart and covering her partially with a blanket as she continued to blankly mumble her prayers.

Cecília moved back until her thighs hit the lip of the cart. Not knowing what else to say, she let another of Tio Aloisio's friends help her over the edge.

Tio Aloisio finished with Bibiana and moved in front of Cecília. "Mr. Quigley is doing me a large favor, bringing both of you girls to Loures on his way out of town. If you cause so much as one lick of trouble for him—"

"I won't," Cecília said softly. "I just wanted to find Francisco and Bibiana."

Tio Aloisio's face didn't lighten, but he nodded to someone behind her, and the cart lurched forward.

Cecília glanced down at the book then back up to where John was still watching. He lifted a hand in a weak parting. Cecília couldn't bring herself to do even that as the cart wheels creaked on their way out of town.

Part Two: 1756

Chapter Nine

Cecília opened her window, and the damp heat still hovering around the house hit her like a wave. The three-day storm that had pelted the area had left everything soaked but hadn't cooled the air. Instead, a warm mist made everything dewy.

What must it be like in the camps? She pressed her lips together. It had been nearly eight months since she had left, and yet none of the news Francisco sent from Lisbon ever seemed to be good. Over half a year, and Lisbon still wasn't more than ruins. Francisco's letter had been more than clear in blaming Senhor Carvalho for the edict prohibiting rebuilding while the king decided on a plan for the city. Cecília was glad Francisco hadn't been there in person, or she might not have been able to refrain from a dark comment about Father Malagrida's preferring no rebuilding at all. Everyone who mattered seemed to feel the need to stall and pontificate while the rest of them were stuck sitting around, waiting for anything close to a normal life to return.

She glanced at the trunk at the end of her bed and considered pulling out the box she had buried under the clothing her grandmother had purchased to replace everything Cecília had lost. In it, she had placed the misshapen silver statue of São Cristóvão along with the book John had given her and the letter he had sent before he left port. She didn't need to pull it out to know exactly what was written there, though. Not after she'd seared it into memory:

Dearest Cecília,

I was glad to hear from your uncle that you have been doing well in Loures, and I assume—as you have stayed in one place for over three months—that you will still be there by the time this letter reaches you.

I have finally managed to find passage back to London. Should all go according to plan, I will have pushed off with one of the relief ships by the time you get this, but I wanted to make sure you knew—though I imagine you have not given me much thought since you left Lisbon. I will likely be sailing again, once I get back and find work. Perhaps I will find my way back to Lisbon someday when it has recovered, and I will get to see if you remember me. Until then, do consider writing. I cannot promise I will be the timeliest correspondent, depending on where life takes me, but I will see letters returned.

Your humble and obedient servant,

J. Bates

Of course, for as many times as she had read it, she hadn't attempted writing a response. Even if she could scare up ink and paper—and trusted herself to write without looking like a child copying letters—she didn't know what writing him would accomplish. They had been thrown together by chance and let things spiral out of control as the world had done the same. People were doing their best to recover what was left of their old lives, and John had been right. Whatever they had been certainly didn't fit into that.

You *don't fit into that,* the annoying voice at the back of her mind said.

She forced it back down. She had told God she would be good, do as she was told, and be the proper Portuguese lady she was supposed to be if only He would see her and Bibiana safely away from the horrors of Lisbon. He had delivered her prayer. She had to make good on her promise. So, no, she wouldn't answer that letter, wouldn't open that wound again. It was best for that entire part of her life to remain locked in that box with the hope that São Cristóvão would watch over John better than he had Papai and João.

Leaving the window open, she walked out of her room and turned into Bibiana's. The air was stale in the small but richly decorated room wedged between Cecília's and her grandmother's. Though Bibiana had finally stopped praying about a month after they had arrived in Loures, she hadn't spoken a word since.

Cecília moved to the window and pulled back the heavy curtains to let in the light. "The sun's back out, Bia. Storm's passed." She waited for an answer she knew wouldn't come. In the silence, she unlatched the window and swung it open as well. "How are you feeling?" She turned back toward the bed.

Bibiana didn't move from where she was sitting, staring at her bedding. She had been changed into a new bed dress, something white with lace that looked far too expensive for a dress that was meant only for inside the house. Even with her matted blond hair and her large dull-blue eyes, she was still being dressed as a miracle.

Voices echoing down the old stone hallway made Cecília frown. Though her Avô Santa Rita and Avó Gouveia had lived at court at one time—decades before, under the late King João's reign—neither of her grandparents received many visitors. In all honesty, they seemed to prefer keeping their household limited to immediate family and a few servants who had worked for them for longer than Cecília had been alive. From how Mamãe had lived, Cecília had to assume it was a Santa Rita family trait she simply hadn't inherited. She moved to the doorway and poked her head out.

Her grandfather faltered mid-sentence, as Cecília's arrival apparently caught him by surprise before he recovered. "Ah, Father, may I introduce one of my granddaughters, Cecília Madelena."

The unfamiliar priest at Avô Santa Rita's side stopped and offered Cecília a kind smile. "Not the granddaughter I'm here about, I take it?"

"You're here for Bibiana?" Cecília's eyes bounced between the two men in the hall, her grandfather still tall and broad, even into his seventies, and the priest slight and no taller than Cecília was.

"Father Moreno is a *Doctor Theologiae*," Avô Santa Rita said. "Your brother thought he might have some insight into her current condition."

Cecília addressed the priest. "You know Francisco?"

"Very well." Father Moreno lowered his head, his expression still good-natured enough that Cecília had to assume Francisco hadn't spent much time telling the man about her.

Though everything in Lisbon had kept Francisco too busy to visit over the past eight months, he had sent a letter every week, telling Avô Santa Rita the news and checking on Bibiana. From the way he had almost pointedly avoided speaking about Cecília, she had to assume her brother hadn't yet forgiven her for how things had transpired. Then again, for all his godly traits, forgiveness had never been one of Francisco's strengths.

"I've been fascinated by your sister's story since I heard it. Your grandfather was very kind to allow me to visit, now that I've managed to find the time."

Something about the way he said *fascinated* didn't sit well with Cecília. She pressed her arms tightly against her stomach. "Do you think you can help her?"

"You believe she needs help?" The priest's tone remained kind, his gentle, round face making him look quite young, even if the gray at his temples said he was likely two decades older than Cecília.

"She doesn't speak."

"I heard she prayed the rosary?"

"She stopped months ago."

Father Moreno nodded contemplatively before motioning toward the room. "If I may?"

Cecília stepped back to allow the priest and her grandfather into the room before slinking back into one of the corners to watch. Some of her grandparents' neighbors had come to pray with Bibiana when they had first arrived, wanting to share the grace of the miracle child. One particularly forward woman tried to cut off a lock of hair to take with her before Cecília had spotted it. But like Bibiana's mumbling, those visitors had trickled off some months before. Cecília wasn't certain how long it had been since a stranger had been in Bibiana's room, let alone a Biblical scholar.

For as much as Bibiana reacted, though, the man might as well have been a speck of dust. As he studied her, her blue eyes remained glassy, focused on nothing particular off in the distance, as though she were a life-sized doll.

Father Moreno inspected her for a moment before he gently placed one of his thin hands on hers and closed his eyes. "Shall we pray?"

By rote, Cecília crossed herself and closed her eyes as well. The familiar Latin washed over her as she sent up her own prayer that Father Moreno would be able to do something. Even if it meant that Francisco had been right all along, she would gladly humble herself and beg forgiveness if one of the priests could make Bibiana right again. But when Cecília opened her eyes at the end of the prayer, nothing had changed. Bibiana still sat silently in the middle of the bed, but with a priest on one side and Avô Santa Rita on the other.

Father Moreno removed his hand but looked as calmly good-natured as ever as he addressed Avô Santa Rita. "Would you be willing to consider moving her?"

"Moving her?" Alarm shot through Cecília strongly enough to shake her mouth loose.

Father Moreno didn't seem bothered by her outburst. "I have already done some reading related to your sister's case, but my books are all back in Belém, and I have my duties to the royal family to attend to. They have enough of their own troubles to deal with as they wait for the *Real Barraca* to be completed."

"Real Barraca?" Cecília repeated. "They're waiting for a... royal shack?"

"Calling it a barraca is a misnomer, in all honesty." Father Moreno smiled. "It is being built as a grand palace, but the king prefers to live inside wooden walls to stone ones, after what happened." He turned back to Avô Santa Rita. "If you were willing to move your granddaughter toward Belém, I would be able to keep up on her case while performing my other work. Father Durante thought you might still have a house in the area. If not, I can easily secure a place for her with the Carmelite sisters. They are in temporary lodgings at the moment, but they are comfortable, from what I have seen."

Cecília's heart raced. Bibiana leaving. Going to a convent. Not even a convent. Some building or shack they had put together like in the campos. The possibility left the room spinning.

"I can see what accommodations we have available." Avô Santa Rita nodded, not seeming at all alarmed by the idea of sending his youngest granddaughter off for Heaven knew how long.

"Can I go?" Cecília asked before she could consider the words.

Her grandfather's blue eyes hit her. "I'm sure Father Moreno doesn't need you underfoot."

"But Bia needs me."

"I'm not certain if the sisters would have room, but if you have somewhere else to stay, it wouldn't be a trouble to me," Father Moreno said. "I believe wishing to stay together is entirely understandable, after everything that has happened."

Avô Santa Rita pursed his lips slightly. "We'll discuss it. When do you need her in Belém?"

"As soon as is reasonable is fine." Father Moreno caught his hands in front of him. "I can stay in touch by messenger as you work out the arrangements."

Avô Santa Rita nodded, motioning for Father Moreno to precede him out of the room.

Cecília sent another look at her sister on the bed before turning out of the room as well. She had agreed to stay in Loures to keep Bibiana safe. If Bibiana was no longer there, there was no use in her being locked away in the country. That would be a brand-new punishment to face. From God or Francisco, though, she wasn't quite certain.

Chapter Ten

"You should take her along, Fernando."

Cecília had nearly choked on her dinner when her grandmother took her side in the argument with Avô Santa Rita.

"Senhor Romão has been trying to get you to go into town anyway, hasn't he? You could stay there with the girls until you work out other accommodations."

There was, no doubt, more happening than either of her grandparents had let Cecília in on, and Avó Gouveia had followed the statement with a thinly veiled attack on Papai and Mamãe's marriage: "Anyway, we should be making certain that Cecília Madalena is meeting the *right* people now that she's eighteen. We don't want history to repeat itself, after all." But if it meant that she wasn't left wasting away in Loures while Bibiana returned to Lisbon, Cecília was more than happy to take it.

Located just to the west of Lisbon proper, Senhor Romão's house seemed to have escaped any real damage, the jagged brighter stripes of white plaster on top of older layers the only visible sign that repairs had been made to the structure. With four stories and a red-tile roof, it was familiar enough to make Cecília's chest ache. If only her home had been a few miles west rather than in the Baixa... If only they had been slightly higher up on one of the hills...

She shook her head to clear it before she could fall too far down the hole of *if only*. She had given into that despair more than once in the months she had been all but alone with her thoughts at her grandparents'. There were better things to focus on.

She turned back toward the carriage just in time to see Avô Santa Rita helping Bibiana down to the brick pathway that led to Senhor Romão's door. Silent as ever, Bibiana had allowed Avó Gouveia to dress her in a full gown that morning and lead her into the carriage. If not for the entirely empty expression, she would have looked like a perfectly normal young lady. Cecília prayed that would be the case sooner rather than later.

The door of the tall house opened, and a well-dressed older man, who Cecília had to assume was Senhor Romão, moved down the front steps to greet them. "Senhor Santa Rita! So glad you made it. I trust your trip was pleasant."

"Oh yes," Avô Santa Rita said, as though he hadn't spent several hours complaining about the bumpiness of the road, the heat of the carriage, and just about every other part of the journey. "It was so kind of you to offer your home to us."

"Of course, of course!" Senhor Romão continued with the same exuberance. "We have missed you over the past years, and it is an honor to host *a criança milagre*." He dropped his eyes to Bibiana.

The urge to put a protective arm around her sister at the new scrutiny passed through Cecília, but Bibiana continued to stare at nothing, so Cecília contented herself by bunching her skirt in her fist.

"And you must be Cecília." Senhor Romão shifted his attention.

Cecília gave a curtsy, feeling slightly off-balance in the new low-heeled shoes her grandmother had gotten her to go with what Avó Gouveia considered appropriate court dress. "A pleasure to meet you, Senhor Romão."

"Enchanted." He bowed. "I believe it was suggested that you were interested in making your introductions around Lisbon?" Though he still addressed Cecília, he looked to Avô Santa Rita for confirmation. Getting a short nod, he continued, "If you are not too tired from your journey, there is a party at Senhor Mendonça's tonight that would be a very suitable entrance to society. I would be thrilled to have all of you join me."

A jolt of excitement, followed closely by a wave of guilt, ran through Cecília's body at the idea of a party. It had been years since she had been to anything close to one, and even then, the "parties" Mamãe had taken them to were never more than a dozen women in someone's salon.

You're here for Bibiana, she told herself. *Not to go to parties.*

Still, she couldn't stop herself from praying her grandfather would agree to go.

"Why don't we get settled first?" Avô Santa Rita avoided answering.

"Of course, of course." Senhor Romão motioned to some of the servants loitering by the doorway. "Let's get you to your rooms, then we can catch up, eh?"

Cecília watched her grandfather's response to the continued exuberance—another simple nod—before she went to Bibiana's side to lead her inside. Something about Senhor Romão's friendliness seemed off, as though he was taking genuine amicableness and making it absurd or perhaps playacting altogether. Cecília could only assume the man was after something, though she couldn't imagine what. The Santa Ritas were an old family but only *fidalgo,* minor nobility. It was hardly a name that led to deference.

Whatever the reason, though, it had gotten her to Lisbon with Bibiana rather than rotting in the country, so Cecília would gladly take it.

CECÍLIA DID HER BEST not to plaster her face to the carriage window as they rattled up the uneven path to Senhor Mendonça's home. Not far from Senhor Romão's, the larger house seemed likewise untouched by the quake, and in the mix of the orange-pink dusk light and golden torches lining the path to the front, the tall white walls glowed. With Bibiana settled into the room they would be sharing and seemingly content to continue staring at a wall, Cecília had internally justified attending Senhor Mendonça's party by deciding she would go and be introduced but wouldn't let herself enjoy any of it. As building excitement continued to buzz through her body, however, it seemed she was already beginning to fail on that count.

The carriage rolled to a stop, and Senhor Romão smiled from his spot next to Avô Santa Rita. "Ah, here we are. Looks like a fine turnout tonight."

Avô Santa Rita gave some murmur of agreement as a man dressed in dark-blue livery hurried down the front steps of the grand house and opened the carriage door.

"Senhorita." Senhor Romão motioned gallantly for Cecília to go first.

She offered a smile of thanks, though she honestly would have preferred to have had the other men out of the carriage before she attempted to navigate the doorway herself. Avó Gouveia had spared no expense in outfitting Cecília for Lisbon, and after nearly a year of bed dresses around her grandparents' house, the wide pannier and rich silk left her feeling off-balance. The new heeled shoes and folded ruffles of lace certainly didn't help.

She could only hope she would be able to hide how ungraceful she felt around people no doubt much more used to court dress. Avô Santa Rita and Senhor Romão followed her out of the carriage, and with a quick word to the doorman, they were all swept inside.

The energy in the room made Cecília's skin buzz. Internal bargain or not, Cecília soaked in the mass of bodies and voices like a starving man who had suddenly arrived at a feast.

"Santa Rita," a voice cut through the din, and a large, rotund man made his way through the crowd. "I thought that was you."

Avô Santa Rita turned and smiled. "Sousa, I hadn't heard you would be here."

"I wouldn't think of missing a Mendonça party!" The round man, Senhor Sousa, laughed heartily. "They're the event of the week."

"That's what I told him." Senhor Romão inserted himself into the conversation. "I don't believe you've met Senhor Santa Rita's granddaughter, Senhorita Cecília Madalena?"

Senhor Sousa gave as deep a bow as his stomach would allow, the thick curls of his wig swinging forward with the motion. "A pleasure to make your acquaintance, senhorita. Your first time in Lisbon?"

The question hit her hard enough that she was momentarily struck dumb.

"It seemed time for her to make a debut at court," Avô Santa Rita answered for her, skillfully avoiding another direct question.

"She will be a welcome addition, I am sure," Senhor Sousa said before bringing his eyes back to Cecília. "I believe the ladies have withdrawn upstairs, if you would like to join them while your grandfather and I talk."

She glanced at her grandfather to check if he took any issue with the idea. When he didn't object, she offered what she hoped was a courtier-worthy smile. "Thank you very much, senhor. That would be lovely."

Senhor Sousa motioned for yet another man dressed in rich-blue livery and directed him to take her to the ladies. With a deep bow, the footman turned for the grand staircase and led Cecília deeper into the house. She took small steps as she followed, as much to look around as to be fashionable. Like at Senhor Romão's, places inside the house had obviously been patched, but whoever had covered the damage had done a masterful job. One would have had to have been looking for evidence of the quake to know the house had been hit.

She slowed at one of the portraits, studying an older man with a stern face but kind eyes. "Who is this?"

The footman started, seeming slightly shocked that she had spoken to him, but he looked at the portrait as well. "The late Senhor Mendonça, senhorita. This way."

Cecília spent a final glance at the portrait then followed the man to another door. Though the energy wasn't quite as intoxicating as in the main hall, the hum of conversation inside the room still left excited butterflies fluttering in Cecília's stomach.

I'm supposed to make a good impression, she reasoned with the lingering guilt in her chest. *Being blithe and friendly will do that better than standing in a corner, sulking.*

She could have a *little* bit of a good time, she supposed. Truly, it was for her grandparents' sake more than hers. It was what her grandmother had sent her to do, after all.

The footman pulled the door open with a grand gesture and bowed as Cecília stepped past him into the large room. The hum died slightly as attention in the room shifted to her, and Cecília thanked her stays for keeping her shoulders pulled back before she could falter. She added a second thanks to her grandmother, for as formal as her new gown was, it didn't come close to matching the folds of patterned taffeta and satin the ladies around the room wore.

One of the women on the left side of the room, wearing powdered curls piled high on the top of her head, leaned toward the ladies seated around her. The group kept their voices low, but all fixed their eyes on Cecília as if to make certain she knew they were talking about her. Cecília pretended not to notice, keeping her chin high and looking for a good place to sit.

A woman in a coral-colored gown apparently took pity on her. With an annoyed look at the gaggle of women on the other side of the room, she stood and stepped in front of Cecília. "I don't believe we've had the pleasure? I'm Maria. Maria das Dores de Mértola de Vilhena."

The family names registered as important somewhere in the back of Cecília's mind. She was nobility of some kind, but Cecília couldn't say just how important, so she offered a smile and curtsy. "Cecília. Cecília de Santa Rita e Durante."

Confusion passed through Maria's wide brown eyes as an older woman snapped her head in Cecília's direction. "Durante?" She ran her eyes over Cecília as though a snake had just slithered into the room. "Any relation to Aloisio Silva Durante?"

Cecília's eyebrows rose. "My uncle."

The woman's nose wrinkled. "Is the first minister now interested in what the ladies are doing?"

Cecília blinked, trying to make sense of the question. "I'm sorry? The first minister?"

"Sebastião Carvalho," Maria answered before the older woman could. "The king's first minister. Your uncle is his man, no?"

"I... wouldn't know." Cecília glanced around the room, getting the strong sense that no one in the room considered the association a good one. "I actually hadn't even heard Senhor Carvalho had been appointed *first* minister. I've been out in the country." When that didn't seem to allay the suspicion in the room, she added, "I'm here with my grandfather, Frederico Cunha de Almeida de Santa Rita? Senhor Romão invited him."

That sent a light murmur through the room. Some of the ladies turned back to their own conversations, but a tall, alarmingly bony woman with fair hair stood and came up beside Maria. "Did he know he was inviting another *Durante* here?"

Maria sighed heavily. "Did anyone request your opinion, Isabel?"

"I just thought there was a higher standard for these parties." Isabel shifted her attention, looking down her nose at Maria. "Senhor Mendonça certainly is known for better."

Rolling her eyes, Maria slipped her arm through Cecília's and started them deeper into the room. "You can ignore Isabel. Most of us have learned to. Come walk with me."

Before Cecília could wonder where exactly they were going to walk in a second-story space, Maria half led, half dragged Cecília toward a set of double doors on the far side of the room. Pleasantly warm air welcomed them as they stepped onto a wide balcony that overlooked a well-manicured garden. The last of the orange-pink sunset had disappeared against the horizon and left a clear night lit by the nearly full moon.

"Lovely night, isn't it?" Maria broke the silence, her voice entirely pleasant, as though the tension inside had never existed.

"Very," Cecília agreed, trying to think of what the proper thing was to say. "I am sorry if my being here has caused trouble. I truly haven't seen my uncle in the better part of a year."

"You really shouldn't trouble yourself with Isabel." Maria waved her hand dismissively. "Her mother's first husband was a Távora, and even though her father most certainly is *not*, dear Isabel believes that still somehow makes her the most important lady in a room."

Even if Cecília could only vaguely recall the names Maria had given her, she certainly knew the Távoras. As old as their house was, the noble family was second only to the king's. With Maria ready to move on, it was likely smartest to proceed to safer, more banal party talk, but Cecília couldn't entirely dampen her curiosity. "Is there a reason people don't like Senhor Carvalho?"

Maria's eyes slid to Cecília.

"I only met him once," she continued, feeling the need to defend herself, though she wasn't entirely certain from what. "Briefly, after everything last November, but he seemed very congenial then."

"The earthquake was his finest hour, some say." Maria gave a resigned sigh, as though she found the topic more tiresome than anything. "Dom José... well, I would never be one to speak ill of His Highness, but he didn't weather everything that happened well."

"He was injured?" Cecília frowned. Her grandparents didn't keep up on much news, but the king being hurt certainly should have filtered through.

"No, the entire royal family made it safely outside when everything happened, praise be, but the king... He still isn't completely right, you know? Still won't step foot inside masonry. People were trying for months to convince him to move to his palace in Mafra while they repaired the one in Belém, but he insisted on building his Real Barraca. All of us at court were left in dreadful little places, waiting for something proper to be built up until a couple of weeks ago. And ever since he named Carvalho first minister, he's all but let the man do whatever he wishes. Not the wisest of decisions, if you listen to most."

"Why's that?"

Maria shrugged. "I can't say I much trouble myself with all the politics, but he is only a *fidalgo*, you know. I can't imagine he truly understands ruling."

With the best of her pedigree certainly no better than the first minister's, Cecília held her tongue. It was likely best not to annoy the only ally she apparently had so far at the party, anyway. She looked for something safer to discuss before the sound of something scraping against stone made her turn back to the railing of the balcony. The sharp memory of buildings crashing to the ground swept any thoughts of Senhor Carvalho and the king from her mind. "Is it safe out here?"

"Safe?" Maria furrowed her eyebrows.

"The balcony wasn't damaged in the quake?"

"Senhor Mendonça has these parties every week. I've been out here plenty of times..." She trailed off as another scrape sounded, then a head popped over the railing. Exasperation flashed over Maria's face. "Mateus!"

"I thought that was your voice, Maria." The man swung his leg up over the railing. He landed lightly on his feet and straightened his fine jacket. "Do you spend all your time out here?"

"Forgive my brother his manners." Maria turned to Cecília. "He likes to pretend he was raised on the streets."

"We just wanted to see how you ladies were doing this fine evening," Mateus said as a second head appeared over the railing. Ignoring his friend, Mateus ran his eyes over Cecília as Isabel had, though his scrutiny appeared more as though he was trying to picture her without her clothing than determining what type of insect she might be. "And who is this?"

Maria released a harried breath but motioned. "Senhorita Santa Rita, may I introduce my brother, Mateus de Mértola de Vilhena, and his friend, Luís de Terra. Mateus, Luís, Cecília de Santa Rita. She's come with her grandfather."

Cecília hesitated slightly at how Maria had removed the Durante name altogether in her introduction, but after the reception inside, perhaps that was wise.

Mateus lowered his head an inch as he continued to study Cecília with an improper level of interest.

Cecília crossed her arms protectively and glanced at the second man, Luís, who was still standing silently by the railing.

Her eyes apparently started him out of whatever stupor he'd fallen into, and Luís bowed to her. "A pleasure to meet you, Senhorita Santa Rita."

Cecília gave enough of a curtsy to be polite, and she finally lost Mateus's attention. He looked back to his sister. "All the regulars back tonight?"

"You know you aren't allowed to be up here."

Mateus smirked and headed for the double doors.

Luís gave another short bow, eyes bouncing between Cecília and Maria for a moment before he said, "Ladies," and disappeared after his friend.

Maria sighed again and moved to the railing. "Do you have any brothers?"

"One," Cecília said. *At this point.* "He's a priest."

Maria laughed. "So the exact opposite of Mateus. He does this every week, you know."

"Climbs up the balcony?"

Maria nodded. "He loves trouble a little too much. José, our eldest brother, says he's waiting to see when it finally catches up to him. We expect it to be spectacular."

A laugh lifted inside, loud enough to carry onto the balcony. Cecília checked behind her as a wave of feminine tittering followed it. "Should we go back inside?"

"I'm fine out here, as long as my brother's in there. You're best off staying away from him as well."

CURIOSITY FINALLY BROUGHT Cecília back inside, though with the interloping men drawing all the attention, there wasn't much more to do inside than out on the balcony. She did her best to preoccupy herself by speaking to the few women in the room who weren't either circling Mateus or pointedly avoiding Cecília as though she had the plague, but soon enough, the familiar restlessness began to make her jittery. Having to assume that she wasn't *only* allowed to stay in the one room as a guest, Cecília made her way back into the hall to see what else was happening.

Male voices continued to drift up the grand staircase, though from glancing over the banister, it seemed the bulk of the party had moved deeper into the house, with only a few lavishly dressed men standing amongst the liveried servants. Cecília debated trying to slip down past them, but even if she thought she could wander that much without facing her grandfather's ire, she didn't trust herself not to trip over herself in her gown, so she attempted to content herself with studying the portraits lining the upper hall. All of the faces—generations of the Mendonça family, she had to assume—were striking, handsome men with strong, square jaws and ethereally beautiful women. No doubt, their family tree was a veritable list of old noble families, the type of people who certainly wouldn't tolerate having their ability to lead questioned.

A door opened behind her, and she turned sharply, just managing to keep her balance on the heel.

Luís froze for a moment in the doorway before he gave a short bow and stepped fully into the hall. "I hope I didn't startle you, senhorita."

"Oh, no. I was just"—she motioned weakly at the painting behind her of yet another handsome man with a charming glint in his eyes—"looking."

"Senhor Mendonça." Luís pointed, moving up beside her. "The current Senhor Mendonça."

Cecília nodded, already having assumed that, based on the newer fashion the man in the portrait was wearing, but seeing no need to answer. Maria had only mentioned staying away from her brother, but Cecília had to imagine it was safest to steer clear of this man as well, at least as long as Maria was the only friendly face she had at the party.

Luís cleared his throat awkwardly. "I hope we didn't make you feel as though you needed to leave."

"Beg pardon?" She turned her head to look at him.

"I saw you left and was worried it was because of us."

"I'm surprised you noticed."

"Oh?"

"There were a lot of people on your side of the room."

"Oh," Luís repeated, giving a chagrined smile. "That's Mateus, mostly. He's always liked an audience. I—"

"He wants to *force* us to sell!" A voice from the bottom of the stairs rose loudly enough to cut Luís off. "Can you imagine the utter gall? That man should be fed to my hounds."

Cecília's eyebrows rose as whomever the man was speaking to hushed him. "That was... dramatic."

"Forgive me," Luís said as though he had caused the outburst. "You shouldn't have had to hear that."

"Do you know whom he meant?"

Luís waved his hand as though he were trying to brush the topic away. "I'm sure it's just politics. Nothing you would be interested in."

I wouldn't be so sure about that. Cecília looked at the staircase for another beat before she affected a yawn. "Oh, pardon me. I don't generally stay up so late. It might be time for me to find my grandfather."

He took a step back to remain in front of her as she shifted to leave. "Would you like me to accompany you?"

"I wouldn't want to trouble you." She glanced at the staircase again.

"It isn't a trouble at all."

"Really, Senhor Terra." She stepped around him. "It's very thoughtful of you to offer, but I'm sure I can make my way. Please, enjoy the party."

Disappointment flashed across Luís's expression. "I hope I will see you at court this week, then?"

"Perhaps. That depends on my grandfather, I suppose."

Luís nodded and offered a final bow. "Senhorita."

"Senhor." Cecília managed a passably graceful curtsy and stepped around him to go after the man who had been yelling.

Though he had dropped his volume to a more reasonable level, he was still easy enough to follow. She stopped outside a room just off the grand entryway.

"He isn't the king, and I'm not saying anything untrue."

"Perhaps, but until we've replaced him, it is wise not to *shout* about the first minister," a second voice said in a hiss.

Senhor Carvalho again. Cecília brought her hand to the gold cross around her neck, fingering the dents for a moment even though it was half-hidden under the oblong pearls Avó Gouveia had given her to wear for the occasion. Maria apparently hadn't been exaggerating about how little the man was liked, at least in Senhor Mendonça's home.

"Dom José can't possibly know what that cur is doing," the first man continued, unabated. "He can't force us to sell just so he can rebuild Lisbon in his own image. He and those *estrangeirados* friends of his have their way, and there will be nothing Portuguese left once he's pushed this preposterous plan through. 'We'll make it one of the great cities of Europe.' Pah! As though it weren't already."

Footsteps moved down the hall in Cecília's direction, and she stepped away from the room a second before her grandfather appeared with a few other men.

He faltered mid-step before recovering. "Cecília."

"Avô." She bobbed another curtsy for good measure, debating for half a second giving another fake yawn before she decided that would be overdoing things. "I'm sorry if I interrupted. I was just starting to get a little tired?"

Suspicion remained on Avô Santa Rita's face, but a man she realized was Senhor Mendonça from the portrait upstairs gave a charming smile. "It is getting quite late, isn't it?" He addressed Avô Santa Rita. "Please don't let me keep you from your lovely granddaughter, Santa Rita. We can speak more in a few days."

Avô Santa Rita lowered his head then looked at Cecília. "You can wait in the carriage. I'll be out in a moment."

"Yes, Avô." Cecília didn't argue, turning for the front door. After nearly being caught eavesdropping, again, on her first outing in months, it didn't seem wise to tempt her luck. She had more than enough to think about from what she had heard already. And she had Bibiana to check on.

Chapter Eleven

The next morning, Cecília barely had the chance to step out of bed and into something decent before Father Moreno arrived to see Bibiana. Cecília wasn't certain why she was surprised—Avô Santa Rita had no doubt been in contact with the priest, and it was why they had come back to Lisbon, after all—but something about seeing Father Moreno while still drowsy from not having arrived home until after midnight the night before left her uncomfortable.

You didn't do anything wrong, Cecília told herself as she ate a quick breakfast, listening to the sound of movement on the floor above them as Father Moreno did whatever he needed to try to help Bibiana. Beyond less than a minute of eavesdropping and the tiny lie about being tired the night before, which wasn't even really a lie, based on how quickly Cecília had drifted off once they'd made it back, she hadn't done a thing she even had to confess before attending Mass. She still crossed herself quickly, just to be safe, before returning to check on Father Moreno's progress in the room she and Bibiana had been given.

Pausing at the threshold, she surveyed the scene. Bibiana was as unmoving as ever as Father Moreno knelt by the side of the bed, a rosary between his hands and an old book open on the edge of the mattress. His mouth was moving, and she could almost make out what he was saying if she strained. It was Latin with the cadence of a prayer, though not one she recognized.

After a few more minutes, he went silent, offered an *amen,* then opened his eyes. Cecília shifted her weight, not certain if she should announce herself or hold her peace. He saved her the trouble of deciding, offering a smile as he spotted her. "Ah, Senhorita Durante."

"I didn't mean to interrupt, Father." She caught her hands in front of her.

"You didn't. I was just praying for guidance." He motioned to the book on the bed. "I found an account from an old convent in Italy about a girl who was very much like your sister. She apparently brought great prosperity to the sisters there despite not speaking a word that wasn't prayer for several years."

Cecília pressed her lips together tightly before asking, "Does that mean she started speaking again eventually?"

"After a visit from São Boaventura, by the accounts." Father Moreno nodded. "I have begun to review São Boaventura's works, in case there is any more insight in them, but of course, we are first and foremost looking to follow God's will in this, as in all things."

"Of course," Cecília said, though she had to admit she hoped they wouldn't need a saint to visit before Bibiana started to speak once again. Then again, people said Father Malagrida was a living saint. *Maybe we should have let him see her before we left Lisbon...* The thought crossed her mind even as the idea of seeing the formidable priest, with all his talk of sin and retribution, made her stomach churn.

"Was there something I could do for you?" Father Moreno asked when Cecília didn't continue.

She shook her head quickly. "No, Father. I just wanted to see how Bibiana was."

"Always feel free to let me know if I can ever assist you as well." Father Moreno smiled. "I will be here as long as necessary with your sister, but I can do more than one thing at once."

"Thank you, Father." Cecília sent a last look at Bibiana before backing away, as much to escape the feeling that the priest was silently judging her, likely for something Francisco had told him, as to give him room to work.

She could hear Senhor Romão's voice before she had made it back to the main floor. "It isn't a bad trip. If we leave within the hour, we'll be at court before midday."

Cecília slowed. He was talking loudly enough that it obviously wasn't a private conversation, which meant she technically wasn't eavesdropping, just overhearing.

"You're certain we should go to court rather than back to Senhor Mendonça's?" Avô Santa Rita asked.

"The first minister may have the king's ear, but you'll find the rest of court is much more sympathetic to us landowners. Trust there's no reason to avoid court."

The first minister again... Cecília tried to call up her memory of Senhor Carvalho, though the day she had run across him and his men in the Baixa was all muddled up with a hundred other things that had left much stronger impressions. He hadn't seemed all that important with everything else happening. But she couldn't say she knew anything about court politics.

"And you could bring Cecília," Senhor Romão continued. "It seems she made a very positive impression last night, from what I heard. I'm sure she would be just as welcomed at court."

Cecília lifted her eyebrows, not certain who would be singing her praises after the cold reception she'd had at Senhor Mendonça's, but it was certainly better than something going around that would get her sent back to Loures.

There was a long pause before Avô Santa Rita answered, "I'll check if Father Moreno needs us. If not..."

"I'll see the carriage ready." A chair scraped against the floor as Senhor Romão apparently decided that her grandfather's answer had been "yes." With Father Moreno set up for a long day, she imagined the man was right. They had plenty of time to go to court.

Cecília just wished she could tell if the fluttering in her stomach was excitement or a sign that she shouldn't want to go at all.

CECÍLIA WASN'T CERTAIN what she had been expecting from the new royal shack, but the Real Barraca certainly hadn't been it. Situated at the very top of Ajuda Hill, slightly inland from the original palace in Belém, the impressive wooden structure stretched out in front of them. One long, single-story building dominated the landscape, overlooking the wide stretch of the Tagus to the south. Though it had to be hundreds of rooms from the look of it, only one pointed roof on the far side had a second level.

No one could be crushed under that, the more morose part of Cecília's mind supplied. The king had succeeded on that count.

She briefly wondered if Father Malagrida would approve. It was rebuilding, not praying, but as grand as the wooden palace was, it was certainly rebuilt with the thought of what God had already wrought.

Or what some subterranean vapors hath wrought... She forced that thought away, accepting a servant's hand to step down after her grandfather and Senhor Romão.

"This way." Senhor Romão didn't wait for any direction before passing the wide wooden doorway, so Cecília didn't, either, instead following closely at her grandfather's heels.

Before the disaster, she had never been invited to court to know what life had been like at the Paço da Ribeira or the old palace at Belém, but the feeling that hovered inside the Real Barraca left her with the impression that things were not quite normal. The way the finely dressed men and women stood near the squared-off windows and tapestry-covered walls felt somehow off.

Or you let everyone from last night get to you. Cecília had to admit, excitement of court or not, everything she had heard the previous night had left her feeling more cautious than she had been as she'd rolled up to Senhor Mendonça's party.

Senhor Romão stopped outside an open doorway and motioned toward it. "If you'd like to wait here, senhorita? I just need to take your grandfather down the hall, and then we can get you settled."

"Oh…" Surprise made her trip over her words before she could put together a sentence.

"We won't be far," Avô Santa Rita said before she could answer, nodding for her to move into the new room before letting Senhor Romão whisk him away.

Unlike the wide hallways, with their smattering of courtiers, the side room was empty. Cecília moved to the window and glanced over the people milling about outside, in between the hedges of a well-manicured garden, before the gray-purple clouds on the horizon caught her attention. It looked like a storm was coming, even though the sun was still streaming over them on Ajuda Hill.

That'll be out at sea, if that's west. She wrapped her arms around her middle, briefly wondering if there were any ships under those clouds. Tio Aloisio obviously hadn't begun sailing again, so she didn't have him to worry about, but there were plenty of men who passed off the coast, heading to Africa, the Orient, or even just past the strait and toward Marseille or Venice. Any of them could be in the midst of a storm while it was still sunny on shore.

Stop thinking about him, her mind admonished before she consciously thought of John by name. *He isn't yours to worry about.*

Maybe it's just in my blood, she argued with herself. *I can't worry about Papai or João or Tio Aloisio. Who else am I going to worry about out there?*

She was from a sailing family. If she couldn't sail herself, she needed someone to travel with in her mind.

Familiar voices caught her attention, and Cecília turned back toward the doorway. They moved closer, and she could make out Tio

Aloisio. Stepping back into the doorway, she peeked around the corner. Tio Aloisio was walking down the hall, speaking in sharp sentences to a man who was trailing a few steps behind him, carrying a large crate. With Avô Santa Rita and Senhor Romão out of sight and no one else around to take issue with her speaking to her uncle, she called his name.

Tio Aloisio nearly tripped over his own feet, his head snapping in her direction. "Cecília. What—"

"Avô Santa Rita is meeting someone," Cecília supplied before Tio Aloisio could accuse her of sneaking somewhere she didn't belong. "He brought me along."

Tio Aloisio hesitated for a moment. "Your grandfather is here?"

She nodded. "One of Francisco's friends, Father Moreno, asked us to bring Bibiana closer to court so he could work with her. They're at Senhor Romão's right now."

Tio Aloisio opened his mouth then closed it without saying anything, some rush of thoughts Cecília couldn't begin to interpret flashing over his expression.

Maybe I shouldn't have said anything...

The man with the crate shifted it with an unhappy grunt as they stood there.

The loud clinking of glasses snapped Tio Aloisio back to the moment. "Careful with that. We already lost two to that storm."

"Sorry, senhor," the man said with another grunt, shifting the crate a little more carefully that time.

Cecília looked between the box and her uncle as it registered. "Have you been sailing again?"

"I haven't, but we still need trade, and the *Vento de Verão* miraculously survived with everything in working order. I hired a new captain to see her off."

Cecília barely caught herself before recoiling, the idea of some stranger captaining her father's ship feeling like a slap to the face. The crate slipped before she could respond, landing on the ground with a thud and crash.

"*Idiota!*" Tio Aloisio let loose a string of insults as the man apologized, bending to recover the crate.

Though the wood had survived in one piece, the tinkle of glass said something inside it had broken, and a warm, sweet smell filtered out between the planks. Something in Cecília's chest clenched as the odor triggered a memory of home—her old home. "Is that perfume?"

"It *was*." Tio Aloisio sent the man a dark look.

"I think that's what Mamãe used to wear. From Venice."

His eyes returned to her, a flash of surprise passing through them. "Good nose." He looked at the man. "Get that to my room—by the window, for Heaven's sake—and open. We can hope *some* of it is salvageable."

"Yes, senhor." The man hefted the crate up and hurried deeper into the Real Barraca, obviously more than happy to escape the situation.

Tio Aloisio waited for the man to disappear around a corner before turning back to Cecília. "Do you know how long your grandfather intends to be here?"

Certain she'd stepped into some other politics she didn't understand, Cecília treaded carefully. "At court or in Lisbon?"

"Either."

"Not long at court, I don't think, but I don't know how long Father Moreno wants us in Lisbon."

"Durante." A familiar face moved down the hall from the opposite direction.

"Senhor Carvalho." The name left Cecília's mouth before she could consider it.

The man slowed, no sense of recognition coming to his eyes. Cecília had to imagine she looked much different, properly dressed for court rather than coated in soot with red-rimmed eyes. Senhor Carvalho, however, looked much the same—his face set and determined and somehow seeming just as tall off his horse as he had on it.

"My niece"—Tio Aloisio made the reintroduction—"Cecília Durante."

"Of course." Senhor Carvalho lowered his head in a clipped bow. "Forgive me. I hadn't realized you'd come to court, Senhorita Durante."

A mix of female voices came down the hall, and Cecília tensed, having to imagine that being spotted standing there, talking to her uncle and the first minister, wouldn't make any future parties at Senhor Mendonça's more comfortable for her.

Luckily, it didn't seem as though Senhor Carvalho expected an answer from her, anyway. He addressed Tio Aloisio. "A moment?"

"Of course, Minister." Tio Aloisio gave a short bow before glancing at Cecília. "Your grandfather knows where you are?"

She bristled slightly at the tone behind the question, but she supposed it was fair after the last time he had seen her. "Yes, Tio."

Senhor Carvalho had already turned away, apparently expecting her uncle to follow, so Tio Aloisio gave a quick "Stay out of trouble" before he moved off as well.

With more people beginning to mill about, Cecília slid back into the room to wait for Senhor Romão. She could certainly do her best to stay out of trouble. It would just be helpful if she actually knew what all the trouble was.

Chapter Twelve

As the sky to the east slowly turned pink, Cecília finally gave up trying to sleep. She sat up and irritably pushed at the hair that had escaped from her braid overnight, but it didn't help the familiar itchiness that overtook her whenever she'd been left in one place for too long.

There must be something wrong with me, she thought, but that was nothing new. She'd always known as much. She just didn't think she'd still get urges to sneak away even with so much freedom. Since they had gone to court more days than not over the past week, she had to imagine it was the fact that people still refused to let her know what was actually happening. Her grandfather continued to go to secretive meetings, the courtiers continued to say vaguely snide things about Senhor Carvalho without any specifics, and Bibiana...

Cecília looked across the room in the soft dawn light. Though Father Moreno had been there every day, Bibiana hadn't changed in the slightest. Crossing herself, Cecília sent up yet another prayer asking for help keeping her faith in God's plan, but especially since news had made it around court that she was the sister of *a criança milagre,* it was getting harder and harder. If she had to listen to one more person talk about how wonderfully blessed she had to feel while her little sister continued to be a lump in bed day after day, Cecília thought she might scream.

Not for the first time, her eyes drifted to where the box holding John's book and letters was hidden in the trunk she had brought from her grandparents. She had packed it only because she hadn't trusted her grandmother not to go through her things while they were gone—or at least that was she had told herself. Sometimes, she felt as though she was starting to lose track of what she actually thought and what she'd convinced herself of, but as her annoyance grew, she found it harder and harder to stay away from it. She couldn't imagine she would find much that would help her in a book of English philosophy or letters she had already memorized, but her mind continued to drift back to the sentence she had found underlined in that book one night when she'd broken down and looked at it.

Scientia potential est. Knowledge is power.

Cecília had to assume that John had marked that passage when he had written where to write him in the cover. It was entirely the sort of thing he would have said to her.

But what knowledge? she asked the box silently, as though John would be able to answer her through it. *Yours or Father Moreno's?*

The rattle of carriage wheels snapped Cecília out of her thoughts, and she slid out of bed to move to the window. Outside, Father Moreno's carriage rolled toward the house. It was alarmingly early, even for the priest.

He must not have gone to Lauds. There was no way he could have attended dawn prayer even at the church down the street and still arrived at first light. She glanced heavenward. *Is that an answer?*

Everything remained unhelpfully silent, save for the arrival outside.

With a huff, Cecília picked up her bed dress and pulled it over her camisa, not feeling the need to call up Senhor Romão's *angolense* girl so early to put on a full gown. As Father Moreno had said on the first day he had arrived, they needed to follow God's will in this as in all things. They had to trust in His plan. After nearly nine months of waiting and wondering, though, it was simply getting harder to do.

Maybe that's why nothing's worked yet. I don't believe enough? She looked at where Bibiana was sleeping. It seemed cruel to make Bibiana suffer as some sort of test, but it didn't seem impossible.

Unless that's pride? Thinking it's about me? She released another annoyed breath. *Why isn't anything ever simple?*

Soon enough, the door downstairs opened, and after a few words with what sounded like Ricardo, one of Senhor Romão's older servants, Father Moreno's footsteps headed for Cecília and Bibiana's room. Cecília made it to the door before he could knock.

Father Moreno paused briefly in surprise before offering as kind a smile as ever. "Good morning."

"Good morning, Father."

"I should offer my apologies for waking you this early. It's a busy day, but I wanted to make sure I still could see how Bibiana was doing."

Cecília stepped back to allow him into the room, not feeling the need to state the obvious when he could so plainly see it. As he headed for his place at the bedside, Cecília asked, "Would you mind if I joined you to pray this morning, Father?"

Father Moreno's eyebrows rose, but he looked more pleased than anything. "Not at all, my child. I'd welcome the company."

Nodding, she took a place near the end of the bed and rested her elbows on the mattress as she clasped her hands. Actually sharing her thoughts with the priest felt too exposing, but if she was being tested, perhaps helping to pray would at least be a start. All she could do was hope.

The sun was fully out, and the little second-story room started to become uncomfortably warm by the time Father Moreno finished whatever set of unfamiliar prayers he apparently was using to help Bibiana. Cecília cracked her eyes open to peek. No change. Her stomach sank as she realized she truly had been hoping for a miracle.

As she began to debate whether she should stay there, some commotion downstairs caught her attention.

Father Moreno paused as he flipped through his book, looking in the direction of the raised voices.

Cecília stood, knees protesting after kneeling for so long. "If you'll pardon me, Father?"

He nodded, letting her slip out of the room alone to see what was happening.

"*You* are not welcome in this household!" Senhor Romão's voice carried up the stairs from the entryway.

"You wish to turn away the king's own physician, whom His Highness most thoughtfully sent?" The surprise at hearing Tio Aloisio's voice made Cecília pause for the briefest moment before she continued toward it.

"Whom the first minister sent, you mean," Senhor Romão spat.

"I have His Highness's letter right here, if you wish to read it."

"We have no need of any physician," Avô Santa Rita's voice joined the argument. "Her condition is spiritual, not physical."

"Entirely possible," Tio Aloisio agreed. "But the king has heard all the talk around court, and he wishes for Senhor Nunes to see her. He can already get a spiritual report from Father Moreno."

Cecília turned the corner, and the scene came into view—Senhor Romão and Avô Santa Rita scowling on one side, Tio Aloisio and who had to be the king's physician, Senhor Nunes, standing on the other, closest to the front door. "Tio Aloisio," she said to introduce herself.

All four men turned their heads to look at her.

"Go back upstairs, Cecília," Avô Santa Rita said.

She turned her attention to him. "The king sent someone to see Bibiana?"

"Cecília—"

"Yes," Tio Aloisio spoke over her grandfather, motioning with the paper in his hand. "As he outlines in this letter." He looked back at Avô Santa Rita and Senhor Romão. "And I apologize, senhores, but I truly must insist."

Senhor Romão puffed up. "Now, listen here—"

"Is there any harm in it, Avô?" Cecília broke in. "Father Moreno is with her right now. I'm sure he won't allow any harm to come to her after everything. And if there is something both physical and spiritual—"

"Cecília—"

"Isn't it worth trying everything?" she finished. "Please, Avô."

Conflict played out over Avô Santa Rita's expression before he blew out a harsh breath. "Let me see the letter."

Senhor Romão made an incredulous noise and pointed sharply at Tio Aloisio. "I'll see the entire court hears of this. Invading a man's private residence."

"I'm certain you will." Tio Aloisio nodded, motioning Senhor Nunes toward the stairs.

Cecília stepped out of the man's way as Avô Santa Rita read the paper Tio Aloisio had given him, and Senhor Romão stormed off toward his office to do whatever he was planning to do about the situation. "Last door to the right," Cecília directed as the physician passed before glancing at her grandfather again.

Tio Aloisio paused to face her just before the staircase. "Thank you, Cecília."

She started at the unexpected show of gratitude, not entirely certain how to react. She ended up watching the physician disappear from sight instead of responding. "Do you think Senhor Nunes can actually help her?"

"He is certainly willing to try if nothing else. I don't believe we can ask much more than that."

So Tio Aloisio wasn't hopeful. Cecília pressed her lips together tightly.

He turned to head up the stairs, as well, before pausing again. "Oh, I did bring something for you, though."

"For me?" She frowned.

Tio Aloisio reached into the pocket of his jacket and pulled out a small glass vial. "Some of that crate managed to survive." He held it out to her. "Since you said it reminded you of your mother...?"

Cecília took the vial carefully, vaguely wondering if someone had come and replaced her uncle in the night as she looked at the pale-gold liquid through the delicately faceted glass. "Thank you, Tio."

He lowered his head quickly in recognition before starting up the stairs and disappearing from sight.

Avô Santa Rita's footsteps moved off in another direction, leaving Cecília standing in the opening between the stairs and the entryway by herself, holding that little bottle. Carefully, she removed the stopper and dabbed a drop of perfume on the insides of her wrists the way she had seen Mamãe do hundreds of times before. The familiar smell floated up around her, leaving some mix of warmth and sadness comingling in her chest. She replaced the stopper just as gently and brought her wrist to her nose, letting it wash over her for a moment before she turned for the stairs as well. At least she could bring a bit of Mamãe with her to face whatever would happen between their Doctor of Medicine and *Doctor Theologiae*.

Father Moreno didn't look any more pleased than Senhor Romão when Cecília entered her room, though his voice was much more measured. "You will not touch this child."

"The king only requested a brief examination," Senhor Nunes responded, his tone just as calm. "We discovered a work by Galen of Pergamon that suggests that trauma may negatively affect the female body and cause hysteria."

"You're suggesting this miracle is nothing but *hysteria*?" Father Moreno recoiled. Cecília had to admit, she didn't care for the sound of that diagnosis any more than the possibility that Bibiana's condition was some sort of test or punishment.

Senhor Nunes nodded. "As we heard she stopped praying quite some time ago, it seemed possible the continuation is physical at this point."

"Can you fix her?" Cecília asked before Father Moreno could respond. "If it is physical?"

A nearly betrayed look flashed over Father Moreno's face.

"There are methods we can try," Senhor Nunes said.

"If it's just an examination, Father...?" Cecília gave the same pleading expression that had worked on her grandfather.

The priest continued to frown, but he took a step back.

"Thank you, Father." Senhor Nunes stepped up to the side of the bed. "If you would perhaps like to sit by your sister, Senhorita Durante? She just needs to lean back slightly."

The tension in the room made Cecília not especially want to move any farther into it, but she was the one who had pushed for this. She sat where the physician directed and let him lean Bibiana against her.

"If it is hysteria," Senhor Nunes explained as he touched Bibiana's stomach lightly, "we would expect the womb to have shifted into an unnatural position, which I should be able to feel."

Trying to ignore the awkwardness of the situation, Cecília looked down and brushed a strand of blond hair back from Bibiana's face, tucking it out of the way.

Bibiana's eyelids fluttered slightly, making Cecília freeze. "Mamãe?"

Senhor Nunes paused his examination. Father Moreno and Tio Aloisio stepped closer to the bed.

"Mamãe?" Bibiana repeated, her blank eyes seeming to struggle to focus as they looked around the room.

"Bia!" Cecília started out of her stupor. "No, it's me."

"Cecília?" Bibiana shifted so she could sit up farther. "Where are we?"

"I think we can say it was hysteria." Tio Aloisio looked between the men in the room.

"He didn't do anything," Father Moreno said, an edge creeping into his calm tone.

"Perhaps it was only slightly shifted," Senhor Nunes said, "and the pressing—"

"Or my praying—"

"Senhor, Father," Cecília cut in, wrapping a protective arm around her sister as Bibiana shrank away from the men in the room. "Could this be done elsewhere?"

Father Moreno opened his mouth then looked at Bibiana and started over. "I can wait right outside, if you need me."

Senhor Nunes didn't move. "I really should examine—"

"Perhaps give my nieces a moment?" Tio Aloisio saved Cecília from having to chase the physician away, clapping Senhor Nunes on the shoulder in a way that seemed designed to indicate that the sentence hadn't actually been a question.

The men retreated from the room, the argument starting again in low tones before the door was even shut, but at least they weren't all standing around Bibiana's bed and scaring her anymore.

"Where are we?" Bibiana repeated after a moment, peering up at Cecília with her wide, innocent eyes. "Where's Mamãe?"

Cecília's stomach twisted. She didn't look forward to having to retell everything that had happened over the past year, but if that was the price of having her sister back, either through medicine or prayer, she would gladly take it. Giving a weak smile, she brushed back another piece of Bibiana's hair. "A lot has happened. I'll explain once we get you something to eat."

CECÍLIA DID HER BEST to pretend she was focused on the embroidery in her lap, but she couldn't help but watch her sister out of the corner of her eye in the silent room. After what had happened with Tio Aloisio the previous week, it seemed Avô Santa Rita no longer wanted Cecília at court while he took whatever meetings he and Senhor Romão were always whispering about, and she had done her best to not let that bother her. Bibiana had needed someone to help her readjust to everything that had happened, anyway. But Bibiana was nearly as silent as she had been when she'd stared off into nothing.

She always was quieter... Cecília did her best to tell herself it was normal, but part of her couldn't help but feel she shouldn't have told Bibiana anything about the past months—even if it had been as polished as she possibly could have made it while still explaining why they were with Avô Santa Rita and why they couldn't go home.

A light knock on the door made Cecília set her embroidery aside entirely. "Yes?"

Ricardo appeared, offering a respectful bow. "Pardon the interruption, Senhorita Durante, but there is a Senhorita Vilhena here to see you. Should I show her in?"

Cecília furrowed her eyebrows slightly before the name clicked. *Maria, from the party.* Though why she would come to visit, Cecília had no idea. She looked at Bibiana. "Are you fine here, Bia?"

Bibiana mumbled a "yes," not looking up from her own careful stitches.

Cecília frowned, but there wasn't much more she could do, so she stood. "I'll come down."

Ricardo gave another bow and slipped away. Looking over herself, Cecília quickly debated changing into something grander before she dismissed it. It was barely midday, and she hadn't been expecting a visit, so she couldn't imagine that Maria would expect full-court dress. When she made it downstairs to the entryway and saw the three people standing there, she did wish she was a little better outfitted. Though they looked to have switched from full panniers to padded rolls for the day, Maria and an unfamiliar taller woman were in beautiful silk gowns, and the embroidery on Luís de Terra's jacket could have put half of Cecília's wardrobe to shame.

"Cecília!" Maria lit up as though they were old friends, catching Cecília's hands before leaning in to kiss her cheeks. "It's so wonderful to see you. We've all missed you terribly at court."

"Oh?" Cecília struggled to find something better to say, though she couldn't begin to think who "we all" could have been. She hadn't spoken to that many people when she had been at court.

"I don't believe you've met Constança—Senhora Constança des Roches e Delgato."

The tall woman with powdered hair curtsied.

Maria continued, "We heard all the talk around court and wanted to see how you were doing."

"The talk?" Cecília asked.

"About your dear sister."

"Oh." Cecília's stomach soured as she glanced back toward the staircase. So they were interested in hearing about Bibiana. *Of course.* She couldn't exactly be rude and turn them out. She motioned toward the salon off the entryway. "Would you like to sit down?"

"Thank you so much." Maria linked her arm through Cecília's before casting a look over her shoulder. "You can find something to occupy yourself, yes, Luís?"

"What?" Luís frowned, but Maria had already turned back to Cecília.

"We needed an escort, and Luís was available, but you can feel free to ignore him, of course."

Cecília furrowed her eyebrows, not certain if she was supposed to copy Maria's dismissiveness, but the other woman didn't give her a chance to decide either way.

Maria swept them both into Senhor Romão's salon and led them to a low settee as though she owned the place. "Now, tell us everything that happened."

Cecília looked between the other two women, trying to determine how she could most quickly get the topic away from Bibiana without insulting anyone far more important than she was. "Not much happened, really. Father Moreno was working with my sister, then His Highness sent his physician—"

Constança gave a very unladylike snort. "The first minister sent *his* physician, you mean."

"Conni." Maria sent the woman a chastising look.

"He said he was the king's physician." Cecília looked between the other two, trying to determine exactly what she was missing. "Senhor Nunes."

"The king has *several* physicians." It didn't seem Constança cared about whatever warning Maria was giving her. "Nunes is the newest, *specially* recommended by the first minister. I think we can all guess why."

"*Conni.*"

"Why?" Cecília asked.

"He's trying to fill the court with *estrangeirados*, and it's only been worse since Father Malagrida started predicting a new earthquake. He'd send anyone who would discount a miracle."

Cecília felt as though her stomach had dropped to her feet. "A *new* earthquake?"

"On All Saints' this year." Constança didn't look in the least bit concerned at the possibility as she fixed how the lace at the end of her elbow-length sleeves lay. "If we don't repent and mend our ways. If it comes to be, mark my words, it will be the first minister's fault. The sooner he's replaced, the—"

"Conni!" Maria snapped. "I'm sure Cecília has had more than enough to worry over without hearing this."

"I'm just saying." Constança huffed, looking up from her sleeve again.

Maria turned back to Cecília. "So, what was Father Moreno doing here?"

Knowing something new was brewing at court left Cecília with the suspicion that there was something deeper than she had been suspecting behind Maria's questions, but thoughts of another earthquake and everything that had already come to pass happening *again* left Cecília tongue-tied. She tried to shake her mind loose enough to answer. The front door opening and low male voices broke in before she could manage.

Senhor Romão appeared in the doorway with a wide smile. "Senhora Delgato! I was just told you were visiting. Such a pleasure to see you, as always."

"Senhor Romão." Constança gave a much more perfunctory smile in return. "We just dropped in. I hope you don't mind."

"Of course not! Of course not! Allow me to have someone bring some refreshments."

The ceiling creaked slightly as someone moved on the second floor, and Cecília stood. "If you'll pardon me a moment?"

Maria's mouth pursed, but Senhor Romão waved a distracted dismissal that Cecília gratefully took. She could check on Bibiana and maybe pull herself back together enough to be genteelly polite.

She stepped back into the entryway and nearly ran into Luís. "Oh, beg your pardon."

"Beg yours," Luís returned. "I shouldn't have been standing so close."

Cecília glanced at the ceiling once again, listening for anything alarming, but it sounded as if the movement had stopped. She assumed that meant it wasn't a rush. "You really could have joined us."

His face lit up, but he said, "I wouldn't have wanted to intrude..."

She shook her head. "There just always seems to be so much more happening than I know about around here."

"Most, you certainly shouldn't have to trouble yourself over."

Cecília couldn't imagine Luís would want to explain what was really happening any more than either woman in the salon seemed inclined to, but at the moment, he seemed her best chance for answers. She attempted to approach the topic sideways. "Even when people are attempting to pull my sister into it?"

His cheek twitched enough to say he certainly knew what ulterior motives had brought Maria and Constança there, but he just caught his hands behind his back stiffly. "I'm certain no ill will befall you or your sister, senhorita. There have just been a few... disagreements over what her former state might have meant."

"If she's a miracle or hysterical, you mean."

She hadn't meant for the question to come off harsh, but Luís flinched slightly all the same. "It's really just a small part of much bigger politics, I assure you. I have no doubt it will pass, likely before you ever have to listen to it."

"What bigger politics?"

Luís hesitated long enough that Cecília worried she had overplayed her hand, but he finally said, "It's the same old conflicts. Who has the king's ear and who should."

She supposed there was little reason not to try for it all. "They want to use Bibiana to convince the king replace Senhor Carvalho?"

"I... uh..." Luís glanced at the salon, alarm evident as he stumbled for words. "I'm sure it's not like that. Really, it's not something you should trouble yourself with. Trust me."

Trust me. Just hearing the words convinced her she shouldn't, but movement started again upstairs. She took a step away. "If you'll pardon me, I'm going to check on my sister."

"I…" He started to say something, stopped, then switched to, "I hope I might see you at Senhor Mendonça's this week?"

She gave a tight smile. "Perhaps. If you'll excuse me."

She didn't make it a question, but he nodded and bowed quickly, letting her slip away as Senhor Romão's loud voice continued to dominate the conversation in the salon behind her.

AVÔ SANTA RITA HAD been oddly silent, even for him, since he had arrived home that evening. Caught up in her own thoughts as he, she, and Bibiana all sat at Senhor Romão's dining table, Cecília couldn't say it bothered her.

"I hope I might see you at Senhor Mendonça's this week?" Though she tried to put Luís's question out of her head, something about the words had stuck with her. If the interest around Bibiana had grown from mere curiosity to some sort of political intrigue, staying as far away from as many courtiers as possible was likely the smartest move. She even considered going back to Loures. But even if that was logical, Cecília couldn't fight the way she balked at the idea of just slipping away, resigning herself to living in the country again for Heaven knew how long. She certainly hadn't found an interested suitor, sitting around at Senhor Romão's day after day as her grandmother had wanted. The way things stood, she would likely end up locked away at her grandparents' for the rest of her natural life or married to some minor country *fidalgo* her grandparents knew who was as just as boring.

Isn't that what you said you'd resign yourself to if you got Bibiana back? The little voice in the back of her head taunted her.

Cecília slid her eyes to where Bibiana was just as silently picking at the food on her plate and released a tense breath. She had promised that. But God hadn't given Bibiana back after that promise. Whether it was Father Moreno's prayers or Senhor Nunes's examination, she hadn't come back until Tio Aloisio had arrived.

That has to say something, doesn't it? Cecília argued back, especially since it all had played out after she had been thinking of John and that book that morning. *It has to. Or am I just trying to convince myself again?*

The uncertainty of it all made her want to throw her fork across the room and say, "To the blazes with all of it."

Instead, she looked at her grandfather. "Avô, I was asked if we were going to Senhor Mendonça's party this week. Do you think we could go?"

Avô Santa Rita started out of his thoughts, looking as though he only just realized he was sitting across from Cecília before he shook his head and went back to staring at his own plate. "I don't believe that's a good idea, Cecília."

"Why not?"

"Am I required to explain myself?" More stress than she had ever heard came through in his tone. "I was actually thinking it might be time for you both to return home."

"What? Why?" Cecília couldn't stop the questions from tumbling out of her mouth.

"What did I just say, Cecília Madalena?" he snapped, making Bibiana's head jerk up. Avô Santa Rita's face softened slightly as he met his younger granddaughter's wide blue eyes, and he set his fork down. "It's late. We all should likely retire for the night. We can speak in the morning."

"But—" Cecília cut off at the dark look he shot her and mumbled, "Yes, Avô."

Not waiting for anyone to join him, Avô Santa Rita pushed his chair back with a loud scrape and stormed out of the room.

Bibiana watched him go, not making a move to stand, so Cecília didn't, either.

"You can keep eating, if you aren't done." She motioned to Bibiana's mostly full plate after a beat.

Bibiana shook her head, setting the fork delicately to the side. "I'm not hungry."

Frowning, Cecília released a breath through her nose. If Bibiana wasn't eating, that meant they likely should leave. Cecília should focus on Bibiana's welfare. "Do you want to go back to Loures? See Avó Gouveia?"

Bibiana looked down at her plate.

"Bia?" Cecília prompted when it didn't seem Bibiana intended to answer.

"I want to go to Convento da Ordem do Carmo."

The name of the convent sent a jolt straight through Cecília's chest. She wasn't certain if Our Lady of Mount Carmel still stood, as close as it had been to the Baixa, but the solid, matter-of-fact way her sister had said it made her shift her weight uncomfortably. "Why do you want to go there?"

"I think I'm supposed to be a nun." Bibiana still didn't look away from her plate, though her voice was more certain than it had been since she had come back.

"You're too young to become a postulant, Bia."

"But I'm supposed to be."

Cecília started to answer before realizing she simply didn't have the energy to add this to all of the other thoughts swirling around in her mind unless she wanted her head to explode from it all. Pushing back from the table more delicately than her grandfather had, she stood. "Maybe we should talk about this in the morning. Do you want to go up?"

Silent once again, Bibiana stood as well and turned to follow, the rest of her thoughts staying as locked behind her eyes as when she had been found after the earthquake.

Chapter Thirteen

Avô Santa Rita had been gone before Cecília and Bibiana had come down for breakfast the next morning, and he hadn't come home in days. Neither had Senhor Romão. Though Bibiana continued to go about her days seemingly content in her own little world, with no more talk of Loures or convents, by the time Sunday came around, Cecília could barely sit from her own jumpiness.

As the sun began to set once again, she simply couldn't take it anymore. Holding her arms out slightly so that Sonia, Senhor Romão's *angolense* girl, could pin the stomacher properly in place, Cecília looked at Bibiana. "I shouldn't be gone long. You're certain you'll be fine here by yourself?"

"Fine," Bibiana murmured, not looking up from the prayer book in her lap.

Not for the first time, Cecília debated whether she should stay there and continue waiting, but Bibiana wouldn't be completely alone. Sonia, Ricardo, and the rest of Senhor Romão's servants would be around if Bibiana needed anything, and after several days without word, Cecília knew something must have happened. The only way she would be able to find out what, though, was to find someone to ask, and Senhor Mendonça's was far closer than court.

With her clothing in order and Bibiana settled in bed, Cecília had Ricardo order the carriage around and stepped in as though she had every right to demand transport to wherever she wanted in the city.

Her heart beating a little too loudly in her ears, Cecília watched out the window as they approached the familiar house. She squinted slightly. Though the torches were lit, as they had been the last time she had attended one of Senhor Mendonça's parties, something was different about the house. The air around it seemed darker, as though a shadow thick enough to dim the lights from the torches was hovering over them. She knocked on the side of the carriage to get the driver's attention. The carriage rolled to a stop, and the driver twisted to look through the small window separating them.

"Let me out here," she directed.

He frowned. "It's still quite a walk up to the door, senhorita. And it's dark tonight."

She glanced up at the partially overcast sky—even without the clouds, the moon was back to only being a sliver. Still, something told her she needed the space before she arrived. "I'll be fine."

"Senhori—"

She fixed him with a hard look.

His face disappeared from the window, and the carriage bounced as he jumped down. A second later, the door swung open.

Cecília took his hand to step out then excused him.

The driver kept his eyes on her, as if waiting for her to come to her senses, but finally, he nodded and pulled himself back up to the seat. "Do you want me to wait with the other carriages?"

Cecília supposed she would be able to walk back to Senhor Romão's if she had to. It was only about a mile or so. Doing so in the dark, in her heels and alone, however, didn't seem to be a situation in which she should willingly place herself. "Please."

The driver urged the horses forward, leaving her standing on the road, staring at the oddly dimmed house.

Cecília took her time as she made her way toward the front door. Something still nagged at the back of her mind, her instinct telling her something was dreadfully wrong, even if she couldn't say what.

          JESSICA DALL

As she ascended the final slight slope to the house, it came to her. Though a few carriages were sitting idle off to one side, the drivers chatting amongst themselves, there weren't nearly the number she had seen before. She looked behind her and realized no new ones had arrived since she had started walking, either.

Trusting her intuition, she skirted the front of the house entirely, sticking to the shadows as she took in the situation. Though the windows along the side of the house were cracked open in apparent preparation for a large gathering, no one was standing in the large salon on the side of the house. What voices she could hear came from deeper inside.

Cecília frowned and turned the corner, walking to the back door. The voices were more intelligible from the dining room that ran along the back of the house. After shutting the door behind her, Cecília padded across the wooden floor, toward the far hallway. She checked that no one was in sight then stepped up to the wall. Pressing herself to the smooth patterned wallpaper, she slowed her breathing and listened.

"You should be packing, not throwing a party," an unfamiliar male voice said.

"You believe I should act like a criminal and flee into the night?" a second answered.

"You'd prefer the first minister treat you like one instead? The fathers were already arrested. Word is that lawyer is being sent to *Angola*, for Heaven's sake."

Cecília dared to lean forward slightly, trying to get a view of who was speaking.

"You need to leave," the first voice continued. "There will be no good—"

A hand clamped down on Cecília's mouth from behind. She shouted in surprise, though the sound was muffled as someone pulled her back. Another arm spun her, and she found herself looking at Luís de Terra.

"What...?" she tried to ask, though his hand was still silencing her.

"What are you doing here?" he whispered harshly.

She started to answer, but he didn't pull back to let her speak. She glanced down at his hand then met his eyes and raised her eyebrows.

He released her mouth, looking suitably abashed though he didn't entirely step away. "Beg pardon."

"Anyway," Cecília said, keeping her tone haughtier than the situation likely called for, "I came for the party. Which *you* invited me to, if you recall."

Luís blinked a little too quickly. "You haven't heard?"

"I've been sitting at Senhor Romão's home for three days with no one but my sister. What in Heaven's name is happening?"

Luís opened his mouth then leaned to look toward the voices before he started in a low whisper, "Senhor Mendonça and the men he's gathered went to see Dom José a few days ago, demanding he remove the first minister. If you can't gather, the king didn't side with them."

"People are being arrested for that?"

"The first minister is not someone to be on the wrong side of, not with the king behind him. I could hear Dom José yelling at Senhor Mendonça for deserting Lisbon during the quake halfway across the Real Barraca. Now, the first minister is rounding up those he is calling 'conspirators.' If they haven't already been arrested, most of Senhor Mendonça's faction is fleeing. You shouldn't be here."

Cecília's stomach knotted, suddenly realizing what all the meetings Avô Santa Rita had been taking at court must have been about. "Where is my grandfather?"

"At court, as far as I know." Luís checked down the hall as though worried someone would stumble upon them. "Your uncle was attempting to keep him from getting caught up in the worst of this, last I heard. Given he relinquishes the land he owns in Lisbon, of course."

"Relinquishes it?"

"He owns property in the Baixa? In the middle of where the first minister wants to rebuild?"

Head swimming, Cecília attempted to make sense of it all. That had to be her home, her old home. She hadn't thought about who owned it, since Francisco had taken a vow of poverty before Papai had died. It made sense that it had gone to her grandfather. But if the first minister wanted it, and Avô Santa Rita was likely being held prisoner at court, that changed things. She brought her hands to her temples. "How did I miss all this?"

"I suppose no one thought to go to Senhor Romão's, since he was already at court when the arrests started."

"And why are you here? Are *you* fleeing?"

Luís hesitated before he said, "I'm not important enough to be noticed in most of this. I've been running messages while I can. I apologize that I didn't think of you and your sister. Senhor Mendonça is the first to choose to remain after I told him he's been banished. The decree should be delivered tonight, and if the first minister convinces Dom José to do anything else in retaliation *before* that, there's no saying how much worse it could get."

"They wouldn't throw Senhor Mendonça in prison? He's nobility."

"Two *priests* already have been. I'm not certain I'd doubt what the minister is willing to do at the moment."

Cecília slipped around him, headed for the dining room to reach the back door.

"Where are you going?" Luís followed her.

"I need to get to court."

"That's likely the last place you should go right now."

"You'll find 'should' isn't often a word that governs where I go." Cecília stepped back outside. She hardly gave her eyes a chance to adjust to the darkness before she started for the carriages. So far, it seemed no one had thought of Bibiana, but if Avô Santa Rita had been caught up, and people were already trying to draw the miracle child into politics, no good was going to come from sitting and waiting to see what happened. Tio Aloisio had genuinely seemed to wish to help when he'd arrived.

Unless that was all politics too?

Everyone had said he was the first minister's man, after all. But Cecília couldn't let that doubt slip in. There wasn't anyone else she could turn to.

Luís followed closely at her heels. "Senhorita, no good is going to come from you doing this."

Cecília ignored him, managing to avoid any pitfalls as she came around the front of the house. She headed straight to Senhor Romão's carriage.

"Senhorita?" The driver straightened, obviously shocked to see her again so soon.

"I need to go to the Real Barraca."

"Now?"

"Is that a problem?"

"It's the middle of the night." He frowned. "The roads between here and there aren't the safest—"

"I need to go now."

"Is there truly no way to talk you out of this?" Luís remained a step behind.

"This is my family," she said.

Conflict moved over Luís's expression, true worry in his dark eyes, but he turned to untether a horse nearby. He addressed the driver as he worked, "I'll ride alongside. I haven't seen anyone out tonight so far. We can hope we won't have problems from any *bandidos* as a pair." He brought his eyes back to Cecília.

She offered a small smile. "Thank you."

Luís offered a strained one in return and pulled himself into the saddle. Cecília stepped into the carriage, a new jitteriness passing through her muscles. She couldn't tell if it was fear or excitement.

AFTER FAR TOO LONG, the carriage rolled to a stop, and the door swung open. Cecília excused the driver to get something to drink then turned to Luís. "Thank you for the escort."

"I can stay with you."

"I'm going to see my uncle."

"It's still not a good night to go anywhere alone."

Cecília had to imagine being alone was safer than being with someone on the wrong side tonight, if everything Luís had said was true, but if he truly was so unremarkable as to be able to ride all over, alerting *conspirators*, there didn't seem to be a reason to waste time arguing. She moved into the hallway.

Lamps had been lit periodically down the palace's halls, but the shadows stretched along the floors in a dark patchwork. Cecília tried to stay on course, though nothing looked quite the same as it had during the day. She paused at an intersection, trying to judge whether she was close to where she'd been when she'd run into Tio Aloisio last time.

"What are *you* doing here?" Mateus's slightly slurred voice made Cecília's skin crawl. Mateus pushed off the wall just around the corner, where he had been leaning in the shadows. "Looking for Carvalho?"

Cecília took half a step back at the sheer venom in the man's tone. "I'm looking for my uncle."

"Same difference, isn't it, Senhorita *Durante*?" He swung his gaze to Luís. "This is probably her doing, you know." He snorted. "Pretending she's one of us."

There isn't time for this. Cecília released a tense breath through her nose but stepped to maneuver around him.

"Where do you think you're going?" Mateus grabbed her wrist.

She jerked back in surprise. "Let me go."

"Mat." Luís stepped forward.

"One of his little spies, aren't you?" Mateus only grasped tighter. "Poking around in the dark. Reporting back—"

"Let go!" She wrenched her wrist to pull where his thumb met his fingers. His hold gave, and he stumbled forward, knocking her into the wall as he caught himself. She grunted as her left arm took the brunt of the impact.

"Mat, you're in your drink." Luís wedged himself between them. "Calm down."

Mateus's eyes narrowed. "Are you working with her?"

"She's not working with anyone. Her grandfather's caught up in all this as well."

"Yet conveniently, her uncle is there to step in."

Luís tilted his head to catch Cecília's eyes. "Go."

"So you are helping her." Mateus advanced.

"Go sleep it off, Mat."

Mateus took a wide swing. Off-balance, he only caught Luís's shoulder.

The punch still sent Luís staggering backward. "Lord, man!"

"Stay out of my way." He pointed at Luís then turned for Cecília.

She didn't wait for him to grab her again. She drove her heel into his toes so hard she heard something snap.

"Holy Mother...!" Mateus jumped back, spurting a line of profanities as he balanced on one foot. He fixed his eyes, burning with rage, on her face. "You—"

"What the Devil is happening here?"

Cecília looked down the hall to see Senhor Carvalho standing in the midst of guards. *Second time his soldiers have come to the rescue...*

"You!" Mateus turned his ire down the hall.

"Mat," Luís hissed, taking a step forward, but Cecília caught his arm as Mateus drunkenly ranted at the man who had just sent two priests to jail and a lawyer to Angola. Senhor Carvalho stoically listened for a moment then motioned. The guards had Mateus by the arms before the drunken man could react.

"You'll pay for this!" Mateus jerked between the two larger men. "You all will, you—"

Senhor Carvalho sent the guards holding Mateus away as the man continued to rant before his sharp eyes turned. "Senhorita Durante?"

Cecília wasn't certain if it was a good or bad thing that he remembered her this time. She continued to grip Luís's arm to keep him from doing something stupid, but he seemed wise enough to hold his tongue against the formidable minister. She gave Senhor Carvalho a weak smile and an off-balance curtsy. "Minister. Thank you. I was going to see my uncle, but we got... delayed."

Senhor Carvalho stared at Luís for another moment then dropped his gaze to Cecília's hold on the man's arm before meeting Cecília's eyes again. "Your uncle is very busy tonight, Senhorita Durante. You shouldn't bother him."

"We could wait somewhere. His room, if you could direct us? I'm sure everyone's"—she glanced at the guards—"very busy."

Senhor Carvalho sent a last lingering look at Luís as he addressed Cecília. "There's been plenty of trouble this week. I'm sure your uncle would be grateful if you didn't bring him more."

"That is certainly not my intent, senhor."

Senhor Carvalho nodded before giving her clipped instructions to what she had to assume was her uncle's room then motioning the rest of the guards forward.

Cecília and Luís didn't move until the last of the footsteps disappeared. Gently freeing his arm from her grasp, Luís stepped forward. "I should find where they took Mateus."

"You'll get yourself arrested as well."

"You'd rather I let him rot wherever Carvalho is throwing his enemies right now?"

"I'm not certain you want my honest answer." She rubbed her wrist, unable to tell in the dim light if it was starting to bruise. She looked down the hallway the way the guards had come. Senhor Carvalho hadn't been cruel or even any curter than he had been when he'd found her in the Baixa. He was a man of few words when focused on something, it seemed. Something in his body language, though, scared her nearly as much as Mateus's rage had. "Walk with me? I've never actually been to my uncle's room. I'm not sure what door it is."

He released a breath, the conflict she had seen at Senhor Mendonça's back as he wrestled with something in his head. Finally, he gave a short bow. "As you wish."

"Thank you," Cecília said, heading in the direction Senhor Carvalho had pointed. With Luís's help, she found what she hoped was the proper door.

No one, save an alarmed servant, was in the anteroom when Cecília arrived, so she stepped inside, praying there wouldn't be too long to wait. At least the lingering odor of Mamãe's perfume in the air said it was indeed the right place.

Luís stood in the doorway, looking around as the servant continued with her work.

"Would you like to come in?" Cecília watched him.

"Beg pardon?"

"You don't have to stand in the doorway as if you're waiting for something."

Luís studied Cecília then looked back into the hallway behind him.

"Are you truly going to try to find where your *friend* was sent?" She couldn't stop sarcasm from dripping through on the word "friend."

His face screwed up. Then he shook his head and stepped into the room. "Normally, I'd expect they would give him back to his family to sleep it off, but after tonight..."

She silently watched him.

"After tonight, I don't know where any of us stands. Carvalho has attacked everything the nobility supports, and the king apparently has sided with him. It's something new."

"What does that mean for you?"

He took a seat across from her, catching his hands in front of him. "Either I need to disavow ever being with you tonight and hope the first minister has gone too far, or I should become your new closest friend and hope Carvalho stops looking at me like I'm next for the scaffold."

"I thought you said you weren't important enough to be noticed."

"He certainly noticed me a few minutes ago."

Cecília nodded, watching Luís closely. Worry had etched itself onto his face, and the muscles in his jaw continued to twitch. She waited a final moment before speaking. "You're sitting here."

"What?" His eyes slid up to meet hers.

"That isn't the thing to do, if you plan on disavowing me."

"That is true," he said but didn't make any move to stand.

She held his gaze then offered a quick nod of understanding.

The door swung open, and Luís stood to face it.

Tio Aloisio froze in the doorway, looking at the younger man before he noticed Cecília and shook his head. "You have a nose for trouble, don't you, Cilinha?"

"I heard Avô Santa Rita was in trouble." Cecília stood as well.

"Not as much as some." Tio Aloisio looked back at Luís.

"Tio, this is Luís de Terra—"

"Oh, I'm aware who he is."

Luís's eyes widened slightly, as though surprised at the recognition, but he bowed. "Senhor."

Tio Aloisio didn't bother to return the pleasantry, pulling his gloves off with quick, jerky movements.

"*Is* Avô Santa Rita in trouble?" Cecília jumped to what was important. "Should Bibiana—"

"Your grandfather has made some imbecilic decisions," Tio Aloisio said, "that come from listening to some less-than-trustworthy people. Had he listened to anyone who mattered, he would know the king has more than full faith in the first minister and the changes planned for Lisbon. Assuming he stops listening to his false friends, though, and does as I've directed, he'll be on his way back to Loures in a few days, as will you and Bibiana."

Cecília wasn't certain if she should find that statement comforting or alarming, as much as he made it sound like a banishment.

Tio Aloisio turned back to Luís. "Thank you for your help. I can handle things from here."

Luís sent Cecília a quick look, a final moment of hesitation in his expression before he gave a shallow bow. "Thank you, senhor. Good night, senhorita."

Tio Aloisio bent enough to be cordial then waited for Luís to leave before he turned back to Cecília. "I know you're still dealing with what happened last year, Cecília, but you're not going to help anything by getting yourself caught up in this. You need to learn to keep your nose in your own business."

She frowned. "I was trying to—"

"You were trying to put yourself in the middle of where you don't belong, and once again, you've managed to pull some young man in after you."

How is John? Cecília nearly asked out of defiance. She crossed her arms instead, trying to stop the wave of feeling like a chastised child from chipping away her earlier resolve. Her voice still came out too petulant. "You're the one who sent me off with Mr. Bates in the first place."

"And I obviously underestimated the effect you have on his ilk."

Cecília pressed her lips tightly together, the situation with Luís de Terra seeming so remarkably different from what had happened with John that it was laughable, but no good was likely to come from continuing the line of discussion. "My grandfather—"

"I told you, he'll be fine if he listens to reason. You and Bibiana as well."

"But—"

"This isn't the time, Cecília." Tio Aloisio rubbed his temples. "It's late. You can sleep in the side room." He pointed to one of the doors off the antechamber. "We'll talk in the morning."

"But—"

"Good night, Cecília." He moved through the other door connected to the anteroom.

She stood where she was, thoughts being pulled in too many directions for her to make any one decision. She could look for Avô Santa Rita, though Heaven knew where he was. And she couldn't imagine much good would come from finding Senhor Carvalho again. He didn't seem like a man who would be swayed by any prostrations for clemency. Once again, her family was in danger, and she couldn't do anything but try to keep her own head above water as they all were bandied about. Only this time, there was no question that this was the will of man over God.

Rather than turn for the side room, she sat down heavily on the little settee in some weak show of defiance, trying to think of anything else she could do to help.

Sadly, she couldn't think of a thing.

Chapter Fourteen

Cecília stirred awake, finding herself on a low mattress in what had to be the side room Tio Aloisio had mentioned, though she didn't actually remember ever having gone inside. She looked around, disoriented for a moment both by the room and by questions of what had woken her. Then she heard it again.

"So Mendonça's gone?" Tio Aloisio's voice filtered through the door.

"He supposedly kissed the decree when he received it, the *cabrão*." Senhor Carvalho swore loudly enough that Cecília was willing to bet he wasn't aware she could hear. Or perhaps he didn't know that she was there at all. "But yes, he's reportedly left for Porto. Not as far as that traitor should be sent, but for now... I've recalled my brother from Brazil to replace him as Secretary of the Navy. I imagine things will go much more smoothly from here on, once we deal with the rest of our problems."

If Tio Aloisio answered, Cecília didn't hear it. Carefully, she stood, the straw in the mattress crinkling more loudly than she liked, and padded to the door to listen.

"Your niece is at court again?" Senhor Carvalho said after a beat.

"Santa Rita didn't send her back to Loures as he said." A bitter note cut deeply into Tio Aloisio's tone. "He apparently underestimated the penchant she has for wandering when left to her own devices. Anyone who's spent more than a day with the girl should know a league isn't nearly far enough to keep her from anything."

"Should we presume that means her sister is still here as well?"

176

"I imagine so, but I doubt that will be a problem. I intend to properly send both girls home with Santa Rita today. He's signed over the plot in Lisbon, and Loures does seem far enough to keep them from trouble."

Senhor Carvalho took a moment before responding. "The younger one, perhaps, but I'm not certain we should be so quick to send your older one away."

Cecília frowned.

"No?" A matching frown came through Tio Aloisio's tone.

"A girl that determined and with the skill to get where people may not want her? She would likely be of more use here than off with a man who obviously doesn't have a thimble's worth of common sense."

Tio Aloisio spoke cautiously. "Cecília also has a unique way of inviting trouble wherever she goes. I'm certain *that* wouldn't work in our favor."

"Don't be so certain. The trouble she found last night gave me a reason to arrest one of the Vilhena sons. And she may have even turned the Terra bastard. He only stopped running his little 'secret' messages last night after he fell in with her. Didn't speak up for Vilhena, either. Fairer girls at court wouldn't be able to say they could do the same."

Cecília frowned at the implied slight.

"She seems to be a very handy girl indeed with her skill set," the first minister finished.

As the conversation trickled off, Cecília debated her next move. Still exhausted from the previous night, she half wanted to sit, have a nice meal, and nurse her sore arm and feet, but there was too much to do to remain in one place. Once Tio Aloisio and Senhor Carvalho's voices moved off, Cecília slipped out of the side room then out of the antechamber entirely.

Winding her way through the palace, Cecília looked for any clues to what she had missed while she'd been away. The halls were all but empty. The odd, subdued feeling there had been at Senhor Mendonça's home—his former home—coated the Real Barraca. She glanced into the open doors as she passed, but it almost seemed as if she were the last person alive. As she passed another room, she noticed a lump lying across a few cushions.

She stepped inside and made out who it was. "Senhor Terra?"

Luís started awake, blinking as he looked around. He jerked as he spotted her, quickly going to straighten out his clothing, though it was in surprisingly good shape for having been slept in. "Senhorita—"

"You slept here?" she asked.

"It was... a long night."

Cecília nodded. "You didn't go back to your room?"

"That's an even longer story."

"Because of Mateus de Vilhena?"

"It will all work out," he said. "Word is that Isabel's trying to call in what Távora connections she has to help him. As upset as the family is at Carvalho after last night, they very well might intervene, even with as little as they actually like Isabel. Having the Távoras as an advocate is nearly as good as having the king."

After last night? Cecília kept that question to herself. "You want him to be helped? Mateus?"

Luís frowned.

"He hit you."

Luís shrugged. "He's Mateus."

Her lips pursed, but he seemed to consider the topic closed with that statement. "Do you still think you did the right thing, coming with me last night?"

He studied her face for a long moment before speaking. "It's going to be Carvalho or the Távoras who win this. Whoever does, I'm not certain I want to be in the middle of that fight."

"Do you have to be?"

"I don't have many other good options, if I..."

"If you...?" she prompted.

"Cut myself off from the Vilhenas," he said.

"You can't go back to your own fam—" Everything came together in a flash of understanding: Maria not giving Luís a second name. *The Terra bastard.* "You're illegitimate."

His eyebrows rose.

She realized she had spoken aloud. "I'm sorry. I didn't mean any insult. I just realized—"

"My parents married," he said quickly, eyes dark, "but my father died within a month. People like to question if the marriage happened at all when they don't care for me."

"I truly meant no offense."

He looked at her for another moment, his expression softening in a way that made her wonder if her uncle had been a little more correct about how Luís thought about her than she realized.

Don't be silly. He barely knows you.

"I should let you get on with your day." She took a step back. There were more things to worry about than Luís de Terra.

"Please be careful, Senhorita Santa Rita," he returned.

"It seems you should likely call me Durante right now," she said then stepped back out into the winding hallways.

CECÍLIA SAT ACROSS from Senhor Carvalho in the dimly lit office, waiting for the man to speak first. He watched her from behind his large desk, his piercing eyes making Cecília's skin crawl as he seemed to peer into her thoughts.

He finally sat back and interlaced his fingers as he set his hands in front of him. "I hope you didn't have too hard of a night, Senhorita Durante."

"I've had much harder," she said.

Senhor Carvalho lowered his head an inch in recognition, some hint of amusement at her reply softening his eyes a fraction. "Your uncle told me you had actually returned to Lisbon all the way from Queluz after the quake."

"I was looking for my family."

"You didn't trust your uncle to do that?"

Cecília chose her words carefully. "I've never been very good at sitting and waiting when something's happening. Patience is a virtue I often lack."

"That isn't necessarily a bad thing," Senhor Carvalho said.

Cecília tilted her head. "I believe you're the first to have thought so, senhor."

Senhor Carvalho leaned back in his chair slightly, still watching her face closely. "If there is anything I have learned over my life, Senhorita Durante, it is that the only way to truly learn about the world is to go and experience it. If you wish to learn the truth, you have to go after knowledge with a net. If you don't, you're only going to learn what others choose for you."

Not certain what else to say, Cecília nodded.

"And how is your sister?"

That question felt even more loaded. She treaded carefully. "Likely worried after me, honestly, since I didn't return last night."

"But she's generally well?"

Cecília nodded again. "The king was very kind to send his physician to see her."

"You believe Senhor Nunes is behind her recovery?"

Whether she did or not, she certainly wasn't going to suggest differently in front of the first minister after last night. "It was only when he arrived that she got better." Obviously, that was the correct answer. More of a smile came to the corners of Senhor Carvalho's serious mouth. "I have a proposition for you, Senhorita Durante, if you're willing to hear it?"

Cecília caught her hands in her lap, squeezing her fingers as she said, "Please."

"There are enemies in court. A number of them attempted to overthrow what progress the king has made to recover from our great tragedy last night. I have ears listening for me, but I imagine it would be much easier for a pretty girl such as yourself to listen without attracting attention."

So now I'm pretty. Some bitterness from the morning bubbled up unexpectedly. She kept the thought off her face. "You want me to spy for you?"

"I wouldn't say 'spy.' Just let me know if you hear anything that sounds important to the welfare of the country. Of Lisbon. I imagine you would wish to stay at court, given the chance?"

Yes. Cecília couldn't entirely deaden the part of her that truly wished to stay. She forced herself to ask, "With my sister?"

"If she wished." Senhor Carvalho didn't so much as hesitate, seeming to have expected the question. "Though I would be a bit worried that too much excitement might lead to a relapse of her condition. I imagine the quiet of the country might suit her better in this case?"

The country likely would have been Bibiana's choice in any case.

If Senhor Carvalho is in charge, it's best for her to stay away. So the question was whether Cecília could justify abandoning her sister. *Is it abandoning? If I'm helping Senhor Carvalho here, he'll care less about Bia and Avô Santa Rita.*

The little nagging voice in her head popped up. *Trying to convince yourself again?*

"Senhorita Durante?" Senhor Carvalho cut in before she had to come up with an answer for herself.

"Yes, senhor," she said, "I imagine you're right."

"Wonderful. Then I believe it's settled? Your grandfather can see that your sister has all the rest she needs, and you can remain with your uncle. I'm sure there is a nicer set of rooms you two could share, assuming you are willing to make note of anything important you might happen to hear while going about your day. Are you willing to do that?"

All the nice words still sounded decidedly like spying—and that still couldn't be good for her soul. But if she was going to be honest with herself, she had already made her decision, especially in the face of someone who seemed truly to believe that curiosity was a virtue, not a vice. She offered her own small smile back. "Yes, senhor. I am."

Part Three: 1758

Chapter Fifteen

"He can't just take it. It's our land!"

"You should know better by now. You'd be safer saying 'no' to the king than the first minister."

Cecília tilted her head toward the voices as much as she dared. She still moved the coral rosary beads through her fingers even as she listened to the two girls whispering a few pews back.

"But we still have two years to rebuild off that other silly edict! How can he just—"

"How can he just anything? He's the *first minister*."

"Girls!" an older woman whispered sharply. "You know better than that. And in church!"

"Sorry, Mamãe," the girls whispered back.

Cecília waited for the three pairs of footsteps to audibly move out of the pew and toward the doors of the grand wooden chapel before she looked behind her—it was the Countess Atouguia and two of her daughters complaining about Senhor Carvalho, but that was barely worth reporting. Any noble who had ever owned so much as a statuette in Lisbon was still bewailing the law passed that allowed the crown to buy the land still needed in the Baixa with or without the owner's approval. "Eminent domain," Senhor Carvalho had called it. Two months of time to digest it hadn't helped much. Since the first minister had put Porto under martial law the previous year, however, following a riot, there hadn't been anything especially shocking for Cecília to report from inside the halls of the Real Barraca.

She supposed she should have been grateful. She had long grown used to her periodic meetings with Senhor Carvalho and actually enjoyed talking with the man when he had the free time to discuss philosophy and architecture, all things he fully encouraged she learn, but the wheeling and dealings of court could still give her headaches. Pageantry and excitement, she liked. Philosophy and theology, she liked. Politics, she could have done without.

Locking away the information about the girls in case she ended up with nothing else to report for a second week, Cecília crossed herself and stood to go to the confessional. She couldn't say she'd had a truly clean soul since she had come to court—likely since the quake, but she could atone for most of her sins. It seemed *most* was the best everyone else at court did anyway. After two years of seeing the scandals and excesses of court, she could understand Father Malagrida's harsh sermonizing about Lisbon's sins.

Of course, the court wasn't destroyed. She wasn't sure if the statement was her thought or one of Tio Aloisio's, but it might as well have been hers for as often as it popped up. *Neither was Senhor Carvalho's home nor the brothels to the north of the city.* If God had meant to punish, he had focused a disturbing amount of anger on the Church, between the destruction of the offices of the Inquisition and the number of basilicas that had been destroyed.

"What do you think it says if God looked to save fallen women over the high inquisitor? It certainly makes me question some of the sermons I've heard."

That was certainly Tio Aloisio, but without the second quake Father Malagrida had predicted and with the first minister solidly in charge, Cecília had at least been able to relax her own guilt enough not to feel damnation weighing upon her anymore.

Something dangerously like Francisco's voice tried to bubble up from a dark corner of her mind. She pushed it back down. She certainly had no inclination to hear his burning words about fire and damnation again.

Pulling her skirt carefully out of the way, she left the end of the pew, looked up, then froze. She blinked, certain her mind was playing tricks on her before she had to admit her brother truly was standing at the doors of the chapel.

Maybe that wasn't in my mind... A stone of guilt hit the pit of her stomach, as she had to wonder if God had suddenly sent her a sign, but Cecília managed a smile. "Cisco! What are you doing here?"

"It's Father Durante." Francisco frowned as he walked up the aisle of the generally empty chapel. "And I'm seeing Father Moreno. I'm glad to see you in church."

To spy. That little voice she had done so well of fighting down sparked back to life with her brother standing there.

I came to pray as well, she answered herself. *I'm a good Catholic. As good as anyone else here.* She somehow kept her voice light and unburdened as she returned, "I'm glad to see *you.*"

It had been almost three years since she had properly seen her brother, but he somehow looked ten years older than when she had seen him in Lisbon. She supposed it had to be how thick he had grown his dark beard and the worry lines etched along the corners of his eyes. He certainly looked older than twenty-five. He ran his eyes over her, obviously critiquing her appearance. "It looks like court suits you, Cecília Madalena."

The pinched look and how he'd used her full name left her suspecting that he didn't fully approve of that fact. Then again, against his simple black robe, she had to look almost gaudy in her deep-red court gown. Even with all the ribbons and lace, it was only a day dress. She couldn't imagine what Francisco would think if he saw her done up as expected for dinner. She kept her courtier's smile plastered in place all the same. "Does it?"

His eyes settled near the low neckline where her stomacher met her gown, making her suddenly very aware of how much of her bust was on display. She was thankful that he didn't comment on *that*. "You had your cross fixed."

"What?"

"The one Pai gave you." He motioned to the necklace. "It was dented."

"Oh, yes." Cecília brought her hand to the smooth gold, her fingers catching on the ruby that had been added at the center. "Tio Aloisio had the court jeweler look at it last year. They added the stone to cover some of the damage, but it's nearly as good as new."

Francisco nodded then glanced around the chapel.

"How have you been?" She tried to keep the conversation going.

"I've been in Setúbal." He brought his eyes back to her. "I must say, I was hoping I might see you there one day. A number of the court ladies travel—"

"To see Father Malagrida," she completed. She had heard more than one of Senhor Carvalho's rants about the priest and how he was still holding his own courts almost two years after he had been officially expelled from the capital "for spinning false prophesies and inciting fear in the populace."

"You've been with him?" Cecília kept her face placid.

"You should consider coming down with some of the other ladies one of these times."

That would certainly go over well... "Perhaps. Tio Aloisio and I don't leave the palace often."

"Father Durante." Father Moreno came from the back of the chapel, his face as good-natured as ever. "I wasn't expecting you until this afternoon."

"I made good time." Francisco gave a tight-lipped smile in return.

"And Senhorita Durante." Father Moreno looked at Cecília. "Did you need someone to take confession today?"

"You're obviously busy." Cecília motioned to Francisco. "Don't worry about me."

"Are you certain? I'm sure your brother—"

"Truly," Cecília said. She had made it two years without confessing to Father Moreno. Francisco being at court certainly seemed like a better reason to avoid the man than some she had given. She touched Francisco's arm. "You'll see me later? Once you're free?"

Francisco nodded once then turned to Father Moreno as if Cecília had been dismissed.

Forgetting confession entirely for the moment, Cecília moved to the doors of the chapel. Rather than leaving, however, she hovered at the doorway, doing her best to listen to what Francisco and Father Moreno had to say to each other. She hoped that Francisco would be in and out of court quickly, before any real problems rose up around him, but leaving out his arrival when Senhor Carvalho next spoke with her wasn't a possibility. Anything having to do with Father Malagrida always seemed to go right at the top of what the first minister wanted in his reports.

A hand caught her arm and jerked her the rest of the way into the hall. She squeaked as she hit the tapestry on the wall with a soft thud and looked up.

Luís shook his head. "How is it that every time I go looking for you, you're hovering in doorways?"

Her tension left in a gust. "Luís! I thought you weren't coming back until next week?"

"I missed court."

"Court?" She lifted an eyebrow.

"Parts of court." He bent as though to kiss her, but Cecília dodged him. He threw her a questioning look.

"My brother's in there." She nodded at the chapel. Francisco's arrival apparently was a better excuse than she generally had for nearly everything. She had made the mistake of allowing Luís to kiss her one night after he'd found her wandering after dark. She had still been new to court and learning the intricacies of spying, and with him as her primary connection to the nobles who wouldn't stoop to speak to a Durante, there didn't seem to be a good enough reason to tell him not to again. He was kind enough and not bad at the actual kissing part, if she was honest. Still, as pleasant as the kisses were, none of them managed to shoot through her or bring back that deep burning she had felt the single time John had kissed her, and so far too often she felt her thoughts drifting where they shouldn't go—to memories she certainly shouldn't be entertaining—any time Luís attempted anything.

Luís took a step back to a more respectable distance, glancing at the chapel. "Your brother?"

"Francisco. Father Durante."

"Oh, the priest." It seemed to click in Luís's mind. "Is that why you were lingering?"

"I didn't know he was coming." Cecília took hold of Luís's elbow to lead him away from the chapel. "How was the wedding?"

Luís shook his head, willing as ever to let a topic go when Cecília didn't want to discuss something. "How do you *think* a Mateus-Isabel wedding would be?"

"Careful. I'm going to be struck with melancholia for not being invited with you so enthusiastic."

"Oh, yes. I'm sure." Luís shook his head. "I suppose there's some benefit in being on the other side of things."

Cecília nodded, not feeling the need to entertain another conversation about where they stood regarding the Vilhena family. With her solidly Cecília *Durante* after what had happened with Senhor Mendonça and Mateus, she was *persona non grata* with the entire household. With Luís unwittingly giving her enough of the gossip to fill her reports, though, Cecília couldn't say she was too upset at her exile. If anything, it made things simpler. She stayed away from the people who would likely have drawn her into the gossip herself, and Luís couldn't tell *them* anything about her without admitting he was still seeing her.

She just likely would have felt less guilty about it if he didn't seem so obviously enamored with her, especially when she couldn't say she returned the sentiment. After two years, she had to wonder if he would have proposed marriage if he wasn't pretending they weren't on speaking terms. A well-off merchant's daughter and a penniless noble would have made a very suitable pair under normal circumstances.

They passed another door, and Luís pulled her into the empty room. He pushed the door closed, leaving it open just enough that they could argue that they hadn't been alone in a closed-off room together. "Am I allowed to touch you now?"

"You should be careful." She leaned against the wall, tilting away from him without looking as though that was her goal. "You wouldn't want to do anything you might need to confess while my brother's at court."

He gently brushed a curl back from her forehead. "You know you do something to me, Cecília."

"I really don't try to." Her stomach squirmed at the deep, devoted way he was watching her. He smiled, and she gave into the urge to slip away. She took a seat on the low couch. "Tell me more about the wedding."

Luís frowned, following her. "You really wish to hear more about that?"

Senhor Carvalho will. She started slowly as she prodded for information. "How awful was Isabel?"

"I didn't have to speak with her much, luckily." He took a seat next to her. "She was happy playing queen for the day with the ladies."

"Anything else interesting happen?"

Luís sighed. "Not unless you consider preening and complaining interesting."

"A lot of complaining?"

"The food, the weather, what everyone was wearing... and that was just the day of the wedding."

"And you wanted to leave *that* so soon?" she teased.

"If I wish to listen to people complaining for silly reasons, I might as well be at court."

"I don't know. Here, everyone's still complaining about their landholdings in Lisbon."

"Same there." Luís took her hand, interlacing their fingers. "The first minster was certainly a favorite topic of conversation."

"Nothing that will cause problems, I hope?" She furrowed her eyebrows, attempting to look purely concerned.

"No, *lindeza*." He leaned toward her. "Nothing like two years ago."

"You promise?"

"I didn't hear anything that isn't freely said at court. Don't worry."

So nothing new for Senhor Carvalho but Francisco. She finally didn't pull back as he continued forward, allowing Luís to kiss her, figuring she had to give the man at least that much. And yet, her thoughts once again began to drift.

Dear São Miguel... I'm still going to Hell, aren't I? She managed one last near prayer before letting her thoughts float away wherever they wanted.

TIO ALOISIO STOOD BY his desk, remaining focused on the letter in his hand as Cecília walked through the door. "Did you know your brother was coming to court?"

Good afternoon to you, too, Tio. I'm well. How are you? Cecília shut the door to their apartments and clicked the latch into place before she turned to face him. "I did not. I wouldn't even have known he was here if I hadn't been in the chapel when he arrived, in fact. He's not here to visit us."

"The first minister is going to ask about it."

"I'm certain he will," Cecília said, accepting she was going to receive another lecture even if Francisco's appearance was none of her doing. Though she had two years behind her and managed everything Senhor Carvalho asked of her admirably, if she did say so herself, Tio Aloisio seemed unwilling or unable to see her as anything more than the seventeen-year-old girl who had stumbled through Lisbon, getting by on luck more than skill.

"Do you know why he's here?"

"To meet with Father Moreno, apparently."

"Meet about what?"

"He didn't say."

Tio Aloisio brought his eyes up to hers without lifting his head.

"I'm not expected to know everything the second it happens now, am I? I wouldn't be very good at my job if I prodded people to the point of suspicion." She moved to take a seat. "I'll see what I can find out when I speak with him later. Perhaps it's about Bibiana. Father Moreno likes updates on her, even if she's been entirely normal for two years."

"I find that doubtful."

"Oh?" Cecília studied him across the antechamber. Construction hadn't stopped on the Real Barraca in the entire time she had been there, and with Senhor Carvalho's favor, she and Tio Aloisio had been placed in a much larger set of rooms than where Tio Aloisio had first lived, giving them each a bedroom *and* Tio Aloisio an office off the antechamber. Still, Tio Aloisio had chosen to keep a desk in the front room with many of his books. Cecília had to wonder if it was a taunt to the former powers that be in his own head. Senhor Carvalho didn't control the Church, but it didn't seem the Inquisition was going to come searching any of his friends' shelves for banned books under the first minister's watch.

When Tio Aloisio didn't offer any more information, Cecília prodded, "And why is that doubtful?"

"She's been at Convento da Conceição for the past quarter year."

The information went through Cecília like a spear. "She's gone to a convent?"

"Intends to join the Poor Clares." Tio Aloisio nodded.

"She's barely thirteen!" Cecília stood again. Of course, Bibiana had said she'd wanted to join a convent two years before—*Lord, has it been that long since I've seen her?*—but with everything else that had happened, Cecília hadn't spent any time ruminating on it. She had been too busy. She had assumed she'd had more time.

"She was *a criança milagre*." Tio Aloisio didn't bother to temper the sarcasm in his voice. "Unsurprising she feels a calling to religious life. Anyway, I imagine your grandfather thought it good to encourage a granddaughter who wishes to be cloistered. I certainly would have less to worry about, if I sent you to a convent."

"Who says I would stay in one?"

"One in the middle of nowhere, it goes without saying." He sent her a look, though a touch of teasing softened the corners of his eyes.

Someone knocked. The teasing disappeared, and Tio Aloisio nodded for Cecília to answer. Who knew where Águeda or the other servants were, but Cecília stood without complaint and answered.

Talk of the Devil… or the priest. She plastered a smile into place at the sight of Francisco and Father Moreno. "Father Durante, Father Moreno. What a pleasant surprise."

Father Moreno smiled back at her, catching his hands in front of him. "Father Durante invited me to join him on the visit. I hope I'm not interrupting a family moment."

"Oh no. We're happy to have you." Cecília didn't think for a second that she actually had a say as to whether the other priest stayed. Quickly, she went through what books Tio Aloisio did have lying about the antechamber. Even if the Inquisition wouldn't break down their door, she didn't much care to think what Francisco might do if he saw something he didn't like. She stepped back and motioned into the room, relatively certain that though Tio Aloisio was bold, he wasn't so bold as to advertise his more blasphemous tomes. "You likely remember my uncle, Father Moreno? Aloisio Silva Durante?"

Father Moreno's expression strained slightly, but he lowered his head. "A pleasure to see you again, Senhor Durante."

"And you, Father." Tio Aloisio bowed then looked at Francisco. "Fathers. It's been far too long, Cisco."

"I prefer Father Durante," Francisco said, his voice colder than when he had corrected Cecília. If he was still irritated with her, he was still *incensed* with Tio Aloisio.

Tio Aloisio quirked an eyebrow at the tone but kept his voice congenial. "As you wish."

"Did you have a good trip here?" Cecília tried to redirect the conversation. "It's been a lovely week."

"We made good time." Francisco's eyes went solidly to the bookshelves as though he had picked up Cecília's earlier thoughts, and he moved forward. "You have quite the collection here."

"Tio Aloisio has taken it upon himself to better my reading ability." Cecília kept the smile in place, as if blissfully ignorant of the tension in the room. "I'm now quite proficient in Portuguese *and* Latin." She decided it was wisest not to mention how Senhor Carvalho had recently started her learning French as well—though she didn't have much skill for it—so she could understand the diplomats wandering the halls.

"What have you been reading?" Francisco glanced back at her.

"The Bible for Latin," Cecília said.

"Not just the Bible?" He picked up one of the volumes from the shelf.

"Some São Tomás de Aquino." She picked the next least offensive work she could think of.

"Some?"

"I've reached his thoughts on the nature of sin. How God's will flows through both natural law and eternal law. How sin is abrogating either one's own reason *or* divine revelation."

Francisco studied her for another moment before looking back at Tio Aloisio. "You're turning my sister into a theologian."

"If she had the temperament for it, I'd say she'd make a good nun," Tio Aloisio answered. "She certainly has the mind for study, if not the patience."

"Patience and a strong understanding of divine will versus human thought is paramount to study." Francisco's voice turned icy. "I hope you're keeping a close eye on what you give her. Nothing dangerous to impressionable minds."

"You heard Bibiana is at Convento da Conceição?" Cecília cut in, more than happy to keep Francisco's mind off what philosophy she might have read.

"She wishes to join the Poor Clares." Francisco set the book back on the shelf. "Avô Santa Rita wrote for my permission to move her. It seems she is doing well, living with the sisters."

"*She* certainly has the temperament." Cecília tried to pump some levity back into the room. She looked at Father Moreno. "You'd heard Bibiana is still doing well?"

"I would have to argue she was never unwell." Father Moreno smiled from the place he had taken in the corner, either to remain out of the way or to watch everything that was happening. "But I don't find it surprising she feels such a strong calling, now that God has given her fully back to the world, even as young as she is. He obviously has had a strong hand in her life already. You have a blessed family."

The ones who are alive? "I pray to live up to it."

Another sharp knock, and Senhor Carvalho appeared in the doorway. Cecília's skin prickled as if it could feel the temperature drop his appearance caused.

Senhor Carvalho still gave a tight smile and bowed. "Father Moreno."

"Minister." Father Moreno lowered his head.

"I don't believe you've met my nephew, Minister." Tio Aloisio stepped forward. "Father Durante."

If the men in the room heard how curtly Tio Aloisio clipped the name, they didn't show it. Francisco and Senhor Carvalho exchanged their own quick greeting, then Senhor Carvalho addressed the room. "If you'll excuse us, I need a moment with Senhor Durante."

Cecília curtsied as Francisco and Father Moreno lowered their heads, and Tio Aloisio went to grab his hat by the door.

"Would you like to pray with us now, Cecília?" Francisco turned to her.

"Please, Senhorita Durante." Senhor Carvalho spoke in the split second Cecília hesitated. "Don't allow me to interrupt your devotions."

"Thank you, Minister." Cecília gave another quick curtsy, entirely able to catch the order behind Senhor Carvalho's friendly dismissal. She wouldn't need to talk about the countess and her daughters the next time she had to report. She likely wouldn't even need to discuss what Luís had told her about the wedding. Senhor Carvalho would want to hear about her brother and just what he had been doing in Setúbal.

Chapter Sixteen

Cecília unlatched her window and swung it open slowly, easing it past the point that always squeaked. With the moon waning, it wasn't as easy to see outside, but after two years, Cecília likely could have found her way around the palace grounds in the pitch black. Pausing to think about it, she realized she actually had.

After spending an hour with Senhor Carvalho, having every word of what Francisco and Father Moreno had said picked apart, even if none of it sounded outwardly seditious, she couldn't consider staying inside. She had needed to remain far too still all day, hearing first from Francisco about how Father Malagrida was saving souls two days south of the capital only to then hear how the man was inciting insurrection from the first minister. For as stern as Senhor Carvalho was, he never actually frightened Cecília outside of when he spoke of Father Malagrida. The loathing the minister had for the priest seemed far deeper than his political feuds with the old families at court. The hatred felt nearly personal.

With her bed dress tied directly over her camisa, Cecília might as well have been nude, as far as court would have been concerned. Without her stays, padded rolls, or pannier, however, she was nimble enough to slip out of the window. She knew well enough how to avoid any other late-night wanderers if she wanted to.

She turned for her favorite spot on the southern side of the Real Barraca, just past the last of the manicured hedges of the gardens, overlooking the river. She glanced up at the crescent moon. *There should be enough light to see the water.*

The pale-silver glint in the distance proved her right. She slowed as she came close to her spot, realizing that she recognized the dark shape sitting in the shadow of the hedges. Certain it was Luís, she released a heavy breath. Most nights, she didn't mind the company when Luís followed her outside. After the day she'd had, however, she didn't much feel like talking. After debating it for a moment, she continued forward and took a seat next to him.

"I was beginning to wonder if it was too dark for you tonight," Luís said.

"Dark but beautiful weather," she answered, looking out at the shimmering river in front of them. Beyond the soft chirping of crickets and the vague sound of waves that reached them when the wind blew the right way, the world was silent. She wrapped her arms around her middle.

"Autumn's coming," he said.

"I always loved autumn."

"Loved? You don't now?"

Too many bad memories. She once again redirected. "My father wouldn't sail in the winter, if he could help it. He always said Brazil was at its most miserable in January, and the winter storms out on the Atlantic weren't worth going to melt in Brazilian heat. Autumn meant I could start watching for his ship down on the Tagus. He normally didn't actually arrive until close to Christmastide, but that didn't matter. It was the only time of year my father was around for that long. He would stay through Easter if he could. Then when João started sailing with him... I don't think Mamãe was ever happier than when they were both home."

"João was your elder brother?"

She was certain she had mentioned João before, but she nodded. "I never got to know him especially well. He was eleven years older and was already sailing by the time I was six, but my mother always said we were the most alike of her children."

"You and your brother?"

She nodded. "I think, honestly, we were both most like my father. Both got his dark eyes and curls. Both felt drawn to travel. I would have gone sailing as well, were I allowed."

A smile came into his voice, though it was too dark to make out his expression. "You wanted to be a sailor?"

"Don't laugh at me."

"I'm not." He found her hand in the dark. "I just can't see you as a sailor."

"Give me a chance to see the world, I'm not certain I'd turn it down even now."

"I hope I'd be able to convince you to stay here."

Cecília didn't answer. She found it was safer not to when he strayed too close to saying anything substantial about their relationship. The world went silent once again as the conversation died off. She took a deep breath and closed her eyes. The wind blew, and she heard a whisper of the waves of the river hitting the banks. For the first time in three years, she let her thoughts drift back to the docks in Lisbon and the Paço da Ribeira, the king's riverside palace, which wouldn't be rebuilt, per Senhor Carvalho's plans. The Ribeira dos Naus, the royal shipyard, would. Through the nausea that came at any thought of what life had been back when things had been beautifully simple, some grain of happy thoughts tried to take hold. She had loved her city, truly, deeply. She could only hope building would properly start sooner rather than later, and she would be able to see the new city risen from the ashes.

"Did things not go well with your brother?" Luís pulled her back out of her thoughts.

"What?"

"You seem distracted."

"Oh." The happy thoughts withered at once. She went with the safest answer. "My brother and uncle don't get along."

"Any reason?"

"My uncle is friends with Senhor Carvalho, and my brother has been living in Setúbal?"

"Ah." Luís obviously caught her meaning.

"No one in my family ever seems able to agree with each other."

"The men, at least." He brought her hand to his lips and kissed the back of her fingers. "I hope they don't pull you into the middle. There was enough trouble with…"

"My grandfather?" she completed as she pulled her hand away. "Could we not talk? I've talked far too much today."

"Of course." Luís slipped his arm around her and rested his hand low on her hip.

That wasn't an invitation. Cecília rolled her eyes. "Luís…"

He released a heavy breath. "Will you at least let me touch you?"

"It's a sin," she argued, pushing his hand away.

"You know I would marry you if I could."

"Doesn't change that we aren't."

Luís was silent for a moment before he shifted, his shadow twisting to face her. "What if I talked to your uncle? Or your brother?"

Cecília stiffened at the sudden change in the common conversation. "What?"

"We could… perhaps work something out. Your brother could marry us. Secretly."

Cecília had to laugh. "And you'd… what? Have a wife you could only see in side rooms? Who lives with her uncle rather than you?"

"We could sort things somehow."

Leaning forward, Cecília placed a hand on his cheek and kissed him quickly, pulling back as soon as she felt his hand back at her waist. "I don't think this is something we should discuss now."

"You're going to be the death of me, Cecília."

I don't think anyone has ever died of frustration. Her life would have been greatly shortened from some of the dreams she'd had if so.

For out of the heart proceed evil thoughts, murders, adulteries, for-nications, thefts, false witness, blasphemies: These are the things which defile a man. The passage suddenly flared to mind, the sound of it feeling surprisingly close to Francisco's voice.

You would certainly think me defiled from some of my thoughts, Cisco. Cecília pulled away entirely and stood. Nothing good had happened since her brother had arrived, and she had the feeling that things would only turn worse if he was there for long. Senhor Carvalho's ranting, Luís's sudden ideas of secret weddings, her own guilt... *Can I even ask God to make a priest leave? What if I should feel guilty?*

That was a road she certainly didn't want to walk down. "I should go back in. It's getting a little cold."

"I could give you my jacket."

"I'll see you tomorrow?" She ignored the offer. "We can talk then?"

The shadow that was Luís looked up at her, radiating enough disappointment that Cecília didn't need to see his face to sense it. "Of course."

"Good night, Luís," Cecília said, turning away before he could offer a good night as well, trying to fight down any of the old guilt she'd done so well in ignoring for the past two years.

WITH FRANCISCO STILL at court, Cecília found that morning prayers had become more than a place to overhear court whispers. Every day, she could feel her brother's eyes on her from wherever he happened to be, as if her presence was the only thing that satisfied him enough not to demand she leave her *estrangeirado* uncle before he irrevocably corrupted her mind.

He likely already has. She kept her hands clasped and her head down. She perhaps hadn't lost her faith, but she had certainly examined it and adjusted it. That had to be why so many books had been banned by the Inquisition. Heretical or not, once thoughts were read, they had a way of sticking inside one's head.

Knowledge is power. Yet, as Tio Aloisio also liked to quote: *A little learning is a dangerous thing.*

She tried to remember where he had gotten that. Some Englishman with an ironic name.

Pope—it came to her. *Alexander Pope. An Essay on... something or another.* It had been in English, so far beyond her ken. She couldn't even read the French treatises yet.

"Cecília."

The voice far too close to Cecília's ear tore her out of her thoughts. She jumped and looked to her left.

The familiar pale face of Graça Cardozo came into view. She smiled, showing her slightly crossed front teeth. "You were obviously deep in prayer."

"I've been feeling contemplative lately." Cecília looked up at the altar and crossed herself, getting a quick glimpse of Francisco still watching her from where he stood, off to one side. Recovered from not having heard anyone come up beside her, she turned back to Graça with a smile. "When did you get back?"

"Last night, just before dark." Graça crossed herself as well before standing to let Cecília out of the pew. "Papai said he couldn't take much more of my grandmother. I wasn't supposed to hear, of course."

From a questionably noble background and with Carvalho-friendly parents, Ana Graça Delgazo e Cardozo had unsurprisingly not been invited to Mateus and Isabel's wedding, either. Rather than staying at court, however, her parents had taken her out into the country to see Graça's perpetually ill grandmother. As those who *had* been invited to the wedding filtered back to court, Cecília certainly would take another ally, especially one who didn't need to keep from being seen with Cecília like Luís.

"Your trip went well, though?"

"A little dull, but I can't complain." Graça glanced over her shoulder as she walked with Cecília toward the doors of the chapel. "Is there a reason that priest is staring at you?"

"My brother. He's visiting Father Moreno."

"He's quite striking." Graça set him a final look before they slipped through the door.

"He's a *priest*."

"Doesn't change that fact." Graça giggled. "Do you know how long he's staying?"

Not much longer, I hope. "He hasn't said."

"Well, we could certainly use nicer things to look at in Mass than Father Rocha."

"And he's my brother."

"Pity for you."

Cecília shook her head, but the sound of female voices coming from the other direction cut the conversation off. If Graça also reported to Senhor Carvalho, or if she knew Cecília did, Cecília didn't know. Either way, they both seemed to share the instinct to listen.

"I'm just glad to get away from that witch." Maria's voice came down the hall then changed pitch as she imitated who was presumably Isabel. "Are you really wearing *that*, Maria? You do know who is going to be here? One would think you'd want to look your best. You aren't growing any younger, you know." Her voice dropped back to normal. "I was ready to pull those stupid little stuffed birds right out of her hair. Pretentious li—"

Maria stopped mid-syllable as they reached the intersection of the halls and Graça and Cecília came into view.

Cecília gave her courtier smile and lowered her head. "Good morning, Maria, Constança, Marga."

The three women lowered their heads quickly, forced to maintain a shred of etiquette, though they looked loath to, before they scurried off silently.

"It seems everyone's coming back to court." Cecília watched them go.

"At least the happy couple won't be back for a while," Graça said.

"You mean you aren't missing Mateus and Isabel desperately?"

"I don't know how I'm managing."

"Senhorita Cecília." Águeda appeared. She curtsied quickly as she stopped, her movements quick and birdlike in the way Cecília had grown to associate with the woman running behind on her chores. "Your uncle is asking for you."

"We'll catch up later." Graça squeezed Cecília's arm with a smile.

Cecília smiled her own quick goodbye and followed Águeda. Keeping her face bland, she tried to prepare herself for whatever could be waiting for her. Any hope for good news died the second she saw her uncle's expression. She waited for him to excuse Águeda before speaking. "What's happened?"

"Your brother." Tio Aloisio tossed a pamphlet on the couch.

Cecília made no move to take it. "What's that?"

"Father Malagrida's most recent thoughts on the rebuilding of Lisbon and the state of our souls. Particularly those at court. Your brother has been circulating them."

Cecília picked up the pamphlet, a cold pit opening in her stomach. "Senhor Carvalho's seen?"

"You aren't his only pair of eyes around here."

"I'm well aware." Cecília stared down at the paper without opening it. She didn't need more reminders to pray for her immortal soul or for *more* guilt to rush back. She needed to worry about Francisco, not herself. "But he's seen? He has a plan?"

"Your brother is going to be expelled from court once Senhor Carvalho gets the royal decree. Sent back to Setúbal."

Cecília released a breath. As far as the possibilities went, that was mild. He wasn't being thrown into Junqueira Prison or exiled to Angola. Expulsion from court was far better than either of those.

"He wants you to go with him," Tio Aloisio continued.

"What?" Cecília blinked as she focused on her uncle once again.

"The first minister is sending you to Setúbal as well."

"But I haven't done anything!" Cecília's voice pitched up dangerously.

Tio Aloisio sent her a look that said she was acting childish. "He wants eyes on what's happening there. Enough of the court goes for 'spiritual retreats' that dissention could well be brewing. Who better to go and report back than a sister who has every reason to be angry with the first minister over the treatment of her brother?"

"You think anyone will believe that? After I've lived with *you* for two years?"

"You are a convincing actress when you wish to be."

"*Cisco's* not going to believe that I'm leaving court to support him."

"Then you better start working out how you're going to convince him."

Cecília released a tense breath through her teeth. Trying to argue with her uncle felt more and more like arguing with a brick wall. She supposed she could appeal directly to Senhor Carvalho, but the first minister wasn't known for taking *I can't* very well, and she didn't much relish the idea of being on the receiving end of one of his piercing, displeased stares. Her tone turned whinier than she cared to admit. "But I don't want to leave court."

"I don't believe that's up to you."

"But—"

"Cecília, we are both here because of the minister's good will. Do you want to lose that?"

Cecília pursed her lips, but she knew better than to argue more. If she couldn't convince her uncle to plead her case, she didn't stand a chance with Senhor Carvalho. "How long do I have to stay in Setúbal?"

"As long as you're told," Tio Aloisio said. "I'm sure there are plenty of places for you to get into trouble down there as well."

She narrowed her eyes at him.

"Águeda will help you pack. I'll make sure you have everything you need for however long you'll stay. You should be ready to leave come morning."

"*Morning?*"

"Be glad the king is away from court until tonight. Remember, Diogo Mendonça was given three hours to leave the capital once his exile was announced."

Cecília crossed her arms, aware but not entirely able to care that she looked like a sulking child as she slunk off to her room. As she looked around her room of the past two years, she tried to console herself.

It isn't the end of the world. You *aren't being exiled. It isn't so far that you'll never come back.* Though Father Malagrida had been banished from the capital, he had hardly been living in the far reaches of the Amazon. Some of the most important families still kept Father Malagrida as their personal confessor, not in the least Leonor Tomásia de Távora, the marchioness herself. She certainly wouldn't allow Father Malagrida to live in squalor.

"*Learn, oh Lisbon, that the destroyers of our houses, palaces, churches, and convents, the cause of the death of so many people... are your abominable sins.*" The memory of the priest's sermon and piercing eyes resounded in Cecília's mind and made the hair rise on her arms. After living with Tio Aloisio for so long, she wasn't certain she could face Father Malagrida, not when three-year-old words could still make her squirm.

Then again, maybe that means you need a spiritual retreat. Truly.

Forcing her mind away from the topic, Cecília focused on the room around her, trying to think what she would need with her.

Chapter Seventeen

Cecília's head pounded as if her heart beat directly behind her eyes. Rubbing her temple with one hand, she moved to the window and looked out. There was no moon at all, leaving the world entirely black past the lanterns that lit the Real Barraca and the pinpricks of stars. Luís wouldn't be out by the hedge. He didn't know how to make his way during a new moon and assumed she didn't, either. She could at least thank the Lord for small miracles. With the king still away—gone to visit his mistress, Teresa Távora, from what Cecília had heard whispered—Francisco's forthcoming banishment hadn't yet been announced, and she didn't want to be the one to have to tell Luís what was happening, especially knowing that if she did, she would have to explain how she knew.

The jumpiness in her limbs progressed to shaking, and she unlatched the window.

She had just pushed herself up on the sill when a pounding on the hallway door rattled the entire apartment. Cecília started. Catching herself against the wooden wall, she regained her balance and eased back down.

By the time she made it to the door of her room, Tio Aloisio was already talking to someone in the hall. "What the Devil is all the racket?"

"The king!" a breathless voice Cecília didn't recognize said. "He's been shot!"

"What?" All the anger in Tio Aloisio's tone disappeared in an instant.

"He's just been brought... Senhor Carvalho... He..."

Tio Aloisio was already pulling his coat over his nightshirt and grabbing for his hat to cover his wigless head. "Lead the way."

As her uncle disappeared into the hall, Cecília took a step forward, hesitated, then followed. If the king had been shot, she doubted anyone would care that she was out in her bed dress. She shut the room door behind her and looked for where her uncle had gone. A glimpse of him turning the corner caught her eye. She picked up her skirt to run after him.

Luís appeared at the intersection, and Cecília stopped short to avoid a collision. His hand went to her shoulder all the same, as if to steady her. "You've heard?"

"The king?" She looked after where her uncle was headed. "Someone said—"

"He's been shot," Luís confirmed. "Out on the road."

"He was out on the road?" She brought her eyes back to Luís's face.

"In his carriage. Someone fired on it. I don't know much else, but they've brought him back here."

"He's alive?"

Luís nodded, though his expression was drawn. "For now."

Cecília's stomach pulled into knots. She tried to picture what it would mean if the king died from his wounds and Princesa Maria became Dona Maria I. Father Malagrida would be brought back to court. That much was certain. Senhor Carvalho would likely take the priest's place, exiled from Lisbon, if he was lucky. The princess's loathing of the man was no secret. Tio Aloisio could take to sailing again if he wished or return to his vineyard, but Cecília would have to switch allegiances. She would have to devote herself to Francisco or go back to her grandparents, if Avô Santa Rita would have anything to do with her. Luís wouldn't be *able* to have anything to do with her. If she couldn't stay with Francisco or go to her grandparents, she *would* have to consider a convent.

"Cecília?" Luís's hand tightened around her arm, snapping her back to reality.

She met his eyes.

"You've gone as pale as a sheet." He watched her and took a step closer, as if preparing for her to faint. "Do you need to sit?"

Cecília looked around him to where her uncle had been led then shook her head. "I'm fine."

"Are you certain?"

She nodded and turned off to see what was happening. The buzz of voices grew as she worked her way through the halls with Luís close behind her. A few more corners, and they reached the crowd that had formed at the doors to the royal apartments.

"Make way! Make way!" someone yelled, and the crowd parted enough to let the royal physician inside.

Graça ran up one of the other halls with her father, and her eyes caught Cecília's. Her father shouldered his way along the side to where Tio Aloisio was, and Graça headed Cecília's way. "What's happened? Do they know anything?"

"We just made it as well." Cecília shook her head. "Luís said the king was shot in his carriage. We don't know more than that."

Graça's forehead wrinkled. "How could this happen? Who would want to shoot—"

"He's the king," Luís said, his eyes on the door as Senhor Carvalho slipped back into the hall. "There are always people who could benefit from a shift in power."

Someone called Luís's name, and Cecília looked quickly enough to see some of the Vilhena family. Luís glanced back at her, his face conflicted.

"Go." She nodded.

He squeezed her hand, the hold low enough that no one would likely have been able to see it, before shifting to make his way through the crowd.

Graça watched him leave before switching back to give Cecília a look.

"We weren't together. I met him in the hall," Cecília said, answering the silent question and pulling her bed dress slightly tighter to her body before scanning the men closer to the door. Senhor Carvalho was easy to spot, as tall as he was, so Cecília took Graça's hand and tried to find a way closer to the doors.

"I don't want a word of this leaving this hallway until we have those responsible impaled on stakes in front of Junqueira," Senhor Carvalho said in a low-yet-harsh voice that left no doubt to his seriousness. "Am I understood? The rest of the country is not to know the king is injured."

"Yes, Minister." A man Cecília recognized as a guard strode off, and Senhor Carvalho turned to give his next decrees. His eyes glanced off Cecília and Graça, pausing just long enough to say he had registered their presence before they moved to some of the men standing about.

Cecília swallowed the lump in her throat.

"Do you hear that?" Graça tugged Cecília toward the door, and she realized she had never released Graça's hand.

She tried to focus as they pressed against the wall next to the doors. Groans floated through the wood planks, muted by the tapestries but audible in the mess of conversations.

"Is that the king?" Graça looked at Cecília with large eyes.

"It has to be?" Cecília listened for any other sound that could give some hint as to the king's state. If he was groaning, though, it at least meant he was still conscious. She would take that for the time being.

A hand touched her back, and she started. Turning her head, she saw Tio Aloisio suddenly beside her.

"Go back to bed, Cilinha," he said then added, "and you, Ana Graça. It will be a long night."

Cecília started, "But—"

"And you might as well tell Águeda to unpack your things." He lowered his voice, his eyes drilling into Cecília. "I don't think anyone will be going anywhere in the morning."

CECÍLIA WORRIED THE cross around her neck between her fingers, vaguely wondering if she had managed to rub out any remaining imperfections in her anxiety.

Or maybe I'm just making new dents. She still couldn't bring herself to stop. The entire court had been on edge for days, speaking in whispered voices between kneeling in the chapel to pray for the king's life and hovering outside the royal apartments for news. Dom José was still alive, but how precariously, Cecília didn't know. Dona Mariana, his queen, had been made regent if nothing else, and Senhor Carvalho was barely a blur around the palace as he led the enquiry, looking for whoever had thrown the world into such disarray.

"It will be fine." Luís caught her hand gently to force it back down into her lap. "You're going to work yourself into a state if you keep worrying like this."

"I can't help it." She stood from the couch in the antechamber. "Everything is just so uncertain. I can't stand—"

"You need to take a breath."

She started pacing.

Luís shifted to the edge of the cushion, resting his forearms on his knees. "Cecília, please—"

"What are they saying with you?"

Luís frowned. "With me?"

"On your side of the palace. With the Vilhenas."

"Same as over here. No one knows anything."

"What are they saying for i-if the king…"

"The king will be fine."

"And if he isn't?" Cecília snapped.

Luís stood, catching both of her hands to force her to stop. "You need to stop. You'll make yourself ill."

She dropped her voice. "What will happen to *me* if it all changes? I won't be able to stay at court."

"Of course you will."

"With whom? They'll sweep me out with the rest of my side of the palace. I'll have nowhere to go."

"That's not true."

"It is!"

"*Lindeza*, trust me. It will be fine." Luís caught her cheek, leaning in to kiss her.

The door opened before he could make contact. He took a sharp step back as Tio Aloisio came over the threshold. He paused as he spotted Luís then closed the door. Still facing away, he took off his hat and placed it on the small table there. "Is there something I can help you with, Senhor Terra?"

"Senhor Durante." Luís pulled at his jacket to straighten it, though it only made him look more nervous. "I was just having a word with your niece."

He glanced at Cecília then raised an eyebrow at Luís. "Alone?"

Luís stumbled a few syllables before Cecília stepped in.

"Águeda just went into the other room, Tio."

Whether or not Tio Aloisio believed the lie didn't matter. She was more focused on stopping Luís from doing something idiotic in his fumbling. Tio Aloisio nodded but kept his eyes on Luís. "I'm sure my niece would thank you for considering how things might look to others. Your being in here, alone with her."

"Of course, Senhor Durante. My apologies." Luís picked up his hat from the couch. "Pleasure speaking with you, senhorita."

Cecília lowered her head as he moved out the door. She waited for his footsteps to disappear down the hall then turned back to her uncle. "Don't chase him away too sternly. He's how I get half of my information."

"Does he know that?" Tio Aloisio moved to his desk.

"Of course not." She resumed pacing.

"Then why was he in here alone with you?"

"You know what the Vilhenas think of us. He can't exactly just come up to me in the hall." She saw the skepticism on Tio Aloisio's face as she doubled back. "You can stop looking at me like I'm a trollop. I haven't had to *do anything*. He genuinely cares about me."

"They always seem to."

She slowed to hold his eyes.

"Just an observation about the company you keep when you're flirting with trouble."

"*I'm* flirting with trouble? You're in all of this deeper than I am if His Highness—"

"The king will be fine." Tio Aloisio turned toward the desk once again. "Senhor Nunes says the worst has passed."

"Dona Mariana is still regent."

"Because he's recovering."

Cecília stopped pacing entirely. "Truly? He'll be fine?"

"So says the first minister, and I have no reason to doubt him."

The panic that had kept her moving left in a rush. Cecília managed to sit before her legs gave out. She breathed the words "thank the Lord" as she crossed herself.

"Better news, they have two men in custody."

"The assassins?"

"They're being questioned now. I imagine we'll hear something soon."

Cecília nodded, wishing she was still in her bed dress and not laced into her stays. She needed a good breath—no, a gulp—of air, and the stiff support suddenly felt too constricting. Placing her hands over her stomacher, she leaned as far forward as her clothing allowed.

"He isn't going to let this happen again."

Cecília didn't look up as she still tried for air. "The king?"

"No," Tio Aloisio said, his tone saying he could only have meant Senhor Carvalho. "*He's* not going to leave us to end up in this position again, should something happen to the king."

Cecília's eyes slid to his, though she didn't straighten. "What does that mean?"

"It means he's going to ask for something. I don't know what yet, but you're going to have to say yes. We're all going to have to say yes. Without hesitation."

She shook her head slightly. "What does that even mean?"

"We'll have to wait to find out."

Chapter Eighteen

Despite Tio Aloisio's warning, Senhor Carvalho didn't seem interested in contacting Cecília or her uncle once news of the arrests began to circulate throughout court. Nor did he call them when the two men arrested were summarily tried and hanged before the populace was even alerted that there had been an attempt on the king's life. After waiting another day to see if anything happened, Cecília allowed herself to relax at least enough to plaster her courtier smile back in place and appear suitably normal in front of others.

It was already a week into September, but the weather was immeasurably pleasant. The mess of people in the gardens said the court agreed. Cecília stayed out of any large groups, aiming for the far end of the manicured hedges. She hoped fewer people would be in the winding dead ends if they were hoping to make the most of the sun and warm breeze. After finding a few quiet conversations and one less-than-proper liaison, Cecília heard Graça's and Luís's familiar voices.

"But have you heard who's been implicated?" Graça said in an excited whisper. "The Duke of Aveiro, the Távoras—"

"People are looking for scandal where there is none." Luís sounded much less concerned with being overheard. "Pedro Teixeria has insulted the duke numerous times, and anyone who's met Aveiro knows the man has a temper. I'm more inclined to believe Mr. Hays's theory."

"Since when have you been friends with Mr. Hays?" Graça sounded suitably skeptical of Luís's connection to the British envoy.

"I've barely spoken to the man, but he's been talking the most sense in the midst of all this. The king wasn't in the royal carriage. It seems entirely likely that Aveiro didn't even know the king was there when he sent those men after Teixeria. An attempted murder, certainly, but regicide? They were two men shooting at a random carriage."

"Then why would the assassins confess to treason?"

"A man will confess to just about anything when put to the screws long enough. And look at who was in charge of the questioning."

"Are you implicating Senhor Carvalho in something?"

It seemed a good moment to step in. Cecília turned around the last hedge with her carefully manufactured smile. "I thought I heard you two."

"Cecília." Luís stood from the little wooden bench placed amongst the hedges.

A flicker of annoyance moved over Graça's face before she looked at Cecília and smiled. "Are you feeling better?"

"Much." Cecília nodded, sticking to the story Tio Aloisio had been telling to excuse her absence. "Took cold is all, I think."

"I said you were going to worry yourself ill." Luís took a few steps closer to her.

"Well, I'm entirely better now. No harm done." She looked back at Graça, searching the woman's face for any sign of what she imagined her own looked like when trying to find information. "What have I missed?"

"People trying to make things far more interesting than they likely are." Luís shook his head.

"You seem entirely too quick to dismiss things." Graça sent him a displeased look from her spot on the bench before returning to address Cecília. She either was not one of Senhor Carvalho's spies, or she was at least as good as Cecília at hiding her true thoughts. "Before they were hanged, the two men—the assassins—confessed to an entire plot against the king's life. They were paid to assassinate him in order for the Duke of Aveiro to stage a *coup d'état*. It supposedly goes all the way to Leonor Távora."

"Which one?" Cecília asked.

"The eldest. The marchioness. And if she is involved, one has to imagine the entire Távora family—"

"Cecília's just gotten well," Luís cut in. "The last thing she needs is to hear scandal and conspiracies."

"I'm fine, Luís. Really." Cecília touched his arm. "I'm surprised my uncle didn't tell me any of this. If there's been a plot—"

"I truly doubt there has been," Luís said.

"Then why has the first minister opened an inquiry?" Graça asked pointedly.

"He is doing his due diligence to protect His Highness," Luís returned. "But an inquiry doesn't mean guilt. I would be hard-pressed to believe Senhora Távora—"

"I think it's too nice a day for all this," Cecília broke in. Whether or not Graça did report to Senhor Carvalho, they were certainly treading too close to too many dangerous topics. Until she knew more about what was happening, the less Luís said, the better.

"Precisely." Luís held Graça's eyes for a moment before turning to Cecília. "You should be sitting."

"I've been in bed for two days straight," Cecília said.

"I should be going, anyway." Graça stood. She caught Cecília's hands and kissed both cheeks. "I'm glad you're doing better. We all need to be careful with our health, with the weather changing." Graça pulled back and sent Cecília a look, holding it long enough to suggest a deeper meaning to her words.

Cecília had the sinking sensation that she knew what Graça meant far too well. Her smile stayed carefully in place. "We certainly do."

Graça disappeared back out into the garden, and Luís shepherded Cecília toward the once-again-empty bench.

"You really don't have to fret over me, Luís." Cecília took a seat all the same. "I promise."

"I wanted to come and check on you." He sat next to her. "But after the last time I saw your uncle... I hope I didn't get you into trouble."

"He was worried about me allowing you too many liberties."

He frowned. "Does—"

"I told him nothing has happened," Cecília said to cut the conversation off as quickly as she could.

Voices moved close enough to hear, and Cecília twisted toward them, listening. A group of women continued to chatter as they passed, nattering on about the supposed plot on the king's life, though they didn't stay in place long enough for Cecília to hear anything new.

"They aren't coming this way." Luís took her hand in his.

Cecília released a slow breath. "Do you ever get tired of hiding, Luís?"

He hesitated. "You know, if I could, I'd—"

"I mean..." Cecília certainly wasn't trying to bring up the marriage conversation again—she didn't have the energy for that—but she was straying perilously close to saying something she would regret. Doing her best to force a smile, she turned back to Luís. "This plot Graça was talking about—"

Luís groaned. "There's no plot."

"Whatever it is." Cecília held his eyes. "Promise me you'll stay out of it."

"Trust me. This inquiry will blow over. There's nothing for it to find. In a week or so—"

"After Senhor Mendonça—"

"This is nothing like that. The retribution was…" He censored whatever he thought of the punishments meted out two years before. "But there *was* a plot. I'm sorry, but no one will ever convince me that Senhora Távora attempted regicide. She's a forceful woman, but she wouldn't attempt a *coup d'état*, and certainly not one to replace Dom José with the Duke of *Aveiro* of all people."

"Just promise me," Cecília said. "Nothing good is going to come from this."

"You're going to make yourself ill again." He touched her cheek. "*Please*. Promise."

Luís caught her chin and kissed her. After a lingering moment, he pulled back to speak. "I promise. Now stop worrying. This isn't two years ago."

No. She closed her eyes, gritting her teeth. *It's likely much worse.*

CECÍLIA PUSHED A LOOSE strand of hair behind her ear and felt the warmth radiating from her skin. She should have worn a hat with a brim outside. As nice as the sun had been in the garden, she had certainly gotten some color from the hour she had spent with Luís. She opened the door to her apartment and froze.

Senhor Carvalho looked up from the book he was holding. "Ah, Senhorita Durante. There you are."

She stepped through, scanning the room for her uncle, the fact that the minister was alone in their antechamber too odd for her to relax. "You were waiting for me?"

"Your uncle just left." He seemed to read Cecília's thoughts, as he had the uncanny ability to do. He shut the book and lifted it for her to see. "Have you read this?"

Cecília closed the door behind her and looked at the title pressed into the cover before shaking her head. "I can't read English."

"Neither can I, actually." He set it back on the shelf. "Spent seven years in London and never learned a word, if you can believe it. Dealt entirely in diplomatic French. I got by surprisingly well, if I do say so myself."

Cecília nodded, not certain what else she could say.

"Please, sit." Senhor Carvalho motioned at the couch as if she were in his rooms and not the other way around.

She silently moved across the space and settled herself on the edge of the cushion.

He studied her. "You look nervous."

"Strained, maybe." She gave a smile, though she was certain the first minister would see through it. Whether or not the man could truly read minds, he certainly knew courtiers well enough to know a false smile when he saw one. "It's been a long week."

"Are you afraid of something?"

"I just don't like not knowing what's happening."

"Hard for you to know what's happening when you don't leave your room for two days." As kindly concerned as the words were said, Cecília could feel the bite to them.

"I..." *wasn't feeling well,* Cecília started to lie before realizing how pointless that would have been. Her uncle would have told him how she had been hiding away, not fully able to return to spying when they had come so close to being on the losing side after two years in power. She changed topics, having to believe the first minister wouldn't take her loss of faith well. "I was out in the garden today. Everyone's talking about how the men you hanged implicated the Távora family in trying to kill His Highness?"

"More than just the Távoras." Senhor Carvalho caught his hands behind his back. "It's no secret that many of the grandees have been displeased with His Highness's decisions on some key issues."

"To the point of assassination?"

"So it seems," Senhor Carvalho said. "Have you heard anything worrying? Something that maybe didn't seem important before Sunday but does now?"

Cecília wet her lips, going through a mess of conversations she had listened to in her mind. "Nothing that jumps out. I can try to think of things."

"See that you do." Senhor Carvalho pinned her with his eyes. "We might need those in the next couple of months."

"Months?" She frowned.

"The truth isn't always an easy thing to uncover. At the moment, I'm simply making certain that everyone is as dedicated to the effort as they should be."

Cecília's insides squirmed at the look he was giving her, but she fought to keep her face placid. "Of course."

"I've come to trust you quite a bit these past years, Cecília," he said. "I hope you feel the same about me."

She nodded. "I do, senhor."

"I'll be in touch." He moved to the door. "Just keep listening. You never know what you'll hear."

He didn't seem to expect a reply, so Cecília didn't give one. Silence certainly was going to be safer for the foreseeable future.

"Oh." He paused in the doorway as if he had just remembered something. "Your brother will be leaving court tomorrow, if you would like to send him off."

Cecília blinked, able to otherwise hide her surprise. "He hadn't said."

"Oh yes," Senhor Carvalho said. "He has taken up a mission to Brazil."

"Brazil?" Her voice raised to a near squeak as her surprise overwhelmed her carefully manufactured calm.

"I'm sure everyone there will be thrilled to have such a devoted shepherd to see to their souls."

Cecília's mouth opened as she tried to form words. Then she shut it and gathered herself. As offhand as the minister had said it, she had to assume Francisco hadn't been the one to decide to leave. If it hadn't been a banishment by another name, she had to imagine it would have been a much different discussion about how she needed to find out what Francisco was planning.

Once again, court was being cleared of anyone Senhor Carvalho considered a threat, and no good could come from ending up on his list. With her thoughts in some kind of order, Cecília started again, much more calmly. "I'm certain they will. Thank you for telling me, senhor."

Senhor Carvalho tipped his hat and pulled the door shut behind him, leaving Cecília alone to roil in her own thoughts. *Where are we all going to end up this time?*

Chapter Nineteen

When nothing came of the whispers of assassination for months on end and Dom José relieved the queen of her regency, the court as a whole relaxed. Cecília couldn't. She knew far too much ever to relax again. Senhor Carvalho hadn't given up on a formless case. He was lying in wait, collecting everything he thought he needed while the people he wanted to see in a noose went back to laughing and living their lives as if nothing had happened.

"Are you still missing your brother?" Luís ran his thumb over the back of her hand as they sat in one of the small sitting rooms, the door almost completely closed. Cecília couldn't say whether Luís truly thought that would pacify her uncle if anyone found out about it, but she didn't bother to comment. Tio Aloisio had far more to worry about than her reputation. *She* had far more to worry about.

"What?" She looked away from the window.

"You've been staring off into the distance since he left as if your mind got on that ship with him."

"I'm sorry. I don't mean to be in a mood."

"It's fine. There's quite a difference between having a family member gone from court and only few days away and one across the ocean."

She looked at him, pulling her mouth tight.

"And... I'm not helping."

"It's fine. I just miss him." Cecília shook her head, forcing her face into something much more congenial. With Senhor Carvalho still slowly planning his final blow, it was likely better to have Francisco across the Atlantic than with a priest Senhor Carvalho hated more than any of the grandees at court.

"Is there anything I can do to make you feel better?" Luís asked.

Give me my family back. Be an entirely different man. Go back three years.

No, she would have to have gone back much further if she wanted everything to be like it once had been, when everyone had been happy. Francisco, Mamãe, Ana Margarida, João, Papai...

Before she could work out an answer she could actually give, voices in the hall outside the small room made her senses prickle. Recognizing Graça's, she stood and moved to the doorway.

"Cecília?" Luís asked.

She pushed the door out just enough to see Graça having a very animated discussion with someone wearing a red-patterned coat. Pushing a little farther, she saw a corner of the man's face. *Mateus.*

She ducked back into the room before Luís could come to the door as well. "Since when have Graça and Mateus been on speaking terms?"

Luís's face twitched in the way it always did when he didn't want to tell her something.

She fixed her eyes on him, giving him a slightly softer version of the look Senhor Carvalho always pinned on her in similar moments.

Luís didn't last more than a second. "I saw Graça leaving Mateus's room last week and then again a few nights ago."

"Graça and Mateus?" Cecília's eyebrows rose. For as much as Graça despised the man, Cecília had to assume that whatever had been happening in Mateus's room after dark was some sort of plot in itself—one that likely intersected with Senhor Carvalho's, Cecília assumed.

"I had the same reaction. Trust me." Luís had clearly read the wrong thoughts into her expression. "But I make it a point to stay out of whom Mateus takes to bed."

"Do we think Isabel knows?"

"As she's only been an average amount of awful to Graça lately? My guess would be no."

The sounds of footsteps and the sway of fabric moved down the hall in Cecília's direction. One pair—Graça but not Mateus.

Cecília motioned to the doorway. "I should talk to her."

"I wouldn't suggest involving yourself with whatever's happening out there." Luís shook his head.

"I'll see you tomorrow." Cecília flashed him a smile then slipped out into the hall before Luís could answer.

Graça slowed for a step then tilted up the corners of her mouth in a tense smile. "I was coming to find you."

Cecília glanced at the now empty corner. "Should I ask?"

"Not here." Graça motioned for Cecília to follow. "We have somewhere we need to be."

FOR ALL HER TIME AT court, Cecília hadn't spent much time in audience with Dom José. She had certainly never had reason to have a conversation with him. It had actually been smarter for her not to. With her reporting to Senhor Carvalho, she had to imagine anything important she said was passed along, and any meeting with His Highness would have gotten too much attention.

Sitting across from him in the royal apartments, though, had her petrified—even if she hadn't said more than a sentence between Graça laying out everything she had apparently learned about a Távora plot, with Senhor Carvalho's prompting here and there. Dom José was likewise quiet, listening to everything Graça had to say as he watched her, his brown eyes peering out of his fleshy face.

"And how did you hear all of this?" Senhor Carvalho once again stepped in as Graça took a breath. "Were you in the Távora apartments for some reason?"

"The Vilhena ones," Graça said, dropping her gaze demurely. "I've always been a bit enamored with Mateus de Vilhena, and when he invited me back to his rooms... Well, I don't think anyone else knew I was there that late at night, and after Mateus fell asleep, I heard them talking."

"Who is 'them'?" Senhor Carvalho asked, though Cecília suspected he had heard Graça's story before.

"João Manuel de Vilhena and one of the younger Leonor Távoras. She was saying she was worried about her mother's plans relying too much on Teresa, as His Highness hadn't visited her in months."

"Teresa Távora?" Senhor Carvalho rested his hand on the back of the couch he stood behind.

"From what was said, it would seem so." Graça nodded. "Cecília agreed."

Cecília started at her name.

"Were you there as well, Senhorita Durante?" Senhor Carvalho's eyes hit her.

"I-I..." she floundered.

"I don't think you and Luís are a particularly well-kept secret, Ceci," Graça prompted as though she knew Cecília needed her line.

"Yes, senhor," Cecília addressed Senhor Carvalho rather than the king.

"And you believe they did mean Teresa Távora in this conversation?"

Nothing about the situation seemed right. Cecília couldn't say what Graça had or hadn't heard—she certainly *had* been with Mateus Vilhena, from what Cecília had seen—but if they were asking for false collaboration, they obviously weren't entirely beholden to the truth. Still, Tio Aloisio's voice pounded through Cecília's head as the first minister's sharp eyes hit her: *you're going to have to say yes.*

"Yes, senhor. That is what it seemed."

If Dom José had any reaction to his mistress being implicated in a plot on his life, his face didn't show it. Then again, after months of an inquest, Cecília imagined it wasn't necessarily news to anyone in the room but her.

"Did it sound as though they were talking about old plans or new ones, by your estimation?" Senhor Carvalho asked.

"They sounded new to me," Graça said. "Then it made me think of a conversation Cecília and I overheard in the garden a few weeks ago. Isabel was teasing Dores Távora about how Dores should try to take her cousin's position, and Dores said something about how her time would be better spent with Senhor *Aveiro*. We didn't know what she meant then, but—"

"You'd be willing to testify to that fact?" Senhor Carvalho crossed his arms, moving his eyes between Graça and Cecília.

Testify?

"Yes, senhor," Graça said without hesitation.

This lie isn't bad enough? The twisting in Cecília's stomach turned to full-blown nausea at the idea of taking an already dangerous story and condemning a possibly innocent woman with it. With Senhor Carvalho's eyes on her, though, she still found herself nodding.

"Yes?"

Cecília swallowed, keeping her eyes on the first minister rather than the king. "Yes, senhor."

She had obviously done whatever Senhor Carvalho wanted from her for the moment, and he turned to the king. "As you can see, Your Highness, time has passed, and the vipers are starting to stir once again. They think they have gotten away with their plot and are now planning their next attempt. The traitors confessed, we have the duke's pistol, we know it was he who gave it to them, only the Távoras knew you would be on that road at that time... This is all treason. When bitten once, one does not give a snake a chance to strike again before lopping off its head."

Cecília dared to glance at the king and found Dom José studying her—or perhaps he was staring past her—before he nodded and stood. He turned to Senhor Carvalho. "How many?"

Senhor Carvalho pulled a paper out of his pocket and began listing, "Marchioness Távora, Count Alvor, Teresa Távora, Duke Aveiro, Marquis Alorna, Count Atouguia..."

As the names continued to stack upon one another, the enormity of what she had been brought into registered in Cecília's mind. Of the list Senhor Carvalho had, all the conspirators he had were either legitimately found out or purposely funneled into the plot, depending on how much testimony was actually true. Cecília caught her hands in her lap, praying only the truly guilty would end up caught in the net being cast.

"Count Vilhena, Mateus de Vilhena, Isabel de Maraliva, Luís de Terra—"

"Luís?" Cecília couldn't stop her mouth in time.

Three pairs of eyes locked onto her.

"I'm sorry." She stuttered, "I-I-I just... Senhor Terra. I can't imagine—"

"People can surprise you," Senhor Carvalho said and lifted the page. "I'm certain no one ever would have thought half of the people on this list would be involved in treason."

"But—" She cut off sharply at the look Senhor Carvalho shot her.

"Senhorita Durante?" Dom José asked.

"I'm sorry, Your Highness." She forced a weak smile. "I was just surprised. I am so sorry about everything—"

He held up a hand. "We are all in shock. Unfortunately, these are the times we live in."

"I'm sorry," Cecília said again in a near whisper.

"It's getting late," Senhor Carvalho said. "As distressing as this has all been, I'm sure Senhoritas Cardozo and Durante are tired."

"Of course." Dom José motioned their dismissal. "We thank you for your help."

"Your Highness." Graça stood and curtsied.

Cecília followed suit then added, "Please let me know if I can help, Your Highness. All of this is so awful. If I can—"

"We'll be in touch, Senhorita Durante." Senhor Carvalho cut off her rambling. "Just telling the truth about what you've heard come the trial will be help enough."

Cecília curtsied again, praying she could control her stomach at least long enough to return to her own room. She followed Graça out of the apartments, not certain if she breathed until the doors shut behind her. Stopping a few steps into the hall, she sucked in what air she could get, trying to fight off the nausea. "What was that?"

Graça turned to face Cecília again. "What did it sound like? The beginning of the end."

"Why would you bring me in there without telling me what was happening?" she hissed, keeping her voice low even though it seemed they were alone. She knew better than most that the tapestries didn't stop voices from penetrating wooden walls.

Graça shrugged. "I didn't have time."

"Why would Senhor Carvalho let me in there, not knowing what was happening?"

"I may have told him I already let you know," she said.

Cecília sent her an incredulous look.

"Do you know how hard I've been working?" Graça's voice rose as much as it could while remaining a whisper. "You get to hide away, 'ill' for days, and then spend all your time with a man who's so obviously in love with you he'd likely give you a written account of everything he's ever heard for you to enter as evidence. *I* had to deal with that dog Vilhena. Do you know what it's like, having the minister order to let *that man* touch you?"

"And you were bitter enough to sweep Luís into whatever story you told?"

"They're arresting the entire Vilhena household." She shook her head. "He lives with them."

"But he doesn't have anything to do with this."

"Then he doesn't have anything to worry about."

"Why do I doubt that?"

Graça searched Cecília's face. "You can't tell him."

Cecília kept her eyes hard.

"If you tell him, you're going to get caught up in all of this as well. Is that what you want? To be an accomplice to treason?"

Cecília huffed, her mind turning everything over, but she finally started down the hall. "Of course I'm not going to tell him. What could I possibly say?"

Graça hooked her arm through Cecília's, either missing or choosing to ignore the fact that Cecília tensed. "The minister's doing this to protect us, you know. It's what all of us have been working for."

"It just would have been nice to have been fully alerted to that fact." Cecília shook the other woman off and took a step away. "I'm going to bed. I have the feeling it's going to be a long day tomorrow."

"A few long days, and then everything will be sorted." Graça offered a smile. "Trust me. Everything will be so much better."

CECÍLIA COULDN'T FIND it in herself to leave her room as the arrests started, no matter what the first minister might have thought of it. The shouting grew loud enough to echo through the tapestry-covered halls and all the way to Tio Aloisio's room off and on throughout the day.

"How dare you! Take your hands off me!"

"Papai!"

From the screams, even children were being carted away in the name of removing the king's enemies. It kept Cecília's stomach churning strongly enough that she hadn't been able to keep a thing down since daybreak.

Someone rapped on her bedroom door, and Cecília's body tensed even though she had no reason to think that Senhor Carvalho had turned on her in the past twelve hours.

"Cecília?" her uncle's voice came through the door. "Are you decent?"

Sitting in her bed dress, she supposed she was as decent as she was planning to get for the day. "Yes, Tio."

The door opened, and Tio Aloisio stepped inside. He looked her over then sighed. "Graça was here a few minutes ago. She told me what happened last night."

Cecília crossed her arms around her middle. "I said yes. I helped set all this off."

"She said you were visibly distressed when Luís de Terra was mentioned."

"I was surprised," she said. "I know he didn't do anything."

After looking at her for another moment, Tio Aloisio moved across the room and took a seat at the end of the bed. "You did the right thing, Cilinha."

Her stomach twisted, hearing the nickname her father had given to her, which only Tio Aloisio still used. It sounded sticky in his mouth. "Lying was the right thing?"

"You've lied before, I'm sure."

"People are going to die."

"We're in the middle of a movement." He shook his head, speaking to her as if he considered her truly to be an adult for a change. "Those books out there, the ones I could be arrested for? Those books are changing the world. Europe is changing, growing, and Portugal is two hundred years behind. You're a smart girl—too smart for your own good, half the time. You know what would have happened if the king had died. Everything we've been working to do would be stopped, torn down. We'd be thrown back right to where we started."

She felt her cross sitting heavily around her neck. "Would you have the entire country turn Deist?"

Tio Aloisio lifted his eyebrows. "Deist?"

"That's what Mr. Bates called it."

"Ah," he said. "No, I'm Catholic, Cilinha. As is Senhor Carvalho. We're just…"

"Reasonable ones?"

He focused on her. "Bates's words again?"

Cecília shrugged.

"We aren't looking to convert the country. Portugal is Catholic. We will always *be* Catholic, but we are trying to stop people from keeping us all back centuries while the rest of the world moves forward. Senhor Carvalho is taking power from the old nobility and shifting it to those who believe in progress. He's making Portugal independent of foreign creditors. He plans to open public schools to educate all the children in Portugal. The poorest family will be able to better its children's minds. People like Bates, who certainly has the mind to be a scholar, won't be forced to teach themselves—or not be taught at all—just because their families don't have the money to spend on an education. I know you support those reforms. You've spent far more time than Senhor Carvalho has insisted on educating *yourself* these two years."

"People are still going to die," Cecília said softly. "And I don't know who is actually guilty, if any of them are."

Tio Aloisio took a moment before speaking again. "Do you have feelings for Luís de Terra?"

Cecília shifted uncomfortably. "What?"

"Some have reported that the boy is in love with you."

Cecília had to imagine that "some" included Graça.

"Do you feel similarly?"

"I don't want him executed, if that's what you want to know."

"I want to know if you believe yourself in love with him."

Cecília took a moment to weigh her words, but even then, she wasn't certain what she wanted to say, let alone what she *should* say. "Why do you need to know?"

"The first minister has said if you can convince Senhor Terra to testify against the other conspirators, he would see you both well positioned, should you wish to marry. From what I've seen, though, I haven't gotten the sense you *wish* to marry him."

"I doubt it matters if I do or don't. He wouldn't testify. He's too loyal."

"You may underestimate your effect on the younger members of my sex," Tio Aloisio said. "I imagine you're the reason Bates was considering taking work in the mess Lisbon was three years ago, though he'd have much better prospects back home."

Cecília jolted, not able to school the surprise off her face at the shock. "He what?"

Tio Aloisio gave her a much more knowing expression than she liked before he moved on. "Senhor Carvalho has written you a letter of passage to see Senhor Terra where he's being held in Junqueira Prison. Strongly consider the option. With support from the right men, you could find yourself married to a count. A *living* count. I imagine at least one of those things may appeal to you?"

Cecília wasn't certain what to say, so she didn't say anything.

Tio Aloisio lowered his head in apparent acknowledgement that he wasn't going to get an answer and held out a folded piece a paper. "Consider it."

After a final tense moment, Cecília took the paper and watched Tio Aloisio's back as he returned to the antechamber just as another commotion went up somewhere deeper inside the Real Barraca.

Chapter Twenty

Over the next week, gray clouds moved in and refused to leave, setting a dull ache in Cecília's rib that she hadn't felt so resolutely in years. She looked up as she stepped out of the carriage, vaguely wondering if God was passing judgment on all that had happened.

I'm sorry. She offered the weak apology, though it seemed laughably feeble against divine displeasure.

A soldier standing at the door of the imposing Junqueira Prison straightened, and Cecília silently held out the letter Senhor Carvalho had provided, allowing her entrance. She still had no idea what she actually intended to say once she was inside, but after the awfulness of the past few days, she couldn't sit in her room and do *nothing*. What she could or couldn't offer Luís, what he would or wouldn't do... she supposed the specifics weren't more important than at least going. The soldier read the page quickly then nodded as he swung the door open. Leaning inside, he called for some other guard to lead her deeper inside the claustrophobic stone building.

Cecília had to remind herself to breathe. The smell of sweat, blood, and human waste filled the air, caught inside the constricted hallways. She did her best to hide her grimace. If the smell wasn't already overwhelming, the memories of the quake—being caught under stone, suffocated—would have been enough to send her running, at least in other circumstances. She suddenly couldn't wait to be back inside the wooden palace, where the worst a quake could do would be to give her a bad splinter. Still, she was already there, even if it was only to salve her own conscience.

They started up a tight, curving staircase, and a piercing scream set every inch of Cecília's body on edge. The guard leading her didn't seem to so much as register the awful sound as he opened another door and led her into a dark hall lit by a single bar-covered window on the far end.

Without looking at Cecília, the guard stepped up to a door on the left and pulled a small flap away to look through a set of bars no bigger than Cecília's hand. "This who you're sent to see?"

Swallowing as well as she could without inhaling too much of the smell, she moved to the little opening and peered through. Her already frayed nerves sent panicked tingles through her fingers as she saw Luís sitting along the far wall. He didn't bother to look away from his own little barred window as they peered through the peep-hole.

Cecília nodded quickly and stepped back to look at the guard properly. "I'd like to go in."

He slid the flap back into place. "I can't suggest you do that, sen-horita."

"The first minister sent me to speak with him." She lifted her chin, doing her best to look commanding. "I don't believe I can do that well through a door."

The guard looked her over, seeming to size up the modest black dress she had chosen for the occasion, then went for the keys on his hip. "As you wish."

The door opened with an unpleasant groan, and Cecília stepped through. The hinges creaked as the guard pushed it the other way, and a fresh wave of panic swept through her at the idea of being locked in, even for a moment. She fought it back as Luís finally looked away from his window.

His eyebrows furrowed. "Cecília?"

She looked through the open flap to see the guard standing sentry outside the door then took another step toward where Luís was sitting with his knees pulled to his chest. She attempted a smile. She couldn't manage one. "Luís."

He pushed himself up to standing. "What the Devil are you doing here? You haven't been arres—"

"No," Cecília said. Her eyes dropped over him quickly, and she attempted to hide her dismay at his appearance. The thin layer of dust that seemed to coat every surface of the prison had settled into his clothes, making his untucked white shirt look gritty and dun. It didn't appear he had slept at all in the week he had been there, either, between the dark circles under his eyes and the gaunt look of his stubbled cheeks. She could hardly blame him. She likely wouldn't have been able to close her eyes, let alone sleep in the place. Somehow, she rallied enough to turn up the corners of her mouth into something that could perhaps be mistaken for a smile. "I came to see you. My uncle got me permission."

"You shouldn't be here." He took two steps toward her then stopped as if he didn't know if he should close the rest of the distance.

She did instead, catching his hands. A chill traveled up her arms, and she registered how sharp the air in the room was for him to only be in a shirt and breeches.

There's no glass in the window. Nearly Christmas, and he's as good as sitting outside.

She rubbed his hands in between hers as if it would help against the damp winter weather. "I had to come. I've been so worried about..." She swallowed. "You need to get out of here, Luís."

He gave a bitter laugh. "That isn't up to me at the moment."

"But you shouldn't be here," she insisted. "You didn't have anything to do with this plot."

"What *plot*?" Luís shook his head. "There never was any plot. This is all Carvalho—"

"They have evidence." Cecília didn't let him finish whatever he had to say about the first minister. If he started disparaging Senhor Carvalho, she wasn't certain the first minster would keep any intent of clemency. "There's the assassin's testimony, the gun... The case is being put together now, but it sounds irrefutable. The death warrants are all but signed."

Luís's eyes shifted away from her, his jaw tightening.

"You *didn't* know anything about it, did you?"

"Of course not." He met her eyes again. "No, because there was no plot. Any idiot—"

"There's testimony that the Vilhenas knew of it." She held onto his hands more tightly as he tried to pull away. "That's why you're here. They arrested the entire household."

"Whose testimony?"

Cecília debated how much truth to tell, not certain what would and wouldn't help her case. She finally went with the truth. Or at least what had been accepted as the truth. "Graça's. She overheard a conversation in their rooms one night when she was with Mateus."

"Graça? She's a reliable witness now?"

"You saw her with Mateus. You know she was there at least twice. She very well could have heard something."

"But she didn't."

"How would you know?"

"Because unless she heard Mateus himself, no one else would be stupid enough to be caught saying something like that." He jerked away from her and moved toward the far wall.

Cecília caught her hands in front of her and did her best not to wring them. Treading carefully, she continued, "Supposedly, it was someone talking to a Távora."

"Then she has to be lying. People go to the Távora apartments. They don't go to others."

"You've never seen any of the Távora family with the Vilhenas?"

"No."

"Not even when they helped get Mateus out of trouble two years ago? Or now that Isabel—"

"Why do you care about this so much?" He turned back to face her.

Because I can't save anyone else. Because I can't take this much death on my soul. "Because I care about you." She moved toward him once again. "I don't want to see you locked in here for the rest of your life. Or worse. This is *treason*, Luís. Do you want to lose your head over some misplaced loyalty to people you don't even truly like?"

Luís went silent for a long moment, his eyes searching her face. "What are you saying I should do, Cecília?"

She swallowed but pushed forward. "If you testified about what you know—"

"I don't know anything!"

"You know Graça was in those rooms. You could corroborate *her*—"

"You want me throw all of my friends into a noose to save my own neck?"

"If they're guilty, yes."

"They're not!"

Cecília clenched her hands tighter to stop them from shaking. She had told Tio Aloisio that Luís wouldn't testify. He was too loyal, and he wouldn't lie to save his own neck. *Unlike* some *people,* her mind taunted her.

But if I can save someone, just one person... Maybe, just maybe, she would be able to live with herself. She took a shuddered breath. "The first minister said if you testify, he'll see you're rewarded. You could fully get your title. No more whispers about illegitimacy. We could marry..." Even in the building desperation, offering that made her trail off, the uncertainty mixing into everything else.

The way Luís was staring at her—some mix of confusion and disgust—didn't help any. "The first minister."

Cecília nodded, tensing to keep herself from squirming. "You know he has the ear of the k—"

"Are you...? Do you...? Do you report to him?"

"Everyone's been questioned. I was called before the—"

"Cecília, do you report to Senhor Carvalho?" He enunciated each syllable as though fighting them through a locked jaw. She hesitated a beat too long, and the confusion evaporated, leaving nothing but disgust on Luís's face. He turned away from her, moving to look out the window, his back to her. "You can go."

"I'm trying to help you, Luís," she said in a rush. "If you'll just testify—"

"Leave!"

"Luís, please..." Her insides squirmed, a rush of heat pounding through her veins as though her body could already feel hellfire building under all of them. The last thing she could possibly attempt flew out of her mouth before she could stop it. "Please. I love you."

Liar.

Luís's shoulders tensed at the proclamation, but he didn't turn around. "Pray for us, if you want to help, Cecília. Or pray for yourself."

Us. The word sat heavily in her chest. He had picked his side as much as she had picked hers, and as resolute a man as he was, it would truly have taken a miracle to change that decision.

Misericorda. Misericorda de Deus. She sent up a short prayer for mercy, even if she was far past deserving it, then nodded. "I will. I'll pray for you. For everyone."

"Thank you," he said, his voice tightly cordial.

Fighting off the new waves of nausea, Cecília turned back to the doorway and stepped through so the guard could lock the door behind her. She kept her head high and silently followed the man back down the tight staircase and out the front of the prison. She would pray for Luís, for Francisco, for all those arrested. She would even pray for Senhor Carvalho and Tio Aloisio. Whether it would help, though, she couldn't say. She would likely have been on her knees until Judgment Day if she started praying for all of the souls who needed saving—and after all she had done, she wasn't certain anyone in Heaven would ever listen to her.

THE TRIALS WERE OVER so quickly that Cecília had to wonder whether the defense had been allowed more than a day to prepare their cases. Blessedly, Senhor Carvalho hadn't asked her to do anything else for him as sentences for the plotters fell into place. She kept silent. Quietly celebrating the Nativity, Holy Innocents' Day, the Solemnity of Mary, and Epiphany, all as if nothing was wrong, was likely damning enough. She didn't need anything more on her immortal soul.

Tio Aloisio watched her as the carriage rolled along to the field in Belém, where a new scaffold had been built just for the occasion. Blissfully, he didn't attempt to strike up a conversation. There had been enough shouting when he had told her she had to attend. With no choice but to obey, she had dressed and gotten into the carriage that morning. There was no need to discuss it at that point. The less she had to think, the better.

He finally spoke as the carriage began to slow. "Try to smile."

Cecília snapped her head toward him. "*Smile?*"

"These are traitors. They don't deserve our sympathy."

She looked away from him, keeping her thoughts to herself.

"Cecília."

"I know why we're here," she shot at him. "I came. I'm not fighting it. What more do you want from me?"

"You can't cry for him. Not here."

The carriage rolled to a stop, and Cecília tossed the door open, not waiting for the driver. Compared to what some of the noble houses were facing, the Vilhenas were lucky—highly ranked enough to avoid a torturous death, yet not so important as to be made an example of. Most of the women had even been given a stay of execution, their sentences commuted to exile. That didn't mean watching a blatantly innocent man hang—watching him hang with a *smile*—would be any easier.

Did you want *to hang, Luís?* Cecília asked for the millionth time. *There were so many ways you could have escaped it. You were no one important...*

To end up with a death sentence over even exile, he would have had to have been making a point. And Cecília could only guess it was directed at her. He held honesty so dear as to go to a noble death rather than live with such heavy sin on his soul.

Though it was barely past eight in the morning, the field was packed with more people than Cecília had seen since before the quake. Easily ten thousand men, women, and children stood around, waiting to see what would happen to the people who once would have been thought untouchable.

Skirting the masses, Tio Aloisio led Cecília to another set of risers and placed them low alongside the courtiers who had stayed on the right side of the fallout and who gathered there. Graça looked over from where she was standing by her parents and offered a quick smile. Cecília pointedly looked away.

A rise of voices went up through the crowd, and Cecília turned in time to see the first line of traitors being led forward under guard, the opening course for a bloodthirsty crowd. Theirs would be simple hangings, nothing like what would come. The thousands standing closer to the scaffolding began to jeer, some throwing rotting food and other things Cecília didn't want to identify. She swallowed, every urge pushing her to shut her eyes. Already, she felt faint, and Luís wasn't yet in sight. Tio Aloisio's hand went to Cecília's elbow as though he sensed she needed to be steadied, but she jerked away.

Almost mockingly quickly, the line of men turned to dangling corpses, the beam holding them aloft creaking under their weight. Another line came, then another—a mix of faces Cecília knew, didn't, and had only perhaps seen wandering the halls of the Real Barraca once or twice. Their lives could easily have been exchanged with hers if only for a few changes in providence.

Finally, a mix of much-too-familiar faces appeared, with Luís toward the end. Cecília sucked in a sharp breath before she could stop it, tightly closing her eyes. A hard pinch to the fleshy part of her forearm made them open again. She glanced at her uncle, but his eyes remained fixed forward. Taking as steadying a breath as she could manage, Cecília forced herself to watch.

That's the very least you can do. Watch. You put him there.

Though none of the men had been allowed to properly dress, lacking coats or anything to cover their heads, Luís still managed to look entirely dignified, his face set in a look of determination and his chin raised as if he couldn't hear the shouting from the rabble. Compared to the trembling, pale men around him, he looked truly noble. Cecília curled her hands into fists, digging her nails into her palms, attempting to use the pain to hold herself together. Charges were read as nooses went around necks, one by one. Even as the rope was tightened, Luís didn't flinch. Cecília bit down her own whimper. Then the rope went taunt, and the world seemed to fall silent, nothing making it past the loud pounding in Cecília's ears. Each twitch hit like a physical blow, knocking the air from her lungs. The world around her spun.

And then the roar came back. Cecília blinked, feeling Tio Aloisio's hand back on her elbow, keeping her upright.

"Try to smile," he murmured.

If she'd had the air, Cecília would have laughed in his face. The bodies were being taken down and added to a pile at the bottom of the scaffold, waiting to be burned once it all was over. Cecília only blinked, forcing her hands to relax, though she could feel a stickiness that said her nails had drawn blood. She didn't bother to look, her eyes glazing over as she tried to forget the day even as it unfolded in front of her.

The rest of the deaths seemed to rush together, each stage growing more and more gruesome. The marchioness lost her head. Five were strangled at the stake. Two were strapped to a *cruz de Santo André* and broken alive. And then came Antonio Alvares Ferreira, the poor man who had the unholy honor of being the day's finale. With the bloody and broken bodies uncovered around him, he was brought to the stake, tied there even as the executioners stacked bodies and kindling as though needing to taunt the sniveling, shaking man about his fate. They began to read his list of crimes, each dark and vile, enough to fully deserve the fate he'd been dealt—if any of them were true. The executioners finished stacking. The magistrate finished reading. And the lit torch appeared. A true hush fell over the crowd for the first time all day. Ten thousand people went quiet enough that Ferreira's sobbing and broken calls for mercy and proclaiming his innocence carried across the field. The executor lifted the torch theatrically then lowered it to the kindling set under the dead bodies.

Cecília closed her eyes again, not receiving another pinch for it this time, and mumbled a prayer for Ferreira, for all of them, fighting to keep down what little she had eaten for breakfast as the smell of wood smoke and burnt flesh floated over the field.

The sobbing turned to shouts then screams, as he was apparently left with no friends even to lessen his suffering by throwing in a charge of black powder.

Of course he doesn't have any. They're all burning under him. Cecília swallowed and forced herself to open her eyes for a final time, watching the thrashing man disappear behind the climbing flames. *The only friends left at court are Senhor Carvalho's.*

Finally, the screaming died away, replaced by the noise of the crowd and crackling fire as the entire platform and all of the bodies were reduced to ash. Blinking away the smoke that floated toward the risers, Cecília felt something tight and hard forming in her chest, just below her rib cage. And though her heart still pounded and her blood rushed through her ears, she went blissfully numb.

Chapter Twenty-One

"Bless me, Father, for I have sinned." Cecília knelt in the confessional, crossing herself then resting her forehead against her hands. "My last confession was three days ago. I…" She took a breath, wishing she knew which priest was sitting on the other side of the screen. "My soul has been troubled these past weeks, Father. I'm afraid I've committed a mortal sin, and I haven't had the strength to face it."

"What sin is that, my child?"

She didn't recognize the voice, but that didn't make her feel any better. "I've told falsehoods, Father, and kept secrets. And people were hurt because of them." "Hurt" seemed like such a weak word for it, but Cecília didn't dare give it more specific form. "I thought I was doing what was best when it all started, but now… I sinned. I sinned, and people got hurt because of me."

"What people?"

Luís's determined face flashed through her mind, feeling like a slap. "Friends. A man I cared for, even if it wasn't as much as he may have wanted."

"Was this man pressuring you for impure acts?"

"No." She added another lie to her conscience, happily taking that over speaking ill of the dead. She likely should have allowed him those impure acts, at least after she'd met with Dom José. It seemed poor payment for losing the man his life. "But… I told him I loved him, because I knew that was what he wanted to hear, and I was trying to make him do what I considered right." She took a shuddering breath. "I've been fasting and keeping the Litany of Hours and doing everything I can think of to atone, but..." She fought for another breath. "Please. I don't want to be damned."

"Telling falsehoods is a serious sin, child. I'm glad you realize that, but you should not feel sorrow for your sins for fear of punishment but because you have wronged our Lord, God."

Cecília pressed her forehead tighter to her clasped hands.

"He wishes to forgive you, but you must open yourself to His grace and make yourself worthy of it because you understand His love, not just fear His retribution."

She took a gulp of air. "Tell me what to do, Father?"

After a pause, the priest gave her penance—prayers she'd already said, restitutions she couldn't make. She agreed all the same, hoping her other atonements could add up to what he had asked.

He offered a prayer for her, granting absolution, and she slid back into the chapel, her chest no less tight than it had been when she'd entered. The court had been quiet in the month since the Távora executions, but she still couldn't be caught wandering around the halls, pale and trembling. She turned back for her apartment and started the slow progression to her room.

Tio Aloisio looked up from where he was seated on the couch as she opened the door. "Ah, Cecília, there you are."

"I was in confession." She went to pick up the Bible she had left by the bookshelf. She had read it through several times in the past weeks, trying to reconcile the stories of God's love with the ones of His wrath, trying to divine what might be waiting for her come the true End of Days. Several times, she had wished she had never learned to read and that she could merely go to one of the priests and be told exactly what she needed from it all. But she had given up simplicity years before in pursuit of her own curiosity. After so many sleepless nights, she wasn't certain it was a fair trade.

Tio Aloisio watched her for a moment then stood as she turned for her room. "I was wondering if you might want to get away from court for the day, Cilinha."

Cecília frowned, her mind and body too sluggish to react any more strongly. "Get away?"

He nodded. "I'm going down to the docks today. The *Vento de Verão* has returned, and I wanted to take a look at the cargo first-hand."

The name of her father's ship jolted through the haze coating her mind. She blinked in an attempt to focus. "With me?"

He offered a smile. "I know you always loved that ship."

A fledgling rush of excitement pulsed through her, followed closely by a stronger wave of guilt for daring to feel anything of the sort. She lowered her eyes. "I have penance I need to do."

"You've been praying every time I've knocked on your door this week. I think God would understand if you took a few hours to get some fresh air."

"You speak for the Lord now?"

Tio Aloisio shook his head, keeping his eyes firmly on Cecília. "Come to the docks today. I truly believe it will do you a world of good."

She didn't answer.

"I will join you for Vespers and Compline tonight once we're back, if you wish. We can pray for both of our souls."

You want to go, Cecília. Are you truly going to let yourself believe what you want is what is right again? The voice that had been plaguing her nagged at her. *Look where that led you.*

But Tio Aloisio looked so earnest, and Lord knew he would benefit from more prayer as well. She looked down at her dress—though it was drably colored, it was still made of a rich, thick fabric that wouldn't care for sea air. "I should change first."

Tio Aloisio smiled, the tension in his body visibly lessening. "I'll send Águeda in. We're leaving in an hour."

THE SALTY AIR MADE the curls at Cecília's neck flutter, and she inhaled deeply, gulping as much as she could take. The guilt wouldn't fully release her, but being at the docks made everything lighter, as if a weight that had been crushing her had at least lessened, if not entirely lifted.

The way Tio Aloisio was moving along the crates his deckhands were unloading said he felt the same.

Runs in the family. She smiled a little bitterly. *Half of us are saints, and the other half can't wait to take to the sea and run as far as we can.*

"Cilinha." Tio Aloisio motioned for her to join him. "What do you think of this?"

She walked up to the box Tio Aloisio had pried open and looked at the glasses inside, all a vibrant red. "They're beautiful."

"Venetian." He picked one up and held it out to her. He waited for her to take it before speaking again. "Most of this is to sell"—he motioned to the crates and barrels sitting around—"but I thought you might like these."

She looked at him, the smooth glass cool in her hands. "They're for me?"

"An early birthday gift."

Cecília gave a surprised laugh and set the glass back in the straw that had been used as packaging. "It's almost my birthday, isn't it?"

"Twenty-first, if I'm not mistaken."

How that sounded so old and so young at the same time, Cecília didn't know. She began to answer when a familiar voice knocked the wind out of her. She turned to scan the rest of the ships moored at the docks, the skin at the back of her neck prickling. Then she spotted him. Though she couldn't understand what he was saying, John was shouting to another man on a nearby brig. Even with him mostly angled away and at such a distance, every inch of her knew it was him. "John," she murmured under her breath.

"What?" Tio Aloisio looked at her then followed her line of sight.

Cecília cleared her throat, trying to make her voice sound normal. "Isn't that Mr. Bates?"

"It certainly looks like him." Tio Aloisio turned to face the brig. "He did say he was sailing again."

She turned to her uncle with a frown.

"He writes now and then when he's in port," he explained at her look. "Last I heard, he was headed to the Colonies, though."

Cecília looked at the brig again and watched John's back as he made his way down to the dock. Though he was obviously in work clothes, loose trousers and a short coat, he otherwise looked exactly how she remembered, down to his clubbed but not powdered auburn hair. "Mr. Bates!" She jumped, her own voice surprising her as it bubbled free.

His head snapped in their direction, shock clear in his expression even from so far away. He took a step toward them, hesitated, called something to one of the other men working on his ship, then turned for her and Tio Aloisio. He wiped his hands on his trousers self-consciously as he stopped within talking distance. "Senhorita Durante, Senhor Durante. What an unexpected pleasure to see you both."

"And you, Bates." Tio Aloisio nodded. "I hadn't heard you were coming to Lisbon."

"We've actually brought some things for Mr. Hays. The—"

"British envoy," Tio Aloisio completed. "I know him well."

John nodded, seeming to struggle to find something else to say.

The urge to throw her arms around him pulsed through her, and Cecília caught her hands in front of her to tamp it down. "Are you headed to court, if you're going to see Mr. Hays? We have our carriage—"

"I'm sure Bates is in the middle of something, Cecília." Tio Aloisio cut her off, though he looked more relaxed than he had in weeks.

He thinks I'm feeling better. The thought dampened Cecília's mood. Meeting John had been half of what had started everything awful that had happened. *I knew what was right before meeting him.*

What I thought *was right. Why can't anything just* be *right?*

"Unfortunately, he's correct." John's voice took her out of her internal argument. He looked over his shoulder at his ship. "There's going to be trouble if I'm gone too much longer, and we still have a cart to load before we head anywhere. Are you both at court these days?"

"Indeed we are," Tio Aloisio said. "You should stop by for a drink, if you have the time."

"I'll certainly do my best." He checked behind him again as someone shouted at him in English. He bowed to Tio Aloisio and Cecília quickly. "Pleasure to see you both, Senhorita Durante, Senhor Durante."

Tio Aloisio lowered, tipping his hat, and Cecília curtsied quickly before she looked up to watch him go.

"The Lord does have a sense of humor." Tio Aloisio watched for another moment before he turned back to his cargo. He motioned to get a deckhand's attention then pointed to the box of glasses. "Pack that into the carriage. The rest should be inventoried. I'll deal with it later."

"Senhor." The man lowered his head.

Tio Aloisio looked at Cecília. "Ready to head back?"

She nodded, her mind whirring into even more of a mess than it already had been.

CECÍLIA SAT ON THE couch in the antechamber, trying to focus on the Bible in her lap as Tio Aloisio sat at his desk. Every set of footsteps, however, made her tense. So far, there had been no sign of John.

He's working. He would have to see Mr. Hays first. She tried to force herself to relax. *He didn't even know if he could actually come. Maybe he shouldn't. You're already a mess. You don't need him rattling your thoughts even more.*

She tried to call up some verse on tested faith out of the hundreds she had read over and over in the past weeks. All that bubbled out of her mind was more decrying her sins. *If I could just do one thing right...*

Someone knocked. Cecília stiffened and tried to focus on the Bible in her lap. Suddenly, she couldn't make out any of the words. Much too slowly, Tio Aloisio rose from his desk and walked to the door. Cecília glanced up as the door swung open then released a soft huff when she saw one of Senhor Carvalho's servants.

"The first minister is asking for you, Senhor Durante."

"I'll be right along." Tio Aloisio didn't ask any questions as he picked up his hat from its spot by the door.

Cecília offered a smile, but her uncle didn't look back, so she returned to her reading as the footsteps moved away. She read quickly, her earlier stumbling with Latin a mere memory.

O Lord, to us belongeth confusion of face, to our kings, to our princes, and to our fathers, because we have sinned against thee...

A new set of footsteps came from the opposite direction. Cecília lifted her eyes but still started at the sharp knock. Suddenly frozen to the spot, she could only stare at the dark wood.

The second knock spurred her to action. She crossed the room quickly and lifted the latch. The door swung open just in time for her to find herself facing John's fist.

He managed to stop the knock before he hit her face, froze for a moment, then dropped his fist to his side. "I'm sorry."

"My fault," she said a little breathlessly, suddenly transported back to the first time she had seen him, caught halfway to knocking on the door of Tio Aloisio's house, which no longer existed. He was even back into a proper coat and breeches, making him the exact man she had seen three years before, and she was once again seventeen, entirely thrown, and staring. She recovered, forcing a smile. "Please, come in."

"Thank you." He removed his hat and stepped out of the hallway. His eyes swept the space quickly. "Is... your uncle here?"

"You just missed him." She shut the door once again. "Senhor Carvalho needed him for a moment. He should be back soon, I imagine." *Not technically a lie. He* could *be back soon.*

"Would he mind my being here without him?"

"I don't think so."

His eyes met hers, and Cecília felt her insides pull tight, as he still seemed able to read her as well as he could three years before.

She cleared her throat and went to pick up the Bible from the couch. "You seem to have a talent for appearing at dire moments."

"Do I?" He turned to remain facing her.

She held the book to her chest as though it would shield her. From John or herself, she hadn't entirely worked out. "You heard there was an attempt on the king's life?"

"I did." He nodded. "Though that was months ago?"

"Things have been... difficult since then." She pushed a black curl back from her face and met his hazel eyes once again. Something brittle and weak, like cracked glass, shattered inside her mind, and she couldn't keep the words back. "Why didn't you tell me you can't give it back?"

His eyebrows furrowed, the confusion plain on his face as he tried to work out her meaning. "I'm sorry?"

"*Scientia potentia est.*"

He gave a small smile. "You read *Leviathan*?"

"And some days, I wish to Heaven I hadn't." She sat on the couch, the fabric of her gown puffing out around her in a very unladylike fashion. "I read it. I've read scores of those." She motioned to the books on her uncle's shelves. "Senhor Carvalho is a strong proponent of universal education, but none of you told me once you read all those theories and philosophies, you can never give it back."

"You want to give it back?"

"I didn't feel this awful before I knew." She looked up at him.

He studied her for a moment before he took a seat next to her, still searching her face. "What's happened, Cecília?"

"You," she said. "And Senhor Carvalho. And that earthquake. And that blasted trial."

"What trial?"

She took a breath, trying to find whatever had shattered and put all the shards back into place. It seemed as likely as being able to re-assemble one of the Venetian glasses her uncle had gotten her, should she smash it. Somehow, she still managed to plaster on a fake smile as she set the Bible gently aside. "I'm sorry. I'm sure you've had a dread-fully long day, and now I'm babbling before even asking how you've been. You've been sailing. Obviously. To the Colonies, I hear?"

"Delivering supplies for the soldiers there this trip." He nodded, though he seemed to be half-focused at best on his own answers as he continued to study her.

"Right. You're fighting with the French again. I heard some talk about that, though of course, everyone's much more interested in what's happening between France and Spain around here..." She lost her train of thought as he continued to watch her silently. "Will you stop doing that?"

"Do people really let you get away with that these days?" he asked.

Her throat constricted, the rush of panic feeling as though he had been able to see straight into all her sins. Her voice wavered too much as she spoke. "Get away with what?"

"Changing the topic when you're obviously not fine?"

"What?"

He shook his head. "You can't tell me you're honestly more interested in discussing the war than whatever awful thing you're dealing with in your own head."

The words landed too close to that shattered part of her. She stood sharply enough that her skirts almost tripped her. "Don't do that."

"Do what?"

"You haven't seen me in three years. You can't know what's happening in my head."

He studied her, seeming to read her far too well all the same. "But something's happened."

She blinked, trying to keep herself together. She wasn't seventeen anymore. She wasn't the lost girl who needed his support to keep going. *I'm practically a new person,* she tried to convince herself.

But then why do you want nothing more than to just crumple into John and have him make everything better?

Whatever had shattered might as well have been ground to sand as a new pain rushed over her from deep inside her chest, and a sob escaped.

"Cecília." He stood in alarm, and she didn't have the energy to fight it.

She stepped forward, pressing her face into his chest so she wouldn't have to look at him as she fought through the tears. "I'm going to Hell."

"What? Why?"

"I can't tell you."

He wrapped his arms around her as naturally as if he had never been away, the familiar smell of salt and sweat surrounding her. "Shh, Cecília. Everything will be fine. Whatever it is, it can't be that awful."

"It is." Her words came out muffled against his wool jacket. The click of the latch on the door made her stiffen before John could answer. A second later, his arms slipped away. She turned her head and saw her uncle standing just inside the doorway. "I'm sorry." She took a shaky breath then looked back at John, who actually deserved an apology after that display. "I'm sorry. I..." Tears still too close to the surface, she shook her head and turned for her own room. "I'm sorry."

She barely made it inside before she slid down to the floor, her skirts eating her up in a sea of fabric. She couldn't imagine what John and Tio Aloisio would be talking about in the antechamber, but for the moment, she couldn't stop her own thoughts long enough to care.

Chapter Twenty-Two

Cecília rubbed her side, not certain if the dull ache there was promising rain or just the memories she hadn't been able to escape all evening. Depending on how little time John actually had in dock, he could already have been back on his ship and sailing off across the Atlantic. That was the way it went, after all. John crashed into her life like a cannonball then disappeared again while she was left trying to rebuild what once was—what she once was.

But that's what he can do. She moved to the window of her room. *Be here when the world comes tumbling down then sail off while the rest of us are still...*

She couldn't think of a way to end the thought. As hard as Senhor Carvalho was working to get the Baixa rebuilt, it had been three years, and it didn't seem as though they were any closer to having Lisbon back. Another three decades could pass before she ever lived there again.

She frowned, that idea never having crossed her mind before. *Am I waiting to live there again? Do I* want *to live there again?*

At the moment, she was ready to live just about anywhere but Lisbon. Others were sailing halfway across the world, and she had never been more than half a day's travel from the spot where she was born.

Maybe that's always been the problem.

She unlatched the window and pushed it open, easing it past the squeak. A cool, damp breeze swept in, and the chill made bumps rise along her arms. Judging from the clouds in the distance, her side, and the humid air, she had to assume a storm was moving in. All the same, she pulled herself up and out.

Her feet had barely landed on the spongy grass outside when John's voice caught her.

"Your uncle said you'd likely sneak out tonight."

She spun, her eyes taking a second to spot him in the shadows cast by the nearly full moon. "What are you doing out here?"

"He asked me to stay and speak with you. Said you slip out the window some nights and think he doesn't know."

She frowned.

"Your window squeaks, and the walls are thin," John offered for explanation then motioned to the place on the grass next to him. "Would you like to sit?"

"You've just been sitting out here, waiting for me?"

"I had dinner first." He leaned back enough for the moonlight to catch his face. "Your uncle's been worried about you. I said I was more than happy to help if I could."

"You can't."

"You're certain?"

"We haven't spoken in years."

"You didn't write," he returned.

She hesitated but clung to the excuse that no longer remained true. "I told you I didn't write well."

"I was still hoping I'd hear from you."

"Why?"

"Because you're an impossible woman to forget, apparently."

Cecília swallowed, not certain what she should take from the tingle that moved through her.

"He told me about the Távora trials," John continued. "And your friend. Terra?"

She crossed her arms, looking out across the gardens. "I think he was in love with me."

He paused briefly. "Not the first man to be, I'm sure."

"I used him," she said, remembering the confessional that morning. "I used him. I lied. I got people killed."

"You didn't make anyone attempt regicide."

"I don't know that anyone..." She realized how close they still were to the palace. Even if she was talking to John, she was still at court. The past three years had still happened. She dropped her voice and finally knelt so he could still hear her at a whisper. "I don't know that anyone did. Perhaps they did. Perhaps they didn't. All I know is half of what was said is questionable at best and blatant lies at worst. I didn't lie to condemn a guilty man. I lied and will *never* know if they were innocent."

John studied her, his face blank enough that Cecília couldn't interpret how he was judging her.

"I'm going to Hell," she said softly.

"*To the Lord our God belong mercies and forgivenesses,*" he quoted. "I don't know what your priests say, but I know mine always said there was no sin so great that God would not forgive a truly repentant soul."

"A Deist priest?"

"C of E," he said. "I wasn't *raised* Deist."

She supposed that made sense. She looked down.

"You went against your conscience. You may have done something terrible, but I am sure there are many men in this world who have managed to forgive themselves for far more grievous sins than yours. From all your uncle said, you far from signed their death warrants. And even if you deserved your own punishment, it sounds as though you have put yourself through worse than anyone else would ever do to you."

"My uncle told you that?"

"As I said, he's been worried about you. And you do look thin, if you'll forgive my saying."

"I'm not certain he's in any position to offer moral guidance." She shifted to properly sit and pulled her knees up to her chest like a child. "Nor are you, for that matter, if you'll forgive *my* saying."

The corner of John's mouth tipped up, making him look anything but offended. "Then who is? Do you need the pope to personally forgive you? The angel Gabriel to come down?"

"You're teasing me now." She frowned.

"I'm really not. Just... what's done is done. You have repented, have worked to atone... what else can you do?"

"I wish I knew."

John brought his hand to her cheek. "I may be the last person you consider qualified to give you advice on the state of your soul, but from what I was told, I would be hard-pressed to believe you forever damned, at least not beyond the Hell you're currently putting yourself through."

How dearly Cecília wanted to believe that. She studied him. "How can you be so certain of everything you believe, John?"

"I'm not certain, but I've spent years reading and questioning my own beliefs. I just had the luxury of having the choice to do that. All of this was rather forced upon you, I admit. At least part of that is my fault."

She shook her head, exhausted down to her bones, tired of thinking, tired of worrying, tired of remorse and shame and regret. "How long are you staying?"

"Just until morning. Your uncle took up a fair deal of Mr. Hays's time this afternoon, which meant he couldn't finish the letters he wanted us to take in time for us to leave this evening."

"My uncle went far out of his way to have you talk to me tonight." Cecília wondered just how much Tio Aloisio would have done to bring her out of her penance. She moved to the question still burning in her mind. "Will you be coming back? To Lisbon?"

John hesitated. "I'm not certain. It isn't my ship."

"So tomorrow morning, off you go until I have some other crisis and you suddenly find your way back?"

"I certainly hope not. I don't enjoy the idea of being the harbinger of Lisbon's misfortune. Or yours, for that matter."

Cecília pursed her lips as she studied him. "How have you been, really? You haven't been sitting around, waiting to talk to me for three years."

"I could have been." He smiled.

She sent him an unamused look. "I'm serious, John. Tell me about London. Where you've been. Tell me about anywhere that isn't *here*."

John released a long breath, looking out across the grounds as the conversation moved away from Cecília. "I haven't spent much time in London lately."

"You've been sailing."

"A good bit," he agreed. "And the *Pendant*—the ship I'm on these days—is actually based out of Boston."

Cecília blinked in surprise. "You're living in Boston?"

"I'm not sure it can be said I'm living much of anywhere that isn't below a deck lately, but we spend a fair deal of time there, yes."

"How would you know if I had written you, if you aren't living in London?"

"We go back and forth. Would be quite hard to trade if we stayed in one port all year."

"What's Boston like?"

"I rather enjoy it," he said. "Not exactly as exciting as sailing to India or the Orient, but it's surprisingly vibrant for such a small city. There's something in the air there." He looked back at her. "Does that make me sound odd?"

"Not at all." She met his eyes, and once again, she was thrown back in time to Senhor Carvalho's house, when she had been battered and bruised and feeling so vastly different but remarkably similar. She swallowed. "You should take me with you."

His eyebrows rose. "To Boston?"

"To somewhere." She moved back onto her knees to face him. "Anywhere. I want to see the world. I've always wanted to see it."

His hand went back to her cheek, his thumb straying dangerously close to her bottom lip. "You know you can't go with me, Cecília." His mouth quirked up in a weak attempt at a smile. "Beyond the obvious, you would freeze in Boston this time of year. You lisboetas don't know how good you have it with your weather."

"I'm serious."

"I know you are. And *you* know I can't take you anywhere."

Her throat tried to tighten as a new type of weight tried to constrict around her. "I could stow away."

All sense of humor drained from his face in an instant. "Don't even joke about that, or I will tell your uncle not to take his eyes off you until we cast off."

"I likely could manage. I've gotten quite good at sneaking around in the past few years." Though obviously not as good as she had thought if Tio Aloisio knew about her leaving at night.

"Cecília." He grabbed both of her shoulders. "You can't. You know you can't. You know I can't let you. If you want to leave, I'm not your way out."

"You're the one sailing away tomorrow."

"Think it through. What happens if you leave with me? You can't be a sailor. Even if you were a man, what could you do on a ship? Did your father teach you the ropes? To climb rigging?"

"I could learn," she said, even if she was just being obstinate for the point of being obstinate at that point.

"How, when I'm the only person on that ship who speaks Portuguese?"

I'll find another ship. She looked away, vaguely wondering what would happen if she somehow commandeered her uncle's ship. *Papai's ship.* It had gone to Tio Aloisio for the same reason the land in the Baixa had gone to Avô Santa Rita, because Francisco was in the Church, and there were no other living sons. *Under different circumstances, it would have gone to me...*

"What are you thinking?" John asked.

She brought her eyes back to him.

"If memory serves, that's a dangerous expression to see on your face."

"I won't stow away."

He kept his eyes fixed on her.

"I promise I won't," she insisted, widening her eyes as innocently as she could manage.

After a moment, John's face finally softened, so he apparently believed her. His eyes flicked to her lips, but then he shifted away. "It's getting late. You should go back in."

"And you?" If he intended to stay out later, she certainly would too.

"I have to be up early to get back down to the docks."

And then he's off across the ocean. "Stay a little longer?"

"Cecília—"

Not able to care anymore, Cecília leaned forward and kissed him. His body reacted immediately, his hand sliding into her hair, pulling her tighter. The smell of salt still clung to him, and she breathed it in, trying to focus on the tingling shooting through her body rather than the guilt in the pit of her stomach.

His hand moved down her side, grasped her waist, then jerked away.

Cecília pulled back far enough to give him a questioning look.

"Sorry." He glanced toward her side. "I just remembered... your side..."

She gave a breathy laugh. "It's been healed for years."

"I know. I mean..." He shook his head. "Just whenever I remember this..."

She watched him as he led off. "You remember this?"

"Well, I remember three years ago," he said slowly. He touched her side again, as though he needed to make certain her rib was no longer broken, then met her eyes. "I need to go, Cecília."

"Now?"

He nodded.

"I don't want you to."

"And I don't want to," he admitted. "That's why I have to go."

A hundred arguments fought to find purchase in her mind, her own good sense fighting with the flood of other emotions inside her. Everything turned into an unholy buzzing, and only one thing registered above it all. She just couldn't care anymore. Either she was long damned, or God was far more forgiving than she was, and either way, nothing mattered.

She leaned back into him, sliding a hand around the back of his neck as her lips met his.

"Cecília," he said against her mouth in a warning tone.

"Please." She slid closer to him. "Touch me, John."

He released a tense breath then said, his voice husky, "Your uncle is right inside."

She rocked back to get her feet under her, straightened, then held her hand out to him. "Walk with me, then?"

John looked up at her, obvious conflict playing out over his face, but he finally nodded, took her hand, and let her lead him away from her—and Tio Aloisio's—rooms.

Without thinking, Cecília made her way to the hedge at the edge of the hill. The thick, damp air didn't quite let her hear the water, but the moonlight did reflect a silvery blue in the distance. She released John's hand and turned around, tucking her bed dress under her as she sat. Vaguely, she wondered if they should go somewhere else, somewhere not filled with other memories. But maybe she just needed new ones. "This is my favorite place on the grounds."

"Oh?" John remained standing.

"You can see the river." She pointed. "Some nights, you can hear it."

John followed her finger to look where the light was glinting on the water before he shook his head. "It's cruel you weren't born a man, isn't it?"

"I've thought so." Cecília didn't let herself fall too deep down that hole of what-ifs. "Sit down?"

He turned to face her. "You're sure that's what you want?"

She bit her lip, the weight behind the question hitting hard. Still, she nodded. "If you're leaving tomorrow, I want tonight."

John stared at her for a final moment before he sat next to her.

Cecília felt her heart beat faster, the little nagging voice making one last valiant effort to get through to her. She pushed it away and shifted so she was straddling his legs. She'd made a decision. Swallowing, she ran her hands up his arms, feeling the lean muscle under his jacket. "You've thought about this?"

"Yes." His voice was deep and throaty again.

"About what, exactly?"

He hesitated. "About things you don't discuss in polite company."

She lowered her lips so they were a hair's breadth from his. "Then show me?"

As if whatever lingering self-control he had been calling upon had suddenly shattered, John slid one rough hand into the hair at the back of her head, and his mouth crashed against hers. Sparks shot through Cecília's body as his other hand found the small of her back, pressing their bodies flush together.

Cecília slid her hands under the lapels of his jacket, working to push it off his shoulders.

He released his grip long enough to shrug it off. His eyes met hers in the moonlight. "Have you ever... done this before?"

Cecília shook her head, the mix of desire and uncertainty keeping her from speaking.

He took a shaky breath. "You're certain—"

"Please." She got that word out, her fingers dropping to brush the simple buttons of his waistcoat.

He released a sharp breath. "You can tell me to stop," he said quickly before his own hands went to the tie of her bed dress, making quick work of the knot.

Cool air soaked through her thin camisa as the thicker fabric fell off. Cecília felt her skin prickle with gooseflesh. She only moved faster, attempting to undo the buttons of his waistcoat with half the dexterity he had managed with her clothing.

Cecília pushed away all of her thoughts, forcing herself to focus on nothing more than the moment. His hands were now at her hips, pushing the hem of her camisa up as his lips moved toward the low neckline, which made it easier.

"Dear Lord, what do you do to me?" he mumbled softly enough that it seemed to be more a question for himself than her.

"John..." she breathed, waves of hot and cold alternating over her skin as he trailed his lips along the curve of her breasts.

He said something she couldn't understand.

"What?" She looked down at him, breathing heavily.

"Talking to myself." He lifted his head so he could kiss her mouth again.

"About what?"

"Cursing we're outside."

"Why?"

"Because you have perhaps the most perfect breasts I have ever seen, and I likely shouldn't take this off."

She swallowed, another rush of heat moving over her. Silently, she worked her arms out of the thin elbow-length sleeves of her camisa, less gracefully than she had to admit she would have liked, and pulled it over her head. John went entirely still, and Cecília's skin prickled—from the cold or the awareness of his stare, she couldn't be certain.

"Jesus Christ." He once again switched into English, but that one she got.

Before her discomfort at the invocation, considering the situation, could fully set in, John's hot mouth was once again on her skin. The rough calluses on his palm scraped the soft skin of her back as he pulled her forward, pressing her chest tighter against him. He sucked one nipple into his mouth, and a new rush, so hot it felt as if her blood were burning, rushed straight through Cecília's core.

She gasped. "Oh..."

He released what sounded like a groan, and his other hand found the inside of one thigh and traced its way up.

Cecília tensed.

John hesitated, his hand stilling where it was as he pulled back to look at her. "Do you want me to stop?"

Do I?

You're going to Hell, the little voice in her head made one last attempt.

I was anyway, she returned. She shook her head. "No."

"No... you don't...?"

"Don't stop," she said softly, shifting her hips on top of him.

Another quiet groan, and John's hand slid the rest of the way between her legs. Cecília sucked in a breath as his rough fingers found a spot so sensitive her entire body reacted. He began rubbing slow circles, and Cecília shut her eyes, the tingles of pleasure beginning to form into a building tension low in her stomach.

"*Meu Deus...*" She fought to keep her breathing steady as the circling grew faster.

"Tell me if it hurts."

She'd barely managed to make sense of his words before a finger slipped inside her. She cried out in surprise. The movement slowed, but she shook her head before he could question her. "Oh, please..." she got out in pants, not entirely certain what she was even asking for. "Don't stop... please..."

She felt him smile against her skin, and his mouth went back to her breasts. A second finger joined the first. The tension coiling in Cecília's stomach pulled so tightly that her body began to tremble. "John...?"

"Let go, love." The rubbing turned fervent. "Let go."

The trembling intensified, tension pulling in so tightly that her toes curled, and then everything shattered. Cecília shouted, jolt after jolt of pleasure shooting through her body as her muscles convulsed around his fingers. She slowly came back down, her body feeling boneless.

John seemed ready for it, freeing his hand to wrap around her and lying her down. The wet grass pricked her bare back, but she couldn't bring herself to care. He positioned himself between her legs then paused and twisted.

Cecília watched him grab his jacket and pull something out of a pocket, her mind still a little hazy. "What's that?"

He paused. "I don't know what you call it. Directly translated... French letter?"

Cecília's eyebrows furrowed. "A letter?"

He opened his mouth then shut it again, fumbling with the buttons at the front of his breeches. "I'll explain later. You want me to use it."

Cecília levered herself up on her elbows, attempting to see but only getting a flash of some sort of ribbon before John was back over her.

He kissed her lightly, nearly chastely, as he touched her face. "Try not to tense, love."

The haze in her mind faded as her nerves began to build, lying under him, entirely exposed. Still, she wet her lips and nodded. Slipping a hand under her knee, John pushed her leg up and pressed into her.

A soft sound escaped from the back of her throat as her back arched. He slipped in easily enough there wasn't any pain, but her body struggled to adjust.

He hissed some word under his breath as he stopped, fully inside her.

Cecília's hips rocked against him of their own accord, the low buzz of pleasure starting again as her body adjusted to the intrusion. "You're going to have to teach me English if you keep doing that."

John gave a strained laugh. "I shouldn't teach you *that* word. You just..." He kissed her. "Dear Lord, you feel so good."

Her hips tried to lift again. "Move?"

His body jerked as if it didn't need the urging, but he still obviously struggled to remain still, the muscles in his arms straining. "If it's too much—"

"*Santos vivos.*" Three years, and he still worried over her as much as when she was seventeen. "John, move."

He didn't need to be told a third time. Pulling her leg higher around him with one hand, he slid the other into her hair, kissing her as he set a pace. The slow strokes lasted for half a second before he sped up. Cecília closed her eyes, the earlier tension quickly beginning to build again. Her chest rose and fell with quick pants, her hands clutching at the grass then at his back, feeling his muscles flex.

"Say my name," he said throatily.

"John," she managed with a gasp.

He groaned. "Again."

"John." She panted, her body tightening again, so close to that edge and desperate to go over.

"Again."

"J—" The rest of his name dissolved into a shout as her body convulsed and those waves crashed back over her, wiping everything from her mind but the rush, every inch of her tingling.

Somewhere, Cecília registered another groan, and after a final thrust, John went still, his hard, warm body resting on top of hers. They both panted, the silence of the night settling back over them.

After a few more breaths, John pushed himself up on his elbows. "Am I crushing you?"

Cecília gave a breathy laugh. "You worry about me too much."

"Old habit?" He kissed her before he pushed himself up and carefully maneuvered off her.

Cold rushed in as his body heat retreated, and Cecília sat up, suddenly very aware of her nakedness. Quickly grabbing her camisa from where it sat, abandoned on the grass, Cecília attempted to right herself. She looked up again just in time to see John tuck the ribbon thing away.

Cecília frowned. "You said that was a letter?"

John released a breath, as though he had hoped he'd escaped the conversation. "French letters. They... well they stop women from becoming with child."

"How does it do that?"

"Do you really want me to spend the rest of tonight explaining the mechanics of it, love?" He gave her a small smile before he reached out and touched her.

Cecília's breath caught in her lungs. She had to force it out again. "*Please* take me with you. You can teach me English. I'll find something to do. I—"

"I *can't*." He shook his head. "Even if I wanted to, it's not my ship. Your uncle would... And, sweetheart, no one could pay me enough to put you on a ship for a month out in the Atlantic with the crew I sail with."

Anxiety made Cecília's muscles twitch. "Stay here, then. You could..." The thought hit. "Tio Aloisio doesn't sail anymore. He pays someone to captain Papai's ship. You could do that, and I could go with you. It has a Portuguese crew. I could learn to do something."

A small smile pulled at the corners of John's mouth, but she couldn't tell if it was sad or patronizing. "I'm sure your uncle has a perfectly fine captain already. Why would he suddenly hand his ship over to me? *Especially* if I planned to help you run off?"

Cecília chewed the inside of her cheek, well aware she was clutching at straws. "Tio Aloisio isn't married. He doesn't have any children. Francisco and Bibiana can't inherit. Marry me, and it would likely be *your* ship, eventually."

The smile disappeared, and John stared at her, his face blank enough that it made Cecília's stomach squirm. She tried to think of something she could say to take back some of her babbling, suddenly feeling more exposed than she had out on the grass. Nothing came to her.

"I'm not Catholic," John finally said.

"You could convert," she said in a small voice, apparently not able to stop digging herself deeper.

He shook his head. "I couldn't in good conscience ever tell a priest I intended to be a good Catholic, love. I'm barely considered a good Protestant most days."

"There can be mixed marriages," Cecília pressed. "If a bishop gives permission, the Church would recognize it. You are still Chris—"

He kissed her, sliding his hand into her hair to keep her lips locked to his before he seemed satisfied that he had fully stopped her speaking. Slowly, he pulled back, looking her in the eye. "I can't just jump ship here. The crew needs me."

"But—"

"Give me a few months." He ran his thumb over her bottom lip. "Let me get back to Boston and see how things are there. If you still want to run away *then*, we'll talk about it."

She forced herself to pull away from him. "That means *no*."

"No, it doesn't."

She swallowed, forcing down a new rush of emotion. She managed to keep her voice steadier than she felt. "If you leave, I'm never going to see you again."

"Why would you say that?" He shook his head. "Lisbon might not be what it was yet, but there are plenty of ships that still come in."

Her voice dropped to a whisper. "You won't come back."

"All these ill divinations." He reached out, brushing a loose curl back from her face. "Promise me you won't do something foolish like run off by yourself, and I promise I'll come back."

The feeling in Cecília's stomach wouldn't let her fully believe him, but she tried to convince herself she was being silly and nodded.

John's hand lingered at the side of her face, his eyes sweeping over her as though he needed to commit that exact image to memory before he kissed her a final time and pulled back. "It's late. We should get you back before your uncle does think we have run away."

"I don't want to."

"Cecília..." He fixed his eyes on her.

"I agreed I wouldn't run off by myself. That doesn't mean I have to go back inside yet."

"I'd feel better if I helped you back in."

"I'd feel better if you didn't go," she returned.

John shook his head, a small smile returning to his lips. "Are you certain you wish to get married? Something tells me you would struggle with the 'submit yourself unto your husband' part of being a wife."

Cecília pressed her lips together tightly, sucking a breath through her nose before answering. "Perhaps I should marry an idiot. He won't be intelligent enough to attempt ordering anything, let alone noticing if I don't obey."

John only looked more amused. "But you'd be very bored, you'd have to admit. Left to while away your days with an idiot?"

"If I find someone mentally feeble enough, I could probably still take Papai's ship, and he wouldn't know the difference. I could travel to Brazil. Or the Orient."

He continued to smile as though indulging her.

"Or I could go to France and take a lover," she added, bristling at the look. "French ladies consider that fashionable, so I hear."

"Then I'll have to find work in Paris, won't I?"

She frowned. "You can be infuriating sometimes. Did you know that, Mr. Bates?"

"Obviously why we get on so well, Senhorita Durante."

Cecília didn't stop herself from rolling her eyes. She twisted to pick up her bed dress and pulled it back on, though it had gotten damp and didn't do much to keep her warm. "You may leave, if you wish. It's safe enough out here. I'll be fine."

John opened his mouth as though he intended to argue before he finally sighed. "I'll be back once I have things settled."

Cecília nodded, though she still didn't believe him.

After a final, lingering kiss, John stood. Quickly, he pulled his own clothing back in order. "You are something special, Cecília Durante. Don't you ever forget that."

Cecília hesitated, not certain what one was supposed to say to a statement like that.

John didn't seem to expect an answer, offering a formal bow before stepping back. "Good night. Take care of yourself."

"And you." Cecília somehow managed a smile. "Good night."

He took a few more steps backward before he finally turned and disappeared around the hedge, headed the way they had originally come. Silently, Cecília watched him, her hand going to the cross around her neck. Part of her wanted to laugh. Part of her wanted to cry. Her mind raced yet felt empty. And all the conflicting emotions left her feeling... calm. Releasing a breath, she turned to put her back to the hedge and looked out at the river. The moon no longer reflected on the water, as approaching clouds seemed to have blotted out everything in the distance. It might as well have been just her and the palace for all she could see.

Fitting, she supposed. Even if John did manage to return within a few months, she was trapped for the time being, and she couldn't keep going as she had been. Spending her days locked away in her room or church had done no good. And returning to spying was certainly not an option. No, if she couldn't get on the next ship out of Lisbon, she would have to do something else, something that wouldn't slowly drive her mad.

The dampness in the air turned into a light drizzle, indicating that whatever storm Cecília had felt in her side wasn't long off. It would likely pour within a few minutes. Tilting her head back, she let the cold droplets hit her face. First thing in the morning, she would find something to do. Something that was just hers. Something that would give her a fresh start—as fresh a start as she could have while still at court.

Part Four: 1760

Chapter Twenty-Three

Cecília tapped the end of her pencil against the paper in front of her, finally throwing the thing down like a child having a tantrum when the numbers just wouldn't work out.

You're the one who asked to learn these blasted things, the voice in her head chided as she sat back in the chair with a huff.

Senhor Rocha had been very kind, taking his own time to teach her what the architects were doing, starting with the basics before slowly working up to all the complicated equations they were using to make the new building plans for Lisbon as disaster-proof as modern mathematics would allow. Cecília had proven to have an aptitude for it, at least most of the time. With the way she currently felt, though, she was lucky when one and one turned out to be two on the page.

You need more sleep.

She laughed at that. *I would if I could.*

For the past half a year, she had done her best to put John as far from her mind as possible, and that hadn't been easy. Even if she had suspected he wouldn't return if he left, she had held out some hope for longer than she should have. She had even attempted sending letters. The first one was six months after he'd been gone, addressed to him at the London parish written in Mr. Hobbes's book, then another in generally passible French, addressed to his sister a few months after that, asking about John's welfare. It hadn't been until a full year had passed that she'd decided it was time to put the matter from her mind entirely, accepting it one night as her own sort of Easter service—a resurrection after Lenten suffering—and dedicating herself to her own betterment. And for six months, she had done reasonably well at it.

Then she'd had that blasted dream.

She placed the heels of her palms against her eyes and rubbed, as if that would clear her head. It had taken her long enough to fully accept that John was gone. She didn't wish to consider what suddenly dreaming about him meant.

Thinking too much about Lisbon?

She tried to convince herself that was the case. She hadn't been invited on the architects' final scouting trip before they began work on the first minister's new *Praça do Comércio*, the grand commercial square that would replace what had once been the king's riverside palace, but Senhor Rocha hadn't attempted to spare her feelings when she'd asked how the city looked. By all accounts, save some new scaffolding in the Baixa, it didn't look much different than it had the last time she had been there five years before. It was down to the dust, from the state of Senhor Rocha's clothing, though it was allegedly from all the digging they were doing for the new sewers that were planned to run under the perfectly geometric buildings they would be constructing soon.

Always soon. She sat petulantly in her chair. In the months since she'd begun working with Senhor Rocha, she had seen all the good work the architects had been doing—designing framing that would stand up to another quake, planning water pumps to make it possible to fight fires, using those blasted equations she couldn't make sense of to ensure all the stonework on the new buildings would fall away from the internal framing rather than on anyone inside, should it crack—but with all the time running numbers and testing models, there hadn't been time to actually begin rebuilding. *I'll be sixty before I ever see Lisbon again, at this rate.*

If Dom José had any real interest in the rebuilding or in ruling in general, Cecília had to imagine Senhor Carvalho would be treading close to the king's last nerve. But with Dom José happy to leave Lisbon to others, and anyone who would oppose the first minister too dead to object, Senhor Carvalho was free to rebuild the city as he wished, as a modern marvel.

She stood sharply, needing to think about something else. At least, after the Távora Affair—as the entire dreadful experience was being called—court had been quiet enough that the first minister seemed to have forgotten about her. If she could just keep going on as she had been, not thinking about John or death or any of it, she could possibly enjoy the rest of her life.

Or at least be content with it. She moved out into the hallway.

The unfamiliar sight of ecclesiastical robes on that side of the palace made Cecília freeze. With the first minister's office and all of his supporters down the hall, what priests remained at court rarely strayed from the chapel. The surprise made recognition take a moment. "Father Moreno?"

The middle-aged priest looked at her. "Senhorita Durante. How are you?"

"Very well," Cecília lied. "Are you visiting?"

"Father Cardona actually requested I return, for the time being." Father Moreno gave one of his congenial smiles, as though he hadn't been one of the priests to leave in protest after Father Malagrida had been arrested for his connection to the Távora family two years before. "It seems he could use the help now that Father Delacruz's health has declined. May the Lord see him healed."

Cecília mumbled the same, crossing herself quickly, though she had to admit she hadn't noticed anything wrong with Father Delacruz beyond the fact that the man had to be at least eighty. She had long assumed his continued presence at court was spite more than a calling, as if he dared the forces on the other side of the palace to attempt removing him.

"How is your sister?" Father Moreno asked before Cecília could add anything.

A knot formed in her stomach at the thought of Bibiana, or Sister Maria Inês, as she had become. Though the odd letter still arrived from time to time, generally around Easter or Advent, Bibiana had disappeared from Cecília's life nearly as completely as the rest of her family. She still forced a smile for the priest. "She is well. Just recently took her vows with the Poor Clares."

"They are blessed to have her."

Cecília lowered her head but didn't otherwise answer. Bibiana would have been miserable at court, and after everything Cecília had experienced, she was glad her sister was nowhere close to the capital, but it would have been nice to have the potential to visit. *Of course she would choose a cloistered order.*

"I should get my things settled." Father Moreno didn't seem at all perturbed by her lack of answer. "I hope I will see you at service, now that I'm back. Are you still keeping the Hours?"

Cecília nearly winced before she caught herself as two-year-old memories fought to join in. "No, Father. But you'll certainly see me at morning Mass." At least on Sundays. Even if the state of her soul was rather questionable, she had been certain to attend Mass and confess at least what she could. The rest, she would have to take up with God when the time came for that.

"I'm glad to hear it." He gave a light blessing as a goodbye then continued the way he had been heading—an odd choice if he intended to head straight to the chapel but also opposite the first minister's office—so Cecília supposed he could simply be avoiding Senhor Carvalho. She certainly had done so on more than one occasion, taking the longer route on the off chance that the first minister would have been out in the hall.

As it was, she took her chances and followed the most direct route to her rooms. With any luck, Tio Aloisio would be out, and she could crawl back into bed for the rest of the day without needing to explain.

As she opened the door, the sight of her uncle sitting on the settee in the center of their antechamber quashed that hope. He looked up from the pamphlet he was reading before he checked the large clock that had appeared in the room after the *Vento de Verão* had docked the week before. "To what do we owe the honor, having you back so early?"

"Everyone is still in Lisbon."

"I'm surprised you didn't join them."

"I wasn't invited."

Tio Aloisio raised an eyebrow. "When have you found that an impediment?"

With everything else already threatening to bring up memories she'd very happily suppressed, she decided to avoid that familiar line of discussion. "What are you reading?"

He lifted the pamphlet enough to show the title: *Candide, ou l'Optimisme.*

"Candid, or the Optimist?"

"Candide is the boy's name in it." Tio Aloisio didn't look up from the pamphlet. "Monsieur Voltaire is satirizing Herr Leibniz's *Théodicée*, using our earthquake, apparently."

Yet more about the earthquake. "Have I read *Théodicée*?"

"It's there, if you'd like to try." He motioned to the bookshelf by his desk. "We have the French translation. It is Herr Leibniz's response to parts of Monsieur Bayle's *Dictionnaire Historique et Critique.*"

"I'm never going to get through them all if everyone insists on writing a response to everyone else."

"Spend more time with your French than those geometry problems Senhor Rocha gives you, and you'll read more quickly."

Cecília decided that was another line of conversation not worth pursuing. French was likely a more useful subject than geometry, as she was hardly ever going to become an architect, but spending too much time actively learning the language also brought up memories of times she would rather have buried. "I saw Father Moreno today."

That caught Tio Aloisio's attention enough for him to finally set the pamphlet down. "Did you?"

She nodded. "Ran into him in the hall. He said Father Cardona asked for him to replace Father Delacruz. Perhaps the Fathers are finally beginning to move on from what happened."

"I imagine it likely has more to do with what is happening with Father Malagrida."

Cecília frowned, asking, even though she wasn't certain she wanted to know the answer, "What is happening with Father Malagrida?"

"The first minister has recalled his brother from abroad. Father Carvalho is to be appointed Inquisitor General."

"Inquisitor..." Cecília trailed off as the implications hit her straight in the chest. With the king supporting every move Senhor Carvalho made and the court brought in line, the only problem the first minister could even possibly have had was Father Malagrida. Though the old priest had been implicated in the Távora affair, he was still locked in Junqueira Prison—not from any clemency on the first minister's count, of course, but because even with as much power as Senhor Carvalho had, he couldn't execute a priest.

He couldn't, but if the Church found Father Malagrida guilty of heresy... "The Inquisition *already* cleared Father Malagrida. He's not a heretic, just a mad old man in a cell."

"He had his new ravings made into pamphlets, spouting prophecies and Lord knows what else. Father Carvalho will be leading the new inquest."

And I wonder what the verdict will be with the first minister's brother in charge. Cecília's body went cold, the smell of ash and flesh a little too recent in her memory for comfort. "You believe Father Moreno is here because of that?"

"Do you believe the timing to be coincidental?"

"It could be."

Tio Aloisio fixed her with a look that said he didn't believe even she thought that. "We may have to start limiting your time in the architects' office, if it is turning you that naïve."

She huffed but moved on. "What would even happen, if"—*when*—"the Inquisition finds Father Malagrida heretical? Senhor Carvalho has outlawed *autos-da-fé*. He called them *barbaric*. Is he willing to slide back his own progress simply to settle some old score he's already won? What threat is Father Malagrida to him now?"

"When he is *still* attempting to stir up panic in the populous?"

"He's mad! Who would listen?"

"More people than one would hope." Tio Aloisio grabbed his hat by the door. "If you'll excuse me."

Cecília frowned. It had perhaps been overly optimistic to believe that Father Moreno's arrival meant something good, but she still sent up a prayer that nothing was starting again.

Was that the dream? She glanced skyward. John had always arrived partnered with some sort of disaster. Perhaps seeing him in a dream was meant to be a harbinger, if he wasn't returning in person. She turned for her room. Even if the men of court insisted on pushing things that had no business being pushed forward, she would have no part of it. She was done with that part of her life, and she had no intention of ever going back to it.

"WE AREN'T BEGINNING a day too soon, let me tell you." Senhor Rocha sat back in his chair, looking around the rest of the architect's office as Cecília worked. "They had to chase out a good half-dozen curs and nearly twice as many vagabonds for us to even get a proper look at the cleared space. What those men think they're doing, living in in cracked foundations..."

"I imagine they don't have many better options, if they've resorted to that." Cecília did her best not to think about the homeless still in Lisbon. Most who had filled the campos five years before had found somewhere to go by then, but that didn't make thinking about those still out on the street any easier. She picked up the paper and held it toward Senhor Rocha. "Like this?"

He scanned the page. "Very good. I'm going to run out of things to teach you, at this rate."

"Why do I find that hard to believe, senhor?" She pulled the paper back to look over the mess of equations.

"Even if I do, though, I suppose I could always hand your tutelage over to Senhor Ventura."

Cecília sent him a questioning look.

"It seems he's outlasted the rest of the office once again." Senhor Rocha nodded across the room with a smirk.

She glanced where he motioned just in time to see one of the younger architects, Senhor Ventura, look away from her and Senhor Rocha and turn back to his work. She rolled her eyes and sent Senhor Rocha an unamused look. "Are you going to attempt to foist me on yet *another* young man in this office?"

"I don't believe Senhor Ventura would find it an unhappy proposition, from the way he keeps staring at us."

"Well, I am perfectly happy with my current education, thank you." Cecília turned back to the desk. "What now?"

Senhor Rocha watched her for another moment before he stretched theatrically. "If you aren't interested in Senhor Ventura's help, it may be time for us to say it's a day. It's growing late."

She looked out the window. Facing west, the architect's office kept enough light to work late into the evening, but the sun was sinking toward the horizon. She nodded, catching Senhor Ventura glancing over once again before she turned to pack up her things. "I'll see you tomorrow, then?"

"I will look forward to it, my dear." Senhor Rocha flashed her a smile as he stood as well.

In case Senhor Ventura intended to attempt catching her, Cecília didn't bother with more of a goodbye. No doubt he, like all the young men Senhor Rocha tried to bring into their lessons, was a perfectly fine man, but even if she was forcing herself to move on from everything in the past, no good ever seemed to come from her romantic entanglements.

She would be twenty-three on her next birthday, and had life not changed, she didn't doubt that people would have been starting to whisper about her approaching spinsterhood. But the world had turned on its head five years before. Nothing was the way it would have been, and Tio Aloisio didn't seem to be in any rush to be rid of her. With her uncle newly into his sixties, Cecília felt safe in saying the man had no intention of ever marrying, which left her his only possible heir. Exactly who would take control of running it all if she didn't marry was a question, but the way things were going, people would perhaps accept an educated woman supervising her own affairs. If she wanted, she could spend the rest of her life as she was, taking over Tio Aloisio's vineyard and everything else once he passed on then letting the family die out altogether once she did. The entire line seemed cursed, anyway, filled with living saints, desperate sinners, and nothing in between.

Caught up in her own thoughts, she noticed the first minister a beat too late.

"Ah, Senhorita Durante." His piercing blue eyes caught her. "A pleasure to see you."

Some good sense still working in her head made her curtsy deeply and return the pleasantry.

"Perhaps I could have a moment?" He opened the door to his office, motioning gallantly, and Cecília could as much say no to the question as she could say no to breathing. She gave another short curtsy and crossed the threshold, doing her best to hide the tension ratcheting up her back.

The first minister's office had been redone since the last time Cecília had been inside, no doubt to match his new status as the *Conde de Oeiras*, a true noble since all the old dukedoms and counties had been redistributed. In fact, given how rich the fabric was on the chairs, curtains, and tapestries, she would daresay that the offices were fit for a king. Having to sit in the smaller chair across the desk from Senhor Carvalho's near throne only made the situation more intimidating, and Senhor Carvalho had never needed help being intimidating.

"Senhorita Durante, how have you been?" Senhor Carvalho took a seat in his chair, his voice light even as his blue eyes continued to pin her in place. The soft wrinkles that had formed on his face over the past few years did nothing to mute the feeling that those eyes could see right into her thoughts.

"Very well, Minister," Cecília said, trying to match his tone, though she couldn't entirely hide her apprehension. "Thank you for asking."

"And how is the rebuilding going? We are breaking ground on the Praça do Comércio soon, I believe?"

"The office seems very pleased with how things are progressing." Cecília squeezed one hand with the other to stop from giving in to the urge to fidget under his scrutiny, the small talk doing nothing to settle her nerves. "Senhor Rocha has been very kind in finding time to explain everything they are doing. When he isn't busy with his work, of course."

"And you're finding you understand everything he's teaching you?"

"Most of it," she said.

"I can't say I'm surprised." He steepled his fingers. "You always have had a quick mind."

She almost slipped and frowned at the unexpected compliment but said, "Thank you, senhor" and waited for the first minister to continue.

"I trust it hasn't eaten into your religious devotions?"

And there it was. With as little as Senhor Carvalho had ever seemed worried over the state of her or anyone else's soul, she couldn't imagine him directing the conversation toward the priests for any other reason than what Tio Aloisio had said was happening. She swallowed, treading carefully. "I attend Mass every Sunday."

"Only Sundays?"

"And Holy Days of Obligation, of course," she said, pretending she didn't know what he was truly driving at with that question.

Those piercing eyes said he didn't believe she'd misunderstood him for an instant. He still moved on. "And I believe an old family friend of yours has recently returned to court. Father Moreno, is it?"

Cecília gripped her hands tighter. "I don't know if I would call him a friend, senhor, but he did work with my sister years ago. Before the king's physician was able to diagnose hysteria and correct it."

Senhor Carvalho took his time responding, and Cecília had to bite the inside of her cheek to keep from squirming. "Did he mention why he had returned to court, when you spoke?"

"He was asked to replace Father Delacruz." At least that was an easy answer.

"He didn't mention any other reason?"

"Should he have?"

The slight narrowing of the first minister's eyes said she had pushed too far, playing dumb. He sat back in his chair-slash-throne. "I believe it may be time for you to attend *daily* Mass, Senhorita Durante."

She fought to keep her thoughts together. "Oh?"

"I'm sure you have heard that His Holiness the Pope has appointed my brother, Father Carvalho, to be Inquisitor General?" Though the sentence tipped up at the end like a question, he didn't wait for a response before continuing, "I'm afraid some at our chapel may be questioning His Holiness's wisdom. If that is the case, I would like to know about it."

Cecília took as deep a breath as she could manage, attempting to get the right words out. *It's now or never.* "I'd rather not, senhor."

Senhor Carvalho's face didn't change in the slightest as he stared at her, and yet it felt as though the temperature in the room had plummeted. "Come again?"

She shifted in the chair, beginning to lose her battle against fidgeting under such scrutiny. "I-I fully appreciate everything you have done for us, Senhor Carvalho." The words came out in a rush. "But I can't in good conscience spy on holy men."

After what felt like eons, he finally leaned forward, resting his elbows on the solid wood desk. "Do *you* believe His Holiness has made a mistake, Senhorita Durante?"

"Of course not, senhor."

"Then you must agree that anyone speaking against the inquisitor general is *not* a holy man?"

Cecília floundered. "Senhor, truly, you don't need me. No one would dare move against you after two years ago."

"You're certain of that?"

After you literally salted the earth under where the Távoras were burned so nothing will ever grow there again? "Your word is as good as the king's."

Senhor Carvalho stood and moved to the side of the desk—not directly over her but a towering figure, all the same. "And what do you believe would happen, should—Lord forbid—the king no longer be the king? I trust you remember what else happened two years ago?"

Cecília dropped her eyes.

"Your uncle asked that you be given time to reconcile what the world demands with whatever you had in your head. You were very sheltered, I know, before everything happened. Do I need to regret not having put a stop to you bothering my architects these past months?"

"No, senhor. It's just—"

"Because I would hate to think I'd have to begin questioning your loyalty to what this country is attempting to do."

"No, you have my full support—"

"Or perhaps it's you don't wish to attend services? Perhaps something my brother should consider?"

Her head jerked up at the implied threat of the Inquisition—the idea of the severely weakened Holy Office doing *anything* had been such a small possibility it hadn't been worth considering in the past few years. "What?"

"What has been happening with those architects? Or with your uncle, perhaps? I believe he has quite a collection of books he allows you to read?"

Half you gave him! She barely caught the accusation before it flew out of her mouth. "Senhor—"

"Is that something that needs to be investigated, Senhorita Durante? You avoiding Mass and reading questionable books?"

"I haven't been avoiding Mass!"

"You didn't just tell me you wouldn't go?"

Cecília gaped, trying to catch up to where the conversation had gone, even though Senhor Carvalho had gotten so many steps ahead of her, there was no chance she would be able to untangle herself from the net he'd woven around her.

"Or perhaps I misunderstood you." He lifted an eyebrow. "So you are intending to attend daily Mass?"

She grasped for anything she could find in her mind that would get her out of the situation as she felt the walls closing in around her. She couldn't manage anything but a weak "Yes, senhor."

"Good." He turned back to his chair, releasing her from his piercing glare. "I'm glad we cleared that up. I'm sure we'll speak again soon, when I'm not interrupting your devotions, of course."

Cecília nodded, her mouth refusing to move again. *How many times am I going to have to say yes?*

He took a seat and began to shuffle through the papers on his desk. "A pleasure speaking with you, senhorita. So glad you could stop in."

Cecília mumbled some equally falsely polite response then stood, beating a quick retreat out into the hallway.

You should have known better, the taunting voice in her head said as she turned for her room. *You can't escape the first minister.*

She slipped through the door into the blessedly empty antechamber and rested against the wall as she attempted to stop the room from spinning.

You chose this.

She couldn't debate that, as much as she wanted to ignore the voice. She just wished she had known then, when she had first said "yes" four years before, what it would mean.

Chapter Twenty-Four

Cecília fingered the gold cross around her neck, irritably rubbing the red stone in the center as her knees protested. It was only her third morning in the chapel, but she was obviously out of practice, her body revolting against the repetitive hour spent in the pews.

Why am I even here?

Morning Mass was quiet, the congregation only a handful of courtiers, and none of them giving so much as a whisper about the service, let alone anything Senhor Carvalho would have found interesting. Of course, he hadn't sounded interested in what courtiers were saying. He wanted her to eavesdrop on the priests, and she still wasn't certain she was willing to resort to that.

"Be blessed by the grace of the Holy Spirit," Father Pinho finished. "Go in peace, and may the Lord be with you and with everyone. Amen."

Peace... Cecília somehow managed not to snort at that idea, and she crossed herself before quickly turning toward the door. That morning, Father Moreno had offered a small smile from where he had been sitting with the other priests when he'd seen her. The last thing she needed was for him to attempt catching her on the way out, at least before she figured out what she was doing. Luís had been willing to go to his death rather than sacrifice even a snake like Mateus de Vilhena. He had been a willing martyr for his principles, even if it was unlikely that anyone would spare him a passing thought in a generation. She wondered whether she was so self-serving that she was willing to send yet more innocent men to their deaths just to save her own neck. The first minister's threats shouldn't have mattered. She should have stared him down and said she was done, whatever the consequences.

And yet every time she tried to think of facing down the Inquisition, all she could remember was the *auto-da-fé* her father had taken her to when she was six, against her mother's wishes. Most of the heretics had been repentant and released after lashes or at least died in the faith and were garroted before being put to the flame. But one man had arrived in a gray cassock with the image of a sinner encircled by demons and fire. She watched everything before him with a perverse fascination, but the screams when the man had burned, so similar to Ferreira during the Távora executions... Papai had had to pick her up and leave before she would stop crying. She would have liked to believe that refusing to report wouldn't catch enough of the first minister's ire that he would push his brother to have her burned alive, but as merciless as he had been with the Távoras, she truly couldn't know.

And not just me. She returned to rubbing the gold cross, her anxiety making her fidget. *They'd pull Tio Aloisio into it.*

Her uncle wasn't any more innocent than she was, but he certainly didn't deserve the Inquisition, not if Senhor Carvalho was willing to bring it all back just to be rid of Father Malagrida.

She turned the last corner before her room and stopped short in surprise. Senhor Ventura, dressed impeccably in his breeches and tailored red coat, stood a few steps from her door with his eyes on a silver pocket watch. Cecília frowned, not certain she wanted to deal with whatever was waiting for her, before she forced herself forward. "Senhor Ventura?"

He started, sliding the watch away as he turned to face her before he quickly bowed. "Senhorita Durante."

She gave a tight smile. "I would have thought you'd be at work already?"

"Yes." He caught his hands behind his back and shifted his weight awkwardly. "I noticed you hadn't been by the past few days and wanted to make sure you were well."

"I'm very well, thank you. Just busy, though I appreciate your concern."

"I'm glad to hear it." He lowered his head quickly before meeting her eyes again. "As you are, perhaps you would like to accompany me to a party Senhora Gaspar is hosting tonight? Senhor Magro extended an invitation."

A party. How long has it been since I left court to go to a party? Even if her mind hadn't been tied up with everything pressing down on her, though, she wasn't certain she had it in her to be an engaging guest on her own, let alone with someone looking to escort her. She put it off in the easiest way she could think of. "I would have to ask my uncle."

"I just spoke with him." Senhor Ventura motioned at the doorway. "I had the good luck to catch him on his way out. He gave his permission, as long as you wished to attend."

So Tio Aloisio knew what was happening. *Wonderful.* Apparently, he had already left, so at least she wouldn't have to talk to him immediately. She kept her smile carefully in place, trying to think of the kindest way to turn the man down. "Senhor Ventura," she began just before a flash of movement at the corner of the hall caught her attention. She felt all the blood leave her face.

John...? Her mind wouldn't form a complete thought as she stared at the man, half-convinced she was seeing things.

He froze as well, surprise moving over his face before he apparently recovered and continued in her direction.

Senhor Ventura twisted to follow Cecília's line of sight, frowning as he spotted the Englishman. Somewhere in Cecília's mind, she registered that the two men were dressed surprisingly similarly, not in full courtier dress but in finer fabric than she had ever seen John wear. Senhor Ventura turned back to her, his voice lowered. "Do you know that man?"

The words were enough to start her out of her stupor just as John stepped up beside them. "Mr. Bates!" She looked back at Senhor Ventura, trying—and most likely failing—to hide how flustered she was. "Senhor Ventura, this is Mr. Bates, my uncle's old business partner and friend." She switched to John, somehow keeping her voice far more level than she would have credited herself for. "Mr. Bates, I didn't know you were in Portugal."

"Just arrived." He gave her something between a nod and a bow before addressing the other man. "Senhor Ventura, was it?"

Senhor Ventura offered a polite bow, though he continued to frown.

"Mr. Bates actually saved my life"—Cecília attempted to ease the tension in the air—"five years ago."

"Ah. You were here in the quake, then?"

"Indeed, I was." John nodded.

"Sorry business, all that," Senhor Ventura said.

John arched an eyebrow. "I believe I'd call it something a little stronger than that, myself."

"Would you like to wait inside, Mr. Bates? My uncle just went out, but I'm sure he'll be back soon."

John switched his quizzical expression to her but didn't argue. "Certainly."

"I'll show you in," she said before sending a last look at Senhor Ventura. "I'm sure I'll see you soon, senhor."

"But about tonight...?" His eyes moved between Cecília and John, more questioningly than she cared for.

"I'll check my plans and let you know." She offered a final smile. "You'll be in the office all day?"

"I will."

"Wonderful. Have a good morning, Senhor Ventura."

The man finally took the dismissal, offering another bow before he moved toward the architects' office down the hall.

Cecília watched until Senhor Ventura was out of sight before she turned back to John. Suddenly, the silence felt much heavier.

"So…" he started when she didn't speak.

Cecília opened her mouth but then shut it again, glancing at the door over her shoulder. She wasn't certain what she had to say to the man in front of her, but the hall seemed far too exposed for whatever it was. She opened the door. "Come with me."

With a nod, he walked into the antechamber, letting her shut the door behind them. She took a deep breath, still struggling to think of what to say. John beat her to it. "Who was that?"

She bristled slightly at the vaguely accusatory tone, the wave of annoyance helping her pull herself together, at least slightly. "Senhor Ventura. He's one of the architects working on the rebuilding."

"And?"

She crossed her arms tight over her stomach. "And what?"

"It seemed I was interrupting some plans you were making."

"He was inviting me to a party tonight." She gave an easy shrug before the flood of emotion she had felt when she saw him in the hallway came roaring back. "What are you doing here?"

John's eyebrows rose. "I told you I'd come back, didn't I?"

"In a few months. Not two *years*."

"Not quite that long."

"Close enough," she returned, not feeling the need to squabble over months.

He shook his head. "It took a little longer to get things settled than planned."

"And you didn't think to write?"

"Nor did you?"

"I did!" Her voice rose dangerously before she caught herself. She continued at a safer volume. "I wrote twice. To you and then to your sister, asking after you."

The slightly exasperated expression slid into confusion. "I didn't receive anything."

"Convenient," she snapped. "Obviously, I should always have just said I'd written. You wouldn't have known the difference."

"I don't know what to say. I *didn't*," he said. "And my sister doesn't speak Portuguese. She might not have known what your letter was."

"I wrote it in French," she said, her tone a little petulant.

He tilted his head slightly. "*Tu parles français maintenant?*"

"A little." She didn't bother embarrassing herself by attempting to answer him in her own horribly accented French. "I've learned enough to manage a letter."

The corners of his mouth tipped up in that infuriatingly familiar way of his. "And to think, you once told me you didn't write well enough to correspond at all."

Huffing, she moved away from him, being so close to feeling dangerous as the initial wave of irritation wore off. "*Where* have you been, John Bates? For all I knew, you were dead out in the middle of the ocean somewhere."

"That's why you found your architect?"

Cecília rolled her eyes, keeping up the pretense, which felt less important as the hurt she'd been nursing for months began to dissipate. "He's not my anything."

"It certainly sounded to be something out there." He glanced at the door.

She considered letting him think that was the case, just for another moment of spite, but she supposed she was hardly the person to judge him for not writing. She had been the one to set the precedent, and he'd already gone beyond what she'd truly expected of him, reappearing at court. She released a breath. "I was going to reject the invitation before you showed up, if you truly care."

Some thought Cecília couldn't make out passed over John's face, but he only said, "Oh?"

"Lately, I've found myself agreeing with my uncle. It's best for me not to get involved with young men."

"I see." The unreadable expression turned vaguely amused. "And are you married to that idea? Or could you be convinced differently?"

Part of her hated that he was still as charming as ever, but she didn't have the energy to fight it. "Part of the point has been not to be married to anything."

The slight amusement became a full smile. "Good."

In one quick movement, John closed the distance between them. One arm encircled her waist as his mouth came down on hers, hot and demanding, two years of desire and deprivation flooding into her all at once, shooting fire over every inch of her. Her body responded before her mind could catch up, arching into him as his hand pressed against the small of her back. Her shoulders hit something hard, and she realized they'd backed up against the wall. Some little voice at the back of her mind tried to warn her of... something. She couldn't fully bring her attention to it as his mouth moved down her neck.

The rattle of the latch let it register. *Tio Aloisio.*

"John," she warned, working her hands between them and pushing him back just as the door swung open.

Tio Aloisio stepped inside, turning to hang his hat before his eyes hit Cecília and John. As flushed as she still felt, what he'd interrupted would have been obvious even if she could have met his gaze. After what felt like an eternity but likely wasn't more than a few seconds, Tio Aloisio's eyes settled on John. "Bates, what an unexpected pleasure. I hadn't heard you were in Portugal."

John swallowed, seeming to need as much of a moment to gather himself as Cecília did before he recovered and stepped toward Tio Aloisio. "Yes, I just arrived this morning. Wonderful to see you, Senhor Durante."

Tio Aloisio lowered his head in recognition of the pleasantry. "Are you collecting Mr. Hays's correspondences again?"

"Working for his office, actually. Apparently, there's a dearth of men who actually speak Portuguese in the British delegation here. Mr. Hays has been trying to find more men who don't need to rely on French."

Cecília blinked in surprise. "You've joined the diplomatic corps?"

"I have." He flashed her a small smile.

"Quite the change from sailing," Tio Aloisio said, something that sounded nearly sarcastic tinting his words.

"After fifteen years, it seemed time to settle somewhere."

"And that somewhere is Lisbon."

"It was a very fortuitous appointment, I thought."

"Quite."

Cecília looked between John and her uncle, trying to pick out what conversation they were actually having under what they were saying. She was obviously missing something, but whatever it was, it seemed less friendly than she had ever seen the two men.

"Well." John glanced at Cecília then turned back to Tio Aloisio. "I should get back to my own room. Mr. Hays has given me today to get settled, but I'm sure there is more than enough to do."

"A pleasure as always, Bates," Tio Aloisio said.

"All mine," he answered before offering Cecília a formal bow. "Senhorita Durante."

"Mr. Bates." She curtsied, waiting for the door to open and close once again before she fully straightened. Her uncle had turned to his desk, as though there were nothing to discuss.

"What was that?" she asked his back.

"What was what?" He didn't look at her.

"You were practically glaring at Mr. Bates."

"I certainly was not."

Cecília scoffed. "You call that a congenial greeting?"

"Not as congenial as the one *you* were giving him, I imagine. Perhaps that's skewing your view of things?"

Cecília was suddenly glad her uncle wasn't looking at her to see how hot her cheeks had gotten. She ignored it as well as she could and pushed on. "You're upset he came to see me?"

"To see you? No." Tio Aloisio finally faced her. "I imagined he would find his way back to visit at some point. Uprooting his life for you is a different matter."

"He came to take a new position."

"And just happened to find one here. Coincidence, I'm sure."

Blowing out a tense breath, she squared her shoulders. "And what if he wanted to be here for me? Is that horrible?"

Tio Aloisio shook his head, looking more exhausted than upset. "You can't be with him, Cilinha."

The familiar name somehow made the statement feel worse. "Why?"

"Beyond the obvious?"

"It didn't seem you, of all people, would take issue with interacting with Protestants."

"There's a difference between my type of interacting and what you're proposing." He released a heavy breath. "I take it you wish to marry him, judging from what I walked in on?"

Cecília pressed her lips together tightly, saying it out loud suddenly feeling too heavy. She turned it back onto him. "You have more reasons not to?"

Tio Aloisio seemed to measure his words before continuing. "Bates is a very... resilient man, and I admit that a diplomatic post is impressive even for him, but he has always gotten by through a quick mind, charm, and friends in higher places. That is hardly a stable existence."

She furrowed her eyebrows. "You're worried how he'd keep me?"

"You've lost a lot in your life. We all have. I don't believe you need to lose more every time the wheel of fortune turns south for our Mr. Bates."

The genuine concern in her uncle's tone made Cecília hesitate, but she still crossed her arms defiantly. "He seems to be doing well now. And I'm not a child. I don't need you to protect me."

"You do need someone to support you, unless you intend to use your skills to start reporting on the diplomatic corps."

She furrowed her eyebrows, a knot slowly forming in her stomach. "What?"

"There's a reason you began keeping the Hours again, I trust? How do you think it would look to that side of the palace, you being that devout yet taking up with an Englishman? I imagine you wouldn't hear anything with that around court. You'd have to hope there's something of interest happening in the diplomatic corps. I imagine you could do exactly as you did with Senhor Terra."

Cecília felt the words like a physical blow, and her uncle's face said that he knew he had aimed low. Her jaw didn't want to move, but she forced the words out. "Don't you talk about him."

"Ignoring reality doesn't change it, Cilinha—"

"Don't call me that!" she snapped.

"And you can't do what you're asked if you involve yourself with Bates," Tio Aloisio continued unabated. "You'll have to offer what you get from him instead."

She felt her hands begin to tremble, but she wasn't certain if it was fear, sorrow, or anger. Clenching her fists, she clung to the last one. "I shouldn't have to *offer* anything. Haven't I done enough of this awful business for one lifetime?"

"Not as long as you're at court. And correct me if I'm mistaken, but if Bates is working in the diplomatic corps, I believe he can't *not* live at court."

Cecília opened her mouth but found herself at a lack for a retort. Spinning on her heel, she headed for the hall.

"Where are you going?" Tio Aloisio called after her.

With no idea herself, she didn't answer.

CECÍLIA BUNCHED HER veil in her hands, her nerves making her fidget. Heavens knew how the lace would hold up to the abuse, but she couldn't bring herself to stop. Still dressed from Sunday Mass, she should have headed straight back to her room. With Senhor Carvalho no doubt having her watched, she felt far too conspicuous in the deep-red gown, and yet she found herself loitering at the end of the diplomatic corps' hallway where anyone could see her.

I thought Protestant Masses were supposed to be shorter. She shoved her veil into her pocket to keep herself from entirely ruining it. Wisely, John had kept his distance over the past few days while she'd fought to work something out, some other option that Tio Aloisio had not wanted her to see, but she'd come up empty-handed. She was caught as tightly as ever in a web she would happily have climbed into, John having reappeared or not.

A sudden rise of voices said the Protestant service held in one of the larger rooms on that side of the palace had concluded. Cecília stepped back to press closer to the wall, though that would likely have done as much to conceal her as waving a pair of signal flags would have. A mix of the different non-Catholic diplomats filtered into the hallway. She watched until she saw John appear, laughing with two other men. *At least someone in the palace is happy.* Veil gone, she bunched the fabric of her skirt in her fist, debating whether she should actually speak with him.

As though he felt himself being watched, John glanced in her direction. His eyebrows rose slightly, but he said something to the men he was with then started toward her. Motioning with her eyes for him to follow, she ducked around the corner. Luckily, one of the sitting rooms not far down the next hall was empty. She slipped inside and waited for John to do the same before she shut the door behind them.

Releasing a breath, she tried to think of how to start as she turned to face him. His mouth on hers stopped her short. As always, the rush of heat through her body tried to chase out everything she had been thinking. *This isn't what you're here for, Cecilia.* She placed a hand on his chest. "John—"

"I'm sorry." He pulled back enough to look at her. "I've just been hoping you'd show up. I would have come to you, but I didn't think your uncle would be pleased to see me."

The easy way he talked about it made her insides squirm. She dropped her eyes.

"Don't look like that, love." John caught her chin. "It's nothing I didn't expect. He's always made it very clear what he thinks about my interest in you."

That statement wasn't important when it came to the grand scheme of things, but she took the excuse to put off the inevitable all the same. "He sent you to see me two years ago."

"Not quite that long, but he knew I was leaving again. That's always been the important part to him."

She started to ask him what he meant before it hit her. "He's the one who convinced you to leave. Five years ago."

John's eyebrows rose.

"He told me you were considering staying back then. He didn't tell me why you didn't."

"He did," John admitted, "but he was right. I was in no position to stay then. That's why I found this post. I can stand on my own two feet now. It will just take him a little while to see this *isn't* five years ago. That I'm not staying 'solely for some ill-formed infatuation,' I believe were the words he used."

Cecília pressed her lips together, once again not caring for the sensation that her uncle understood everything far better than she'd assumed him to.

"He's only trying to look after you," John said, brushing her cheek. "I can't begrudge him that."

She swallowed, trying to keep her nerve to say what she'd actually come to say while looking straight into his eyes. "That's not why I... It's not that. I..."

His eyebrows pulled together slightly as the words died in her throat. "What is it, love?"

"I..." She started again. "We need to keep our distance right now."

The concerned expression turned into a full frown. "Did your uncle—"

"No, it's not him. There are other things happening. It would be dangerous for us to be seen together until it's all settled."

"Dangerous for you or for me?"

"Both, possibly."

"What's happening?"

She shook her head. "I can't talk about it."

"If you tell me, I can try to help."

And she didn't doubt he would try. He always had, when she'd needed him. *All the more reason he needs to stay far away from this.* "I *can't*. Just, everything should be settled soon." *One way or another.* "We only need to keep our distance until then. It won't be forever."

His eyes searched her face. "Are you in trouble?"

Yes. "I'm fine. I just don't want you to take a needless risk for me."

"Love, if I weren't willing to take risks, I'd likely be working the Southampton docks with my father right now. So far, risks have treated me rather well."

And they have nearly killed you. Flashes of them battered from the earthquake mixed into memories of Luís in Junqueira Prison and the Távora executions inside her head as though she had woken every awful memory she had at once. John was not Luís—dear Heaven was he not Luís—but the thought of history repeating itself and having to see another man in prison or on the scaffolding made it impossible to speak. Especially since if it all did happen again, it would certainly be the first minister punishing her. No politics, just someone else dying to hurt her. She couldn't hold his gaze. "Please, John. If something happened to you because of me, I'd never be able to live with myself."

"You believe it that dire?"

She pressed her lips into a thin line.

"Cecília. Look at me."

She couldn't bring herself to look away from the spot on the delicately patterned rug on the floor.

"Cecília." He leaned to put himself in her sight line. "If you're in trouble, tell me."

Lord, did she want to. She steeled herself enough to at least meet his eyes. "Please, just stay away until I tell you different? I'll explain the moment I can. I promise. If you could just wait..."

The concerned, critiquing look didn't leave his face, but he finally nodded. "It's been five years. I can handle waiting. I only hope you know you can trust me. No matter what's happening."

"I do. This is just safer for everyone."

He didn't appear any more pleased, but he nodded again. Cecília took a deep breath, preparing to make her exit before noticing his eyes flick to the low neckline of her gown. He beat her to speaking. "Do I at least get to kiss you again, since you're already here? It is somewhat cruel to wear that dress to tell me I can't see you."

She let the breath out with an exasperated huff. With everything else, it hardly seemed the time. But if he was going to offer to leave things on a lighter note, she wasn't going to dissuade him. "I came from Mass. You don't wear your best for Sunday?"

"Your best outdoes mine by a good margin."

Cecília rocked forward enough to kiss him. She pulled back again before he could deepen it. "I really should go."

"A few more minutes." His hand slid to the small of her back to pull her closer to him. "Surely, that can't ruin anything."

She'd already put both of them at risk, loitering around that side of the palace. The sooner she left, the better. But then the chances of someone seeing her leaving now were the same as someone seeing her in five minutes. Or thirty. "A few minutes. As long as that's it."

"Yes, ma'am." Another light pull brought her flush against him. Then his mouth was on hers, and Cecília did her best to turn her mind off. Just for a few minutes.

Chapter Twenty-Five

Cecília blew out a breath, brushing her skirt self-consciously, though John had assured her—multiple times—that everything looked entirely in order before she left. She had wavered slightly from her original plan, but she had still gotten a promise to stay away, so she'd done what she'd set out to do, even if she'd allowed herself to get sidetracked. She only needed to worry about keeping her own head out of a noose.

She turned the corner to her own hallway and stopped dead. Especially since he had been given his new noble status, Senhor Carvalho had been a rare sight around Cecília and Tio Aloisio's rooms. Sending someone with an invitation to see him was a far more proper transaction between a count and a merchant, no matter how long they had been acquainted. Yet there the man was, making it as impossible for Cecília to pass as if a brick wall had suddenly appeared.

His sharp eyes hit her as she stood frozen in place. "Ah, Senhorita Durante. I was just inquiring after your uncle, but it seems he is out. Perhaps you would favor me with your company instead?"

For as light and honestly kind as the words sounded, they made her stomach bottom out. *Not now.* Whether he truly had been more interested in speaking to Tio Aloisio or not, there would be no escaping giving a report if she was with Senhor Carvalho. And as quickly as her mind was racing, she couldn't think of a thing to tell him. Though she had not dared disobey the specifics of the first minister's orders, diligently attending daily service, she certainly hadn't done what he truly wanted. Most days, she was halfway out the door before the priest had closed his mouth from bidding them *requiescant in pace*. If she didn't loiter, there was little chance she would hear anything worth reporting. Where that left her when the first minister wanted information, though, she hadn't yet worked out. It was too late. With no other choice, she curtsied deeply and followed as Senhor Carvalho turned for his office.

What little color she'd had in her face was no doubt long gone by the time she reached the first minister's office. As desperately as she tried to work out something that would allow her to escape the man's ire, all she could picture was the executioner tightening the noose around her neck. *How did Luís...* She couldn't bring herself to finish that thought. Galant or idiotic, Luís's convictions had allowed him to face his own death with solemn purpose. Cecília couldn't find anything close to that.

Senhor Carvalho didn't speak until they had made it to his office. "Please sit." He motioned at the offered chair as he took his own chair-throne.

Cecília forced herself to perch on the edge of the smaller chair, feeling about the size of a five-year-old.

He shuffled through some papers on his desk, quickly finding what he wanted. His eyes ran over whatever was written there even as he addressed her. "You'll forgive me if I jump straight to business today?"

"I..." Cecília took a breath to steady herself. "I'm afraid there isn't much to report, senhor. I've been attending Mass every day, as you directed, but I haven't heard anything that sounds dangerous. A little grumbling about the new grand inquisitor, general statements about the state of Lisbon's soul, but you have complete control of the court."

Senhor Carvalho's blue eyes came up, pinning her in place as he seemed to read her thoughts one by one before he spoke again. "Is that so?"

Something about the way he asked the question made Cecília feel as if she was walking into a trap, but she said, "Yes, Minister."

"You haven't heard *anything* of interest."

"Senhor, truly, I've been listening, but—"

"What can you tell me about your brother?"

Cecília jerked in surprise, having to catch herself before she did anything else he would no doubt see. "Francisco?"

Senhor Carvalho seemed to interpret the question as rhetorical—his eyes continued to drill into her.

"He doesn't write to me these days," she continued carefully, saying the absolute truth. Since Bibiana had taken her vows, Francisco hadn't written a word to either Cecília or Tio Aloisio. "But I imagine he's still doing his ministry work in Brazil?"

"Oh no." Senhor Carvalho turned the paper in his hands around for her to see. "He's gone missing. Sources who would know state that he was last seen attempting to board a ship bound for Lisbon."

Cecília tried to keep her breathing steady as it became harder and harder to draw air. *Dear Lord, Cisco. What are you—*

"You wouldn't know *anything* about that?" Senhor Carvalho motioned with the paper.

"I just said, he doesn't write to—"

"He writes to the priests," Senhor Carvalho snapped, his tone rising as close to a shout as Cecília had ever heard. "He writes to those cursed men still clinging to the idea that Malagrida is anything but a mad, backward buffoon. Tell me, senhorita, how *I* know that, and his own sister is entirely in the dark on that matter."

"I-I..." Cecília pulled on whatever remaining thread she still had keeping her together, shock and exhaustion threatening to overwhelm her. "I swear, Minister, on my dear father's soul, I didn't know. I hadn't heard—"

"You are no use to me, Senhorita Durante, if you refuse to open your ears and *listen*."

"Please—"

"You will be keeping the Hours." He jabbed his finger at her. "You will be in that chapel every time those bells ring. I don't care if you need to sleep there to do so. You will be there, and you will not leave until you have something useful to tell me. Believe me when I say that this is your *very* last chance unless you wish for us to revisit our last discussion. Is that clear?"

"Yes, senhor," she whispered.

"Do not try my patience, Senhorita Durante. You will find it has worn very thin."

"Yes, senhor."

"You may go."

"Yes, senhor. Thank you, senhor," she said, her voice so breathy that Heavens knew if he could even hear her before she scrambled up from her chair, not able to care that she must have looked like a frightened mouse.

She stepped back into the hall but only made it halfway to her rooms before the shaking caught up to her. She placed her back to the wall, taking shallow gulps of air as she tried to pull herself back together. They only came faster and faster, not allowing for any true breath as her already shaking fingers began to tingle.

"Senhorita Durante?" Senhor Ventura's voice sounded somewhere nearby.

Dear Lord, why? She couldn't lift her head.

"Senhorita Durante." A pair of boots stopped in front of her. "What's the matter?"

She shook her head, trying to draw enough breath to remain upright let alone speak.

"Senhorita Durante?"

Slowly, she managed to find that little thread she'd been clinging to, though tears felt far too close to the surface. She blinked quickly, trying to force them back as she met Senhor Ventura's dark eyes. "I'm sorry. I..." She fought to swallow. "I just got some bad news."

His eyebrows pulled together, genuine concern playing over his face. "Is it anything I could assist with?"

Another man was offering to help without knowing just what that help would risk. She shook her head as she struggled to find something safe to say. She ended up with, "My brother has gone missing."

"Your brother?"

"My elder brother. Father Durante. He was on a mission to Brazil. Now he's disappeared, and no one seems to know..." She sucked in a sharp breath as she tried not to fall right back into an attack. "I don't know where he is or if he's hurt..."

Senhor Ventura continued to watch her with the same expression, but he at least didn't offer any empty platitudes. "I will add him to my prayers."

"Thank you." She dropped her eyes, the statement so familiar and yet oddly foreign, leaving her even more off-balance. *How did you not already think to pray for him?*

"Would you like to come to the office to take your mind off of things?" he asked after a beat. "I just started the plans for how we're going to rebuild the damaged side of Junqueira Prison."

Dear Lord, the prison was the last thing she needed to think about. She shook her head. "Thank you for the offer, senhor, but I think I need to lie down. I feel a little faint."

"Of course. Would you like me to walk you?"

"I think I can make it."

Senhor Ventura looked at her for a final moment before he stepped back with a short bow. "Please don't hesitate to fetch me if you find any need of me."

"Thank you, Senhor Ventura," Cecília said, though she had zero intention of doing so. She watched him move toward the architects' office to start what was no doubt going to be a much less complicated day than anything she would have been able to manage.

Chapter Twenty-Six

It was hardly the first time Cecília had kept the Hours, but it had never felt quite so oppressive. Her entire body ached as she found herself back on her knees for Vespers, and it was only her second day. If things kept going as they were, she would have ended up looking more hunched and hobbled than ninety-year-old, arthritic Senhora Abarca by the end of the week.

"Amen," Cecília mumbled by rote with the rest of the small congregation and crossed herself as Father Moreno finished the service. Soft shuffling filled the chapel as the handful of courtiers present began to move out of the pews. Cecília remained where she was, blowing out a long breath as she tried to relax her muscles enough to move.

Finally, she managed to get her legs to shift, just in time to notice Father Moreno moving toward her.

Oh, dear Lord. Please, no. She already had been racking her mind for how she could protect Francisco without damning Tio Aloisio and herself. She didn't need the other priests throwing themselves into the mix as well.

Of course, no one listened to her prayer, and Father Moreno stopped at the end of her pew. "Good evening."

"Good evening, Father." Cecília fully straightened and caught her hands in front of her to keep them from fidgeting.

"How are you faring today?" His kind eyes searched her face. "I've noticed you've been joining us for the Hours."

Of course you have. "I've been praying for my brother." The first thing she could think of left her mouth, even if it was likely the worst option she could have gone with, save blatantly admitting to what Senhor Carvalho had ordered. She only just caught the grimace before it made it to her face.

"Oh?" Father Moreno's graying eyebrows rose.

"He's gone missing." She was locked into the lie now. "I'm worried about him."

The interested look fell into obvious disappointment. "You haven't heard from him, then?"

"No, Father. Have you?" *Cecília!* She cursed herself, not wanting him to answer.

Father Moreno's mouth pinched. "I'm sorry to say I haven't."

Thank you, Lord.

"I admit, I am worried as well. He should have landed by now."

"What?" Cecília's voice squeaked.

Father Moreno studied Cecília's face again, seeming to realize that she didn't know something he did. He motioned to the confessionals to the left of the pews. "Would you like to make confession, child?"

"Oh, I already—"

"Please." He cut off her lie, moving toward the little cabinets.

Gritting her teeth, Cecília followed along, watching his black robe flutter out behind him. Her mind briefly glanced over the one she had been wearing the day everything had started. It had been turned into rags that November, too shredded from when she had crawled out of the rubble to mend. Apparently, real priestly robes didn't offer as much protection as before, either.

She stepped into her side of the confessional then turned to kneel in front of the grille. Her knees quickly protesting, she sat on the little bench instead. She heard Father Moreno enter the opposite side, and the grille slid open. When he didn't speak, Cecília asked, "Would you like me to actually make—"

"No. Not unless you wish to, of course. There are simply... many ears about the palace. I thought we should be cautious."

Moving won't help you with that. Cecília remained silent, biting the inside of her cheek.

"When was the last time you heard from Father Durante?"

"Months ago." Cecília interlaced her fingers in front of her, telling herself that it wasn't technically a lie. She could even say when she was a child was months ago—just many, many months.

"You haven't heard of his vision, then?"

"Vision?" Cecília repeated, already not liking the sound of where the conversation was headed.

"São João o Apóstolo blessed him in a dream. Told him it was his calling to save Father Malagrida from this shameful case being brought against him."

Cecília squeezed her eyes shut tightly, the situation so much worse than even the dire possibilities that had been niggling at the back of her skull. "He's coming to Lisbon?"

"That is what we were told. He should be here by now, though, and no one has heard a word from him. I was rather hoping he had contacted you."

"Me?"

"As his sister?"

You have the wrong sister for that. "I haven't heard a word."

"Oh dear." Father Moreno sighed. "I will continue to pray for him. I hope nothing happened to his ship."

Cecília couldn't have said a shipwreck would have been a worse fate than Senhor Carvalho's wrath. At least with a wreck, he could wash up on some friendlier shore. Trying to do anything with Father Malagrida in Portugal would likely lead to a much more painful death than what could happen at sea. For him and the rest of them.

"You'll let me know? If he contacts you?"

"Yes, Father." Since that possibility seemed about as slim as her ever *actually* getting on a ship, she didn't let herself worry about agreeing.

"Thank you, child," Father Moreno said.

Silence fell over them, and Cecília shifted her weight uncomfortably. "Is that everything, Father?"

"Oh, yes. Yes. Unless you would like to make confession."

"I did this morning." *That* was a lie, but she was going to Hell, anyway. She could certainly have done without confession for another day. There seemed little it would help at that point.

"Go with God, my child."

"Thank you, Father," Cecília said in a rush before she stood and left the confessional. She slowed in the hallway outside the chapel, trying to think of somewhere to go or someone she could ask for help. Francisco might have been attempting to sign his own death warrant, but she couldn't hasten that. He was her brother, no matter how they had left things years before. Her first instinct was to find John, but that would hardly have been fair. Too many people were already at risk. She wouldn't pull him back less than half a week after she'd warned him away.

Tio Aloisio? The thought made her stop as she mulled it over. Her uncle had been the first minister's man since before he'd been the first minister. Cecília wasn't certain whether Senhor Carvalho had friends, but if he did, Tio Aloisio would have been considered one. She couldn't trust, if she went to her uncle, that he wouldn't go straight to tell the first minister, as he had about Father Moreno.

But it's Cisco... Her brother had all but told her that she was damned when she had brought Tio Aloisio to the camp after the quake, and she still would risk her life to save him. She could hope her uncle had at least *some* familial love left for his only surviving nephew, at least enough not to want to see him hang or worse.

Cecília shivered but started forward once again. She didn't have to tell Tio Aloisio everything, just enough to see if he would help. She could plan from there.

Tio Aloisio was once again at his desk when she arrived, a lamp lit a little too close to the papers there as he stooped over whatever he was reading.

She hesitated when he didn't give more than the barest level of greeting, but she wouldn't have many other options if she lost her nerve. "Do you have a minute, Tio?"

"Could it wait?" He still didn't look up.

She glanced at the door behind her and moved farther into the room so that no one in the hall could overhear. "People were talking about Francisco."

That got his attention. "Have you told Senhor Carvalho?"

She pressed her lips into a thin line.

"Cecília." Tio Aloisio stood, his expression warning enough that she had to assume he knew everything that had happened in her meeting with the first minister.

"They don't know where he is," she said quickly. "But he's trying to come back to Portugal. He had a vision."

"Or Brazil baked his mind," Tio Aloisio grumbled. "You need to tell the first minister."

"Tio... it's Cisco."

Enough conflict played over his face that Cecília dared hope he understood, but then Tio Aloisio shook his head. "He made his decision a long time ago, Cilinha. There's nothing we can do for him."

"You could watch the docks. He has to be on a ship, don't you think? If you found him first, we could send him back—"

"And he would turn right back around as soon as he made landfall. You know your brother. If he wants to martyr himself, he will. No good will come from taking ourselves down with him."

"But—"

"Report this, or I will." He picked up his papers from the desk and moved back to his room without giving her the chance to reply.

Cecília chewed on the inside of her cheek, running through what other choices she might still have whose names *weren't* John. *There's still a shipwreck.*

She released a sharp breath, but there truly didn't seem to be any better options than praying that Francisco found himself anywhere else but Lisbon.

I don't want him hurt. Just... not here.

And you're going to Hell, the voice in her head insisted.

Pressing her lips together tightly, Cecília fingered the cross around her neck, not fully able to argue the point. At least she suddenly had a better reason for attending the Hours. Whatever she was or wasn't going to tell Senhor Carvalho, she genuinely needed to pray for Francisco and for her own soul.

"AMEN." CECÍLIA CROSSED herself, the action automatic as she neared her third week of daily services. As one day dragged into the next, the routine wavered between comforting and dreary, no two services feeling quite the same. As they'd made it through the second week with no news about Francisco, she had finally stopped trying to figure out what she felt about everything, mumbling her way through the responses and continuously shaking her head whenever Father Moreno sent her hopeful glances. If she could just keep things going the same way they had been—going to chapel, giving Senhor Carvalho bland reports that he disliked but accepted about how her brother was still missing but likely trying to make it back to Portugal—she might actually make it through everything with some modicum of sanity.

As she stood, she felt Father Moreno's eyes on her. Cecília looked up to shake her head once again, answering the unasked question, but the priest was making his way down the aisle toward her.

Meu Deus... Cecília vaguely wondered if she had cursed herself, daring to think things might actually be fine.

"You wished to make confession, child?" Father Moreno asked, voice light as he glanced at the other courtiers still lingering in the chapel.

Cecília almost groaned, as the overly casual way he was attempting to stand, paired with the glancing, made him look far more suspicious than if he had simply stood there. She sent up a quick prayer that he wanted to see what she knew about Francisco, but instinct told her there was something else, something new. *Heaven save us all.*

Knowing it was pointless to attempt avoiding it, she silently turned for the confessional and stepped into her side of the cabinet. *Bless me, Father, for I have sinned...*

Father Moreno didn't hesitate, speaking nearly as soon as he had shut the cabinet on his side. "I've heard from Father Durante."

Of course you have. Cecília squeezed her eyes shut. She tried not to sound as anxious as she felt. "Oh?"

"He is in Lisbon, staying with some friends."

Cecília didn't dare ask what friends.

"You have been to Junqueira Prison before, I believe?"

That memory slammed into Cecília's chest, surprising her enough that she lost her breath for a second. She didn't need to think about Luís when she was already dealing with whatever Francisco was attempting.

"Years ago?" Father Moreno prompted at her silence.

"Yes, Father," Cecília managed, forcing herself to draw a proper breath.

"The first minister gave you a letter of passage?"

She certainly didn't like where the conversation was headed. Hesitantly, she said, "He did."

"Do you still have it?"

Honestly, she couldn't remember what she had done after she had visited Luís. That entire evening—the entire rest of that week—was one large blur leading up to that singular, ungodly clear memory of the scaffolding, Luís's stubbornly determined look, and the nausea... She squeezed her eyes shut. "I'm not sure. It was two years—"

"Could you look?" Father Moreno's question came out too rushed.

"Why?"

"It would greatly aid your brother. He needs to make it into the prison if he is to complete his divine mission."

"And he wants *my* letter?" She had to imagine he would attempt to scratch out the original information, but Senhor Carvalho would know in an instant where he had gotten it if—or perhaps when—Francisco was caught, and then Cecília would be up on the scaffolding along with him.

"He was hesitant about bringing you into it," Father Moreno said. "I'm certain he doesn't want to put you in any danger."

Or more rightfully, he's suspicious of me.

"But I told him how devoutly you have been praying for his safety. Certainly you wish to see him successful?"

Cecília avoided the question. "I don't even know if I still have that letter, Father."

"Will you look and tell me at None? If you can find it, we can get it to Father Durante tonight."

"Tonight?" Surprise made her voice squeak.

"He was so delayed arriving, there really is no time to waste. The new inquisitor general"—Father Moreno's tone turned darker at the mention of Father Carvalho—"does not intend to wait, it seems."

Cecília's mind turned over, trying to work out a plan even as she spoke. "Can I see him? Francisco?"

Father Moreno hesitated for the first time since they had reached the confessional. "That likely isn't wise, my child."

She couldn't debate that, but if she couldn't see him, she didn't have any chance to try to stop him, and that would leave implicating herself in the plot to try to keep him from being caught or turning him over to the mercy of Senhor Carvalho, and neither option was anything close to acceptable. "I won't give the letter to anyone but him."

"Child—"

"I won't," she said, leaving no room for argument.

Father Moreno released a weary breath but said, "I will see if that can be engineered. We will speak at None?"

"Yes, Father." Cecília opened the cabinet door and slipped away. Attempting to carefully measure her steps, she moved toward the door of the chapel. Still, with each inch she put between herself and the confessional, her heart began to beat faster. She already knew she couldn't tell Senhor Carvalho what she had heard, even if it would likely be enough to free her from reporting—it was proof that Father Malagrida was attempting to avoid the Inquisition, that he knew he was a heretic. She wouldn't take thirty pieces of silver for her brother's life. But even if she could convince Francisco to see her, Heavens knew what she would be able to say to convince him to abandon his plans altogether. She hadn't seen Francisco in years, but she couldn't imagine Brazil had softened his convictions, not if he was already willing to risk death for what he believed was a divine mission.

Who says it isn't? You?

Cecília froze, considering when she had decided that she didn't believe Francisco was being divinely guided. The idea certainly shouldn't have been absurd. He was a priest. He had given his life in service to the Church. If God did wish for someone to save Father

Malagrida, there was no reason He wouldn't have called on Francisco.

But something inside Cecília wouldn't let her believe it. Perhaps she couldn't believe God cared so little that *everything* was some natural law He'd sparked off, but at some point in the past years, she had unthinkingly chosen her side. She had chosen doubt over faith. She crossed herself, halfheartedly asking for any forgiveness she might need, but if she was wrong, she was already damned. There seemed to be little reason to let her brother die on the off chance that *he* was right.

Of course, that didn't solve the problem of getting Francisco to agree to return to Brazil. Cecília certainly wouldn't have been able argue him out of anything. She would have been lucky if he let her get another word out after he learned she wasn't giving him the letter, and she couldn't *force* him to listen to her. She wouldn't exactly be able to overpower him, after all. And she couldn't imagine many people would be willing to help her physically drag him off and tie him up somewhere until she had more of a plan. He was still a priest. That would still mean *something*, at least to anyone at court who wouldn't run immediately to Senhor Carvalho and report on her.

Except... She was back to John. She had been careful to keep a wide berth from him, even when their speaking would look innocuous, but she had to believe his offer to help was still good. She had certainly felt him watching her at the full-court dinners as though he was attempting to divine what was happening, even if she'd made a point not to look back. And if there ever was a time when having a Protestant for a friend would come in handy, it had to be when planning to physically attack a priest.

She bunched up the fabric of her skirt in her fists hard enough that the silk brocade would no doubt be puckered once she released them. She would still never forgive herself if something happened to him, but in her sea of awful possible outcomes, John was likely the only option she had left. Anyway, he worked for the diplomatic corps. Even as much power as the first minister had, he couldn't execute a British citizen with simply the snap of his fingers.

He couldn't execute a priest, either, but he's found a way around that. It will be Luís all over again.

She locked her jaw, but in more ways than one, John wasn't Luís. Tio Aloisio had been derisive about how John had gotten through life, but anyone would have to say that John was a survivor. She couldn't see him willingly martyring himself purely off principle or judging her for doing what she needed to survive—at least no more than she already was judging herself.

You'd still be putting him at risk.

From what he had said, he wouldn't care, which somehow made it worse. He would help simply because she'd requested it, no questions asked, no idea what he was actually facing.

Unless you tell him the truth. The full truth.

As simple as the idea was, it hit her like an epiphany. She could stop trying to do everything by herself, tell John exactly what was happening, and let him decide what to do. It wouldn't make anything less dire, but if he still decided to help, he would be going in with eyes wide open.

Her mind made up, she turned toward the diplomatic corps' hallway. John had only given her a vague description of where his room was the last time she had seen him. And with the sun just down, there was no saying whether he was even in his room at all rather than finishing up work for the day or off playing cards or whatever the other English diplomats did with their time. She would just have to hope he was dressing for dinner or already retired for the night.

Only a handful of men were in the halls, and none gave her a second glance as she strode past as though she belonged there. The much demurer black gown likely helped. Finally, she found what she prayed was the correct door—third from the end on the left—and knocked.

The door opened quickly, as though John had been expecting someone, before surprise flashed over his face. "Cecília."

If someone else was coming, being found inside would no doubt look compromising, but standing out in the hall for anyone to see seemed the worse of the two options. "May I come in?"

His eyebrows furrowed, but he stepped back to leave the doorway open.

She moved inside, her eyes sweeping the room. It was one of the smallest she had seen at the Real Barraca and sparsely furnished with a simple wood-framed bed, a square trunk sitting at the end of it, and two small desks with chairs.

"Do I need to leave before your bedfellow returns?" she asked.

"What?"

"Two desks?"

"Oh, it's just me for the moment. Though I was about to leave to meet some friends."

Less than a month, and he already has friends. Cecília kept herself from shaking her head. Four years at court, and she wasn't sure there was anyone she would have called more than a casual acquaintance. She tried to release some of the tension in her shoulders, all the same. "I won't stay long."

"I can certainly reschedule, if you'd like."

"No, I shouldn't stay long anyway. Just..."

He waited for her to find something to say.

She finally settled on, "I am in trouble. At least I could be."

John's expression remained serious, but there was no hint of surprise. "Would you like to sit?"

"It won't take long to explain." Well, it would have taken too long to fully explain. She decided just to explain one part. "I need your help, if you're still willing to give it."

"Gladly. With what?"

"Kidnapping a priest?" Her voice tipped up uncertainly.

He blinked for a few seconds, seeming to need a minute to fully comprehend what she'd said before he shook his head. "How could I refuse a proposition like that? Any particular priest?"

"My brother. Francisco. You remember him?"

"Oh, I remember him." His tone of voice said they were not particularly fond memories.

With an unsteady breath, Cecília launched into the full explanation—or at least everything she could fit into the short time they had. Everything she had been keeping to herself came pouring out at once: the spying, Father Malagrida, the Inquisition, Francisco's supposed vision. To his credit, John listened to it all without commentary. "So I don't have anyone else to ask, and Cisco isn't going to listen to me. The only way I can keep him from getting himself killed is if I can force him somewhere and keep him there long enough to get through to him."

"Hence the kidnapping."

She nodded.

"What time do you need me?"

Cecília hesitated, the completely casual way he asked throwing her. "You'd possibly be risking your life, helping me."

"More likely my job," he said. "And it if comes down to that or you, I'm more than willing to chance it."

"John—"

"I already said I would help, Cecília," he said, his voice certain in a way she wished she could feel. "Now, what do you need me to do?"

CECÍLIA SCARCELY DARED to breathe until she made it back to her own hall and into her rooms. John had been more than agreeable to her entire crazy plan, even if she had come up with most of it on the spot, but there was still more to do before she saw Francisco. By some divine providence, Tio Aloisio was out, letting her pass the antechamber without having to pretend nothing had happened. Blowing out a breath, she rested against the door of her bedroom, trying to keep her mind steady. She had willing help, but she still needed to keep herself together. Everything would be lost if she dissolved, and she would have to be back in the chapel far too soon.

In the years she had been at court, she had managed to collect an odd assortment of effects, mostly things Tio Aloisio either hadn't managed to sell or had gifted to her from his cargo trades. She couldn't remember where he had gotten the dark-stained wooden furniture that filled out the space, but she moved to the little vanity sitting near the window and started riffling through the drawers. An assortment of jars and knickknacks that should have been cleared out long ago cluttered the space. She didn't pause until she found an old stack of papers. Buried among the mess was what she was looking for, the letter she had no doubt thrown in that drawer and done her best to forget after that awful day when she had visited Luís. It was all coming back to haunt her.

Her first instinct told her to burn the damned thing. She could tell Father Moreno it had been lost over the years, and they could come up with some other crazy plan to get themselves killed. Instead, she carefully folded it once again and slipped it into the middle of the papers. She obviously couldn't give it to Francisco, but she couldn't bring herself to destroy it, either, just in case. Of course, she couldn't show up empty-handed. She picked up a blank piece of stationary, steadied the slight tremor in her hands, and folded it carefully into thirds. It wouldn't fool anyone for long, but it also meant that no one would be able to say she was attempting to help Francisco with any sort of coded message or whatever else the first minister's men might say if everything went wrong and they were all captured.

Querido Santo Judeu, she sent up a quick prayer to the patron of desperate cases and lost causes, just on the off chance that *someone* was still listening to her. *Please help us all get out of this alive. Please.* And as always, the silence that answered sounded deafening.

Chapter Twenty-Seven

"Behind the chapel, after Matins."

Father Moreno hadn't given Cecília more direction than that, but there she was, standing outside in the middle of the night, waiting. She fidgeted with her dress, trying to keep the jumpiness from hitting her legs as every creak or gust of wind made her half expect Senhor Carvalho's guards to come storming out to arrest her. Even the fact that John was hidden in the shadows no more than a few arms' lengths away and no doubt would tell her if anyone were to come up behind her didn't help dispel the nervous energy coursing through every inch of her. Every second felt like an eon as she waited for Francisco to appear. She glanced up at the half-moon in the sky, wishing it would tell her the time as she gave in to tapping her foot.

Finally, the back door pushed open, and a shape moved into the darkness. Cecília's heart stopped for a moment before she realized it was too short to be Francisco.

"Father Moreno?" she whispered.

The tension visible in the man's shoulders relaxed an inch. "Good, you're here."

She tried to see into the shadows behind him. "Is Francisco?"

Father Moreno leaned back inside, and a moment later, a man in a monk's habit stepped through the door. Though his face was hidden with the cowl pulled far over his head, the new man somehow moved how Cecília remembered Francisco did.

She started to step forward before she realized she would box John off if she got too close to the building, and she rocked back again. He wouldn't have been able to do anything while Father Moreno was still there, since the half-baked plan they had developed depended on John being able to catch Francisco alone and by surprise, stopping any real fight, but she couldn't block the way. She tried to keep her voice level. "Cisco? Father Durante?"

The man pushed the cowl back enough for Cecília to see her brother's face, thickly bearded, tanned, and hardened, but undoubtedly Francisco. Cecília couldn't help herself—she threw her arms around his neck to hug him.

Francisco didn't return the gesture, instead letting her embrace him for a moment before he caught her waist and forced her a few steps back. "Do you have the letter?"

Cecília pulled out the folded piece of stationary she had brought but held it back when Francisco reached to take it. The second he unfolded it, he would no doubt be gone. "Could we speak?"

"This isn't the time, Cecília." Francisco frowned. "Give it here."

"I will after you talk to me." Cecília took another step back, angling so Francisco would entirely have his back to John if he faced her head-on.

"Cecília, this isn't a game," Francisco said firmly.

"I didn't think it was." She glanced at Father Moreno. "Could I have a moment with my brother, Father?"

Francisco began to admonish her again, but Father Moreno lowered his head an inch and stepped back inside. Cecília could only pray he'd moved far enough away not to hear any scuffle. She should have assumed Francisco wouldn't have arrived alone—one more for the long list of things she *should* have thought through when she'd passed the plan along to John earlier. If only she'd had the time.

"Please listen." Cecília didn't wait for him to finish his little lecture. "You've been gone. Senhor Carvalho has control of *everything*. The government, the Inquisition... if you try to move against him, you won't survive."

"I am doing God's work, Cecília."

She could nearly *hear* John's eyes rolling in the darkness. "Father Malagrida isn't the man you knew, Cisco. He's gone mad. Yes, there's no reason for the first minister to spare the man a thought other than pure vengeance, but that is on Senhor Carvalho's soul. There's nothing anyone else can do to help Father Malagrida."

"I know Aloisio has been working to corrupt your mind for years, but don't question the will of God, Cecília Madalena. Give me the letter." He snatched the paper from her hand before Cecília could pull back again.

"Cisco." She stepped closer.

"What is this?" Francisco's eyes moved over the blank paper, his forehead creasing. "What do you think—"

John cut off the rest of the sharp question, locking his arms tightly around Francisco's neck. Cecília's stomach clenched as Francisco thrashed for a few seconds then finally went limp. John pulled Francisco back into the shadows then pulled out a rope.

"What did you do?" Cecília took a few hesitant steps forward.

"Choked him out." John fished a knotted rag from another pocket then handed it to Cecília. "Get that in his mouth. He'll come back around in a few seconds. I doubt he'll be pleased when he realizes what's happened."

Cecília released a tense breath through her teeth but bent to tie the gag around Francisco's head, the knot fitting unsettlingly well in his mouth.

Making short work of Francisco's hands and feet, John hefted Francisco over his shoulder with a grunt then nodded for Cecília to follow him around the edge of the Real Barraca. As John had said, Francisco began to stir before they made it halfway to the door closest to the diplomatic corps' hallway. Cecília saw his head move languidly, as though he were too dizzy to fully make sense of things, before something clicked. He jerked, making John sway to maintain balance, and mumbled words into the gag.

John gave another annoyed grunt as he shifted his grip. "Listen, *Padre*, there are a lot of people in this palace who want to do much worse to you than your sister here, so I'd keep quiet if I were you. We're just going somewhere you can have a nice chat."

Whether Francisco fully understood what was happening or not, he seemed to grasp the wisdom of not waking Heavens knew who in the palace and calmed enough for them to reach John's room.

"Door." John nodded Cecília forward.

She pulled it open, the soft scrape of the wood on the ground sounding like a gunshot to her panicked mind, but they somehow made it inside without incident. There were no Carvalho guards, no priests looking for Francisco, and no confused diplomats wondering what in the Good Lord's name was happening in their hallway.

Unceremoniously, John deposited Francisco onto a chair he'd obviously had the foresight to move away from its desk. John shook his head as he rubbed his shoulder. "Either working here's making me soft, or your brother's heavier than he looks."

Not certain what to say, Cecília ended up murmuring, "*Padre* is Spanish again."

"I'm aware," he said, leaving her to assume that dealing with Francisco again was bringing out John's irritable side.

She could only hope he managed to control it long enough for them to get something done. She attempted to offer her brother a small smile but then caught the glare he was giving them, and she felt nearly frozen solid where she stood, just inside the door.

Apparently recovered, John bent to attach Francisco solidly to the chair with yet more rope he had gotten from Lord knew where before he met Francisco's eyes. "Now, if I remove that gag, can I trust you'll be calm and have a nice, gentlemanly conversation with your sister?"

Francisco's eyes narrowed.

Cecília shifted awkwardly between her feet. "Take it off. Making a racket in this part of the palace would be worse for him than us."

John glanced at her. "As you wish."

Francisco spat the knotted fabric out the second it went loose enough. "You will burn in Hell! Attacking a man of God. You—"

"All due respect, if you lot are right, I'd be burning long before this."

Francisco studied John's face in the low light before recognition seemed to hit him. "You're that Englishman. From the camp."

John lowered his head—in assent or greeting, Cecília didn't know. "I apologize it isn't a more congenial reunion."

Francisco's jaw clenched, his eyes swinging to Cecília. "Is *that* what living with Aloisio has done to you? Turned you into some Englishman's whore?"

"I believe I said *gentlemanly*." John's shoulders tensed.

"Is it untrue?" Francisco returned.

"Mr. Bates." Cecília sent him a warning look. What small chance she had at convincing Francisco to listen to her wasn't going to be helped if he and John got into an argument. "Could I have a moment with my brother, please?"

John's mouth pinched at the dismissal, but he didn't argue. "Of course. I'll be right outside."

Cecília waited for him to leave the room before she forced herself to move closer to Francisco. "Cisco."

"If you do not release me at once, you will burn in Hell along with that Protestant." He somehow made the word *Protestant* sound like the worst insult of all.

Cecília swallowed, but it wasn't the first time he had said something like that, and it was rather late to waver in her choices. She'd had to accept Hell as a possibility long before then, after all. "If I release you, you're going to get yourself killed."

"There are things far worse than death, Cecília. I would think you would have realized that by now, as much time as you have supposedly spent in prayer. But no, this is Bibiana all over again. You with Aloisio and that Englishman, worried more about our petty lives than God's will."

"We're all we have left, Cisco. You, me, and Bibiana. I'm supposed to just leave you to die?"

"If it is God's will, I am more than willing to die. I'm certain Bibiana would feel the same. You were never called to the Church, so perhaps you don't understand, but you were raised well enough to know what is right and wrong."

I'm doing my best to figure that out. She pressed her lips tightly together. "Can't you go back to Brazil? Your missionary work must have been—"

"I was *called* here, Cecília. Now *let me go.*"

"I can't," she said. "Not until you agree to go back to Brazil."

"You question God's judgment."

"I question *your* judgment," Cecília snapped.

"I am a priest."

"And not the pope. You aren't infallible."

Francisco stared at her, shook his head, then closed his eyes, mumbling under his breath. It took a moment for Cecília to realize he was praying.

Grinding her teeth, Cecília sent her own glance skyward, but she had to imagine there would be no help coming there, though divine intervention was likely the only way she was going to change Francisco's mind anytime soon. But she had managed to stop him from doing anything that night. What to do from there, however, was another *should* that she had missed. *Piecing everything together like this isn't going to end well.*

With Francisco otherwise occupied, she slipped out the door.

John straightened from where he was leaning against the wall. "That isn't a pleased expression."

Cecília shook her head. "How long do you think we can keep him in there?"

"He's not going to work those knots free, the way he was pulling on them, but there are a lot of men on this hallway. Someone likely will notice something amiss sooner rather than later. More than a day would be remarkable. And even that, risky, especially if the other priests are looking for him."

She blew out a tense breath, having to agree with the assessment. Every minute he was in the Real Barraca was one in which they all risked their lives. "We need to get him out of the palace. Save São João interceding, I'm not going to convince him to go overnight."

"Does your uncle have a house in town?"

She shook her head. "Nothing's been rebuilt there yet. And he wouldn't help, anyway."

"His own nephew?"

"I asked him for help before I even knew Francisco wanted to meet. He said to tell Senhor Carvalho. Going to him is as good as going to the first minister."

John pursed his lips slightly as he thought. "The docks?"

Cecília frowned. "What about them?"

"I told you, those ropes will hold him long enough to go wherever we need. If you put him on a ship back to Brazil, you don't need to convince him. It takes, what, five or six weeks from here to Brazil? You'd have three months before he could even make it back once again, and that's if there's a ship he can immediately take once they dock. It would likely be longer. Surely, things will be more settled by then?"

She considered. It was hardly a perfect solution, but it was more time—and likely the best they could manage by themselves. "You think we could find a ship that would take a bound man aboard?"

"You haven't spent much time down at the docks, have you, love?" The corners of John's mouth tipped up, though the good humor didn't fully reach his eyes. "Find the right hand to put enough coin in down there, and I'm sure you could find someone willing to do more than just transport your brother."

Leaving Francisco to a man like that didn't make Cecília feel wonderful, but even a bought man would be better than the first minister. "Do you have any money?"

John grimaced. "Some, but not much."

Cecília didn't, either. Living at court, she had never needed coinage. The crown, or perhaps the first minister, supplied most of what she needed, and she simply asked Tio Aloisio for anything else. She did, however, know where in his desk her uncle kept his purse. The commandment *thou shalt not steal* echoed through her mind, but if she already had a priest bound and gagged, it was likely a little late to go only halfway. Trying to ignore just how much penance she would have to do to begin to redeem her soul after everything that was happening, she gave a nod, much more solidly than she felt. "I can get some." She glanced at the room. "Do you think you can stay here with Francisco alone and not have it turn ugly?"

"*He* was the one insulting *you.*"

Not entirely unfairly, all things considered. She didn't bother getting into that discussion. "The last thing we need is to have someone find him because you two start arguing."

"Worse comes to worst, I could always gag him again."

The slight shrug said John was attempting to joke, but the thought only made the knot in Cecília's stomach pull tighter. She did her best not to think too hard about it. "I'll be back as soon as I can."

John nodded, his expression going serious once again. "Be careful. I'll handle things here."

With as much of a smile as she could manage, Cecília turned down the hall. As jumpy as she still felt, she only managed to keep herself from running with the thought of how much noise that would make. She couldn't imagine Father Moreno would be bold enough to come down her hallway, with it being so close to the first minister's office, but with the night half gone, their best chance of getting Francisco out of the palace unseen was quickly dwindling. She didn't need to wake anyone else.

She barely breathed as she passed Senhor Carvalho's room, her luck held out, and she made it to her door. With the curtain drawn over the single window by her uncle's desk, the antechamber was pitch black as she entered. Shuffling her feet to make sure she didn't knock into anything unexpected and wake everyone, Cecília made her way toward that side of the room. She pulled the curtain just enough to let in a sliver of moonlight and set to riffling through the drawers to find Tio Aloisio's purse. In one of the lower drawers, her fingers brushed the velvet bag. She pulled it out with a jingle and emptied the contents to see what was there. It wasn't a fortune—she imagined her uncle kept the rest of his currency somewhere more se-cure—but it was more than enough for passage to Brazil. She had to hope it was enough for passage *and* whatever bribe they would need to keep Francisco safe until he was well off the coast once again.

She had just begun to gather the coins as quietly as she could when the sound of a door opening made her freeze.

"What do you think you're doing?" Tio Aloisio stood at the threshold of his bedroom, still wearing his nightcap, the candle in his hand leaving him in a small circle of light.

Cecília's mind raced, trying to think of an answer, but nothing came to her.

"Cecília." He moved forward.

"I..." Her mind still spinning, she couldn't think of anything bet-ter than the truth at this point. "I was meeting Francisco."

Tio Aloisio stopped where he was, staring at her as though he couldn't understand the words coming out of her mouth. "You know where he is?"

She nodded.

"And you've told Senhor Carvalho?"

"If I do, Cisco is dead."

"We already had this discuss—"

"You ordering me about isn't a discussion," she snapped. "And you can stay entirely out of it, if you wish. We have things handled."

"You and your brother?"

Cecília hesitated, realizing it likely wasn't the best idea to mention John with her uncle already up in arms. "If you go back to bed and let me get on with things, he'll be on his way back to Brazil by morning. No one else needs to know."

Tio Aloisio frowned skeptically. "You've convinced him to leave?"

"I..." She swallowed, trying to make herself sound more certain than she felt. "I have things handled."

"You're playing with fire, Cecília."

"And you don't think that's better than letting *him* burn at the stake?"

"Do you believe he would do the same for you?" Tio Aloisio continued the rest of the way forward. "Has he done anything in the past five years to make you believe he wouldn't leave us both to hang if it suited him? You want to ruin us both to save someone who couldn't care less about us?"

"He's my brother."

"Francisco is your brother. That man is Father Durante. He has made that very clear."

"And if you let me go right now, neither one will have to die." She held his eyes, trying to project more confidence than she felt. "I can do this."

A flash of uncertainty, just enough to give Cecília hope, passed over Tio Aloisio's expression. A heavy knock broke in before he could respond. Cecília's hand tightened around the purse, but she otherwise found herself once again frozen in place. From Tio Aloisio's suddenly tense stance, he felt the same. A second, louder knock spurred him into action. Pulling his bed robe tighter around him with one hand, he moved to the door and pulled it open.

"Yes, yes. What is all the racket?" he asked, his tone much more indignant than Cecília would have been able to manage with her heart still in her throat.

"Please step aside," a man's voice instructed.

"I beg your pardon?" Tio Aloisio asked even as a pair of guards shouldered past him. "What is the meaning of this?"

The guards sent a suspicious look at Cecília before the one who had previously spoken directed the other toward the bedrooms. He turned back to Tio Aloisio. "Your niece and another man were seen in the company of a wanted criminal tonight."

"A *criminal*?" Surprise let Cecília's mouth move.

The guard held a paper out for Tio Aloisio to take.

Her uncle held the candle closer, reading quickly before he looked at Cecília. "Your brother has been officially exiled. He is a criminal if he's inside the country."

Cecília pressed her lips together, not certain how the first minister had convinced the king to issue that decree when Francisco hadn't actually done anything save return from what was supposedly a religious mission, but she supposed it didn't matter. She faced the guard. "There's no one here."

"Do you deny you were outside the church tonight?"

Cecília hesitated, her first instinct to deny it, but if she had already been spotted, that would have done her no good.

"There were two men?" Tio Aloisio broke in before she could think of something safe to say. Cecília snapped her eyes to him.

"So was reported," the guard said.

Tio Aloisio gave her an exasperated look that said he'd correctly guessed exactly who had helped, but he addressed the guard. "Come with me."

Cecília took a step forward. "Tio—"

"Stay," he snapped, as though she were a disobedient hound. "You have done quite enough tonight."

She still tried to object.

He spoke over her, back to the guards. "If you are looking for Father Durante, you can come with me."

The guard sent Tio Aloisio a suspicious look.

The second guard reappeared. "Nothing."

The first continued to glare for a moment before he gave a short nod and motioned for Tio Aloisio to lead.

Not bothering to ask to dress, Tio Aloisio turned for the door.

"Tio—" Cecília tried desperately to grab his arm.

He shook her off with enough force to make her stumble back. "This is for both of us," he said in a low hiss.

As the three men swept out into the hall, Cecília caught her balance and rushed forward. The shut door wouldn't budge. He'd barred her in. She pulled at the handle all the same. Though the wood rattled, it stayed shut. She hit it in frustration. She could go out the window to follow, but by the time she wrapped around the outside of the palace, the guards would already be to the diplomatic corps' hallway. John would no doubt do his best to delay them, but he would have to save himself as well. She could only hope he was right that his job was more at risk than his life. Her mind spinning too quickly to come up with a plan that wasn't simply walking herself into a noose, she placed her back against the door and slid to the ground.

Dear Lord, what do I do now?

Chapter Twenty-Eight

Cecília paced the antechamber like a caged animal, waiting. Dawn had certainly broken. The bells had rung for Lauds. She had no idea what Father Moreno had to think or if he already knew what had happened. And still, Tio Aloisio hadn't returned. She was beginning to wonder if he was purposefully avoiding her. Whatever had happened with the guards and Francisco had to have been long over by then.

Just as she was considering going out through the window, there was a scrape as whatever had been bracing the door pulled away, and Tio Aloisio stepped through.

Cecília spun toward him.

He spoke first. "Don't you dare try to explain yourself, Cecília Madalena."

"Explain *myself*?" Her voice tipped up, dangerously loud in her incredulity. "You've killed your nephew."

"I've *saved* my niece. There was already a price on Francisco's head. You don't need one placed on yours."

"I could have managed things. Gotten him out of the country—"

"How, exactly? By dragging him down to the docks and asking every ruffian you come across if he'll help? Bates might be infatuated enough to attempt your ill-conceived notions, but I can still tell you when you're trying to get yourself killed."

Anger still made Cecília want to snap at him, but the mention of John sidetracked her. "Mr. Bates... Is he...?" She couldn't think how to end that question.

"Mr. Hays will likely have a headache to deal with, and I imagine Bates will be having a much shorter stay in Lisbon than he was planning, but most likely, he'll come out the best from this entire fracas. He always has had a way of landing on his feet. You'd do best to worry after yourself."

She tried to ignore the twist in her stomach. "What about me?"

Tio Aloisio held her eyes. "I convinced the first minister I could be trusted to watch you—and that wasn't a simple feat, believe me—so you are not to leave these rooms until all of this passes."

"I'm being held prisoner?"

"If you don't wish to join your brother in Junqueira, you *will* remain here."

The thought of the prison, the awful smell, and the screams made Cecília's throat close. She fought to get her voice back, but Tio Aloisio had already moved on.

"You know the first minister is not someone who easily forgives, Cilinha, and what good will *I* have left is wearing thin. I can't save your brother, but if you just listen to me for once and do as you're told, *we* may get through this."

The sad sincerity on Tio Aloisio's face made some other emotion flicker through the righteous anger Cecília had been clinging to through the morning, leaving a sickening, unbalanced feeling inside her chest. For all her time living with him—five years of sharing a roof, conspiring together, going through some of the worst times of her life—somehow, she hadn't fully factored her uncle into her thoughts of family. The equation had always been her, Bibiana, Francisco, the last vestiges of the family she had lost, not the one who had taken her in. A fragment of guilt attempted to take hold. "How long does he want me to stay here? Until he's killed *all* the priests on the other side of the palace?"

"That isn't our business."

Cecília pressed her lips tightly together, her conscience churning.

Tio Aloisio watched her face closely. "I don't want to have to bar the exits, but I will."

"Then there isn't anything else to discuss, is there?" She crossed her arms, retreating into her anger.

Something sad went through his eyes—hurt or disappointment, Cecília didn't know—and he shook his head. "Do you at least understand why I'm doing this?"

Whether she wanted to admit it or not, she did. Silently, she gave the barest of nods.

"I suppose that's something," Tio Aloisio murmured under his breath, moving deeper into the antechamber toward his desk. With his back to her, he raised his voice to address her again. "You'd best find something to occupy yourself with. You're in for a long wait one way or the other. It'll only feel worse with nothing to do."

Worse. Cecília bit back a scoff, not certain it was possible to feel worse. But with nothing else to do, she turned on her heel and stormed off to her room.

Chapter Twenty-Nine

The twitchiness in Cecília's limbs had grown so bad that she had begun picking at the hair on her arms to keep herself from making a run for the door. Since the start of her imprisonment more than a week before and his promise that he would try to do *what he could*—whatever that even meant—Tio Aloisio had rarely been around, and no one else had been by to visit. She had to imagine that Senhor Carvalho had forbidden anyone from entering the rooms, same as he had forbidden her from leaving. She might have escaped a cell in Junqueira, but there was certainly no denying that she was a prisoner all the same. And she was being punished.

As the sun sank below the horizon once again, Cecília stood from the side of her bed and moved to the window. She pulled the bed dress tighter around her, supposing it didn't matter that she once again hadn't gotten properly dressed. She hadn't even *seen* Águeda in two days. Heaven knew where the maid had gone. Perhaps that was part of the punishment Senhor Carvalho had devised, keeping even that contact away from Cecília. But then it wasn't as though Cecília was going anywhere that required court dress, so she hardly required help dressing.

With the sky going from pink-orange to dark blue, she heaved a sigh and turned to light the lamp by her bed. She could have returned to the book she had been reading—if nothing else, Tio Aloisio had been keeping his shelf remarkably well stocked over the week—but sulking seemed like a far more appealing option.

She had just gotten the wick to catch when something tapped on the glass. She spun back toward the window. Squinting to try to see past her own weak reflection in the lamplight, she made out the shadowy shape of a man. The jump in her chest said who it was. She hurried back up to the window and lifted the latch, swinging it as widely as the chain that had been added would allow. "John?"

"You're a very difficult woman to see at the moment."

"What are you doing here?"

He started to answer before he glanced over his shoulder as though worried he had been followed, and given the circumstances, that certainly wasn't out of the question. "May I come in?"

"The window doesn't open any farther." She pulled on the frame to demonstrate.

John's eyes went to the chain before he leaned back to look down the building. "What about that one?" He pointed to his right. "That's over your uncle's desk, isn't it?"

Cecília frowned. "Do you think you'd fit?"

He judged it for a moment before nodding. "I bet I could manage, if you unlatch it."

Though the outside door was barred, there was nothing stopping her from going into the antechamber. She nodded back. "I'll meet you there."

Without another word, he slid down the side of the building, and she hurried out of her room. With as rare as her uncle's presence had been, there was no reason to believe Tio Aloisio would pick that exact moment to return, but with her luck lately, she wasn't willing to chance being caught.

Though the rectangular window didn't look as wide as John's shoulders were broad, he somehow managed to maneuver his way through, using the desk as a step down to the floor. Cecília opened her mouth to ask another question before she checked the door to the hall and grabbed his hand to lead him into her room. There perhaps wouldn't be an easy escape if Tio Aloisio returned while John was inside, but he could at least hide there, unlike in the antechamber.

She didn't speak until the door was safely shut behind them. "Now, what are you doing here?"

"You aren't pleased to see me?"

"Of course I am." After a week of near isolation, she nearly would have been glad to see Senhor Carvalho, let alone John. "But you could get into a lot of trouble, being here."

"They're already shipping me out in the morning. I'm not sure there's much else anyone here could do to me."

The matter-of-fact way he said it somehow made the information worse, settling into Cecília's stomach like a lead weight. "You came to say goodbye, then?"

He hesitated for a beat. "Only if you don't wish to come with me."

Cecília blinked, the words taking a minute to make sense. "Go with you?"

"They haven't actually told me what's coming once I reach London—it's really anyone's guess if I still have a job or not—so not an ideal situation by any means, but if you and your brother need to get out of the country..."

She shook her head. "Francisco is in prison. Senhor Carvalho isn't going to let him leave the country. It's doubtful he would let me, if we asked."

"So we don't ask." John shrugged as though it were the simplest thing in the world. "You have a letter to get into the prison, don't you? That's what your brother wanted?"

"You're suggesting we break Francisco out of Junqueira Prison?"

"Sounds like an adventure to me."

"Possibly getting killed is an adventure?"

"What do you think sailing is?" He gave one of his lopsided smiles before continuing. "It's your decision, of course, but I have a ship leaving port come morning. I was hoping to at least take you, if not you and your brother. I imagine you'd prefer that to waiting in here for the first minister to have a good day and agree to release you?"

For the first time in weeks, something like hope moved through her chest. She moved to the drawer with her papers and pulled out the letter Senhor Carvalho had given her two and a half years before. "This is what Francisco wanted."

John moved up beside her and looked at the paper from over her shoulder. "It looks simple enough. We change the date on it, and I don't think we'll have any issue getting in."

She chewed on the inside of her cheek, trying to play out all the possibilities if they actually attempted a rescue. Of course, the guards at Junqueira probably cared less about people trying to break *into* the prison. "Getting out is likely the more difficult part."

"Could we forge something for that? We have the first minister's signature there. We could make some sort of order to move your brother."

"And any guard would believe the people Senhor Carvalho sent to move him were an Englishman and a girl?" She turned her head to look at John.

He pursed his lips slightly, saying he couldn't argue the point. "We need to sneak out, then?"

"It's a prison. I don't think there are a lot of windows to go out of."

"Wasn't it damaged in the quake? Perhaps we could find a fracture or something that hasn't been fixed yet?"

Cecília opened her mouth to answer before the thought hit her. "I know where the plans are."

"What?"

"The plans for rebuilding the prison. They would include what parts are still damaged. We could use those to find a way out."

John's eyebrows rose as he nodded. "Where are they?"

"If we're lucky, the architects' office. If not, Senhor Ventura has them."

"Who?"

"The man I was speaking to when you first arrived."

"Ah." Recognition moved over his expression. "So it shouldn't be a problem even if he does have them."

She shook her head at his tone. "You are going to sound jealous, Mr. Bates, if you aren't careful. And for no good reason. I don't think he's going to go out of his way to help me off two conversations weeks ago."

"I don't know. You're very convincing when you wish to be."

She sent him an unamused look but moved on. "Do you know where the architects' office is?"

"I can't say I've ever been."

"And you likely aren't familiar with architectural plans."

"They haven't been my field of study, no."

With the architects so close to Senhor Carvalho's office, it certainly wasn't a safe place for Cecília to go. But if the first minister already knew John was working with her, someone finding him stumbling around trying to find what they needed wouldn't be any better for her. If they were going to stupidly risk their lives by trying to break Francisco out of prison, she would have to begin by stupidly risking her life by sneaking into the architects' office.

"Help me dress?" She opened the chest at the foot of her bed to pull out something that was decent for the halls but less cumbersome than full court dress. "You can change the letter while I look for those plans then meet me in the gardens. Where we went last time?"

Though she wasn't looking at him, she could hear the frown in his tone. "You don't want me to come with you?"

"People would likely notice us more moving together." *And you'd still be able to stay out of it if I do get caught before we even leave the palace.* She undid the tie to her bed dress and draped it over the chair at her vanity before picking up her stays. "Help me?"

"I'm not sure I make the best lady's maid." He moved up behind her all the same.

"Just do the opposite of taking them off."

"You believe I have a lot of experience with that?"

"You managed fine the first day we met." She looked at him over her shoulder.

He met her eyes for a moment before he dropped his gaze to the stays and began lacing them. "This likely isn't the moment to get distracted, unfortunately."

Cecília felt herself flush more than she imagined she should with their history and looked forward again. "I don't know where my uncle is, but we shouldn't linger."

"And you should pack what you can." He pulled the laces a little tighter than they needed to be but managed to get the stays up. "I doubt you'll be able to come back once someone notices you're missing."

The reality of what they were attempting hit like a blow to the stomach. Still, she nodded. "Get started with the letter. I can manage the rest of my clothing." *I think.* "Then I'll grab a few things."

After putting on something that could be called decent, Cecília returned to her chest and pulled out everything she thought she might need that would also be simple enough to carry. Her jewelry, she could easily enough fit in her pockets along with a few other knickknacks she had collected over the years. She would have to live with just the dress on her back, as anything more elaborate would be too cumbersome. *But then I won't need court dress if we aren't at court.*

She reached the little box she hadn't seen inside in more than a year. Opening it, she pulled out the little misshapen São Cristóvão and slipped that into her pocket as well. *Leviathan* she could leave with the other banned books on her uncle's bookshelf, and the letters John had written five years ago... She picked up both and moved to the other papers she had in her vanity.

"What're those?" John asked.

"Things I'd rather no one go through if they come in here." She took the entire stack of pages and tossed them into the unlit fireplace. Using the flame from her lamp, she set the papers alight. The rest of the room would likely be torn apart, everything that was left confiscated, but at least all those records and thoughts would be gone, hers alone. Giving a satisfied nod, she turned away from the growing flames. "I'll leave the lamp lit. With any luck, Tio Aloisio will think I'm still here, if he comes back. Do you think you can help me out the window over the desk? I can't go out the front."

"You're sure you don't want me to come with you?"

She nodded, trying to look far more certain than she felt. "Just meet me in the garden."

John didn't look any more enthusiastic about the plan, but he didn't argue as he turned for the antechamber.

With his back to her, Cecília took the chance to cross herself, glancing up at the ceiling as she offered a weak prayer then slipped her hand into her pocket. São Cristóvão hadn't done anything to protect Papai or João, but perhaps he'd keep her, John, and Francisco safe—half-melted or not.

THE ARCHITECTS' OFFICE looked exactly the same as the last time Cecília had been there, and the normalcy of it left her unsettled. Her heart beating in her throat, she forced herself deeper inside the room to what she recalled was Senhor Ventura's desk.

Thank you, Santo Expedito. She released a relieved breath as she saw Senhor Ventura's portfolio resting against the table legs. In one motion, she scooped it up and began flicking her way through pages of equations and designs. Finally, she found plans—the new European designs for the buildings going up in the Baixa, the archway that would mark the new riverside plaza, and the prison. She pulled the last free with a jerk, scanning the markings in the dim light. When she had asked to learn what the architects were doing, she hadn't thought she'd be using the knowledge to be able to break out of a prison. From what she saw on the page, though, she had learned exactly what she needed to be able to do so. As she folded the plans to slip them away, the office door opened.

Cecília froze and found herself staring right at Senhor Ventura.

He recoiled slightly in surprise before he seemed to register who it was. "Senhorita Durante."

"Senhor Ventura." She did her best to recover, giving as blithe a smile as she could manage. "I hope you don't mind my poking through your things. I was running short on reading material, and I remembered you offered to let me see your plans."

"Of course." He stepped fully into the room. "I imagine it must make for some long days, being quarantined."

Quarantined. She repeated the word in her head. So the rest of the court didn't necessarily know what had happened, then.

"You're feeling better, though?"

"Certainly on the mend"—she fell into the lie—"but I'm still not supposed to be out. I should get back. Would it be a problem if I took this for the evening? I really need something to do." She slowly started for the door, not intending to give it back even if he disagreed.

"Feel free." He turned to continue facing her. "I could come and explain what we're doing, even, if you'd like."

"I'd feel awful if I got you ill. In a few days, perhaps?"

"I look forward to it." He nodded with enough enthusiasm that Cecília had to fight down a new wave of guilt. She would just have to be careful that, if they were unlucky enough to get caught, she got rid of the plans before anyone found them. Keeping Senhor Ventura from being dragged into the mess was the very least she could do for the man. There were already too many people at risk with what she was doing. He walked with her to the door. "Might I walk you back to your room?"

Dear Lord, no. She kept her smile in place. "I'd love that, but like I said, I'm not supposed to be out yet. My uncle would have a fit if he saw me talking to someone."

Disappointment moved over his face, but he accepted the answer with a polite bow. "In a few days, then."

"A few days," she agreed. *When we'll be well on our way to England, I hope.*

Doing her best not to look too suspicious, she poked her head out into the hallway to check that no one was outside the first minister's office before she quickly ducked around the corner to the outside door. She made it to the hedges in record time.

John met her as soon as she turned out of sight of the palace. "I was beginning to worry."

"I have it." Cecília didn't feel the need to recount what had just happened. "You're certain you want to do this?"

"As long as you are."

She released a tense breath but steeled her resolve. "We should go, then?"

John nodded and let her turn halfway before he caught her wrist and pulled her in for a searing kiss.

She blinked up at him as he broke it.

"For good luck." He gave a weak half smile. *And in case we don't make it out of this*—the silent addendum seemed to hover between them. "Let's go. If I recall, it's a long walk into Lisbon."

Chapter Thirty

Junqueira Prison rose as imposingly as ever, even if it was just a shadow against the blue-black sky. Cecília slowed next to John as they made it through the final streets, her legs already tingling unpleasantly from the long walk after so much sitting around.

"We should hurry," John said, his voice just loud enough for her to hear. "Things aren't going to get any safer."

Cecília nodded, suddenly not feeling able to speak as her stomach went into knots.

The guard at the front door stiffened as John and Cecília approached, shifting the musket in his hands. "Halt. State your business."

John pulled the doctored letter from his jacket. "We need to speak with a prisoner here."

"No visiting at night." The guard made no move to take it. "Come back in the morning."

"This letter is from the first minister." John kept the letter out for the guard. "Would you like me to contact him and see if *he* wishes to wait?"

A flash of apprehension moved over the guard's face before he snatched the letter and looked it over. After a beat, he called over his shoulder for another guard from inside and pressed the letter into the second man's hands. "Take them in."

The second guard glanced down at the paper then nodded. "With me."

If anything, the halls of the prison felt smaller at night, the distance between the lanterns along the hall leaving long splotches of darkness to walk through. Cecília tried not to breathe through her nose, as the smell was even worse than she remembered—especially with the guard leading them down into the bowels of Junqueira Prison rather than up. Cecília could only be glad there were no awful cries.

They reached the bottom of the stairs, and an odd thumping sound started.

"What's that?" Cecília asked before she caught herself.

The guard snorted. "The mad priest. Between his ravings, he throws himself into things. Here." He moved up to one of the doors and pulled the panel open.

The hollow thumping grew louder, and perverse curiosity drew Cecília forward. With his long white hair fanned out in a ratty mane around his head, the man inside looked every bit the lunatic Cecília had been told Father Malagrida had become. Gone was the imposing figure who had enraptured crowds in the campos outside Lisbon. The poor broken man sitting inside, beating his head against the rough stone wall, didn't look as though he would have been able to draw a mosquito's attention, let alone a crowd's. She had to wonder if Senhor Carvalho had actually seen the priest in the past few years. If he had, she couldn't imagine what the first minister expected to gain from sending the Inquisition after him. Setting Father Malagrida loose to wander the streets as a crazed beggar would likely do more to drive away what followers he still had than convicting him of heresy.

"If you don't mind, we're in a hurry." John's voice brought her back to the present.

"Right." The guard let the flap close again and moved down a different cramped hallway. "This is who you're here to see?"

As the man pulled the next flap out of the way, Cecília caught a glimpse of her brother, looking nearly as haggard as Father Malagrida but thankfully much saner. "Ye—" she started to answer before the guard jerked, and she realized John had his arm locked around the guard's neck as he had Francisco's before. Quickly enough, the guard went limp as well, and John let him slide to the floor.

"It didn't seem the time for a fair fight," John answered her wide eyes before quickly binding the man's hands.

"It is a little disconcerting how adept you are at that."

"I told you, docks aren't always the safest places." John finished with the length of rope and started to pat down the guard's clothes. He came up with a key. "Ready?"

Cecília couldn't say she was, but they were in much too far to hesitate.

Francisco's head jerked up as the door opened, surprise making him look more like the brother she remembered for a split second before his eyes narrowed. "You."

She supposed she shouldn't have expected any more of a welcome. "We've come to save you."

"*I'm* not the one who needs saving." His eyes flicked between John and Cecília, not looking the least bit happier with either of them.

You're going to die. Cecília didn't bother to make the obvious argument. It had gone nowhere before. It didn't seem there'd be any reason for Francisco to listen to it now.

"I have more rope," John murmured, "though carrying him would slow us down."

"*You* stay away from me." Somehow Francisco made just that *you* sound like an insult.

A sound in the hall said the guard was coming back around. *We don't have time for this...* A new thought that just might work popped to mind. "Father Malagrida is down the hall."

Francisco finally paused long enough for her to continue.

"You wanted to get inside here, didn't you? To find Father Malagrida? The guard just showed us where he is, right down the hall."

Francisco stood. "You can't pretend you intended this."

"Are you going to question God's ways?"

He kept his eyes narrowed, but he moved for the door. "Where is he?"

"Cecília," John said in a warning tone.

"Trust me," she hissed before motioning Francisco forward to the cell they had just left. If anything, the thumping had only intensified. She pulled the flap back and moved far enough back to let Francisco see. "*That's* Father Malagrida."

Francisco stepped up to the door, alarm cracking the disdain visible on his face.

"He's mad. You bring him out of this prison, he's as likely to walk straight into the Tagus and drown himself as change anything."

Francisco shook his head slightly. "That can't be him."

"If *I* know it is, you must." Cecília glanced down the hall to see John once again wrestling down the guard. He sent her a look, so she hurried as much as she could. "He can't be saved. Not even if you get him out of here."

Conflict played across his face as he seemed to be trying to work out what to do as quickly as Cecília had.

"You likely remember his sermons better than he does at this point," she pressed on. "Do you think *that's* what your vision could have meant? That you need to save him by bringing his words to the people? You joined the Church to help people, Cisco. If you get yourself killed along with him, how will that help? Everything you know will die right along with Father Malagrida."

A rise of voices on the floor above them made Cecília look up.

"Time's up." John fingered the rope he still had. "We need to get out of here."

"*Please*, Cisco," she said, making a final attempt.

Francisco took a few steps back, conflict still washing over his face though he slowly started to nod.

"Great." John grabbed Cecília's hand. "Which way?"

Cecília looked around, trying to place where they were versus the plans. "We need to get back up the staircase. Then the far side of the prison is still damaged. We can get out that way."

"Off we go, then." John started forward.

The grumble of voices grew clearer as they move toward the stairs.

"You let them in?"

"They had a letter from the first minister. What was I supposed to do?"

"It must have been a fake. You better get them before Senhor Carvalho arrives, or *you're* going to be in one of those cells before morning."

Cecília's stomach clenched at the idea of Senhor Carvalho himself making the trip to the prison. If they were facing that level of wrath, a simple hanging would likely be too good for them. Maneuvering around John, she led the way, slipping through the door at the top of the stairs and around a corner just ahead of the guards. In the cramped hallways, the reverberation of their voices and footsteps made it impossible to tell if it was three men or thirty.

Using the long patches of darkness to remain out of sight, Cecília found the next tight staircase they needed—the one she had taken to see Luís, if the recognition that hit her stomach said anything—and led them out of the belly of the prison.

As they left the echoing guards below, the prison went eerily quiet—no angry voices or mad thumping. There had to be men locked up behind at least some of the wooden doors they passed, but there wasn't so much as a cough. The silence only grated on Cecília's frayed nerves. She did her best to focus on logical things and work out where they were versus the plans she'd reviewed.

The hall they were in came to a T, and Cecília headed right.

"Are you certain you know where you're going?" Francisco whispered behind her.

I certainly hope so. "I have the rebuilding plans." She made a left turn that should have brought them to the back of the building.

The hall suddenly came to a dead end.

"We can turn around—" John started as voices began to filter through the distance. More guards were being roused. There was shouting and footsteps.

"Now we're trapped," Francisco snapped.

Heart beating too quickly at the encroaching panic, Cecília swallowed, trying to work out where she had made a mistake. She had followed the plans to where rebuilding was marked to start. There was something she was missing. The hall shouldn't have ended so suddenly. There should have been an opening of some sort in that hall. Suddenly, it registered. The wall was oddly pitched and brick, not stone like the rest of the prison.

"No, we're not." She moved to the last door on the slanted wall. Pulling back the flap, she smelled a gust of blessedly clean fresh air. "Here! They must have bricked over where the hall cracked. The cells on the other side are still open!" She tried the handle. The wooden door wouldn't budge. "John. That key?"

He jumped as though he hadn't thought of it and patted down his pockets.

"Please tell me you brought it." She glanced down the darkness-mottled hallway. She still couldn't see anyone, but the voices were growing closer and clearer.

"Yes!" John found the key he'd taken from the guard. "Just pray it works."

"*I* will," Francisco murmured a little more pointedly than the situation called for.

Thankfully, John ignored him, working to fit the key into the lock.

Footsteps neared. The guards couldn't have been more than a turn or two away.

"John..." Cecília glanced between him and the hall.

"It fits. It's just... rusty."

Voices echoed around the stone, sounding dark, nearly demonic.

"John."

"It's going. Just a second."

"Hey!" The shout went out as a man rounded the corner.

"Got it!" John rammed his shoulder into the old door, and it swung open with an unholy creak.

A gunshot went off, a musket ball hitting stone somewhere close enough for Cecília to hear the ricochet.

"Run!" John grabbed her hand again, and she grabbed Francisco's, moving them as a chain out into the dark night.

Cecília panted, the burning in her legs back in full force as she struggled to keep up with the men's longer strides. She didn't dare stop as more and more gunshots went off behind them. John made a wide swing, heading first away from the river before doubling back. She didn't have the breath to question him.

As they neared the docks, he skidded to a stop, nearly sending Cecília straight into his back. She dropped both men's hands to steady herself. "What—" she started to ask before she saw what he did. "Tio?"

Tio Aloisio stood in front of them, a bag over his shoulder, seeming to have appeared out of nowhere like a phantom. He shook his head. "I knew there would be trouble, having both of you together again. I didn't imagine it would be to this level."

"Tio Aloisio, I couldn't—"

"I thought that might be the case." Tio Aloisio held his hand up to cut her off before checking the street behind him.

John frowned. "How did you—"

"Senhor Ventura isn't the best secret keeper, it seems." Tio Aloisio glanced at John before addressing Cecília once again. "He let it slip he had seen you while out in the hall and, when brought to the first minister, that you had taken his plans for the prison. From there, it wasn't too difficult to put together what you were attempting to do. There are a fair number of soldiers out in the streets around here looking for you. My first stop after *I* heard was to the diplomatic corps, and when I heard someone was set to ship out in the morning, I was willing to venture where you might be headed after the prison."

Cecília's entire body tensed. "Are you planning to stop us?"

"Hardly." Tio Aloisio heaved a sigh. "I had a suspicion you wouldn't take well to being locked in, so I've been in contact with a friend I have in France. Outside Paris. I was originally going to suggest it for you, but after this fiasco, I imagine we're all better off out of the country."

"*All* of..." Cecília looked toward Francisco, only to find empty air. "Cisco?"

"He slipped away as soon as he saw me," Tio Aloisio said. "I thought it best to let him go."

"He's wanted!" Her voice rose a little more than was prudent.

"And he's aware. You've freed him, which is more than he could have expected. What he does with that freedom is going to be up to him. You know your brother. There's nothing we could possibly say that will change his mind. There are people who are willing to question their faith and come to a stronger understanding of it through those trials, and those who gain their strength from believing there are no questions to ask. Your brother has always been the latter."

And you think I'm the former. After everything that had happened, Cecília couldn't fully disagree with him.

"Now, the *Vento de Verão* is in port, ready to cast off as soon as I give word," Tio Aloisio continued. "I would highly suggest we all be aboard it before the first minister thinks to block off the docks. Unless you wish to catch your own ship, Bates?"

Cecília looked at him in time to see John and her uncle share some other silent conversation in a look before he offered her a small smile. "I've never made it as far inland as Paris. I'm told it's a city to see."

"Then might I recommend we go?" Tio Aloisio turned, obviously meaning his question to be rhetorical.

Cecília still lingered, sending a last look after where Francisco had been.

"You saved him from prison and put him off Malagrida," John said. "That could be enough to save his life. Even if he stays here."

Could be. Cecília wished there was more certainty than that, but with Francisco, she supposed that would have to be enough. Tio Aloisio was right. They all had their own versions of faith. She couldn't change his any more than he could change what hers had become. With a certain nod, she turned back to follow her uncle. John took her hand once again and gave it a gentle squeeze.

As they moved away from the prison, the streets became quiet, nearly ominously so. But it seemed the soldiers Senhor Carvalho had sent were still searching closer to the breakout, not the docks. They came around a line of wooden buildings, no doubt temporary structures to replace what had once been there, and her breath caught. Though the moon wasn't more than a small crescent, the light had managed to catch the Tagus, making the entire wide band of water glint silvery-blue behind the masts of the ships at dock.

"This way," Tio Aloisio said, and Cecília noticed she'd stopped. She started after him again then saw it: Tio Aloisio's ship, Papai's ship, her ship. She picked up her pace, jogging the last few steps past the men to look up at it.

"Are we climbing aboard?" John asked behind her.

Tio Aloisio gave a low whistle in response, and a gangplank appeared over the side. "As I said, I was prepared." He motioned for Cecília to go ahead of him, and out of everything else she had felt that night, that year, a heady buzz began as she walked up the plank and onto the deck.

Tio Aloisio followed close behind her, handing his bag to one of the handful of men on deck. "Get that into the captain's quarters. Bates, I trust you still know your way around rigging? I thought it best to let as few men as possible know what was happening."

"Aye, sir." John touched Cecília's arm lightly before slipping into the activity on the deck as though born to it.

Tio Aloisio remained beside her. "You aren't choosing an easy life, you know, Cilinha."

She nodded, the nickname not feeling as grating anymore. "I'm not sure if I would know what to do with myself at this point, if things were suddenly easy."

Tio Aloisio shook his head, but she could almost see the hint of a smile in the moonlight, as if being on the ship made him feel lighter as well.

A man finished pulling the gangplank and faced Tio Aloisio. "Are you taking the helm, sir?"

"I suppose I should. It's certainly been a while," he said then looked at Cecília. "Would you care to join me? It was your father's ship, after all."

Cecília blinked in surprise. "Really?"

He took a step back and held his hand out toward the large wheel near the end of the deck. Not giving her uncle the chance to change his mind, Cecília headed where directed.

"Hoist the mast!" Tio Aloisio called. The order echoed through the sparse crew as he took a place behind the helm. "I'll steer us through the mouth of the river, then we'll see if you can have a go."

He glanced at Cecília. "As long as you don't wreck us on the coast, it's hard to hit something out at sea."

Butterflies stirred in Cecília's stomach, and she nodded, not trusting her voice as the ship slowly began to pull away from the dock. The deck under her feet rocked slightly. Wind began to blow her hair, carrying the intoxicating smell of salt and spray up from the water. She breathed it all in, watching the silvery-blue water pass underneath them. And for the first time in months—for the first time in years, perhaps—she felt entirely at peace. Maybe, just maybe, everything would finally go right.

Epilogue: 1775

Cecília's heart pounded as their carriage rolled through the crowds that lined the streets leading to the Praça do Commércio, slowly enough that she had plenty of time to scan the buildings that made up what they were calling the Pombaline Baixa—after all, the designs, the work, all of it had been led by the long-serving first minister Senhor Carvalho, now the Marquês de Pombal for all of his tireless efforts. Traveling into the city was likely a needless risk. Though it had been fifteen years, she couldn't trust the first minister's wrath had lessened any. He had, after all, seen the entire Durante family—save Bibiana—officially exiled even after they had already left the country, and he was not a man known for forgiveness. Still, at the news that Lisbon had finally been rebuilt, Cecília had found it impossible to stay away.

"Is it everything you thought it would be?" John's voice snapped her out of her thoughts.

Cecília looked away from the window long enough to meet his eyes. "I don't know. I haven't seen everything yet."

The corner of his mouth tipped up at the slightly snarky reply. "I'm just seeing if you think it was worth the risk of coming."

"I'm not sure you're one to lecture me about taking risks right now."

"You can't say you aren't just as interested in what's happening in Boston."

"I'm not sure anyone on this side of the Atlantic, save perhaps King George, is as interested in what's happening as you are, John Bates."

The amused look turned into a full smile as he turned back to his own window. Cecília shook her head but let the conversation drop. They had already gone through it dozens of times, the compromise that he could get involved in whatever was happening with his old friends in Boston as long as they stopped first in Lisbon. All of it was no doubt asking for trouble, but for everything else that had changed in the past fifteen years, John was no more risk averse at forty-two than he had been at twenty-seven.

She returned to staring out the window, spotting the designs all the architects had been slaving over what felt like three lifetimes ago brought to life. Perfectly symmetrical buildings lined carefully measured roads. Still, even rolling down the street, she could see all the imperfections, every façade that had been erected to cover an incomplete structure. Lisbon might have been "rebuilt" enough for the grand opening, but there was certainly construction still happening.

Finally, the crowd became so thick that the carriage couldn't move.

John leaned to see farther ahead of them. "We're going to have to walk if we want to get much closer."

Cecília nodded, knocking to get the driver's attention. "Pull off onto one of the side streets," she said when he leaned down to look through the small window into the carriage. "We'll walk from here."

The man frowned. "Are you sure that's wise, senhora?"

It wasn't, but that had never stopped her. And it felt oddly fitting, following the masses into Lisbon with John next to her. "We'll find you when we're finished." She swung the door open before he could hop down to do it for her. John quickly joined her, and they filtered into the crowd walking toward the grand arch marking the start of the Praça.

The smell that was Lisbon—sea air, sardines, red sand—hit her strongly enough that it nearly knocked her off her feet. Memories of the life she had once lived, back when the streets had been small and twisted, back when she had snuck her way down to the river while her mother and aunt were speaking inside, washed over her. She took John's hand, keeping one foot moving in front of the other as they entered the Praça. For all the *awful* she had seen in her life, there had certainly been good too. If everything hadn't happened exactly as it had, she never would have met John. She likely would never have left Lisbon. She certainly wouldn't have had the last happy fifteen years, seeing at least her small part of the world.

Leading John behind a man playing a pipe for coins, Cecília found a spot alongside one of the cheerful yellow buildings that surrounded the Praça. All of those, at least, seemed to be completed, the monuments to neoclassicism Pombal had had designed for their new, enlightened Lisbon.

Settled in place, she scanned the platform that stood in the center of the square, erected for the unveiling of Senhor Carvalho's statue. She had to imagine there had been more than a few unkind words said about it at court, but opening the new Baixa by dedicating a statue of himself right in the center seemed entirely in character for the man Cecília had once known.

A flash of the Távora executions shot through her mind. She shook her head to clear it. Following Father Malagrida's execution, the *autos-da-fé* had been abolished for good. No one else had burned. Even Francisco, wherever he had gotten to, had once again escaped death even if she had heard his name mentioned in any one of a hundred stirrings against Senhor Carvalho over the years. Where he was, though, or even if he was still alive, she supposed was anyone's guess. Either way, she supposed more speculating would do her no good. If nothing else, she would have to attempt to explain herself in front of Saint Peter, assuming Francisco arrived there before her.

Mind once again clear, she opened her eyes and focused on the platform. Senhor Carvalho stood near the center, looking far older than he did in Cecília's memory. She gave a light laugh. *It has been fifteen years. All but King of Portugal or not, he isn't immortal.*

The crowd fell silent as the speeches began. They clapped and shouted as the statue was unveiled. Though some looked angry, over-all, the people Cecília saw seemed happy. The people of Lisbon supported their first minister. Looking at the younger faces around, Cecília had to imagine half of the people standing on the Praça barely remembered the quake that had brought them all there—if they had been alive at all—let alone all the ups and downs that had dominated Cecília's early adulthood.

Let them never know any of it as more than a story, she sent up as a soft prayer. *Let them only know the good that has come from it all. Let that be the legacy all the horror leaves behind.*

The men on the platform retreated, moving for one of the doorways on the other side of the Praça, and John turned to Cecília. He studied her face for a moment before asking, "Ready?"

Cecília studied the crowd for a final moment, looking at what her city, her Lisbon, had become. And it looked... strong. No matter how long it took to get there, one day, Lisbon would be fine. It would once again be her beautiful city, one that would survive another one, two, three centuries, God willing.

She nodded, offering John a small smile before he turned to find a way through the masses still in the Praça. Cecília let him lead, giving herself over to her own thoughts. As good and bad as her memories in the city were, she could at least call herself satisfied. And for the moment, that was more than enough.

Acknowledgements

First and foremost, I need to thank my loving husband, Niles, who was with me every step of the way while writing this novel. From helping spark the idea to assisting with research to listening to me talk endlessly about character arcs and plotting issues, he was an integral part in the process. As the dedication says, this book truly would not exist without him.

I would also like to thank my in-laws, Jeanne and Michael, who thought of me when they found Mark Molesky's book *This Gulf of Fire* soon after its release and gifted it to me while I was struggling with finding sources; my parents, Carolyn and Hans, early proof-readers and general cheerleaders; and my daughter, Louisa, who managed to start sleeping through the night right as I was attempting to tackle final rewrites, allowing for the end of this book to be somewhat cohesive.

Further, thank you to everyone who assisted in the writing and editing of this book, including my beta readers, Emma Stickney and Hannah Bersee, Dr. Ferreira of Brown University and Dr. Shelford of American University, who helped point me toward academic sources on the Lisbon earthquake, and authors such as Mark Molesky and Nicholas Shrady, who have written books about a historical event that is otherwise sorely underrepresented in English works.

Last but certainly not least, I need to thank my publisher, Red Adept Publishing, specifically acquisitions editor Kris James and content editor Sara Gardiner, who both gave valuable feedback that allowed for revisions that created a much stronger final work, and line editor Kate Birdsall, who helped polish the writing until it shone. I certainly could not have done it without all of you.

Author's Note

Going into writing *The Stars of Heaven*, I knew I would be doing a lot of research. Any work of historical fiction means hitting the books. However, this novel required a special level of digging, mostly because when I started writing it, I knew next to nothing about Portuguese history. In fact, the idea for the book itself came from an unlikely source—a video game. While playing *Assassin's Creed: Rogue* one Saturday, my husband and I came to a scene where the player causes a massive earthquake in Lisbon. While the cause in the game was obviously fictional, we knew the creators of that series used real historical events as a backing, and we doubted they would entirely invent something as large as a city being destroyed for a plot point. As both my husband and I are history nerds, this sent us down the rabbit hole of trying to find out about this event we'd never heard about. What we found was one of the most important historical events that seemingly no one—at least no one who hasn't read Voltaire's *Candide*—has ever heard about. Yet, as I read more about this devastating event and how much it altered an already quickly changing Europe, I knew there had to be a story there.

As my knowledge of Portuguese history ended with the few paragraphs about fifteenth-century explorers in my high school curriculum, I quickly threw myself into research... and found books about the Lisbon earthquake, at least in English, to be few and far between. As I don't actually speak Portuguese, I was very, very lucky that around the time I was struggling to find what I needed to write this novel, Mark Molesky's book *This Gulf of Fire: the destruction of*

Lisbon or apocalypse in the age of science and reason was released. For anyone interested in learning about the actual history of the quake along with a quick rundown of all the Portuguese history you likely missed in high school, I highly suggest this book.

Now, after four years, hours and hours of research, and dozens of rewrites, *The Stars of Heaven* sits before you in its final form. As it is a work of fiction, I admit to taking a few liberties, such as inventing characters, filling in gaps where the actual historical record is lacking, and even transposing Father Malagrida's 1756 pamphlet, "An Opinion on the True Cause of the Earthquake," to a live sermon—but I have done my best to accurately represent all the ups and downs people living at the time may have experienced after such a world-changing event. I hope, beyond being an enjoyable read, this work brings an amazingly important but often forgotten piece of history to life.

Also by Jessica Dall

Beyond the Style Manual
Building the Bones: Outlining Your Novel

Order and Chaos
Raining Embers
Graven Idols
Shattered Tempests

Standalone
The Stars of Heaven

Watch for more at jessicadall.com.

About the Author

Jessica Dall finished her first novel at the age of fifteen and has been hooked on writing ever since. In the past few years, she has published two novels, *The Copper Witch* and *The Porcelain Child,* along with a number of short stories that have appeared in both magazines and anthologies.

In college, Jessica interned at a publishing house, where her "writing hobby" slowly turned into a variety of writing careers. She currently works as both as an editor and creative writing teacher in Washington, DC.

When not busy editing, writing, or teaching, Jessica enjoys crafting and piano, and spending time with her friends and family. She can most often be found at her home in Maryland with a notebook and her much-loved, sometimes-neglected husband.

Read more at jessicadall.com.

About the Publisher

Dear Reader,

We hope you enjoyed this book. Please consider leaving a review on your favorite book site.

Visit https://RedAdeptPublishing.com to see our entire catalogue.

Don't forget to subscribe to our monthly newsletter to be notified of future releases and special sales.